11/24

To Nicki
love
Liz x

SHADOWS
ON THE
MOON

Elizabeth Raill

First Published in the UK 2012 by Belvedere Publishing

First edition: 2012

A copy of this work is available through the British Library.

ISBN: 978-1-908200-72-3

Belvedere Publishing
Mirador
Wearne Lane
Langport
Somerset
TA10 9HB

SHADOWS ON THE MOON

BY

ELIZABETH REVILL

Author's Acknowledgements

This book is dedicated to all who have supported and encouraged me, especially my loving husband, Andrew Spear, who still puts up with my constant tap, tapping away on my laptop at all hours.

To my sweet Dad, who helped me with the all the Welsh names, colloquialisms, their spellings and who has provided me with a profound love of all things Welsh and huge pride in my Welsh heritage on both sides of my family.

My son, Ben Fielder who shares my passion for writing and all the excellent discussions and ideas we have together.

To my mum who lived the life of Nurse Carol Pembridge and instilled in me my love of literature, the creative arts and all things psychic.

To my dear friend, Hayley Raistrick-Episkopos, who constantly encourages and wills me on to succeed.

To the lovely village of Crynant that has been so inspirational to me.

To everyone who read Whispers on the Wind and wanted more.

And very special thanks to Sarah Luddington and her brilliant team at Belvedere who made this sequel possible. Thank you one and all and here's to the next...

Future titles will hopefully include, Against the Tide, a stand-alone historical novel that will draw you into the world of The Riding Officer and his fight against the cutthroat, bloody and vicious trade of smuggling in 1796, and **Rainbows in the Clouds** the continuing saga of the Llewellyn family.

Terms and colloquialisms used in

Shadows On The Moon

ach y fe:	you dirty thing.
bach:	male term of endearment - dear.
blas:	flavoursome, tasty.
cariad:	term of endearment – my love, little one.
cawl:	Welsh stew/ broth.
chopsy:	mouthy, cheeky.
cwtsh:	snuggle, cuddle.
cwat lawr:	shut up
dera:	come on
Duw:	God.
Dadcu:	Grandfather.
esgyrn Dafydd:	bones of David - an exclamation.
fach:	female term of endearment - dear.
fy merch 'i:	term of endearment - little lady.
Gelli Galed:	Hard Living
iechy dwriaeth:	an exclamation.
Jawch:	an exclamation like crikey.
jib:	an unpleasant expression on the face.
Mam-gu:	Grandmother.
Na:	No.
paid:	don't - stop it.
potch.:	soaking wet.
rhwyn dy garu du:	I love you.
tschwps:	a lot, cried the rain.
twp:	stupid, dull
Wuss:	friend, mate, pal - local to the region not what it means today.

BRONGLAIS

CHAPTER ONE

New Beginnings

Carrie stood outside the Maternity Unit in Carradog Road and looked up at the brick facing of the pillared, impressive building known as Bronglais. She was excited. This was to be her home while she worked at the Aberystwyth Maternity Home. Her new life was beginning.

Her eyes were vibrant and alive, full of hope and expectation.

She mounted the stone steps and eagerly pushed open the huge double doors. Her heels clicked professionally towards the glass window of the reception office and she confidently pressed the buzzer summoning the clerical aid to the window.

"Can I help you?" inquired the prim faced secretary, her owl like spectacles seeming too large for her small face.

"Caroline Llewellyn, probationer auxiliary nurse. I start work here tomorrow," a hint of pride had entered her voice.

"Ah yes. Take a seat and I'll call a runner to help you settle in."

Carrie gazed around at her surroundings, which were to become familiar territory within the next year, the wooden floor polished like glass, the aroma of lavender, and disinfectant mingling with the unmistakable smell of ether to produce an indisputable hospital smell.

Nurses smart in blue and white, starched crisp and clean bustled briskly off to their duties.

"Caroline Llewellyn?" said a soft voice with a gentle Irish lilt.

Carrie turned and came face to face with Nurse Gilhooley.

"Follow me and I'll take you to the Nurses' Home. You'll be sharing a room. Are you used to that?"

"No. I always had my own room at home. There's just my brother and me."

"Lucky you. No such luxury for me. In fact, coming here and sharing with three others was real bliss! I come from a large family, six brothers and seven sisters. I had to share a bed with my sisters. It was just like that nursery tale where the little one kept falling out."

Carrie smiled, she didn't know which story was meant but Carrie instantly warmed to her. Her intuition told her that they would become friends.

Carrie enjoyed listening to Nurse Gilhooley or Gilly, as she liked to be called. The chatter made Carrie feel welcome and at ease. Gilly's voice had a musical lilt and she seemed to talk in pictures just as her Aunty Annie had done. This alone made her feel at home and quelled the nervous fluttering, which had manifested in her stomach. Carrie could hardly believe it. It was really happening. She was really here. Her dreams were coming true.

Up the stairs and along a corridor they went where no one door was distinguishable from another, except for the numbers. They stopped outside room twenty-nine.

"Here we are!" The door was unlocked and Carrie surveyed the sparsely furnished room, with two beds, two bedside cupboards, one wardrobe, two easy chairs and a table.

"Storage of trunks and excess baggage is on floor three. It's clearly marked. There's a kitchen at the end of the corridor and a communal bathroom opposite. A word of warning, if you want hot water get in before five a.m. That's if you can get up?"

"Early rising's no problem for me," replied Carrie, "I lived on a farm."

"That's just as well then. You won't be afraid of hard work. Look, I'll leave you to unpack. That's your bed and locker there. We'll be sharing the wardrobe. If you take the left side of it, it should avoid any confusion. Here." She passed Carrie a room key, "All right?"

"Fine," agreed Carrie pocketing the key and placing her case on her bed.

"Right. In room twenty-eight there's Thomas and Jones. In thirty there's Kirby and Pemb. You'll like them. Pemb's a probationer like you. She's looking to go into proper nursing as soon as she's eighteen."

"That's my dream," murmured Carrie.

"Then you'll have something in common. What'll we call you? Llewellyn's a bit of a mouthful?"

"Call me Carrie."

"NO!" bellowed Gilly in horror. "No first names here. I'll call you Lew. That should do. I'll be back in about half an hour. I'll take you to get kitted up, we'll have a quick cuppa and then I'll take you down to Matron. Right?"

"Right," affirmed Carrie.

Gilly left. Carrie began unpacking, a profusion of thoughts rambling and climbing through the trellis of her mind.

Thirty minutes later, Carrie was being drilled on the laundry system of the home.

"Every Monday morning the trolley comes round. A clean sheet, pillow slip and towel will be left outside the door," recited the laundry maid, "Put the top sheet to the bottom and the clean sheet on top. The underneath sheet, pillow slip and towel take to the laundry basket, one on each floor by the stairs from four till ten-thirty a.m." Her bored voice exaggerated every syllable. She droned on, "If you have an accident the laundry's open six till two, otherwise you'll have to wait. All mattresses are covered; don't remove them even if you get the sweats. Any questions?" There was a barely imperceptible pause before she was in full flow again. "Changing the laundry is your responsibility. No change, no clean bed right?" She fixed her nut-brown eyes on Carrie.

Carrie acquiesced, "Right."

"Right," The laundry maid reaffirmed and then launched into the second half of her script about uniforms and their care finally ending with, "All uniforms must be labelled and marked. Tags and pens are available in the laundry room..."

"Six till two?" finished Carrie.

"Right," came the stony reply as those currant bun eyes fastened on Carrie once more. With her speech interrupted, the laundry maid, Edna, became confused and had to pause for a moment. She struggled to remember her lines, and finally concluded, "Articles to be boiled in the blue bin, ordinary wash in the white bin and colours in the brown. Any questions?"

Receiving none Edna lazily lumped away behind the counter selected a number of items from the shelves and slapped three uniforms in front of Carrie.

"Try these. One to wear, one off, and one in the wash. Clean aprons are available from Ward Sister when you go on duty." The performance petered out and Edna the dough faced, laundry maid plumped away from the counter dismissing them. She reminded Carrie of an old barren cow from the farm bovinely chewing her cud, only in Edna's case she was snacking a bag of toffees.

Gilly and Carrie shared a quiet cup of tea. Carrie enjoyed her new friend's company whose bright sparkling eyes revealed a wicked sense of humour and a personality to match. Carrie thought her vivacious and alive. She admired Gilly's burnished brown hair. It reminded her of her school friend, Megan. Gilly's figure and build were not unlike her own, and her humour was unmistakably Celtic and in tune with Carrie's. Gilly's conversation was anecdotal and every gem of wisdom, which she shared, resonated with Carrie. The only thing she had was a bit of a dry cough possibly because she smoked too much. Carrie had never smoked, but thought even though it looked glamorous and sophisticated, she didn't fancy a getting a cough like Gilly. It reminded her of some of the miners who suffered with pneumoconiosis from years of breathing in coal dust.

By ten-thirty Carrie had seen Matron and had been taken down to ward B1, Pengelly, to meet Staff. This was where she would report for duty the next morning.

There were six beds, with one young mother to be, suffering from pre-eclampsia toxaemia, one patient in for bed rest, two with babies in the breech position, waiting to be turned, one lady expecting twins whose waters had broken but whose cervix was not dilating; she was to be prepared for a caesarean section that morning. However, Carrie's attention was alerted to a young mother who had given birth to her first baby with a condition known as Omphalocele.

Carrie gasped in horror and understanding. It appeared that the little one's organs were outside the baby's body as if the wall of the abdomen had not formed properly.

Doctor Caldwell was checking on the child whose organs were placed in a sterile bag while waiting for surgery to close the hole in the stomach wall.

"Is everything all right, Nurse?"

Carrie blushed, "I was just wondering about this case, Doctor."

"You have an interest in this congenital abdominal wall defect?"

"Yes, Doctor."

"What do you want to know?"

"What exactly has happened here?"

"Quite simply, the baby is born without muscle and tissue of the abdomen so that organs from inside are allowed to protrude outwards. There is another similar condition called Gastroschisis, where there is no sac covering the intestines, which are usually the only abdominal contents to protrude. In itself, Gastroschisis is not lethal. In fact, great progress has been made in its treatment of late and usually there are no more birth defects or problems. Omphalocele, however, is different. There may be more organs that protrude making closure of the abdominal wall more difficult. Babies are more likely to have associated birth defects. These can involve the heart, urinary system and genetic makeup of the baby making the overall survival of Omphalocele much less than Gastroschisis."

"I see." Carrie's eyes filled with tears.

"May I ask why you are so interested in this?"

Carrie struggled to speak for a moment. She swallowed hard, "My mother died in childbirth. She was in labour for days and my little brother was born without a roof to his stomach."

"I see." Dr. Caldwell's expression softened, "We know a lot more about the condition today than we did."

"He was just left to die. The midwife said she had seen nothing like it before." Carrie took a gulp of air, "Will this one live?"

"We hope the baby will survive. But we have to check the child over thoroughly for other defects or the little one may not survive the necessary surgery. The mother will be fine."

Carrie nodded, "Thank you doctor. I only wish you had been there for my mother."

"Yes, well, as I said, many advancements have been made in the last five years."

Carrie had plenty to think about while she settled in.

CHAPTER TWO

Brotherly Longing and settling in

At Gelli Galed, Carrie's brother, John had a raging pain in his heart. His stomach wouldn't settle. He felt in a continual state of turmoil. The feelings he was experiencing were akin to being in constant fear. He knew why... Carrie! The love he felt for her, her leaving, was like the grief of losing his mother and father all over again.

John's strong hands neatly undid the knotted twine that bound the bales of hay that he tossed in the feeder for the sheep.

Trix looked up softly at him and gently whined as if she understood his pain. She, too, missed Carrie.

There was a kerfuffle and a clucking from the hens in the yard as the farm cart rattled over the rough ground. Ernie was at the helm with a tanned muscular young man at his side.

Cousin Tom jumped down and retrieved one of his bags from the cart. He looked questioningly about him.

"You'll be sleeping in the house," offered Ernie indicating the house with a nod.

Tom half smiled an acknowledgement but before he could speak Trixie had come running up, whining and yelping at this familiar person.

"Hello, old girl," he muttered ruffling her fur.

"Well, it's about time," said a deep voice.

Tom turned to see his cousin John standing tall and straight behind him.

Tom threw down his bag and opened his arms. The two men clasped each other warmly.

"It's good to see you," breathed Tom huskily.

"You too, wuss," returned John.

John had begun to realise just how important family were to him. He felt so alone especially now Carrie had gone.

"Well, well, let's get you in and settled. Ernie, put the kettle on, the farm can wait until I've heard my cousin's news."

Afternoon drifted into evening and evening into night. The lights burned long and late at Gelli Galed.

Carrie wriggled her toes as she clasped a cup of hot cocoa in her hands. She was too excited to sleep but she knew she must try and rest; tomorrow would be a long day.

The door opened quietly and Gilly slipped in.

"You still awake? I thought you'd be flat out."

"I couldn't get to sleep, thought the cocoa might help."

"It must be strange after the quiet of the farm. I'm never any good at sleeping in a new bed, takes me a week to get used to it."

"There's an element of that," whispered Carrie. "But I can't calm my mind. It's creating all sorts of scenarios for the days to come."

"A week of duties and that'll soon be knocked out of you," Gilly laughingly warned as she started to undress.

"Would you like a bedtime drink? I'll make it," smiled Carrie.

"An offer like that is not to be ignored, as long as you don't expect me to chat into the early hours..." sighed Gilly.

"I won't," replied Carrie. "I've only just made this, there's still some milk in the pan." Carrie put down her cup and stepped lightly to the door. "Do you take sugar?"

"Yep... I need all the energy I can get, two please."

Carrie left Gilly to get ready for bed and tiptoed to the kitchen. She heard voices, a hushed stern tone and an angry retort. She paused outside the kitchen.

"We're all in the same boat here. Just don't be so thoughtless. If it happens again I'll report you for theft."

"Why don't you go boil your head, you're just a junior, a probationer at that."

"It makes no difference. You have no right to help yourself to other people's supplies, we've been wondering where things were disappearing, now we know."

"It's just your word against mine. Do your worst." The door burst open and a tall, thin, raven-haired nurse with a pinched face pushed past nearly knocking Carrie flying.

"Watch where you're going," snarled the nurse.

"Sorry," whispered Carrie. "Who was that?" she enquired as she watched the woman disappearing up the corridor.

The curvy snowball blonde nurse pursed her lips that were turning white with anger, "That's Hawtry, best avoided if at all possible, frustrated old harridan!" The blonde turned her doe-like brown eyes on Carrie, "Sorry you had to witness that," her tone lightened, "You must be Lew, Gilly's new room mate. She said you'd arrived. I'm Pemb."

"Pleased to meet you. I didn't mean to barge in like that."

"Oh, don't worry. We're all heartily sick of her petty pilfering. She thinks because she's a senior she can help herself to anything we've got. It's the first time she's been caught red-handed, although we had our suspicions. Maybe now she'll lay off. At least we can hope! Can I help you with anything?"

"No thanks, I just came to make Gilly a cup of hot chocolate."

"She's got you well trained."

"No," laughed Carrie, "I offered, she's bushed and I couldn't sleep."

"I see. I know just how you feel. My first night I was raring to go. I couldn't settle for the life of me, twisted and turned. I ended up writing home and drinking about fifteen cups of tea. I felt it the next day though, and gave everyone the impression I'd got a weak bladder! The first week's the worst, after that you'll have no trouble sleeping, out like a light when your head touches the pillow."

Carrie put the milk pan on to heat and continued to chat to the petite probationer. She liked Pemb, and instinctively felt that here she had found a true soul mate.

By the time Carrie returned to her room Gilly was fast asleep, her breathing deep, with a slight rattle.

"Oh well, at least she doesn't snore," thought Carrie as she settled down to write a letter to John. She sipped Gilly's hot sweet chocolate and grimaced at the extra sugar.

The clock chimed two and Carrie crept gingerly into her bed and switched off the light. She snuggled down and replayed the events of the day like a film reel before drifting off into a peaceful sleep.

The raucous clanging of the alarm clock juddered Carrie to consciousness. The bristling bustle of hospital life burst into activity. Footsteps clattered and echoed in the corridor outside. A squeaky wheel on the laundry maid's trolley grated on Carrie's ears as the sunlight fought its way through the thin curtains and the tree outside the window leaving a gobo like leaf effect patterning the floor. Carrie raised her head sleepily to see Gilly wiping herself down with a rough hospital towel.

"You'd better hurry or there'll be no hot water left," remonstrated Gilly.

"I'm up, I'm up," breezed Carrie stretching lithely. She swung her legs out of bed and reached for her robe and padded off to the bathroom.

Five minutes later she was back, "Brr, you were right. The water was freezing. I must have been more tired than I thought. I won't be late again. Ah well, at least it's woken me up. I've just got time for breakfast before duty. See you later."

Carrie tried to still the jittery flittering inside her. She could feel her meagre slice of toast and jam rising and swallowed hastily. She looked at her watch pinned to her uniform.

Time to report to Ward Sister and Pengelly Ward.

Carrie moved nimbly past the Nurses' Station and into the ward. She lifted her head, as her mother would have done and walked towards Sister. She caught sight of her reflection in the window and hardly recognised herself.

"Ah, Nurse Llewellyn, Dr. Caldwell will be arriving in about eight minutes to do his rounds, make sure breakfast things are clear by then and the patients are comfortable."

"Yes, Sister."

Carrie worked hard and well. She was a quick learner. The days passed and she became familiar with the standard routines earning praise from her seniors, which was apparently a rarity.

Christmas came and went and Carrie took on extra shifts forgoing a trip home. She prayed her enforced absence from Hendre would make John realise that she really was her own person now and could make her own decisions. Letters from home pleaded with her to return for a visit when she had time off and Carrie decided that later in the year at the next Christmas would be the right time and now she was actually willing the days away and looking forward to going back and seeing everyone.

She penned another letter home, closing with the words:

'So, it's high time I was back to see you all and make sure you are all playing your part in looking after the farm. I guarantee that at Christmas time I will be back and I look forward to a proper family celebration rather than walking my feet off here on duty.' She signed the letter and sealed it ready for posting knowing the delight with which her announcement would be received.

She was going home. That decision alone put a happy smile on her face. She had a feeling that things would be very different and longed to see the family and her beloved Trixie who had always been her closest companion through all the trials that life had thrown on her.

Carrie would sleep well that night.

CHAPTER THREE

The fair comes to town

She had been at the hospital for ten months when the fair came to visit Aberystwyth.

"Never been to a proper fair?" shrieked Gilly. "Well, now's the time. Come on. It's Saturday night and we've got the evening off. Let's go."

"I don't know. I'm barely conscious, my feet are singing a song, all out of tune," she added, and started to smile remembering the first time she'd heard the phrase when her beloved Aunty Annie uttered them after they had traipsed around Neath Market all day.

"Nothing that a good soak won't cure. Come on," Gilly pleaded, "There's a whole gang of us. It'll be fun."

"Oh, all right! You've persuaded me. But you better put that fag out. If Hawtry or Duty Sister sees you you'll be for it."

As if on cue the strait laced Sister Toomer brusquely rounded the corner. Gilly carefully flipped the cigarette back inside her mouth, a trick Carrie had seen and wondered at many a time.

Sister Toomer, waited for her duty report and as she went to move on she glanced at the almost puce faced Gilly struggling to try and stop the smoke from streaming through her nostrils like a bull on heat in the cold.

"I should get a drink if I were you, nurse. Your sinuses are on fire." She half smiled and took her place at the Nurses' Station whilst Gilly succumbed to a fit of severe coughing.

Carrie giggled, "At least she's got a sense of humour."

"A sense of humour? ...Yes, sometimes," coughed Gilly, as she stamped out the offending cigarette under her shoe. "But, she can be a terror. She doesn't suffer fools gladly. You need to be on the ball when you work with her."

"But she's good at her job?"

"The best! There's no one who would dispute that."

"Then I can learn from her," said Carrie sagely.

"Oh, spare me the ideals!" winked Gilly, "Such earnest enthusiasm this time of the day, I can't cope," and Gilly pretended to writhe in anguish, crumpling into a heap like some invertebrate, jellied creature. Carrie laughed, and pulled her chum up onto her feet, but made up her mind to try and organise her duties to coincide with the roster of the famed Sister Toomer.

Carrie's eyes widened as she took in the sights and sounds of the fairground. The whirring machinery and rides, the stalls, which beckoned for everyone to try their luck, the freak sideshows, and the Fortune Teller booths, which promised to reveal all. It was all so different from her one trip to Porthcawl and the Coney Island Fair, which she had visited on a Sunday School outing many years ago.

At night the place was alive and dazzling with lights. The gang of four attracted admiring glances from the groups of university students also taking advantage of a Saturday night out.

"Come on! Let's ride the carousel," yelled Gilly above the cacophony of sound.

"It's the only horse you'll get me on,' shouted Pemb. "They terrify me... but these, these I can cope with."

They waited until the ride came to a stop and made a dash for one of the wooden horses. Carrie chose a cathedral candle cream mount with gold reins. Its horse gum pink smile seemed to be welcoming her aboard. She sat and waited while the rest of the mounts were taken. Four young men wearing Aberystwyth university scarves raced to grab a seat. One with a winning boyish grin, beamed at Pemb, who was being studied by one of the other lads, he then caught Carrie's eye and winked. She felt herself smiling back.

Carrie squealed deliciously as the merry-go-round began. She hung onto the pole, which rose and fell as the ride circled its way around. This was fun! No sooner were they off than Gilly had grabbed her hand and dragged her to the helter skelter. They picked up their coconut mats and mounted the steps, patiently waiting their turn.

With a whoop of glee they came sliding down one after the other. Carrie catapulted off the end and landed at the feet of a bemused student. He leaned over and helped her up. It was the same young man who had winked at her on the carousel. She smiled shyly, "Thanks."

"My pleasure... Miss...?"

"Llewellyn, but everyone calls me Lew."

"Don't you have a Christian name?"

"Carrie."

"That's much better. I'm Lloyd. Lloyd Osmend."

Carrie found herself blushing under the young man's scrutiny but was soon jolted out of it with a poke in the back from Kirb.

"Come on Lew. Bumper cars next."

The four nurses ran to the dodgems laughing and giggling. They watched the small cars racing around and waited for them to stop. Nurse Kirby continued, "You have to watch the university students - they're a load of wolves, especially the R.E. students."

"R.E.?"

"Religious Education... They're the worst!"

Moments later, the cars whined to a halt and their drivers and passengers alighted, their faces lit up with enjoyment. The three each grabbed a car and shouted to Carrie who stood hesitantly.

"Come on, there won't be any left."

Two of the students dived toward Pemb's car and the tall dark one beat the fairer student, Lloyd, who turned and ran and grabbed Carrie's hand.

It was the same student from earlier. He rushed her to a car and pulled her in. The other nurses, before they had a chance to complain, giggled as the cars groaned into action and the fare collector was hopping onto the back of the cars to take the money.

Conversation was forgotten amidst the squeal of the cars and shrieks from the riders. Kirby, head down, like a demon bull, rammed Carrie's car jolting her into Lloyd at her side. He glanced across at her and grinned.

"Right, let's get her!"

They sped around the steel floor; tails of the cars sending sparks showering down. It was a free for all and all too soon the ride was over.

"Go again?" asked Lloyd.

"No, I'd better get back to my friends."

"Okay. Maybe, I'll see you and your friends around?"

"Maybe," she clambered out of her seat then stopped awkwardly. "By the way, what are you studying?"

"Geography. Why?"

"Nothing," and with that she joined the others.

Joking and laughing together they headed for the coconut shy, leaving the four students to have their own battle on the bumping cars.

The night went on enjoyably and they didn't cross paths with the boys again although they had chatted about them and discussed their 'attributes'. This small talk was all new to Carrie whose circle of male friends was confined to family and farming acquaintances.

"No one special at home then?" asked Pemb.

"No... Not really," she hesitated as the face of Michael

Lawrence inexplicably popped into her mind.

"Aah! Then there is someone..."

"No." But Carrie had flushed guiltily. The result was she was teased all the way out of the fair until she conceded that apart from her best friend's brother, Gwynfor who she'd been told was interested in her, she quite liked a gentleman from a neighbouring farm.

"But it's hopeless. He's much older than me and every time we meet we fight," she confessed. This unconscious embarrassed revelation surprised her and she immediately dismissed it, as a sharing exercise because she wanted to be one of the girls.

"That's a good sign," mused Gilly. "A bit of vinegar with the syrup. To be sure, it's a fine line between love and hate. I should know. My brother's best friend, Patrick and I fight like cat and dog, yet since I've been here, he's written me every month. There's something to be said for the old cliché... absence makes the heart grow fonder."

Pemb looked at her watch, "Talking about absence, if we don't get a move on we'll be locked out. Come on. Cyril locks the gates at ten. It's five to. I'm on duty at six." She started to run from the fairground closely followed by the others.

"Damn and blast!" puffed an exhausted Gilly. There in front of them the lodge door to the Nurses' Home was securely locked.

"I can't breathe. My heart's about to burst. I'm going to die."

"Give up the fags, then," remonstrated Kirb.

"What do we do now?" asked Carrie.

"We have to climb the fence," complained Pemb. "Come on, it's not so high on the corner."

They ran to where Pemb suggested and struggled to scramble over the wooden fence, which was rickety in the extreme from other nurses' illicit entries and exits. All seemed to be going well until Gilly, the last, reached the top of the swaying boards, which relinquished her weight with a splintering crack and the whole panel came down throwing her on the grass beside the others who collapsed in helpless laughter. Gilly with clothes askew unsteadily got to her feet and clutching her grazed knee did a circling dance whilst intoning blasphemies Carrie had never heard.

"Holy Mary, mother of God, Jesus Mary and Joseph..."

"Ssh! You'll wake the dead," urged Pemb.

"It's dead we'll all be if Sister catches us," warned Kirb, stilling Gilly's dance by clamping her hand over her mouth.

"Now what?" whispered Carrie.

"If we're lucky the laundry window will be open," murmured Pemb, "This way."

It was obvious it was not the first time Pemb had been locked out as she led the way across the garden, round the vegetable patch and to the laundry window, which was open just a tiny crack. Pemb winkled her fingers underneath and tugged at the window. It made a scraping and a whistling sound as she pulled it up. They stopped and waited, anxious in case someone would hear. All was still.

Pemb was the first in, over the sill onto the sink and down onto the flag stoned floor followed by Kirb. Next came Carrie who helped Gilly. The four of them stood like naughty schoolgirls. Pemb found her voice first.

"Right girls, take it in stages. I'll go first, wait five minutes, Lew you follow, then Kirb and Gilly."

"Why do I have to go last?"

"Because you're the noisiest," Kirb hissed. "If anyone will get caught it's you, therefore it's better if we're away and out of sight."

"Oh thanks very much! See how put upon I am, Lew?"

"Button up," whispered Pemb, "Your voice carries like the wind. A bell on every tooth you've got."

Gilly closed her mouth with a pop, like an overgrown goldfish and made a face. There was a hush. Pemb disappeared up the stairs first. A few moments later, Carrie, her heart thumping vanished up the black stairwell towards the dimly lit staircase and corridors. When she reached the second floor she was somewhat disorientated and paused trying to work out at which end of the corridor her room was situated. She was helped by the fact that Pemb stuck her head out of her door and waved. Carrie scuttled along to her own room. Fingers shaking she fiddled with her key and managed to open the door but not before Hawtry had poked her nose out to see what the racket was. She glimpsed Pemb's blonde hair vanishing into her room and picked out Carrie's fiery red tresses. So, the new girl was a friend of Pemb. That wasn't a very wise choice. Hawtry closed the door a fraction to see who else would materialise on a night walk.

Carrie hurriedly changed for bed. She waited for what seemed an eternity before Gilly pushed open the door and closed it firmly, leaning against it with a huge sigh of relief.

Attacked by a fit of the giggles they collapsed on their beds and laughed until they were exhausted.

"I can't laugh any more, I've got pains in my tummy," whimpered Carrie.

"Me too," agreed Gilly.

They looked at each other and erupted again. But this time there was a warning knock on the wall. So, suitably chastened they made for their beds and were soon asleep.

CHAPTER FOUR

Working it out

Senior staff quickly noticed that Carrie was fast to learn and turning into a great nurse. They moved her from Auxiliary status to a full Probationer. She showed initiative. Sister Toomer had noted her enthusiasm whatever task she was set, no matter how menial, and Carrie's honest approach to her work and newfound friends made her popular amongst the other nurses.

"I'm done for," sighed Carrie, "Off duty now; Sister Toomer wanted me to do a double stint but I've had nearly a week of double duties so, I had to decline, besides I need to write a letter home."

"Lucky you," grumbled Gilly, "I had no option, work tonight or lose my Saturday off. Well, I'm not going to do that for man nor beast."

"Or Sister Toomer."

"Or Sister Toomer," agreed Gilly.

"What's this about Sister Toomer?" boomed the unmistakable tones of the feared Sister.

"Nothing, Sister. Just singing your praises as always," flattered Gilly.

"I hardly think that's the case," judged the Sister, "Just be certain you're not late on duty. Remember gossips find the time passes quicker than they think," and so saying she marched off down the corridor much to their relief.

Gilly frowned, "She's right. I'd better scoot. See you later." And she trotted after the disappearing figure of the Sister.

Carrie made her way to her room. She took off her uniform and hung it up carefully before making her way to the bathroom. Hopefully, she could have a long, hot soak and then she thought... maybe she would write *two* letters home."

Carrie had no longer settled in the warm water when there was a fierce knocking at the door.

"Don't spend all night in there. There are others who need to use the bathroom as much as you. And I need it urgently."

It was Hawtry. Normally Carrie wouldn't have taken much notice and enjoyed her bath but there was something in the nurse's voice, which indeed suggested urgency so, reluctantly Carrie called out, "Give me five minutes and I'll be out."

Carrie didn't linger. She did what she had to do, thoroughly and speedily, and true to her word, five minutes later she was out and towelling herself dry. At that moment Carrie promised herself that when money would allow she'd put in a proper bathroom at home. She wrapped her wild hair now wet and looking deceivingly more manageable in a towel, donned her dressing gown and cleaned the bath.

Carrie padded barefoot from the bathroom and tapped on Hawtry's door, "All yours, Hawtry."

It was as if Hawtry had been anxiously waiting as the door opened immediately and she came out of her room. She looked pale and drawn, managed to mumble her thanks and scurried to the bathroom. Carrie watched her go. She didn't look well and as Hawtry moved up the corridor Carrie noticed a few spots of blood drip and stain the polished wood floor.

"Ah! A period," thought Carrie and inwardly sympathised. But she wasn't entirely correct.

There was a howl, reminiscent of a large dog in pain. She could hear stifled sobs of anguish and hesitantly tapped at the bathroom door.

"Hawtry? Hawtry are you all right?"

The sobs became muffled and Hawtry tried to answer but her voice wavered like a bleating nanny goat.

Carrie became more alarmed, "Hawtry! Do you need help?"

"Just piss off and mind your own business," came Hawtry's pinched nasal twang.

"Sorry, I was just concerned, that's all. There are blood spots all down the corridor to your room."

"Nothing to do with me. Just clear off and mind it."

Carrie couldn't force Hawtry to speak with her so she shrugged and returned to her room. Half an hour later she heard the bathroom door open and the sound of scrubbing. Carrie opened her door a fraction and saw Hawtry on her hands and knees mopping up the blood spots with a rag, which was so bloody, it looked like it had been used in a slaughterhouse. Carrie softly closed the door not wishing to alert Hawtry and incur her wrath again, but she was curious as only Carrie could be. She waited until she heard Hawtry return to her room and the door close, then she softly but swiftly made her way to the bathroom and opened the door. She gasped in incredulity at the smears of blood daubing the sides of the bath and the congealing mess on a towel dropped on the floor. Too late she heard a sound behind her. It was Hawtry who stared at her like a rat up a pump, carrying fresh rags. They stood like that for a few minutes. Hawtry's face was an ashen yellow. She looked ill.

"Here let me help you with that," asserted Carrie and took the rag from the frozen faced Staff Nurse. Carrie chattered lightly as she cleared away the offending remnants of the blood, "Goodness, you must have a humdinger of a period to make this mess. You must feel absolutely rotten. Why don't you go and lie down? I'll clear this up and bring you a nice hot water bottle. That will ease the discomfort. My Aunty Annie used to swear by it. A couple of codeine and a hot milk drink should do the trick."

Hawtry said nothing. Carrie turned and saw that the Staff Nurse's eyes had filled with tears, obviously not trusting herself to speak, Hawtry nodded and returned to her room. Carrie watched her go before returning to scrubbing at the mess of blood, which spattered the floor and bathroom. Carrie had been at the Maternity Unit for long enough to know that this was no ordinary period. This was something much more serious. She also had her own experience to go by and her suspicion was confirmed when she saw an empty bottle of ergot in the waste paper bin. She lifted the lid of the adjacent lavatory pan and saw the globule of tissue and blood clots floating on the water. What she saw was more akin to an abortion and a self-administered one at that. It was strange; according to the other nurses Hawtry didn't have a boyfriend. Had she suffered a similar fate to Carrie?

Carrie finished cleaning up the bathroom and corridor before scurrying to the kitchen and putting on the kettle. She filled her hot water bottle, made a milk drink and carried both to Hawtry's room. She knocked hesitantly on the door.

"It's open."

Carrie was just going inside when Kirb turned into the corridor and looked with surprise at Carrie's disappearing figure. Surely, she wasn't going into Hawtry's room? Someone needed to speak with her. Carrie would have to be warned about Hawtry.

Hawtry was in bed with the curtains pulled. The bedside light was on but even in that weak light Carrie could see the senior nurse's sickly pallor.

"Here, drink this. It will make you feel better. A nice hot drink used to make my toes curl. And pop this on your tummy. There's nothing like a bit of warmth for soothing the cramps."

Hawtry gratefully accepted the drink and hot water bottle.

Her eyes filled with tears, "Why are you doing this?" A malicious glimmer crept into them, "A nice piece of gossip for you and your friends... now you've got something on me," she added spitefully. But Carrie was not to be rankled. She'd dealt with and dispatched better than Hawtry in her young life.

"No. I thought I could help, that's all. What passes between us will go no further... I'm not here to judge but I know what you've done."

Hawtry looked at her suspiciously. "Just what do you think you know?" Her pinched face became more haggard.

"Let's just say. I know you've experienced the pains of Hell but whoever gave this to you could be in serious trouble." She pulled out the empty bottle of ergot from her pocket.

"I don't know what you're talking about," lied Hawtry.

"Fine. If that's the way you want it. But remember, don't judge everyone by your own standards." Carrie moved back to the door. "Put my hot water bottle in the kitchen when you're finished with it." Carrie's palm was on the handle she was just about to open it when Hawtry stopped her.

"Stop, please. Don't go... I'm sorry," she added reluctantly.

Carrie turned back. "You don't have to tell me anything. But life here must be very lonely if you refuse to open up with anyone."

Hawtry snorted, "That's what got me into this mess. I know everyone hates me."

"Maybe they wouldn't if you gave them a chance."

"Too much water under the bridge now. Too late to change."

"Not necessarily. I won't pressure you but if you need to talk, you know where to find me."

"You'll keep this just between us?"

"Of course, everyone's had a bad period at sometime, haven't they?"

"Thanks." The word came out with difficulty. Hawtry wasn't used to kindness in any shape or form and when Carrie closed the door after her, Hawtry dissolved into tears.

CHAPTER FIVE

The Farm Revisited

"Come on, wuss. It'll be fun. I don't think you've had any fun in almost a year, not since Carrie left," Thomas insisted.

"He's right," added Ernie helping himself to another slice of bread and butter. "You could do with a bit of lightening up. Your face has been miserable for too long. Go on; enjoy yourselves. It isn't like there's a dance every week. It'll give me a bit of time to catch up on a bit of cleaning. The place is a disgrace since Carrie left. She won't thank you come Christmas when she comes home. May not even come back again if she sees the filthy state you've let the place get into."

"He's right, John. Besides, what would you rather, the village dance or clearing up the house?"

"No contest, even with my two left feet. But only if you're sure...?" he said looking questioningly at Ernie.

"Go on with you. No need to soft soap me. Go and get yourselves spruced up. I'll clear away."

"I haven't fed Trix," protested John as his cousin dragged him up from the table.

"I'll see to it. Where is she?"

"Out by the barn the last time I saw her. I'll give her a call." John opened up the porch door but before he could call out there was a scurrying of flat feet and Bandit had scuttled in flapping his wings warming them by the kitchen fire.

"That duck has got to go. Thinks he's human, he does," smiled John as the bird settled on the rag mat. "Trix!" he shouted out and the soft tempered collie padded in joining Bandit in front of the fire. They made an incongruous pair, especially when Bandit hopped onto Trixie's back. The old farm dog didn't bat an eye as she placed her head on her paws to snooze in the warmth.

"Go on, be off with you," ordered Ernie. The two young men clattered noisily up the stairs. Ernie grinned. Perhaps tonight would be a turning point for John and he'd open his heart to someone other than Carrie. At least that's what Ernie hoped.

Half-an-hour later Thomas and John were in the kitchen dressed in their Sunday best. John pulled awkwardly at his collar, starched to perfection but it was chafing his neck.

20

"I feel like a plucked chicken prepped for the oven, over stuffed and over dressed," grumbled John.

"Here," said Ernie coming to the rescue, "Pop a bit of Vaseline on the collar and it won't rub your neck raw."

"Useful tip," remarked Thomas. "Can I have some? Don't think I've worn this since going through immigration."

"Help yourself," offered Ernie, "And then be off with you or you'll only make the last dance."

"That's the important one," winked Thomas. "Say, do you think Megan will be there?"

"You sly fox. Is that who you've set your sights on?"

"No, no. I just don't want to tread on anyone's toes, that's all. I know she's always been rather smitten with you," Thomas pointed out.

"For goodness sake. Listen to the pair of you. Just get out there and have a good time. We're not talking marriage here. It's only a dance," remonstrated Ernie and the two young men sauntered out of the house, laughing and teasing each other before climbing into the cart, which Ernie had prepared. He lit the lamps on the side of the carriage and watched the glowing lights swing rhythmically from side to side as the wagon made its way down the hillside to the village.

Ernie returned to the kitchen and his eye caught the letter on the mantelpiece addressed to all three of them in Carrie's writing. "Well, I'm blessed!" he exclaimed. In all the fuss he'd forgotten to tell John about the letter's arrival. But there would be plenty of time for that tomorrow. Ernie placed the kettle on the range. Even though the letter was addressed to all three he knew John liked to be the first to open his sister's missives. But Ernie was curious and keen to hear Carrie's news, so no harm would be done, he'd simply steam it open and John could still think he was the first to read it.

"Ieuchy dewriath!" he exclaimed as the hot water vapour nearly scalded his fingers. He rescued his mittens from his pocket and popped them on to complete the task. The flap peeled up easily and Ernie carefully extracted the letter. He eagerly scanned the contents. He could almost hear Carrie's voice as he read about her antics with the other nurses. It seems she had made some good pals. He could picture perfectly each and every one of them such was her gift with words. This would be put to the test when any of them visited with Carrie, which Ernie was sure would happen at some point.

"I miss you all and Trix and Bandit but I'm really loving

it. As soon as I'm able I'll apply to a good teaching hospital. Birmingham comes highly recommended. That'll be a change from Wales. A really big city, I'm told, and what's more, Pemb is going to apply with me, two probationers together. Oh John, you'd like Pemb. She's got just the same sense of humour as us and she's so pretty, lovely snowball blonde hair and curves to match. She's one of twins, although her sister has stayed at home and elected to go into service at a big house in Merthyr. There you are Thomas, we'll have to introduce you to her sister. Sounds like I'm matchmaking. I'm not really; I just want you to meet her. I know you'll like her as much as I do.

Thank you for your last letter. I've read and reread it a hundred times so I almost know it off by heart. Miss Price would be proud of me. After all, I never could learn that blasted poem about daffodils I got lost after the first four lines!

You haven't mentioned anything about Hendre for a while. Is there any more news from the solicitor? And what about Mr. Lawrence? How is he faring? Is the aid package you've worked out together holding good?"

"Aye, my lass, it is. I wondered when we'd come on to Mr. Lawrence," twinkled Ernie. "Although, I don't think your brother will be too keen to know you're thinking of him," he murmured aloud.

"In fact, I hope you don't mind, John but I thought I might drop Mr. Lawrence a line, after all, it's been some time now and he was kind to me before I left and I was less than courteous."

"That you were my girl; that you were," mused Ernie. "Like I said, your happiness is in your own back yard but you're too stubborn to see it." Ernie eagerly continued with the letter until Trix raised her head from her slumbers dislodging Bandit from his precarious perch. A throaty rumble grew in her throat and she let out a bark.

"Esgyrn Daffyd, Trix, you frightened the life out of me. I almost dropped the letter on the coals. Surely, the boys can't be back. They've only been gone an hour." He stared hard at the dog. "Why am I talking to you? It's not like you can answer me. Having a granddad's moment I am." Ernie jumped again as a loud knock echoed into the kitchen. Ernie hastily replaced the letter and resealed it placing it back on the mantel. There was another insistent knock.

"Coming!" shouted Ernie as he scrambled to the door. He didn't see the gust of wind catch the envelope and carry it to the greedy devouring fire.

Ernie unlatched the porch door to see the figure of Michael Lawrence standing there.

"Sorry to disturb you but I wonder if I might have a word?"

"Certainly, certainly. Come in."

Michael followed Ernie's portly figure into the cosy warmth of the kitchen.

"Sit down, sit down, do. Would you like a cup of something? Kettle's just boiled."

"Why thank you. Tea would be nice," Michael replied as he eased himself into a kitchen chair.

"What can we do for you?" Ernie enquired. "Is there something wrong at Hendre?"

"No, no. Just the opposite. Thanks to your help the farm is once again flourishing. No, I came on a personal matter."

"Yes?" Ernie was curious.

"I received a letter from Miss Llewellyn, today."

"Oh yes?" Ernie tried to keep his voice casual, so Carrie had finally put pen to paper. That was a good thing.

"It was a pleasant surprise after all these months. But, the thing is, I'd like to respond but she neglected to put her address at the top of the page and I wondered if you could supply me with it?"

"Certainly, certainly. I have it right here." He reached up for the letter but of course the fire had eaten it. "That's strange..." He looked around but could see no sign of it on the floor. "Oh no!"

"What?"

"When I answered the door it must have tumbled into the fire... The back draft from the porch," Ernie explained.

"I'm sorry. Do you have a record of it anywhere else?" Michael obviously didn't realise the implications of what had happened.

"Er yes... yes. I'm sure it's here somewhere. The Maternity Unit is in Aberystwyth, Carradog Road I believe."

"And the Nurses' Home?"

"Um... Bronglais. It's called Bronglais. She's in room 29."

"Is that in the same road?"

"What?" Ernie was distracted. He was wondering how he could explain to John what had happened to Carrie's letter.

"The Nurses' Home. Is it in the same road?"

"Er yes, I believe so."

"Are you all right? There's nothing wrong is there?"

Ernie blustered as he poured water from the kettle into the teapot but he was not concentrating. Michael Lawrence's words were drifting in and out of his head, odd words echoing in his mind.

"I must say I was surprised to hear from her. She even apologised for our last meeting and thanked me for the use of the butterfly brooch, which she felt had helped with her confidence. In fact, she says she was sorry she appeared to throw my gift back in my face. I'd like to send her that brooch. If she'll have it... Ernie watch out!"

Too late! Ernie agitated by the thought of the consequences of facing John, Ernie misjudged pouring the scalding contents of the pot, which cascaded over his hand. Michael Lawrence was on his feet. He wrested the pot from Ernie before it was dropped and dragged Ernie to the kitchen sink where he pumped water vigorously.

"Here, hold your hand under there, while I sort this out."

"Butter," said Ernie, "There's some butter in the pantry."

"Nonsense. Old wives' tale. Butter will make it fry. You don't want your hand cooked," retorted Michael. "Thought you'd know that."

"Contrary to expectations I don't know everything," returned Ernie.

"Keep your hand in the water till the sting has eased. Have you got any dry dressings?"

"First aid box in the cupboard under the stairs."

Michael rummaged amongst the stored boxes and cases until he spotted the tell tale red-cross box.

Ernie was soon sporting a clean lint dressing and bandage to cover his raw and enflamed wound.

"Will you be all right? Can I get you anything, call anyone?"

"John and Thomas are at the village dance. First time out in many a month. Don't bother them, I'll be fine."

"What about the doctor?"

"Na, na. I'm sure your ministering will have put things right."

"What we really need is some lavender oil but the scald may even be too sore for that. I suggest you get yourself to Dr. Rees in the morning."

"Yes, well, we'll see how I am later. Thank you, Mr. Lawrence for all your kindness."

"Please call me Michael. Tell me, Ernie. How do you think Miss Llewellyn would react if I were to pay her a visit?"

"I couldn't possibly say. But if she's written to you she's hardly going to shut the door in your face, now is she?"

"I suppose not." He paused reflectively before moving to

the door. "Thank you. Thank you. Mind you take care of that hand now."

"I will and thank you again and if it's any use I think, in her heart, young Carrie will be more than pleased to see you. But I didn't say so," Ernie winked at Michael who smiled delightedly.

"You think so?"

Ernie nodded. Michael Lawrence stepped back into the night a new spring in his step.

CHAPTER SIX

The dance

Thomas and John were having an excellent time at the sixpenny hop. They sat in a group with Gwynfor, his sister Megan, their cousin Dilly and another old school friend, Brian Davies. Thomas noticed with envy the way Megan was looking at John and wondered how he could get her to look at him with the same interest.

"Come on, Megan, have this one with me. I'll polka you off your feet," and into my arms thought Thomas silently.

Megan looked at Thomas and giggled, "Dancing feet I've not got; at least not this sort of dancing. My training is in ballet, and tap, on my own. If you don't mind me stepping on your corns and bunions I'll give it a whirl."

"The only corn I've got is in the field and the onions are in the vegetable patch," grinned Thomas.

"You'll regret it boyo," added Gwynfor. "She may look dainty..."

"Go on with you," she chuckled, "If John sees how easy it is maybe he'll give me a dance later." Megan eyed him affectionately but John was totally oblivious to her charms muttering, "Aye, I'll dance with you once I see how Thomas fares. Broken bones I can do without."

Thomas whisked Megan to her feet with a whoop and shout. All heads at the dance turned in their direction. Megan was easy on the eye and her lustrous hair swirled as she turned on the dance floor held close by Thomas who was obviously utterly captivated by her. She danced beautifully.

Thomas danced her into the middle of the floor and lifted her aloft, despite her screams of protestations, and slid her back down to the floor brushing her lithe body gently against his. Megan swung her head towards him as their faces almost touched and he felt the butterfly kiss of her sweet breath on his lips and she knew instantly how he felt about her. As her feet made contact with the ground she straightened her dress and in a show of apparent unconcern caught his hand and ran them both back to their seats where she flopped feigning exhaustion.

"That's me absolutely pooped!" she murmured. "When I've recovered it's John's turn."

"No, no, Megan fach. I'm not a dancer unless it's a square dance in a field with the sheep and Trix."

"I'm not taking no for an answer," Megan persisted shaking her burnished conker coloured tresses.

"You may as well give in, wuss," said Gwynfor, "A proper little madam she'll be if she can't have her way. Your ears will drop off with the battering they'll get."

The group laughed together. Megan stole a look at Thomas. He was hurt. That much she knew, but her heart was set on John and she'd not take second best if she could help it.

Dilly and Brian took to the floor with a slow foxtrot while Gwynfor and John retreated to the bar for a ladle of cider to fill their mugs.

"One for me too, please," pleaded Megan. "I've a thirst like a dredger."

"I'll get you one, Megan," offered Thomas.

"It's all right, my brother will see to it. Thank you, though," she added a little more graciously and fastened her attention on the dancers clapping her hands delightedly. Thomas, saddened and chastened, stared into his ale and wondered how he could win Megan to his side.

Gwynfor slopped the cider into John's glass, "I've been meaning to ask you wuss... about Carrie."

John inclined his head to listen, his heart racing at the sound of his sister's name. He knew what was coming.

"You being the man of the house with your da gone an all. Would it be all right if I wrote to Carrie?"

John took a deep breath, "Course wuss, have you got her address?"

"Megan's got it somewhere, those two keep in touch. I'd like to visit her too, if she'd let me. When's she coming home?"

"She was talking of making it for Christmas. But you know Carrie; she's a mind of her own like Mam. Strong willed and stubborn."

"Are you saying she wouldn't take to me?"

"No, no," John blustered. "Just don't want you to get your hopes up. Take it steady would be my advice."

"Course you know Megan has picked you out?"

"No... No. It's fun she has with all of us."

"You're blind, John Llewellyn. My little sister talks of you like no other."

"What about Thomas?"

"What about him?"

"He's smitten with her I know."

"I know and she knows, I think, but it's you she's after."

"I'm not ready for anything like that, p'raps you could dissuade her."

"Her affection's locked on you as tight as a tick. She'll take some dislodging."

John took a swallow then drained his glass and proffered it for more. Gwynfor duly obliged, saying sadly, "Let her down gently, wuss. We've been friends long enough."

John faced the dance floor and eyed up the girls of the village sitting in a giggling gang. He thrust his glass at Gwynfor, empty once more and walked across the floor dodging the dancers and stood in front of the group. He stretched out his hand to one of them who smiled shyly. Her friends tittered and egged her on, "Go on, Jenny."

Jenny stood up hesitantly and took his hand. They moved to the dance floor and joined the throng. John gave her his undivided attention and Megan looked on enviously.

Thomas watched the proceedings with interest and when Megan caught his hand to drag him back on the floor, he went willingly, even though he knew the reason she was in his arms was to catch John's eyes but he didn't mind. He was grateful for any crumb of affection Megan chose to give, whatever the reason.

The village girls chattered and whispered amongst themselves, as they eyed their friend who was enjoying John's focused gaze. Gwynfor edged back to the seats where Dilly and Brian flushed from all their dancing had collapsed. "Who does she remind you of?" he questioned, gesturing to John and young Jenny on the dance floor.

"Hair like Carrie's she's got. Fiery, wild and in a tangle."

"That's what I thought. A bit of a safety factor p'raps?"

"Perhaps," murmured Brian. "Although, how he can involve himself with that lot, God only knows. Sillier than a sack full of sisters they are."

"Or a cow in curlers," added Dilly. They're always giggling. Over nothing. She may have hair like Carrie but that's where the resemblance ends."

"Looks like he's enjoying himself," observed Brian as John swung Jenny around in the middle of the floor until she fell against him in a tumble of laughter. He brought her across to the group.

"This is good," said John. "First fun I've had in months, no years," he corrected himself. "We must do this again. When's the next dance?"

"Not for a month," answered Dilly. "But there's a slide show on at the Hall next Friday."

"Slide show? I thought it was a film?" replied Brian.

"Friday is the slide show. Something about magic I

believe, but on Saturday they're showing a proper film from Hollywood."

"Then we'll go," said John. "Are you up for it, Jenny?"

She swallowed incredulously before sighing, "I'd love to."

"Right. I'll meet you outside Segadelli's at seven. You'll be there?"

"I'll be there."

"And now, I'll have the last dance and walk you home. If that's all right?"

Jenny inclined her head submissively as John led her back out for the last couples' dance of the evening. He tapped Thomas on the shoulder, "Wait for me by the cart, will you, wuss? I'm walking Jenny home."

"And you're walking me home, aren't you, Tom?" interjected Megan.

"Certainly, if you want me to," smiled Thomas who took full advantage of Megan pressing her body into his and he gently nuzzled her neck. Megan arched her back as she allowed his caress but her eyes were bright with hurt and she closed them tightly to prevent the tears from spilling out.

John walked Jenny home. His manner changed considerably as they progressed down the lane.

"So are we to go to the film or the slide show?" she eventually managed to ask.

"What's the film?"

"It's supposed to be good. A real thriller by Alfred Hitchcock, The Lady Vanishes."

"And who's in it?"

"Margaret Lockwood and Michael Redgrave. Do you still want to go?"

"Why not?" He gave her a perfunctory peck on the cheek and waved cheerily as he made his way back to the cart and Senator waiting outside the hall.

Thomas was already astride the passenger seat.

"Thought you'd be a while yet," called John.

"Not with Gwynfor keeping us company. I left her at the corner." He paused as John climbed into the driver's seat, "Jenny... I'm surprised."

"She's as good as another."

"What about Megan?"

"What about her?"

"She's keen on you. I'd give anything to have her look at me like that."

John took the reins and ordered Senator, "Walk on." He glanced at his cousin, "Megan is Carrie's best friend. I wouldn't mess with her and sweet as she is, she's not for me. It would ruin the friendship between our families. But you, you're taken with her. You have my blessing. Are you going to the film on Saturday?"

"Aye. A whole gang of us I believe. And you?"

"Meeting Jenny at seven."

"Roll on Saturday."

John smiled. Jenny would serve his purpose quite well. He'd ensure that Megan would take more notice of Thomas. Whatever it took.

A shooting star travelled across the night sky and Thomas quietly made a wish, as the cart rumbled along the rutted track beneath the jewelled ceiling. "Hardly need the lights. I've never seen the sky so bright," observed Thomas.

"A lover's ceiling."

"That it is," agreed Thomas. He was excited, yet filled with the fear of trepidation that his happiness depended on John's non-interest in Megan as a girlfriend.

The cousins fell quiet as the cart rounded the track of the hillside to Gelli Galed where welcoming lights shone through the velvet black of the night.

"Ernie's up late," mused Thomas.

"Probably waiting up for us. A bit of an old woman he is, sometimes."

"Maybe, but we couldn't do without him."

"No. Part of the furniture and fittings now, he is." John pulled up in the cart, "I'll see to Senator. You go in and tell the tale. That's what he'll be wanting."

Thomas laughed and jumped down. He was happy enough tonight. He vowed that somehow he'd make Megan fall in love with him.

He clattered onto the porch and into the kitchen where Ernie was asleep in the chair, his hand bandaged up like a mummy.

"Jawch, Ernie! What have you done?"

Ernie roused himself and squinted in the gentle light from the paraffin lamp.

"Thomas! There's a fright I had. Dreaming I was..."

"Never mind that. What have you done?" he reiterated.

"Scalded myself, my own fault. Not concentrating, see?"

"Is it bad?"

"Bad enough. I'll pop in to Dr. Rees in the morning. Too late to bother anyone now. How was the dance?"

"Great. We met up with a gang. Going to the pictures next week, if that's okay with you?"

"Why shouldn't it be? And who is it, may I ask, that's set a sparkle in your eyes?"

"Megan..."

"Carrie's friend?"

"The same."

"Good, good..." there was a barely imperceptible pause before Ernie continued, "And what about John?"

"He walked one of the village girls home, Jenny, Jenny Davies."

Ernie raised an eyebrow in surprise, "Met someone then. That's good."

"Not as good as it could be," replied Thomas honestly. "Megan has taken a fancy to John. I've no illusions about it. She's only seeing me to make an impression on him."

"And John?"

"He went after Jenny to shake Megan off and give me a chance. He knows I like her."

"It may work out. We can hope," said Ernie philosophically. "What's this Jenny like?"

"Funnily enough, from the back it could be Carrie."

"Why?" Ernie's eyes narrowed in alarm.

"Hair just like her."

"No," interrupted John as he pushed open the door. "No one has hair quite like Carrie. Hers is unmistakable."

"Maybe so, but it's as unruly as hers and a similar red gold," observed Thomas.

"That's where the similarity ends. What are you trying to say, cousin?" barked John defensively.

"Nothing," replied Thomas wondering at his cousin's sudden hostility. "I'm just saying that's all."

"Right. Well, I'm off to bed," muttered John. He hadn't even noticed Ernie's hand and Ernie knew better not to mention Carrie's letter. That could wait until morning. There'd be fireworks soon enough then, he was sure.

John pounded up the stairs and Thomas turned apologetically to Ernie. "Sorry, wuss I don't know where that came from."

"Don't worry. There's a lot on his young mind." He smiled weakly, "Get yourself off to bed. It's an early start tomorrow."

"I'd forgotten. Early load of grain to the mill. Night, Ernie."

"Night. I'll just put this one back in the yard and let Trix out."

"That duck thinks he's family. He'll quack a different tune when we have him for supper one night."

"Not if you don't want to incur Carrie's wrath you won't," warned Ernie.

"Only kidding. Besides he's probably as tough as leather, the amount of time he spends in here warming his wings."

Ernie laughed, "I told Carrie that would happen. See you in the morning," he called and stepped out into the star rich night.

Thomas awoke with a start to angry voices travelling up the stairs. He rubbed his eyes blearily and looked at the clock. Five forty-five. What on earth could be happening this time of the morning? He slipped on his dressing gown, lifted the latch on his bedroom door and tiptoed to the top of the stairs. John was certainly venting his fury and the recipient of his lashing tongue was Ernie.

"What a stupid, nincompoop thing to do. How could you let that happen? Carrie's letter for God's sake. You know how important it is to me. You KNOW," he shouted.

"I've said I'm sorry and I'll apologise no more. An accident it was when a gust of wind took it into the fire."

"Aye, when Michael Lawrence came calling."

"John bach, the man was being neighbourly," Ernie didn't feel that now was the time to impart the real reason for his visit.

"We don't even know what it said," John was close to tears, "You silly, silly man. Why didn't you tell me a letter had come?"

"I put it by there as I always do, pride of place on the mantelpiece but what with all the excitement forgot to mention it."

John continued to bluster and fuss until Ernie raised a hand and murmured quietly, "Enough. I'll no more listen to your bad mouthing and bad temper. Yes, it's a shame the letter's gone but you're wrong. I do know what it said."

Thomas opened the kitchen door and asked tentatively, "Whatever's wrong? It sounds like the end of the world."

John didn't hear. He was staring at Ernie with a strange haunted look on his face. "You know what it said? How? You know I like to be the one to open them," he accused.

"Yes, but it was addressed to all three of us and with you going off to the dance I couldn't help myself. I wanted to hear her news too."

"I don't understand what all the fuss is about," interrupted Thomas.

"Cwat lawr," hissed John, "Don't interfere."

"But if a letter's gone missing and I'm one of the

addressees then it's just as much my business as yours." There was a pause and John white faced and tight-lipped just managed to stop himself from saying anymore. If he did, he knew he'd regret it later. He realised he was being unreasonable but he just couldn't help himself. He turned away from Ernie's steadfast gaze and Thomas' questioning eyes. He was giving too much away. He eventually broke the silence, "You're right. You're both right. My outburst is unwarranted... Sorry, Ernie, I'm not myself this morning. Too much of a good thing last night makes it hard to rise the next day."

"Go on with you," said Ernie kindly. "It was what you both needed," and he added a little more carefully, "A bit of female company and good friends having fun is the ticketed medicine."

John turned back forcing a smile, "Quite right. Quite right. So tell me, what did she have to say?"

The moment passed and breakfast was served and eaten as Ernie recounted as best he could remember Carrie's antics at the Nurses' Home and the fair. He noticed the hostile look, which crept into John's eyes at the mention of the young geography student who had been at the fair and the fact she'd written to Michael Lawrence. Ernie was certain John needed to know this to be able to get on with his own life.

"Seems like she's having a good time," said John begrudgingly, "And not short of suitors, she'll be spoilt for choice now Gwynfor's joined the queue."

"Oh?" queried Ernie.

"Asked for her address and if he thought it would be okay to visit her."

"And what did you say?"

"Told him to go ahead but not to get his hopes up. You know Carrie," John added sheepishly.

"I doubt whether Carrie's thinking of settling down. She's a bit young yet. Just enjoying making new friends that's all. We mustn't read anything into it. Besides nurses aren't allowed to marry," mused Thomas. "But it sounds like she may have found someone for you in the Jean Harlow blonde. What did she call her?"

"Pemb. Wonder what that's short for?" pondered Ernie.

"No matter, you'll have to tell her about Jenny," prompted Thomas.

"Aye, I will," said John dismissively. "No more gossiping or we'll be late with the grain."

"On my way," chirped Thomas as he finished the last of his breakfast.

"Not without dressing first, or they'll think we're a haircut short of a shilling," observed John. "I'll get the wagon ready."

John pushed aside his plate and left the unsettled atmosphere. Ernie looked after him thoughtfully as he began to clear away the dishes. It would be difficult for John to accept anyone into his sister's life and that boded trouble for the future.

"Don't take it hard Ernie," offered Thomas sympathetically. "You know what he's like where Carrie's concerned, very protective of her."

"Aye, I know," murmured Ernie but he knew John had to move on from his obsession with Carrie. He prayed that this Jenny may do the trick but he doubted she would.

CHAPTER SEVEN

Opportunity

Carrie treated Hawtry with more kindness after the recent bathroom encounter and true to her word she said nothing to anyone else. Her friends were not so charitable and even pestered her about it.

"Don't know why you want to give her the time of day," criticised Gilly, "She's just an old bitch."

"And a thief," added Pemb.

"She'd be the first to do you down if she could." Kirb joined in the annihilation of Hawtry's character.

"All right, I know she's not got the sweetest of tempers," responded Carrie.

"Sweetest of tempers!" exclaimed Gilly, "She's as rough as a badger with a growl to match."

"Like a rasp," agreed Kirb.

"All I'm saying is, she may have had a tough time of it and that's why she's like she is," defended Carrie.

"Huh! So she has to make sure everyone else has a rough time too. I'm sorry, Lew but you are just too kind. We'll have to re-educate you," continued Gilly.

"Or call it quits," persisted Carrie.

"Have it your own way," retorted Gilly, "but don't expect us to see the devil as an angel in disguise!"

"Leave it alone, Gilly. Let her make up her own mind. All I'll say is Hawtry's lucky if she's got one person on side," said Pemb.

"Or she knows something we don't," obsessed Gilly.

"I'm saying nothing," smiled Carrie knowing that her remark would further infuriate Gilly who went sounding off in an epiphany of blasphemies punctuated by a coughing fit, which reduced the rest of the group to laughter.

"Look at the time! I didn't realise it was so late," screeched Kirb. I've got to shift or I won't make night duty. Why didn't I have a nap instead of being drawn into your pyjama party?"

"We all have choices," said Pemb sagely.

Kirb pulled a face and made for the door, which she yanked open, "Catch you tomorrow." Kirb backed out of the door and directly into Hawtry who appeared to be on her way to the kitchen.

"Mind your step," snapped the Staff Nurse. Kirb made

another face, mouthing, 'Told you so,' and headed back for her room.

The door closed again.

"Do you think she heard?" whispered Gilly.

"Do you think she was listening?" queried Pemb.

"Too late to worry now," rejoined Carrie. "I'm off for a nightcap. Anyone else want one?"

"No thanks. Best get my head down. Early shift tomorrow," replied Pemb. "Night both."

"Good night," called Gilly as Pemb headed off after Kirb, before she turned to Carrie, "If she did hear we'll all be for it, except maybe you. That woman can make life very unpleasant. Oh God! Piss pot duty here I come."

Carrie smiled, "Do you want a drink?"

"No, better not. My bladder's not up to it. I need a good night's sleep."

"I'll try not to disturb you, is it all right if I leave the light on a while, I want to read my post."

"I'll bury my head under the pillow," murmured Gilly in a long-suffering tone.

"Go on with you, you'll be out like a light by the time I come back and be zedding away."

"I don't snore," protested Gilly.

It was true that she didn't but Carrie still enjoyed teasing her on that, "All I can say is heaven help any husband you have. It won't be alarm clocks he'll be needing but ear plugs."

"Get on with you!" laughed Gilly good-naturedly batting her with a cushion.

Carrie laughed and tiptoed off to the kitchen so that her efficient feet wouldn't clatter on the wooden floor. She was ambushed by Hawtry who was hiding behind the kitchen door.

"Oh! You made me jump!" cried Carrie, "What's the problem?"

"I wanted to say, thank you," muttered Hawtry begrudgingly. Kind words were difficult for her.

"You heard," said Carrie matter of factly.

"I heard," Hawtry affirmed. "And..." she continued slowly, "I may be able to help you."

"I don't understand..." faltered Carrie.

"A notice came round all senior staff today," Hawtry paused.

"Yes?" prodded Carrie.

"The teaching hospital at Birmingham has three places. I know you're interested and we've been asked for recommendations. Sister Toomer has put your name forward and I've seconded it."

"What about Pemb? She's been here longer than me and it's her dream too."

"She was mentioned. One place has gone. There's two left. I can swing it for you, if you want."

Carrie didn't know what to say; she knew chances like this came rarely, usually once every couple of years. She felt a churning in her stomach as she struggled to find the right words whilst busying herself with putting some milk in a pan. Eventually she spoke.

"Thank you Hawtry. I know you mean well. I'll just wait and see. There's bound to be lots of competition."

"Maybe not," Hawtry replied, "Just be prepared." With that the thin-faced nurse left Carrie alone in the kitchen to ponder over the implications of what she'd been told.

Carrie made her drink and returned quietly to her room where, as she'd predicted, Gilly was now fast asleep. She undressed as quietly as she could and pondered over the letters in her possession. Usually, she received one a month from John and the rest of the crew at Gelli Galed and always looked forward to reading their news. Occasionally, there'd be one from Megan but this time, this time there were five, and three in hands she didn't recognise. She placed John's letter to the back of the pile and opened Megan's first which was full of the news of the village dance and her disappointment at a local girl, Jenny, finding favour with John. Carrie was cross that Megan seemed to be using her cousin Thomas to try and make John jealous. Tom didn't deserve that. Carrie hoped Megan would come to realise that Thomas was indeed a much better proposition than John. She tried to remember what she knew of Jenny. She had seemed nice enough at school. They always compared notes on their hair, she remembered. Both sympathised with each other over their unmanageable locks.

Carrie looked at the postmark of the next letter written in a formal hand with neat small writing, which was postmarked in Aberystwyth. It read,

"Dear Carrie,

May I call you, Carrie? Lew reminds me of an old schoolteacher I once had, but there the resemblance ends. She was nothing like you.

I hope this letter reaches you, as all I have done is think about you and your friends since the Saturday night of the fair and wondered if you would be willing to come out with me one night to the pictures, perhaps? Or maybe even bring a friend with you?

I know that you work hard and change shifts often, so all I can say is that for the next month I shall be at Mary's teashop in the High Street on Friday afternoons at three o'clock. I hope sometime to see you there. Friday I don't have any lectures and usually use it for private study. If it's difficult to arrange meeting me then you can always leave a message for me with Gladys who manages the shop. She's very kind to all of us at the university, possibly because she is walking out with my friend, Joshua.

I look forward to hearing from you or even better seeing you.

Yours respectfully,
Lloyd (Osmend)

There was a PS in a different hand, which was scrawled at the bottom, 'For God's sake, put him out of his misery. J.'

Carrie assumed this must be his friend Joshua. She smiled to herself, feeling very flattered. Lloyd Osmend the geography student. Yes, he was very pleasant. His hair reminded her of her own father's, blond with a quiff at the front, which fell over his eyes. And he had a lovely smile, which lit up his whole face. She decided she would think seriously about taking him up on his offer, although she had originally thought that Pemb was the one he was interested in but Pemb appeared to have teamed up with another of Lloyd's friends, James, the tall dark one.

The next two letters were postmarked Crynant. The first was a stiff formal letter from Gwynfor who clearly had trouble writing and expressing himself. He rather clumsily was trying to ask her permission to write regularly to her with a view to courting her when she returned home. He talked of their long standing friendship and his desire to make it something more permanent.

Carrie sighed and pursed her lips, dear Gwynfor, he was a friend and a good one. They'd played together throughout their childhood but Carrie had never seriously thought about him romantically even though she'd allowed herself to be taunted by family and friends that Gwynfor was to be her intended. She was loathe to hurt him and wondered how best to turn him down. That would be a hard letter to compose.

Carrie turned her attention to the next letter penned in beautiful copperplate handwriting. Who could this one be from?

She took a sharp intake of breath when she read the name

at the bottom of the page, Michael Lawrence. He'd replied to her even though she was sure she hadn't put her address at the top. Her heart began to thump as she read his words. She could hear his cultured tones and see his face clearly as she avidly scoured the letter.

An excited churning began to bubble in her tummy and try as she might she could not suppress the smile, which rose to her lips. She read the letter twice more before deciding to clamber into bed. John's letter remained unopened at the side of her bed as she tried to quell the excitement building within her. Her thoughts scrambled uncontrolled through her mind as she willed sleep to come, but the clock's hands clicked slowly around the dial for almost two hours before she finally succumbed and drifted off into the world of dreams.

She was woken next morning by Gilly frantically scrabbling through her closet looking for her belt, which she seemed to have misplaced. Carrie's eyes blinked open still drowsy from her slumbers, "Whatever's the matter? Sounds like I'm sharing with the farmyard goat with all the bleating, scraping and tutting."

"Sorry, Lew. I can't find my belt. I could put my own leather one on but you know what a stickler Sister Toomer is. I'll pay for that with a dose of more late shifts I'm sure."

"Borrow mine," offered a yawning Carrie. "I need it back this afternoon," she continued.

"No problem. If you haven't found it for me I'll grab one from Edna. She still owes me half a crown from last month."

"How does the laundry maid owe you half a crown?" queried a puzzled Carrie.

"Long story."

"Then save it for later. I'm pooped," and she buried her head under the covers while Gilly flapped a bit more before disappearing with Carrie's belt, which she cursed was too tight for her.

The sudden silence in the room, rather than sending her back to sleep, served to wake Carrie even more. Muttering one of her Aunt Annie's favourite expressions she remonstrated with herself, "This won't knit the baby a bonnet." She swung her lissom limbs out of bed and padded to the door and peeped out. Nurses were scurrying down the corridor, late for duty, whilst others had stuck notes on their doors begging not to be disturbed or to be woken at another time. She popped on her dressing gown and heavy lidded trotted to the kitchen with her cocoa encrusted mug to wash it and make a cup of tea where she encountered Hawtry once more.

"Morning, Lew. Have you thought about what I said?"

Carrie had to admit that she hadn't but that she appreciated what Hawtry was trying to do for her.

Three junior nurses wanting to make a cup of tea before their duties interrupted them. Hawtry sent a warning signal to Carrie with her eyes and said primly, "Leave it with me," before exiting the kitchen. Carrie was too tired to stop her and took her tea back to bed where she read her remaining letter. She was surprised there was no mention of the dance but he did tell her that her last letter had ended up in the embers of the fire.

Carrie reread her mail and promised herself that once she was washed and dressed she would set about answering them, all of them, although she wasn't quite sure what she was going to say to Michael Lawrence. But, she did know one thing. His letter had disturbed her and sent her tummy into convulsions and little pinpricks of tremulous excitement had gone rippling through her body.

She went off for a bath although she knew the water would be nearly cold by now. Hopefully, it would wake her up and bring her to her senses, Michael Lawrence, for goodness sake, what was she thinking of?

Ablutions finished, Carrie skipped down the corridor to her room. She flapped around trying to get warm. Her mother had always told her to dry her hair thoroughly before going out but Carrie didn't have time. She knew she'd regret it later but just prayed she wouldn't catch a cold. Carrie had made up her mind she would drop a note in to Gladys at Mary's tearooms before she changed her mind.

She dressed quickly before the shivers really set in and then in a firm round, neat hand she wrote,

"Dear Lloyd,

I would be happy to go to the cinema with you. My next night off is a week Tuesday. I'm afraid I can't make the teashop this Friday as I am on duty but if Tuesday is inconvenient then I will be able to make the rendezvous at Mary's a week Friday at three p.m.

Yours sincerely,

Carrie Llewellyn.

She carefully sealed the letter and placed it in her pocket before selecting paper and pen to write her usual letter home. Once that was completed she dashed off a note to Megan, warning her to take more care of Thomas' heart. She finished the letter in an upbeat mood describing the young university student whose eye she had caught. She hoped that Megan would tell Gwynfor so that when her letter arrived for him, as it would once she had written it, it would help to soften the blow.

It was a tricky letter to pen, as she cared deeply for Gwynfor but only as a friend. She would have to choose her words carefully.

My dear friend Gwynfor,

Thank you for your letter. It was kind of you to write. I always like to hear the news from Bronallt as I do from home. Of course, I would welcome any letter you may wish to write but it seems impractical for you to come and visit especially as my shifts are all over the place and I couldn't guarantee seeing you. I would hate you to have a wasted journey.

I am nothing, if not stubborn, which you know only too well having been friends all our lives, but I would not want you to get your hopes up regarding a future with me. For one, I feel I am too young to think seriously about settling down and I am more than determined to have a career and mean to progress up the nursing ladder. As you know, currently nurses are forbidden to marry and I would not want to lose my job. I am working hard at making a new life for myself and loving every minute of it.

Please don't think harshly of me as I know it has been expected by both families that we would eventually unite the farms in marriage and I love you dearly as a friend but I cannot see myself as anyone's wife and my feelings for you are that of a friend and not a lover.

I look forward, as always, to seeing you and the gang back together again and we will speak further at Christmas when I hope to get home, duties permitting.

I am sorry not to have given you the answer you want but I know that out there is someone who will be perfect for you.

I hope this won't spoil our friendship and in my heart of hearts feel that this letter was prompted more by family expectations than by your own wishes.

Please take care and give my love to everyone at Bronallt.

Your friend,
Carrie Llewellyn.

Carrie looked through the letter again and made a slight adjustment inserting 'good' before 'friend' in her closing words. Pleased with it, she sealed it in an envelope and addressed it carefully.

She glanced at her watch. No time to write to Michael now if she wanted to catch Gladys at the teashop and get back to Bronglais in time for her ward duty. She didn't know what to write anyway. She grabbed her outside coat and locked her room. Next stop was the teashop.

CHAPTER EIGHT

Taking chances

Carrie entered the quaint little tearooms and took in the cheery atmosphere. She noticed a group of university students with their Aber scarves laughing and joking together. She thought she recognised one of them from the night at the fair but she wasn't certain.

A waitress came over to her with her order pad raised "Yes? What would you like?"

"Pot of tea for one and a toasted tea cake please." The waitress scribbled it down but Carrie stopped her leaving, "Excuse me, could you tell me which one is Gladys?"

"Over there by the cake counter with the blonde hair. Do you want to speak to her?"

"Please," affirmed Carrie.

"Glad," called the waitress, "Someone to see you."

The waitress went off with the order and Carrie looked around at the chintz wallpaper and curtains, the fancy plates decorating the walls, china ornaments adorning the shelves, the crisp red check tablecloths with mahogany ladder-back chairs and cottage cushions, the glass cake stands with their lace doilies and the whole oldie worldly feel of the place.

A bosomy, well made up, platinum blonde sauntered across. She had a distinct wiggle in her step and looked as if she had walked off the set of a Hollywood film. Her sweater clung to her ample breasts and a belt cinched in a tiny waist, which accentuated her hourglass figure. Her red pouting lips broke into a smile and Carrie noticed she had one tooth chipped at the front.

"Yes love," her voice was warm and expansive. "How can I help?"

"You're Gladys, friend of Joshua?"

"Yes?" a hint of suspicion entered the waitress's voice.

"I want to leave a message for his friend Lloyd, if that's all right?"

The waitress' demeanour instantly changed and she became friendly once more. "Are you one of the little nurses he's been going on about?"

"I don't know, maybe. We met at the fair."

"Yes, Carrie something ... Of course you are. Your hair gives you away."

Carrie wished she'd tucked it away under a beret or hat.

She hadn't dried it properly and it was wilder than ever, more akin to Moses' burning bush she thought, as her cheeks began to turn pink.

"Oh, don't mind me. I'd be happy to pass a message along. What do you want me to say?"

"Could you give this to him, please?" She took the letter from her pocket and handed it to Gladys as her tea and bun arrived.

Gladys meandered across to the students and had a quiet word with the student Carrie felt she'd seen before. She passed him the letter. Much to her embarrassment, he waved maniacally at her and called out, "Lloyd will be mad. He decided to stay in and study. Wait till I tell him you were here." He strode across and stuck out his hand, "Peter, Peter Gilbert. At your service."

"Don't mind him, love," apologised Gladys. "He's a real ladies man but he won't step on Lloyd's toes. He's too chivalrous for that. Moustache or no moustache."

It's true; Peter had very dark hair, piercingly blue eyes with a wicked twinkle and a dark, military looking moustache. He gave her a broad wink, "I'll see Lloyd gets this." He patted his pocket, now safely harbouring her missive. "Tell me how's that Irish friend of yours?"

"Gilly?"

"Is that her name?"

"It's what I call her. She's fine."

"If she's ever up for a foursome, give me a shout," and he wandered back to his friends who were watching the proceedings with interest.

Carrie flushed self-consciously and drank her tea with a greater speed than she would normally, even when on duty with little time to spare. She hastily finished her teacake and left as quickly as she was able, escaping outside to the fresh sea air.

A seagull chuckled overhead. At least it always sounded like laughter to her. She hurried along the High Street, turned up the hill briskly. The town clock chimed. Carrie would need to put a spurt on if she was to get back, change and grab a quick cup of tea before work.

She ran up the steps to the Nurses' Home and bumped smack bang into Pemb.

"You better move it," warned Pemb. "Sister Toomer's looking for you."

"Why?"

"I don't know, thought you could tell me. I have to see her at six. I can't think that we're in trouble. Can you?"

Carrie shook her head, "I'd better go and brush this lot. I'll never get it under my cap, else."

"No," Pemb eyed her critically, "Your hair does seem to have a mind of its own, and at the moment it looks as if it's disagreeing with you. There's some Vaseline in the bathroom. Try smoothing a small dab on your hands and just running it over your hair. It may help to tame it. Don't use too much or it'll look like greasy rats' tails."

"Thanks, I will. Is Gilly back?"

"Not seen her."

"Damn! She's got my belt. Have you got a spare?"

"Sorry, Lew. Got to scoot. Have to be on the ward in..." she checked her fob watch, "Now!" and she bolted on towards the Mat Unit.

Carrie cursed under her breath. How could she possibly go on duty and see Sister Toomer if she wasn't dressed properly? There was nothing for it she'd have to improvise, both clothes wise and verbally if challenged. She didn't want to get Gilly into trouble.

Carrie scuttled along the corridor to her room and changed frantically out of her daywear into her uniform. She practically ransacked Gilly's half of the wardrobe hunting for the lost belt. But wherever it was, it was not to be coaxed out of its hiding place.

All Carrie could find was a bright red leather one, which clashed with her uniform and hair, but not wearing one made her look inefficient and unkempt. She prayed no one would notice but knew that was an impossibility. She scurried out to the bathroom, cap in hand and took Pemb's advice with the Vaseline. She was surprised to see that it actually helped. So that's how Pemb always had immaculate hair. She'd remember that trick. She raced down the corridor and out of the building colliding with Gilly, fag in hand, on the steps. There was a frantic scramble as the two, switched belts all of which was observed by the fearsome Sister Toomer who pounced before Carrie had a chance to flee to the wards.

"Nurse Llewellyn, Nurse Gilhooly," she boomed.

"Yes, Sister," they chorused standing to attention.

"In my office, both of you, at six, in full uniform," she stressed the word, full.

"Yes, Sister," they replied in military style.

"Don't be late. And I should put that cigarette out if I were you," she said accusingly to Gilly before marching off. Gilly stamped on the offending item but not before Carrie noticed a burning smell.

"Gilly!" she shrieked, "Your cape's smouldering. You've burnt a hole."

"Holy Mary Mother of God," she blasphemed as she batted it out, "I'll go to Hell for all my sins. What'll I do about this?"

"Borrow a cape, and find your belt. If there's time I'll darn your cape. I'm good with a needle."

"Thank Christ for that. I quarrelled with one years ago."

"And you better get to Confession. You need a clean slate," giggled Carrie. "See you later."

Carrie had no more time to lose and she practically flew into the Unit and the ward.

When she arrived Hawtry was pinning up a list on the corkboard. A cluster of nurses had gathered. One of them pointed at her, "That's her. She's only been here five minutes. It's not fair. Favouritism that's what it is. I'm going to complain."

Hawtry smiled meaningfully at Carrie before leaving the rest of the nurses, like gannets, devouring the contents of the list.

Carrie had no idea what they were talking about and pushed her way through the throng to see for herself. There was a short list of nurses for interview for three places at a Dudley Road Teaching Hospital in Birmingham. Carrie's name was first.

"What gives you such preferential treatment?" asked one nurse snidely.

"Leave her alone," said another. "She's worked hard since she's been here. It's well known she does a sterling job."

"Getting on the right side of Toomer."

"Yeah, and Hawtry to name a few."

"Did I hear my name mentioned?" boomed the voice of the respected but fierce sister as she moved through the melee of nurses. "Ah, I see. The list is up. A good list too. All nurses had the opportunity and these ten have earned their chance to be on it. The final three will be decided by an interview process. Anyone any objections?" she bellowed.

"No, Sister," came the subdued response.

"Then get about your business, quickly," she roared.

The nurses scattered quickly, including Carrie.

"Not so fast, Llewellyn." Carrie halted in her tracks. "I'm glad to see you've found your belt. I'll see you at six."

"Yes, Sister." Carrie's heart was beating as quickly as a sparrow. She could hardly keep the lid on her bubbling enthusiasm. What an opportunity; what a chance. She had to ensure she wouldn't blow it. She took extra care to complete her duties properly. She knew she was being watched and judged. She waited anxiously for six o' clock.

CHAPTER NINE

Laughter in the rain

Carrie stood proudly outside Sister Toomer's office alongside Pemb, Kirb, Gilhooly and six other nurses. All four friends had made the list. Gilhooly fiddled with her new belt gleaned from Edna the laundry maid who it seems was a betting woman and owed Gilly for an ill placed bet on the horses. She was the first in and after checking over her uniform she went in before Sister Toomer, Matron and a representative from Dudley Road Hospital. The rest waited in agonised silence outside. Ten minutes later she was closing the door and screwing up her face.

"How did it go?" whispered Carrie, but she was not to know as her name was called next. She smoothed her skirt, straightened her back and head held aloft sailed proudly in before the panel.

"Sit down, Nurse Llewellyn," invited Matron.

"Thank you, ma'am."

"I expect you are surprised to be included on this round of interviews?"

"Yes, I am," she replied honestly.

"Mm. You have talent, of that I've no doubt, and you have now turned eighteen. You're part way through your midwifery training. However, I feel that this is not the direction you wish to pursue. Is that correct?"

Carrie was uncertain what to say but followed her heart and what she knew her mother would advise and told the truth. "Yes, ma'am. I am enjoying my time here but I am set on a career in general nursing. I hope then to find my niche and specialise."

"What field do you think that may be?"

"I'm not certain, but general nursing will give me ample opportunity to find out."

"You do realise that you would be required to finish your midwifery course?"

"Yes, ma'am."

"This, however, shouldn't be a problem. I'm assured that should you be selected, you can complete an accelerated course at Birmingham. Does this interest you?"

"Yes, ma'am." Carrie's heart was thumping so loudly she felt sure that all in the room could hear it. Her knees were feeling shaky. She could hardly stop her hands from trembling.

The representative from Birmingham spoke next, "Nurse Llewellyn would you tell me why you think you should be selected for one of the offered places?"

Carrie took a deep breath and struggled to keep her voice even. "I'm a quick learner and greedy to learn more. I don't shirk my duties, whatever they are. I feel I can hold my own amongst the other nurses. I was lucky enough to be moved up from auxiliary to probationer after commencing here. My mother taught me to be honest and reliable. I am both and I know have staying power."

"I can vouch for that," certified Sister Toomer. "She's punctual, works hard and is good with people, patients and staff alike, an excellent communicator."

"Able to act on her own initiative? In a crisis?"

"I'm confident, she is," affirmed Sister Toomer.

"You come well recommended. Do you have any questions?"

Carrie had a million but didn't feel she could vocalise them all, "When would the placement begin?"

"After Christmas, January 3rd. We have newly qualified nurses moving onto other hospitals and will be ready to take on thirty new recruits."

"I thought there were only three places?" Carrie asked before she could stop herself.

"This isn't the only place we're recruiting from. There are other places to visit around the country. Anything else?"

"Yes," she swallowed hard, "Although, I value and welcome this opportunity, in fact it is my dream, I feel that there are many other equally good student nurses who also deserve the chance."

"Meaning?" questioned Sister Toomer fastening her dark eyes resolutely on Carrie and making her feel distinctly hot.

"It's just that I'm the new girl on the block and there are many others who have been waiting longer than me. I wonder if it's quite fair that I should be picked above them."

"Do you have any doubts? About your own capabilities? Your own ambition? Are you up to the job?"

"I'm up to it. I'm more than capable and can nurse as well as any other."

"Then I should keep quiet before you talk yourself out of it. I doubt whether the other nurses would be as charitable."

"Yes, Sister. Thank you, Sister."

"Very well. We have your reports in front of us. Is there anything further you wish to add?"

"Yes, Sister. Just that I'm proud to be considered and would be even prouder if selected. I wouldn't let anyone down."

"Thank you, Nurse Llewellyn, you may go."

Carrie smiled good-bye and left the room holding her proud bearing. Gilly was waiting outside as another nurse was called in.

"Well? How did it go?" asked Gilly.

"I was just going to ask you."

"Oh tosh! I just told them the truth," answered Gilly.

"Which is?" pressed Carrie.

"I'm happy here. I've always wanted to be a midwife. I want to complete my training, go back home and possibly work on the district. I love babies and big bellies. Plan to have one myself some day."

"The belly or the baby?" laughed Carrie.

"You mean you can have one without the other? What a surprise."

"So you've counted yourself out?"

"That I have. Gives someone else the chance. Someone who really wants it. Come on let's grab a cuppa. I'm dying for a fag. You can tell me about yours. The others'll be ages yet."

"Good luck, Pemb," whispered Carrie, "You too, Kirb. See you back at the block. Damn, I forgot to ask when we'll be put out of our misery."

"I'll do that," promised Pemb, "Now scoot, you're making me nervous."

Carrie and Gilly impishly scuttled away. "I feel like celebrating," said Gilly.

"Why? What's there to celebrate?" puzzled Carrie.

"Oh, I don't know," murmured Gilly mysteriously. "I just have a good feeling about a few things. It's my Celtic intuition."

"What? What do you know?" coaxed Carrie.

"Ask me no questions and I'll tell you no lies," avoided Gilly. "All I'm saying is you best check your pigeon hole at Bronglais."

Carrie couldn't imagine what she meant, but she played along anyway. "It can't be a letter from home I've just had," she quickly calculated, "Four from there."

"Ah!" nodded Gilly knowingly. "You'll have to wait and see then."

"Duw, gellwch yn fod yn broblem fawr."

"Now, now - you know my Welsh is limited to swear words and numbers."

"I said, God, you can be a big problem. In other words, you're infuriating."

"All part of my charm," Gilly smiled. "Now, do you

fancy going into a teashop in Aber or are we saving our pennies and having tea at home?"

"With all this intrigue going on?"

"The Nurses' Home, it is then. Race you. Last one in makes the tea," and with that she sprinted away leaving Carrie to dash after her calling, "You're not playing fair. Cheat."

The two friends scrambled along the road but as Gilly reached the steps she doubled over gasping for breath. Carrie flew up the steps and in through the door shouting, "Winner!" She turned back and saw her friend, sitting at the bottom her head in her hands. "Gilly?" She ran back to her, "Are you all right?"

"Can't seem to get my breath," she wheezed. "I've got stitch and my lungs feel as if they're about to burst."

"It's not another ruse so you can leap up and run past me indoors?" But one look at Gilly's face and Carrie knew her friend was really suffering. Gilly abruptly turned her head away and violently coughed up a huge amount of phlegm. Carrie noticed there were a few specks of red in the regurgitated mess. "Here, lean on me. Let's get you inside."

Gilly gratefully allowed herself to be pulled up and she leaned on Carrie as they negotiated the steps. Once inside Gilly rasped, "Check your pigeon hole. I'll wait."

"No," insisted Carrie. "Let's get you to bed. I can check that any time." Gilly tried to protest but Carrie took no notice and helped her up the stairs and to their room where Gilly flopped on her bed.

"I'll get you some water."

"And a cup of tea."

"In a minute, here sip this." Carrie poured a glass of water and gently moistened Gilly's lips. "Do you think you can manage to get to the window?"

"Why?"

"The fresh air will help." Carrie struggled with the metal catch and pulled up the sash. Gilly limped to the window ledge, stuck her head out and took a huge lungful of air before retreating back to her bed.

"I'll put the kettle on, won't be a minute."

"If I don't die of the cold first. That wind's enough to freeze the nose of a polar bear," complained Gilly.

Carrie ran to the kitchen. Luckily the kettle was still warm and it didn't take long to heat up. The shrill whistle piercingly announced the water was boiling and Carrie made a big brew. When she returned to their room with the tea things she was horrified at what she saw.

"You stupid idiot," she yelled. "What do you think you're doing with that?"

"Smoking it," came the glib reply.

Carrie wrested the offending cigarette from Gilly and vigorously stubbed it out. "This is what's causing your wheezing. No wonder you're short of breath. If God intended us to smoke he'd have put chimney pots on our heads. How can you be so foolish? You silly, silly woman."

"Ah, but you love me really," responded Gilly amiably.

"Yes, we all love you. That's why we don't want you to go killing yourself with these."

"No harm done. If they were dangerous they wouldn't be legal. Come on, Lew; don't be such a spoilsport. Everyone smokes, Clarke Gable, Bette Davies. All the big stars. If it was bad for them wouldn't they be stopping it too?"

"One day they'll be putting warnings on these things," and Carrie snatched the rest of the pack and crushed them into the bin.

"What do you want to go and do that for? They were to last me till payday. That was my last packet and I'm not up to popping out for some more."

"No. And you won't be again, if I have my way." Carrie shook her head, her face full of concern.

"Don't look so serious. You'll be putting warnings on men's underpants next."

"What?" Carrie was bewildered by the change in conversation.

"Warning. Poking can seriously damage your health. Do you think that would help them keep their trousers on?"

Carrie couldn't help herself, she laughed and sat down by her friend, "Sincerely though, you've got me worried."

"Oh tosh, worry about yourself first."

"Gilly, I know what I saw."

"You saw nothing."

"I did. There was blood in your sputum. You have to get checked."

"And if I'm ill, I can't work. I'll lose my job. My family depend on me. You don't understand."

"And what if the coughing is more than damaged lungs? You'll be infecting other people. It's irresponsible." A light dawned in Carrie's eye. "That's why you want to stay here. If you were selected you'd have a medical. You can't afford to do that."

"Because I'd lose my job and my family would lose the bread winner," finished Gilly.

"I can't believe that. There must be some way we can get help."

"You can't tell anyone. Not a soul. You promise me."

"But what if it's..." Carrie took a breath, "What if it's TB?"

"I'll cross that bridge, if and when I come to it."

"Gilly," Carrie tried to reason with her, "You have to do something. I can't forget what I saw."

"And I'm asking you as a friend, to let it go. There's no point in pursuing this conversation, go down and check your pigeon hole."

Carrie knew it was impossible at the moment to make Gilly see sense. They were both as stubborn as each other. Carrie needed to think and sighing deeply she went downstairs to see what all the fuss was about but before closing the door she added, "It's not the end of the matter. Whatever you think."

It was with a worried frown she approached the letter rack in the foyer and there was a hand delivered letter in a small, neat script, which she recognised as belonging to Lloyd. She opened it with mixed emotion and scanned the contents. So the cinema date was on and not only that, it was to be a foursome. Peter Gilbert had persuaded Gilly to accompany him. Carrie raced back up the stairs. She flung open the door, "You can't go out with Lloyd's friend if you've..." She stopped. Gilly wasn't there. She peered down the corridor and then ran to Pemb's room and knocked. No answer. She headed for the kitchen but as she passed the bathroom, showers and toilets she heard a chesty wracking cough and the sound of someone retching. She tapped on the door, "Gilly? Gilly are you in there?"

There was a scuffling and Gilly opened the door, looking blanched. "Lew, I need help," she finally stuttered before collapsing on the floor.

Carrie knelt at her friend's side before urgently shouting out, "I need some assistance here. Anyone? Please!" A nurse quickly appeared and lent a hand. Carrie looked up it was Hawtry.

"Let's get her back to your room. What's the problem?" Hawtry said efficiently, taking charge.

"I'm not sure," Carrie said hesitantly, "I just know she's not well."

"She doesn't look it. Not that colour. We'll call one of the doctors to see her."

The two of them lifted her up and half carried and half dragged her back and lay her on the bed.

"It's not..." Hawtry stopped, "Anything like I had, is it?" she continued.

"No, no," Carrie protested, "Nothing like that. Some sort of chest infection I think."

"All the more reason to get her checked."

Carrie eased Gilly's head onto her pillow and looked searchingly at Gilly whose eyes fluttered open. She nodded and whispered, "Do it."

Hawtry commanded, "You stay with her and I'll get help."

Gilly caught hold of her friend's hand, "Not Hawtry! Didn't know the old bitch had a soft side."

"She's not a complete dragon,"

"Missing a tail, is she? Or is it just the fire breathing breath," she joked and then coughed again.

Carrie grabbed a towel and Gilly spat into it. The blood was frothy and red, blood from the lungs. "Gilly, Gilly, Gilly," Carrie repeated, "Why didn't you say something? We all just thought you had a smoker's cough."

"Easier not to," murmured Gilly. "Cat's out of the bag, now. No double date for us on Tuesday."

"No, not unless there's a miracle."

Minutes later, Hawtry returned with Doctor Caldwell. Taking his stethoscope he examined Gilly, "Diminished breath sounds, bronchial breathing, tracheal deviation and coarse crackles, what does that sound like to you Staff Nurse?"

"It could be pneumonia or TB."

"Or any number of lung disorders. An X-ray should confirm it. What else do we need to do?"

"Take a culture of her sputum?" offered Carrie.

"Good, Nurse. How do we do that, Staff?"

"Three early morning sputum smears on three different days. Prepare the specimens on a slide stained with acid fast dye."

"Well done. I needn't tell you how urgent this is," he decreed, "We need to get her get her X-rayed and put her in isolation. What do you think an X-ray will reveal?"

"Could show cavitation, calcification, nodes in upper lobes."

"Correct."

"How do you know so much, Staff?" asked an amazed Carrie.

"My speciality, Chest. I'm hoping to move back into that area." She turned to Carrie and added quietly, "My fiancé died of tuberculosis. Four years ago."

"I'm sorry."

She became brisk and efficient once more. We'll both have to be tested, as will all other nurses and patients who have been in contact with her. That's if the worst happens. But, remember not all forms of TB can be passed on."

"My grandmother on my mother's side had TB," said Carrie. "She was made to climb a mountain and drink her own urine. It worked for her."

"Old wives' tale, Nurse. Your grandma must have had the constitution of an ox; a strong immune system, with a bit of luck that's been passed on to you. Right! To the Septic Block now," he ordered.

Gilly, Hawtry and Carrie were whisked away to the Septic Block with speed and efficiency. Carrie stared at the ward's hygienic but boring surroundings. Every wall was clinically white and the floor highly polished. Gilly was made as comfortable as possible. Carrie sat on her friend's bed and took her hand.

"What happens now?" asked Carrie in a hushed tone.

"You'll have to go out with both of them, Lew. I don't think I'll be better in time for the pictures," smiled Gilly.

"You may not be out yourself, but don't worry too much," said Hawtry. "You'll have a skin test. That'll examine your immunity. Treatment has come a long way this decade."

"That's if she's got it."

"That's if she's got it," affirmed Hawtry.

"How do I get a message out, to let the others know what's happening?"

"I'll see what I can do."

"How come you can get out?"

"Been through it all before. I'm immune so it's not a problem."

"Can I give you a note?" asked Carrie grabbing a piece of paper.

"Sorry, nothing must leave the block. It'll have to be a verbal message, or I can write a message for you."

Carrie took Lloyd's letter from her pocket. "Here's the address. Can you explain what's happened and tell him I'll be in touch as soon as I can. You can leave a message for him at Mary's teashop. With the manageress, Gladys."

"I know the one. Consider it done. You better get yourself something to do, play cards, anything. You'll go mad stuck in here."

"Thanks, Hawtry."

The thin-faced nurse nodded cursorily and left the two

friends. Gilly was stretched out on a bed, her eyes were closed and she was breathing in rasps. She murmured, "Who'd have thought it? Hawtry has a heart. I thought she was the original ice maiden. What have you done to her, Lew? She seems half sensible now."

"Nothing. I just gave her some time when she wasn't feeling too good. Seems she appreciated it... You know everyone deserves a chance. If you expect someone to behave a certain way, they generally do. My old school teacher used to say..."

"Oh please, get off your soap box. I'm not up for a lecture now."

"It's not a lecture," Carrie stubbornly reprimanded, "But wise words. If you have high expectations of someone they'll generally live up to them. Hawtry is tough and people treat her accordingly, expecting her to be mean and so she is. If you give her the time of day she'll surprise you. At least, I think so."

"Yes, yes, yes... Now shut up so I can get some sleep."

Carrie removed her cap and shook out her spangled curls. She sat at the table and picked up the cards and began to deal out the deck for a game of Patience. It was going to be a long night.

CHAPTER TEN

Fast changes

Ernie's hand was getting better. Thanks to Michael Lawrence's quick action there would be no long-term damage. Dr. Rees had changed the dressing and designated Ernie to household duties until he was completely better. Thomas and John could manage the farm on their own. John was also feeling even more guilty about his outburst after seeing Ernie's injury and did his best to put things right.

Saturday night had come round and the two cousins were busy sprucing themselves up and enjoying the usual male banter, which acted as a precursor to a night out.

"If it's a woman you're out to catch you'd best go easy on that stuff," chortled John as Thomas slapped on some cologne. "She'll think you're trying to mask something nasty."

"Or she'll float away in my arms mesmerised by the sheer power of the perfume."

"If she can breathe. You don't want to give her an asthma attack."

"And what about you? I don't notice you going lightly on the stuff," rejoined Thomas.

"Maybe I know something you don't."

"Like what?"

"Like she has a poor sense of smell. Remember when Jenny stepped in fox dung and trod it all over school? Everyone noticed except her. She suffered all the usual cracks and still didn't catch on."

"Aye, I remember something about it. What about when Angela Jennings got stuck in the chair?"

"We laid bets the chair would break."

"It certainly didn't look too happy when we pulled it off. Stress marks it had. She had a rear and a half. What happened to her?"

"Family moved to Pontypridd, I think."

"I thought we were going to need a hacksaw to get her out."

"Are you two still clowning about up there?" shouted Ernie, "If you don't get a move on you'll be late."

"I can't find my collar studs," returned John.

"In the pot on the dresser in the spare room."

"What are they doing there?"

"It's where you left them," replied Ernie.

"Oh aye, not myself I was."

"Well, I don't know who you were then," laughed Thomas.

"Oh ha! Ha!"

"Come on lads, Senator's ready and waiting, all kitted up. It's nearly quarter to seven."

"All right, all right. Don't fuss! Where's the Vaseline?"

"Where you left it."

"Yes, but where?"

"I've got it," yelled Thomas. "Come on, wuss. Let's hit the road. Ladies watch out, you don't stand a chance. How do I look, Ernie?" he asked as he trundled down the stairs.

"A proper gentleman that's for sure."

"Let's hope some of that stink wears off on the ride down. Overpowering it is, isn't it, Ernie? Megan will pass out."

"Go on with you. You both look fine. Have a good time."

Ernie waved them off as Senator started his march down the hill. He returned to the kitchen and sat there thoughtfully, a troubled look on his face. The prickling of a premonition was forming in his mind and he knew something had happened to Carrie. He tried to rescue the pictures, which accompanied the feelings but they were proving elusive. Something was wrong. He was sure of it, but he seemed to know that Carrie was all right although she was in some way affected by someone else's plight. He struggled and tussled with his thoughts but could see nothing conclusive. He switched on the wireless and fiddled with the tuner. The BBC World Service was broadcasting its news and it was full of gloom. Britain was now on the brink of war with Germany. The Prime Minister, Neville Chamberlain had appeased Chancellor Hitler once too often and had given a stern warning not to invade Poland. It seemed that Germany was amassing its troops for just such an event. If so, what would happen then?

Ernie shuddered to think. The Great War had been a war to end all wars and everyone had said, 'Never again.' He remembered the trenches, the mustard gas attacks and friends who had died in vain 'going over the top'. What would it be like for the young men today? He wondered how they would manage. It was likely that all young men could be called up. Farmers had usually been an exception but if there were older folk and women to run the farm then they could quite easily call on Thomas, Gwynfor and maybe even John. 'Best face that devil when it snarls,' he thought and put the kettle on to boil. He opened the kitchen door and Trix padded in closely followed by Bandit and the two settled in front of the fire at Ernie's feet, who closed his eyes and allowed himself to drift away on a sea of dreams.

John and Thomas anchored the cart in the square and sauntered across to Segadelli's store where Jenny was waiting shyly, in a neat primrose dress and green double-buttoned coat. Thomas noticed with sadness that Megan was not alone and had big brother Gwynfor for company. So, no loving walk back home with her tonight. He smiled a little too brightly, "Gwynfor, Megan. Has anyone seen Brian or Dilly?"

"They said they'd meet us there," came her prompt response. "They're keeping us a place in the queue."

John took Jenny's hand and smiled at her. She looked up at him and beamed. She really had a rather comely smile he noticed. Pretty cupid bow lips and a smattering of freckles across her nose like Carrie. She wasn't at all bad looking. And with a surge of earnest enthusiasm, which surprised even him, he began to chatter about his week and ask her what she had been doing since the dance.

Megan reluctantly allowed her hand to be taken by Thomas as they walked along in silence. They reached The Hall where Dilly and Brian were standing near the front of the queue and who waved frantically. There were groans and jeers of "Get in line," as they took their place alongside their friends.

"P'raps it's unfair and we should go to the back," whispered Jenny.

"Nonsense," replied John. "They'd all do it if there was someone they knew saving them a place." Inwardly he quite liked what she had said, it's probably how Carrie would have felt.

There was a bit of foot stamping and hand clapping as they waited for the doors to open and they all got pushed forward in the rush as people tried to get to the payment booth and purchase their tickets.

"Here's the money for mine," offered Jenny.

"No," insisted John. "I asked you out. If you like, you can buy the ice creams." She nodded trustingly and with her heart all of a flutter stepped into The Hall where John led her to the back row. Gwynfor flopped into the seat next to him.

"You were right, wuss," he whispered.

"What?"

"Carrie. She just wants us to be friends. Says she's too

young to be serious about anyone and nurses aren't allowed to marry. She's promised we'll talk at Christmas."

"Right. Sorry about that. I did warn you."

"I know. Guess I'll have to set my sights on someone else. Jenny hasn't got a sister has she?" he murmured.

"No, she's the only girl with five brothers. You'll have to look elsewhere." John felt a feeling of relief that his sister had acted accordingly. It just might be that she wouldn't be serious about anyone, perhaps not ever.

The lights began to dim and a cheer went up as Pearl and Dean began their run of advertisements followed by the trailers of films to come. John smiled amiably as Jenny snuggled into his shoulder as his arm went around her. Thomas was not having such luck, as Megan sat there stiffly hardly bearing to let their arms brush against each other. Thomas decided he'd have to be patient and work hard at winning her affections but convinced himself that he'd manage it.

Carrie sat solemnly in front of Doctor Caldwell, "You're lucky Nurse Llewellyn, the schick test has brought you up in a raised red lump, that coupled with a clear X-ray shows that you have indeed inherited your Grandmother's immunity. You are free to go."

"What about Gilly?"

"Not so lucky, I'm afraid."

"Then she's..." Carrie trailed off.

"Yes, she's got TB. We'll have to send her off to a Sanatorium where she can best be helped. We are pumping her full of antibiotics but her lungs have suffered badly. It may mean they'll collapse a lung to give the other a rest. I don't know."

"What'll her family do? They rely on her."

"They'll have to rely on someone else, now."

"Can I see her?"

"Yes, but don't tire her out." He hesitated, "I don't quite know how to say this but the disease appears to be accelerating quite rapidly. I've never seen such a quick decline."

"Is it the transmittable kind?"

"I don't know, not yet, we have to wait for the results of the cultures to come back. It may not be. We can hope."

Carrie felt her eyes fill up and a solid lump formed in her throat. "Thanks for your honesty," she managed to say. Up went her head, back went her shoulders and she briskly moved into the ward where Gilly was in isolation.

"This is one Hell of a way to get out of a double shift," she said as she marched in.

Gilly turned her head, "You know me, I always have to go one better. How are you doing?"

"I'm clear."

Carrie was shocked at the sight of her friend. The doctor was right. The decline had been rapid. The skin on Gilly's face was translucent, almost transparent. She looked ethereal.

"How do I look?"

"Awful."

"Don't sugar the pill, Lew, tell me what you really think. I could do with some face paint."

"No one to see you in here."

"There's Dr. Caldwell," Gilly smiled, "I kept most of you fooled, a little rouge is a wonderful thing, brings colour to the cheeks."

"And here's me thinking you were a natural Irish colleen."

"We all need a little help, some more than others."

"So what now?"

"They're sending me up in the mountains somewhere. Switzerland would be best but I can't afford that, so it's the Welsh mountains for me."

"Doesn't Ireland have mountains?"

"You're not getting rid of me that easily. Besides, I don't want to alarm the family."

"Gilly, you have to tell them. They need to know."

"No, they don't. Why worry them unnecessarily? Plenty of time enough for that if it gets serious."

"It doesn't get any more serious than this."

"Oh tosh! You Welsh always have a tendency to exaggerate, and be over dramatic. I'll get over this you'll see, just watch..." Gilly doubled over with yet another hacking coughing fit. Carrie picked up the sputum bowl and rushed to her friend's side and stared anxiously as her friend coughed and spluttered into the bowl.

She fondly mopped her brow, "You stubborn, foolish woman. What are we going to do with you?"

Gilly flopped back on her mountain of pillows, propping her up, to stop her lungs from drowning. "It's hell trying to sleep like this, I'll have a whopper of a double chin by the time I'm through," she wheezed.

"Is there anything I can do? Anything you want?"

"A cigarette would be nice."

"Think again."

"Quite fancy some chocolate, if you can get any. You know what they say about hospital food. Oh, and my toilet bag. At least I can look presentable, even if I'm not."

"Done. I'll check your post too."

"Thanks. What about our double date? Do you think he'll wait?"

"I'll speak up for you."

"No, you're just greedy; two gorgeous men and one of you. Why don't you take Pemb?"

"It's you he wanted to see, you'll just have to get fit and well."

"Okay." She closed her eyes, "I'm feeling sleepy now. Do you mind?"

"No, you rest. I'll be back."

"You'd better."

Carrie left the Septic Block with tears streaming down her face. She felt bereft and helpless. It was then she came to the decision that if she had an aptitude for it that she would make Chest her speciality too, like Hawtry.

CHAPTER ELEVEN

Facing demons

The film was a great success, enjoyed by all. The group of friends chattered animatedly about the story and the spinster, Miss Froy, who was the most unlikely candidate to be a spy. They agreed that this Alfred Hitchcock certainly had a flair for suspense.

"Beats all that Saturday morning stuff we watched as kids," said Thomas.

"The Three Stooges and Laurel and Hardy? You can't compare them. They were comedy and in black and white. This was a thriller in full Technicolor, as they say in America."

"Quite the little expert are you, then?" queried Megan.

"No," said Thomas defensively, "I know what I like and what's good, and this was far superior to anything I've seen in a long time."

"Don't forget Tom's been in Australia awhile, probably don't have pictures there," said Gwynfor meaningfully with a look that told his sister to shut up.

"They did, but it was hundreds of miles away from where we were settled. I didn't have the opportunity to go," said Thomas uncomfortably.

John suddenly swung Jenny around and pulled her in close and kissed her full on the lips. Megan peeved, stiffened, "You walking me home then, Thomas? Or are you watching the next show here in the square?"

"What?"

"Those two; that's if you can stomach it," sniped Megan jealously.

"Course I'll walk you home. See you back at the cart, wuss?"

"Don't rush on my account," said John. "Meet you back here in about an hour? Does that give you long enough?"

Thomas nodded, and John and a giggling Jenny, ran off towards Seven Sisters end of the village. Megan frowned, tucked her arm in Tom's and proceeded towards the railway lines and track to Bronallt. Gwynfor hung back and decided to follow some of the rest of the village youth to Segadelli's café, which stayed open later on picture night. He joined some of his old school friends and cast a fresh eye over the unattached girls of the village.

Carrie sat in Pemb's room her eyes red from weeping.

"Don't take on so," reassured Pemb, "Gilly's a fighter. She'll pull through this, you'll see."

"I hope you're right," murmured Carrie, "But you didn't see her. She looked so ill."

"Well, she would, she's got TB."

"But that's just it, how could she have hidden it from us for so long? Make up to give her an artificial colour and I never noticed."

"Don't blame yourself. There's nothing anyone could have done."

"All the symptoms were there under my nose and I just thought it was the smoking that gave her that cough."

"As did we all."

"Yes, but I shared a room with her. I should have suspected something."

"If Gilly didn't want you to know, you wouldn't. Secretive she was. It's not your responsibility."

"And what if she dies?"

"Don't say that."

"But, it could happen. It could."

"Lew, wise up. She's getting treatment. The best. It's in God's hands now."

"God has never done me any favours before," retorted Carrie and then seeing the hurt look on Pemb's face she apologised, "I'm sorry, I don't know what I'm saying. I've seen too much of death in my short life. I don't want her to die."

"None of us do, you're not the only one who loves her. Come here." And Pemb took Carrie in her arms who sobbed as she had with her Aunty Annie years before after her mother's death.

John approached Jenny's house and pulled her into him, "Don't go in yet. Stay a while. Let's walk to the playing fields and sit on a swing."

Jenny hesitated but when she looked at his eyes smouldering with passion she went with him. She was nervous. She'd never been this close to a man before, never stepped out with one and didn't know what to expect. They reached the small shelter by the field and John pulled her close fumbling with her clothes. His kiss became more insistent, more urgent.

"Stop, John, you're hurting me."

But he took no notice and carried away with the sight of her wild hair and freckled nose he tore at her clothes.

"No, I don't want this, please," she begged. John had gone past the point of no return and pushing her to the ground he was on top of her. Jenny's eyes glazed over and she protested no more.

John forced himself on top of her and was just about to penetrate her when he caught her fragile terrified look. He remembered Carrie and Jacky Ebron and his heart filled as though it would break. He rolled off her.

"Duw, cariad, I'm so sorry. What am I thinking? I'm not an animal. I don't know what possessed me. I've never felt like this before." Jenny drew her legs together and whimpered like a small child. She pulled her clothes around her and drew her knees up, sitting shivering on the ground. John was filled with remorse and sorrow. He took off his coat, wrapped it around her, cuddled her, and rocked her, begging her forgiveness. She took a huge gulp of breath and seemed to awaken from her stupor. He showered kisses on the tears, which straddled her cheeks murmuring endearments over and over. "Cariad, forgive me. I'm so, so sorry."

Jenny appeared to respond and as he whispered his apologies, she brushed his unruly hair from his eyes and caressed his cheeks. He leaned over and kissed her tenderly, his hot salt tears mingling with hers, joining together in a union of love. This time he was gentle and giving and Jenny sighed, "I've never done this before. I don't know what to do."

"Neither have I," John confessed, "I guess we'll just let nature take its course."

"I always said I'd wait for the right one and only then, when I was married."

"And what do you say now?"

"I don't know," she answered in a small tight voice.

"We'll go no further unless you want me to, Jenny."

Jenny closed her eyes arching her back into him. He had his answer. Together they lay moving rhythmically until they juddered in the pulsating joy of adult love.

John held her close and kissed her eyes, her nose, her ears, her chin and Jenny sat there, stunned. In silence they rearranged their clothes and John walked Jenny back to her house and kissed her gently on the cheek.

"Will you meet me next week?" she asked, her eyes pleading.

"Aye, Saturday, seven o'clock at Segadelli's. See you then." He turned with a cheery wave and began to whistle as he walked back through the village towards the square and the waiting cart.

The fresh air filled his lungs and awakened his senses. What had he done? He'd selfishly taken the virginity of a sweet village girl who reminded him of his sister. He gave himself a brisk talking to on the way back to the cart. "She wanted it as much as you. She's a tidy girl and you could do a lot worse, John bach, a lot worse. Come on pull yourself together. Perhaps, it's just what you need. Just what you need."

CHAPTER TWELVE

War

Ernie was worried. Storm clouds were gathering on the European front and although he didn't talk about it in front of John and Thomas, at the farm, the news each day seemed to be filled with fear and trepidation of a possible military conflict with Germany.

Chamberlain's policy of appeasement seemed to be having little effect on the German Chancellor, who constantly flouted agreements. The Treaty of Versailles wasn't worth the paper it was written on, as Germany had rearmed, reoccupied the buffer zone of the Rhineland and had reunited with Austria, all in defiance of the treaty. The transfer of the essentially German Sudetenland in Czechoslovakia had reluctantly been endorsed by Britain and France.

Ernie felt that the Prime Minister had no teeth and although everyone would prefer a peaceful solution it seemed Herr Hitler would not stop at this. Propaganda made much of Communism being a bigger threat to the West than Fascism, but Ernie was troubled. He'd had a strangely vivid dream, the type of dream he knew not to ignore, a dream of running away from a building toppling forward as if pushed. The windows were filled with Union Jack flags.

As he ran he was joined by John, Gwynfor, Thomas and other young men in the village. They escaped into a deserted church where artists' easels were scattered around with unfinished paintings. John picked up a palette and began to complete a landscape scene of a field of red poppies when a young man, wearing a swastika on his sleeve, standing at the next easel dipped his hands in red paint and smeared them across John's picture changing the scene to one of bloodshed. As they began to fight there was a cry and a group of refugees, mainly women and children came streaming into the church crying in a language he didn't understand. The swastika arm banded man stopped his fight. He plucked a machine gun out of another picture and turned it on the refugees, splattering the women and children with a parade of bullets until they were dead.

Carrie entered the church in a halo of golden light dragging a huge flag of Poland and tenderly covered the bodies, as the German soldier in slow motion turned the gun towards her and took aim. John, screaming, took a flying leap at the enemy to knock him off balance and that's when Ernie woke up.

The dream had lived with him through the early hours as he tried to decipher its meaning. It had troubled him all through the day and now at supper time, he was hearing on the wireless that although Britain had declared a formal military alliance with Poland only days ago, Hitler had dismissed the Anglo Polish treaty as an empty gesture and Warsaw had now been struck by a series of early morning bombing raids. Two major German army groups were invading Poland from Prussia in the North and Slovakia in the South.

"What's the matter, wuss?" asked John wearily as he entered the kitchen. "You look as if you've been forced to ride the ghost train all day and night at the fair."

"Listening to the news, I was. It's frightening."

"What's frightening?" asked Thomas as he entered, grubby from the fields, yawning, and scratching his straw filled hair.

"Listen," urged Ernie as he poured them both a mug of tea and turned up the volume. The broadcast told of Germany achieving air supremacy. The newscaster spoke out in measured, cold tones.

"Most of Poland's air force was caught on the ground. Panzer spearheads have smashed holes in the Polish lines and permitted the slower moving German infantry to pour through into the Polish rear.

In advance of the line of attack the Luftwaffe has heavily bombed all road and rail junctions and concentrations of Polish troops. Towns and villages have been deliberately bombed to create a fleeing mass of civilians to block the roads and hamper the flow of reinforcements to the front.

Junker Ju-87 dive-bombers have fulfilled the role of the artillery and have destroyed any strong obstacles in the German path. This surprise German blitzkrieg has resulted in Poland requesting immediate military assistance from France and Britain at eight o'clock this morning. An emergency meeting of the cabinet has been in progress all day. An aide close to the Prime Minister has indicated that he hopes Hitler would accede to Britain's demands and leave Poland. He is due to go to Buckingham Palace later today." Ernie switched it off.

"I can't listen to anymore. The world said, 'never again' and here we are again at the same crossroads, just twenty five years later."

The three slumped into their seats in silence. Finally, Thomas spoke, "What do you think will happen? Is it to be war?"

"Without a doubt. It will be war. In the next couple of days, you mark my words," said Ernie solemnly.

"What'll we do?" asked Thomas.

"I don't know. Will we be called up?" asked John. "What about Carrie?"

"Carrie'll be safe enough in Aberystwyth," said Thomas.

"That's my worry. You know Carrie. Always does what she feels is right and noble," murmured Ernie despondently.

"What do you mean?" queried John.

"She's a barrow of courage and filled with honour," continued Ernie.

"Meaning?" John's eyes narrowed suspiciously.

"You know your sister. No thoughts for herself, she'll go where she's needed."

"But she can't. She's not qualified."

"Do you think that would stop her?"

"But what about us?" interrupted Thomas. "Where do we stand in all this?"

"Farmers are usually exempt from service but you are young men, so I don't know."

Supper was served in silence while each of them weighed up the consequences of Germany's actions and how it would affect them.

The list went up at Bronglais, just before noon, on September third. The nurses crowded around. Many turned away disappointed, "Hey, snowball you're through," shouted one to Pemb as she tried to push her way forward. It was true, Pemb had been successful, so had Carrie, but the biggest surprise was that the third nurse to transfer was not a probationer or second year student nurse but Staff Nurse Hawtry. And the start date had been brought forward. Instead of beginning in January they were to move to Birmingham October the first.

"In that case I'm glad I didn't get it," muttered Kirb. "Good luck to you both."

"There's always next year," offered Pemb consolingly. "You'll be able to keep an eye on Gilly. Keep her on the straight and narrow and off the fags."

Carrie came running up to the board as people were dispersing, "Have you heard? Have you heard?"

"Yes, we're through. Isn't that great?"

"No. The news. It's awful."

69

"What are you talking about?"

"On the wireless now. The Prime Minister, Britain's at war with Germany."

A hush fell over the small group as the implications of that announcement for them and their families, filled them with fear. The sound of an air raid siren being tested was heard outside. Its mournful wailing warning pressed into the passageway and reverberated around the walls filling the void.

Carrie tucked her arm in Pemb's, "What happens now?"

"It looks like we're scheduled to leave for Birmingham ahead of time. Have you even seen the list?"

Carrie shook her head and returned to the board, "October first? That doesn't give us long. Do you think we'll still get home for Christmas?"

"I don't know. War changes everything doesn't it?"

"I must write home."

"Me too."

"Then, I'll go and see Gilly."

"You'll have to hurry. I hear she's being moved to a sanatorium in the Welsh mountains. That's if it's not too late."

"Don't say that. We have to be positive. She can't die. She just can't."

"What's all this talk about dying?" came the forceful tones of Sister Toomer.

"Nothing, sister," they chorused.

"If you're talking about your friend then I think there may be better news." They were both instantly alert. "The cultures are back and it's not the sort that can be passed on. However, it does seem to be an extremely virulent strain."

"Can anyone see her?" asked Pemb.

"I should imagine you'll be allowed in, especially now you're both off to Birmingham. Congratulations by the way."

"Thank you, Sister," they chorused again.

"Sister?" called Carrie as the Sister turned away. "What treatment is Gilly having?"

"I believe they've collapsed one lung to give it a rest. She'll be a bit sore; they had to break her ribs. They're pumping her full of antibiotics. I know, however, they're transferring her fairly soon."

"That's what we heard. Have I permission to change my shift today?" asked Carrie.

"If you can find someone to change with you. Go ahead."

"Yes, Sister. Thank you, Sister," smiled Carrie and she scooted off down the corridor.

"Hey wait for me," shouted Pemb.

"Don't run!" boomed the sister. Carrie skidded to a brisk walk, which allowed Pemb to catch up with her and they hurried off to find someone to exchange duties with them.

There was a hammering on the door of Gelli Galed. John answered to see Gwynfor standing there.

"Come in, come in, wuss, make yourself at home," he welcomed. Gwynfor settled himself in a kitchen chair. He accepted the offered mug of tea and gazed solemnly at them all.

"You'll have heard the news?"

"Yes," John answered, "Frightening stuff."

"I've decided to join up."

"What? What about the farm?"

"There's mam, dad, Megan and farm helpers. They don't need me. I'd more than likely be called up, anyway. I came to see what you were doing. I thought I'd visit Carrie. Tell her what I'm doing before going off to London."

John studied his friend of many years, his face full of earnest enthusiasm and hope. He spoke softly, "I don't think it will make any difference to Carrie. I believe she's made her decision."

"You're probably right," murmured Gwynfor eventually, "But it's something I have to do. I have to speak to her face to face... I need to know... I may not come back." The truth of his words hung suspended in the air.

Ernie cleared his throat; he seemed to be choked with emotion, "Aye, Gwynfor. You see her. She'll not be unkind. Will she, John?"

"No, no I'm sure she won't," he threw a puzzled look at Ernie whom he felt knew more than he was saying.

"What are you both going to do?" asked Gwynfor turning his head from Ernie to John and Thomas.

"I don't know... I don't know what's expected," exclaimed Thomas.

"I've heard that the British air force is dropping leaflets in Poland, not bombs. Begging for peace they are, but people say it's just another hesitation on Chamberlain's behalf. We'll be at full war within three days. They'll be calling on every young man, good and true, to fight for their country."

"Farmers are exempt though, aren't they?" said Thomas.

"If there's no one to run the farm. Ernie can't do it alone," agreed John.

"But there are contingency plans. The papers say women will be brought in to work on the land. It just needs someone to oversee them. Ernie could do that. And city children are to be evacuated to the countryside. If that's the case, then in a few months you and Thomas could be sent away."

"We'll worry about it when it happens. That's what mam would say," said Thomas.

"Aye, that's what Aunty Annie'd say," rejoined John.

"Aye well, I just thought I'd let you know." Gwynfor stood up and clasped John warmly by the hand. The two men eyed each other and John drew him into his arms and hugged him for the friend he was. Thomas did likewise and Ernie shook Gwynfor's hand. He had a word of advice, "Don't go taking up smoking. It may be tempting but it won't be good for your health."

Gwynfor laughed, "You say such odd things, sometimes Ernie. No, I won't be smoking."

"When are you leaving?" asked John.

"Tomorrow. Just came to say my goodbyes. I'm going to Aber first, then on to London. Brian's going too and a number of the other lads. The village will be devoid of young men apart from you two. Look out for Megan for me, won't you? Come to think of it, with all the village lasses and Land Girls arriving from up country, you two should have a whale of a time."

"Only one girl for me," said Thomas.

"Aye, I know. And I wish you well. Look in on mam and dad sometimes, will you, please?"

"That we will, Gwynfor bach; that we will."

Gwynfor nodded, not trusting himself to speak, and made for the door. They watched him mount one of his mother's prized Arab horses and he trotted off back down the mountain track. Trixie ran after him and whined softly in her throat before returning to John's side.

"What'll we do for the harvest this year?" Thomas questioned.

"It'll be a very different harvest and fry up, as you'll see," prophesied Ernie.

"We'll just do the best we can. That's what dad would want," answered John. "That's all we can do," he said almost to himself.

Carrie finished her letter to all at Gelli Galed, conveying her good news, now blighted with the announcement of war. She took another sheet of paper and paused as she thought of Michael Lawrence, then she began to write. It was short, polite and to the point. She gave him her forwarding address at the hospital in Dudley Road, Birmingham. She signed her name with a flourish and without thinking she tacked a small 'x' after her name. She sealed the letter before she could change her mind and addressed it. There was just one more note to write. "Dear Lloyd,"

There was a tap on her door and Pemb popped her head around, "Ready?"

"Nearly, just give me a minute to finish this and I'll be with you. I should have written them yesterday, like you, but I couldn't get anyone to swap shifts."

"Not to worry. I'll wait. Anyway, I didn't see Gilly, they were doing some more tests, but I left a message that we'd be round today." Pemb plonked herself on the bed and chattered on while Carrie tried to complete her letter. She wasn't sure she'd made a lot of sense but felt she'd explained what had happened and gave him her new hospital address. She closed with the lines that she hoped she'd see him before she left.

"All done," said Carrie as she licked the envelope. "I have to get this to Mary's teashop."

"We'll go there after we've seen Gilly."

"Great. Have you heard anymore?" asked Carrie grabbing her nurse's cape.

"Kirb saw her yesterday. Said she wasn't up to much, very listless in between bouts of coughing and spitting. Horrible disease. The sooner they get her in the fresh mountain air the better."

Carrie slipped her key in her pocket and they hurried along the corridor, down the stairs and into the foyer. Carrie put her stamped letters in the post tray and they headed for the Septic Block.

Their heels clicked with efficient precision as they walked along the corridor to the little used ward where they spoke to the nurse on duty.

"We're here to see Nurse Gilhooly, if that's okay?"

The nurse nodded, "But not for long, she's very tired and she's got a bit of a journey tomorrow. Okay?"

"Fine. We won't tire her. We just want to wish her well and say goodbye," said Pemb.

The walk along the ward block seemed interminable to Carrie and she encountered the same feelings she had on entering the courtroom at Netta's trial. She took the same strategic action. She needed to be strong for her friend. Head held high, shoulders back and like her mother she glided to Gilly's bed and drew up a seat. Pemb sat alongside and Carrie took Gilly's hand. Gilly's skin now was almost transparent. She was propped up on a mound of pillows. It reminded Carrie of the story of the princess and the pea but this was done to enable Gilly to breathe more easily and prevent the mucus from rising up into her nose and throat.

"I was wondering when you'd be across. Done well for yourselves, so you have. I'm proud of the pair of you," said Gilly in her much quieter, lilting Dublin tones.

"I couldn't swap shifts," explained Carrie.

"No matter. I was fit for nothing yesterday, like a wet dish cloth I was." She started to cough a little. Carrie was up on her feet and dabbing at Gilly's mouth where the sputum and blood trickled.

"I know you like being waited on but isn't this going a bit far," joked Pemb.

"You always said I'd got her well trained," murmured Gilly nodding her head at Carrie. "Tell me all the gossip and scandal. Kirb wouldn't tell me anything. Said I shouldn't get excited."

So Carrie and Pemb took turns in recounting the events of the past few days on the wards and in the Nurses' Home. And of course they discussed the terrible prospect of war.

Gilly made a great effort and squeezed Carrie's hand, "Thanks for being such a good friend. Would you do me another favour?"

"Anything."

"Write to my family, explain what's happened. You'll find the address in my desk drawer in our room on one of the family letters."

"Of course."

"When are you both off?"

"Arrangements are being made. We start the beginning of October. We'll leave our address."

"Besides, once you're well, you'll be joining us," said Pemb optimistically.

"I don't think so," wheezed Gilly, "Be sure to tell them at home that I love them."

"You'll be able to tell them yourself," said Carrie, "You've got to get well for Patrick."

"Ah! Patrick, he's a darling so he is. Tell him I miss him and I wish we could have had a life together."

"Enough of this doom and gloom. Come on Gilly, where's your fighting spirit?"

"All punched out. I'm coming to the final knock out, Carrie. No, don't say anything," urged Gilly as Carrie attempted to make light of it. "I know I'm dying. I know it's gone too far." She began to cough violently. Carrie was on her feet holding a bowl at her mouth and Pemb ran to fetch the nurse, calling "Quick! It's a mop!" The crimson froth bubbled from her mouth and Carrie stared on helplessly, dabbing it away and talking soothingly. "Come on Gilly, for me. Hang on. Please hang on."

Gilly fell back limply on her pillows and an angel's glow seemed to surround her and her face shone with a golden light. "They're here," she whispered.

"Who?" said Carrie turning but seeing nothing.

"There's my Grampy and my Gran. They've come for me and they're smiling. Can't you see? It's beautiful." Gilly reached forward with her other hand and a smile lit her face and a look of utter peace settled on her countenance.

Carrie cried, "No, Gilly. Don't go. Please."

Gilly turned her shining eyes to Carrie and whispered, "I've had a good life. My time has come. But you, you have so much ahead of you. Your Michael Lawrence, Carrie. He's the one for you. You'll see." She lay back with an enigmatic smile and Carrie watched in horror as the light went out of her eyes.

"No!" she shrieked as Pemb came running back with the nurse and doctor. "No!" and she juddered into an inconsolable sobbing that no one could quiet. Pemb held her friend close as Carrie's tears soaked her shoulders. The doctor tested Gilly's pulse and shaking his head, closed her eyes and drew the sheet over her face.

With shoulders depressed in sorrow Carrie and Pemb returned to Bronglais. They entered the foyer and to Carrie's surprise waiting patiently, by the pigeonholes, was the familiar figure of Gwynfor.

"Jumbo!" she exclaimed without thinking, using his nickname from their school days. Correcting herself she repeated, "Gwynfor, whatever are you doing here?"

He turned and smiled broadly at her, "I got your letter, Carrie fach. I want you to know I understand..." He stopped when he saw her eyes red from weeping and her friend's protective embrace.

"I'm sorry. Gwynfor, this is my friend Pemb."

Pemb politely acknowledged him and turned to her friend, "You'll be all right?"

"I'll be fine," nodded Carrie. "See you later." She turned back to Gwynfor, "Now, how did you know that it's a friend I'd be needing now? What are you doing here? Wait!" She stopped him from speaking. "Let's walk. We'll go to the front and kick the bar, I have to do it in memory of a friend."

Carrie tucked her arm in his and propelled him out of the door and they walked through the glorious sunshine to the sea front and Carrie shared her heart and thoughts with her old friend. "How can the sun shine so brightly when such tragedy is around?" she concluded.

"I'm sorry about your friend. She sounded fun."

"You would have liked her. Everyone would. She was so alive, so mischievous but so very, very kind and a damn good nurse. The shock is it all happened so quickly. TB can take years to fasten its stranglehold, but this seemed to happen all of a sudden."

"Life can be like that. Rise up and hit you in the chops when you least expect it."

They progressed along the promenade like any other young couple. Gwynfor stopped and turned Carrie to face him. Her hair blazed in the sunlight, shining with copper fire and threads of molten gold.

"I'm going off to war and wanted one last time to see you."

"You've joined up?" said Carrie with a gasp.

"Aye, they don't need me on the farm and I feel I need to do something with my life, something to be proud of... something to make you proud."

"Oh, Gwynfor, anything you do, you must do for yourself. At the moment, all I can see for me is a lifetime of nursing. My grand ideas about running the farm, well, that's all they were, ideas. I'm not saying I won't ever change my mind but I'm discovering myself and that's the most exciting thing in the world."

"But you'll think of me and let me write?"

"Of course I will. We've been friends for too long."

"And we'll talk again, when or if I come back?"

"You'll come back. And yes, we'll talk but I don't want to give you false hope. My heart's set on nursing."

"No matter, you'll speak with me again. That's all that matters. Can I ask you one last thing?"

"Ask."

"Hold me before we part."

Carrie, stepped up onto her tiptoes and pulled his gentle lumbering frame into her arms. Her lips softly brushed his cheek.

"Now, no more old nonsense, you come back safe and sound. Promise."

"You always were a bossy little madam. But I'll do my best." He laughed, "I feel so much better now. You just have that knack, Carrie, of making all well in the world."

"You wouldn't say that if you saw me on the ward sometimes. I never knew women could make such a din having babies. It's enough to frighten the dead." Carrie went on to recount some dramatic stories of births she'd assisted on.

"It's not put you off, then? Having children?"

"It did at first. There was no way I wanted to go through the pains of Hell, for anything. But then, when you see the mothers with their bonny babies, nursing them, somehow you forget and it all blurs into the wallpaper."

They walked in silence for a few more steps until they reached the bar at the end of the promenade.

"Come on, kick the bar, good luck for you and good luck for my friend wherever she is now."

They walloped the bar with their feet and laughed; at ease in each other's company once more.

"What time's your train?"

"Jawch! I'd better get moving or I'll be missing it."

"I'll see you off. We'll get a taxi. There should be one on the rank by the bus station. This way." And Carrie sprinted off laughing, with Gwynfor closely following.

A cab ride later they were at the station and Gwynfor was aboard. He lowered the carriage window and strapped it down so he could wave to Carrie until her spangled hair was nothing more than a glittering light in the distance. Then he eased himself into his seat and a peaceful smile settled on his face. It had been the right thing to see her; the right thing, and now he would sign up with a lighter heart.

CHAPTER THIRTEEN

New Harvests

Ernie's words were indeed prophetic. The reaping on their neighbouring farms was a very different affair from the previous years. Grandfathers rolled up their sleeves and women worked where usually the men toiled. Most of the young men from the village had gone to join up, like Gwynfor and Brian. All were seeking the thrill of an adventure, imagining that to fight for one's country was a glorious and patriotic thing to do. They had no idea what to expect and had built their fancies on Hollywood movies and heroic tales passed down from their fathers and grandfathers. No one could possibly imagine the horrors that many were to experience on the battlefield and in prisoner of war camps.

John and Thomas worked alongside each other and with Ernie's guidance Gelli Galed enjoyed a bumper harvest. Thomas had watched with heartache Megan's looks of longing towards John and he believed that nothing he could do or say would sway her heart to him.

"I've been thinking, John..." he paused.

"What is it, wuss?"

"Megan will never look at me the way she looks at you. I don't think she ever will."

"She knows I'm not interested and she knows I'm seeing Jenny," John replied.

"Aye, but that only seems to make her all the keener. She sees you as a challenge, takes every opportunity to talk about you and I don't think I can stand it anymore."

"What are you saying?"

"I've been thinking I ought to go, join up like Gwynfor and Brian."

"What? How will we manage?"

"You'll manage. Land Girls will be deployed fairly soon. Now the harvest is out of the way, there's only the ploughing and livestock to see to and Ernie's a master stockman."

"Give it more time, Megan will change you'll see."

"I doubt it. She might have more respect for me, if I enlist. Proud of her brother she is. I want her to feel the same about me. It may just help change things. It will give me a chance to see something of the world."

"Australia wasn't enough?"

78

"Aye, but that was different. I can do something honourable by serving my country."

John weighed up his cousin's word and nodded. "I'll not stop you. You know your own mind. When were you thinking?"

"I thought I might wind up affairs and go to Cardiff, join a Welsh regiment. I think October would be about right. Who knows, I may get called up before then? Gossip has it that letters are going out to all those of eighteen and over. Mine could well be on its way. After all I've done no national service."

"Nor have I cousin, nor have I."

They continued the conversation until they were interrupted by Trixie's barking, announcing the arrival of a visitor. There was a clang of the bell on the porch.

"Are you expecting anyone?"

"Not me."

"Better open up and see."

John went to the door and sucked in his breath when he saw the spangled fiery tresses belonging to a young woman. She turned her head. It was Jenny.

"Jenny, what are you doing here? It's more than a hike from the village."

"I had a ride with Mr. Lawrence as far as Hendre. The rest of the climb wasn't too bad," she explained, clearly embarrassed. "John, I must speak with you."

"Come in, come in." He opened the door wide to admit her. "Couldn't it have waited till Friday? You know how I'm fixed until then."

"No, it couldn't wait," she lowered her eyelashes as she saw Thomas. "Hello, Tom."

"Jenny." Thomas could see the awkwardness between them and made his excuses, "I'll take Trix down to count the flock. I'll see Ernie on the way."

Jenny waited until Thomas had gone then she looked at John fearfully with her huge eyes before bursting into tears. "Oh, John; I don't know what to do."

"What? What's the matter?"

"I'm late," she hesitated, "I think I'm pregnant."

"You can't be. We've been careful... How late?"

"I've missed two periods and I've been awful sick of late, not just mornings, all sorts of times."

"How could you let this happen?" John blazed.

"It's not my fault. Remember it takes two."

John checked his temper and began again more reasonably, "But I don't see how..."

"We've been careful, but not that first time. Remember?" And she fixed her eyes on him.

He flushed guiltily and put his arms around her, a worried frown on his face.

"I'm frightened, John; really scared. Mam and Dad will go berserk. I don't want a baby on my own, not like Suzy Evans in the village. Look what people think of her. I've never been with a man before. You are my first," and she sobbed on his shoulder.

John held her in his strong arms and kissed away her tears, "You won't go through it alone. I promise. If you're pregnant I'll stand by you. But first you better make sure. Go and see Dr. Rees. Best not to worry unnecessarily. When we know, then we'll make a decision. I've heard that worrying can delay periods, maybe it's something like that."

"I don't think so. I'm noticing changes. Of course if you don't want me I could always go to Bopa Jane."

"And have you cut about by some quack? No, if you are, then it's my responsibility and I'm man enough to accept that. It may be a little sooner than I expected but well, why not?"

"I prayed you'd say that. You don't know how scared I've been to face you."

"That's just silly. Now dry your eyes. I'll get you back to the village and you go to Dr. Rees. I'll meet you Friday as usual and if it's the news you expect I'll come with you to see your mother and father. All right?"

Jenny nodded, her face flooding with relief.

"Yes, John. Thank you." She turned to the door and looked back, "I know you don't love me but perhaps you can learn to love me, in time." She breezed out holding her head up and at that moment she reminded him more of Carrie than ever, and he felt a protective warmth wash over him.

"We have friendship. We have passion. Love will come." he told himself more than her, and followed her outside.

The remaining September weeks flew by. Carrie could scarcely believe that she would be setting off for the big industrial city of Birmingham.

Gilly's funeral had been a surprising affair. Not only did everyone from the Nurses' Home turn out, as well as hospital staff, but also a contingent of Gilly's family from Ireland managed to attend and a crowd of university students turned up. Gilly had been more popular than she had ever imagined.

Carrie had attempted to put a brave face on the

proceedings but now she didn't have time to worry or think as October fast approached.

She was hauling her luggage out of her door when a runner came from the foyer.

"Nurse Llewellyn! Nurse Llewellyn!" Carrie stopped and turned to face another junior.

"Someone downstairs to see you. I said you were packing up to go to Birmingham but he insisted, said it was important."

"Okay. Thanks. Tell him I'll be down in a minute. Did he give his name?"

The junior shook her head, "No, just asked to see you and said no matter how long it took, he'd wait."

Carrie's curiosity was aroused. She shoved the cases into the corridor where they were to be collected by the hall porter and taken to the station. She locked her door and ran down the stairs to the vestibule. As soon as she saw the broad shoulders and short cropped hair she knew who it was. Instinctively she moistened her lips, straightened her uniform and patted her hair.

"Michael! Mr. Lawrence! Whatever are you doing here?"

He turned to face her and as his eyes met hers, he broke into a warm smile.

"Carrie! I wasn't sure how long you'd be. I almost expected to be kept waiting."

"I was intrigued as to who had called to see me. I don't get many visitors. I'm nothing if not curious."

"Is there anywhere we can go? For a pot of tea or something?"

"I don't have very long. My train's at three." Carrie noticed the disappointment registering in his eyes and added, "If we're quick I can probably give you a few minutes."

"I have a car waiting outside. I won't take up too much of your time. Where do you suggest?"

"It's a quarter past one now," said Carrie glancing at her watch, "If you can get me back here for two, we can nip into Mary's Tearooms but we'll have to hurry."

She brushed a rebellious curl from her eyes as she preceded Michael out of the Nurses' Home, just as Kirb was coming up the steps. Kirb looked curiously, "You'll be back to say goodbye, Lew, won't you?"

"Has a gnat got a bite? I'll be there."

John was uncomfortable under the scrutiny of Jenny's parents. "So you see, I would like to put things right and take Jenny as my wife if she'll have me."

There was an uneasy silence. Jenny stood head bowed, next to her mother who, tight lipped, had a protective arm around her daughter.

Jenny's father, Howell Davies was a big redheaded man. He finally spoke, "It's not what I would have wished for her, but you have made your case and I believe you're honest and sincere. So, if Jenny's willing then we'll agree."

"You do good by our daughter and we'll stand by the pair of you," added Mrs. Davies, an older version of Jenny, "You can afford her keep and the child?"

John nodded, "We'll manage and I'll work hard. I promise."

"Then there are arrangements to be made. Best see Reverend Richards and pick a date. The sooner the better. She's not showing yet and we don't want the whole village to know there's a baby on the way," Mrs. Davies continued. "There's bound to be gossip. You'll have to live with it."

"I'm no stranger to that," John replied. "As long as Jenny can cope. That's if she wants me."

"She has no choice in the matter. It's the right thing to do. I suggest you go to the Chapel House now. Do you want me to come with you?"

"I think we'll be all right on our own. Jenny?"

"I'll get my hat and coat. Only if you're sure, John? I don't want you to think I'm trapping you or anything."

"What's happened has happened and we'll make the best of it. I'll do my utmost to make you proud to have me as your husband, and father to our baby."

"That's good enough for me."

Mrs. Davies dabbed at the corner of her eye with a lace hankie as she ushered them out of the door. John took Jenny's hand in his and they headed for the rectory.

Carrie and Michael sat at a table at the back of the shop. Carrie was aware that the manageress was eyeing her curiously.

"I have to admit I'm surprised to see you. Who's managing the farm in your absence?"

"I've finally got some help, recommended by your brother and Thomas."

"That's kind of them." The tart words came out before she could stop herself. "Sorry, I didn't mean for it to come out quite how it sounded. Go on."

"As I said, I have someone to manage Hendre, in my absence, someone with experience who will liaise with John over the running of things."

"Why?"

"Surely, you've heard?"

"I don't think so, what are we talking about?"

"The preliminary hearing. I felt sure John would have contacted you."

"Do you know that had gone completely out of my head? It was last week wasn't it?"

"Yes. The Judge has given both parties three months to prepare their cases. The judiciary has ruled that the eight hundred and fifty pounds found on Jacky Ebron is rightfully yours but there is still the question of the first instalment. John and I have come to an arrangement."

Carrie raised her eyebrow questioningly.

"Once the residue of the money held in escrow is paid with interest into my account then until the rest of the cash can be found, he and I will be partners in the long term planning for Hendre."

"Why hasn't John told me? I've heard nothing about it?"

"Perhaps that's because he's other things on his mind."

"Like what?"

"He's taken up with a village girl."

"Yes, Jenny Davies, Megan told me. She was rather put out."

"I understand that things are moving on between the two of them."

"That's good. It's just what he needs. I don't understand why you need to see me."

"Because I'm to be a sleeping partner. Ernie and John will be running things at Gelli Galed and Hendre."

"They can't. It'll be too much without help. Especially if what Megan said in her last letter is true and that Thomas is joining up."

"Maybe. But we've been notified that reinforcements in the shape of Land Girls are to be sent into the countryside. Hendre and Gelli Galed both qualify for help as do the other neighbouring farms."

"I still don't understand," pronounced Carrie, pushing back another stubborn curl from her eyes.

"You have wonderful hair," sighed Michael distractedly.

"Never mind my hair. What aren't you telling me?"

"I believe John was waiting for you to come home at Christmas before he told you. He'd know by then whether or not the scheme would work. If so, it would be drawn up legally."

"You mean this is just a verbal agreement?"

"A gentleman's agreement. I think you accept I can trust your brother."

"You certainly can. But can he trust you?"

"I believe the odds are stacked more in his favour than mine." Michael paused.

Carrie prodded further,"I still don't see how it can be of any benefit to us or why you've come all this way to see me."

"If John keeps both Hendre and Gelli Galed profitable then if the money is not found we will do as originally suggested and do a straight swap..."

"Yes?" prompted Carrie beginning to lose patience.

"And if I don't return I have written in my will that Hendre is to be left to you. So it looks like you will have your beloved Hendre after all, one way or another, and hopefully without a complicated court case."

"What do you mean if you don't return?"

"I'm going to enlist. I have flying experience and a licence. I thought that as a pilot returning from war I may finally gain the respect of the village."

Carrie paled, "You can't. You may not come back." Suddenly, this fact seemed very important to her.

"If I didn't know you better I'd think you were concerned."

Carrie began to fluster before she found the right words, "I just think that by working with John word would get around the village and when folks hear your intentions their attitude will change."

"Maybe. But I've a conscience. I'm a young man. I have skills the armed forces can use. I have no family so I've nothing to lose and everything to gain."

"Nothing to lose? What about your life?"

"I thought you'd be pleased."

"I'm not... I am... I'm confused. Why are you here? I'd have found all this out in the course of time."

"Because I wanted to see you. You wrote to me, remember?"

"Out of politeness."

Michael reached in his pocket and took out her letter. He opened it out and it was clear from its condition that it had been read many, many times. "Then if it was just politeness, explain this," and he pointed to the x after her name.

"Just a slip of the pen. I'd written a number of letters to family and friends and I put that without thinking. I didn't want to write the whole letter again."

"Why didn't you just cross it out?"

"Because..." Carrie was flummoxed and Michael stared hard into her eyes. Before she knew what was happening their heads were unnervingly close.

"Will you be wanting anything else?" interrupted Gladys who had been watching them intently.

"No, no thank you. I have to get back," responded Carrie, flushing with embarrassment.

"Will we be seeing you later? I understand Lloyd is coming in," she continued pointedly.

"No... No I'm off to Birmingham this afternoon. I don't know when I'll be back."

"I heard you were leaving us. It's a shame. You'll be missed. Good luck." And with that Gladys sniffed imperiously and returned to her watch by the dresser.

"I really do have to go," said Carrie apologetically.

"I'll take you back."

"It's all right. I don't want to take up any more of your time."

"I insist. Come on, it makes sense. It'll only take five minutes by car."

Carrie nodded. Michael left some money on the table, which Gladys eyed greedily. As soon as they were out of their seats she was across to pick it up. She called out as they opened the door, "Any message for Lloyd?"

"Tell him I'll be in touch," and she fled from the tearooms, her cheeks uncomfortably hot, to the waiting car.

Michael climbed in the back beside her and instructed the driver. His knee brushed against hers and she felt a disturbing tingle course through her body. They sat quietly neither knowing what to say until they reached Bronglais in Carradog Road.

Michael jumped out and held the door open for Carrie who tried to alight gracefully but Michael's next question caught her off guard, "Who's Lloyd?"

"I don't see that's any of your business, Mr. Lawrence. But if you must know he's a friend, a good friend."

She scrambled out of the car caught her heel on the kerb and staggered forward. Michael gripped her arm to prevent her falling, and her eyes were level with his chin, which he tilted up with his fingers. Carrie seemed unable to move or look away. They stood gazing at each other for what seemed an eternity.

"Lew! Lew! Better get your skates on we have to say our goodbyes," exclaimed Pemb hurtling down the front steps. "Oh, I'm sorry, I didn't realise..." She trailed off, sensitive enough to know that she had walked in on something.

"Pemb, this is Michael Lawrence, Michael my friend Pemb who's coming with me to Birmingham."

"Pleased to meet you," said Michael politely shaking her hand.

"Michael!" exclaimed Pemb, "Oh I see... You'd better scoot I'll meet you in the Arthur Halstead room, they've got a bit of a gathering for us. Nice to meet you," called Pemb as she raced back into Bronglais.

"I must dash," said Carrie lowering her eyes defensively and she started up the steps. She was just about to open the door when she heard his footfalls behind her. She hesitated slightly and he grabbed her arm, turning her and pulling her into him. Before she knew what was happening he was kissing her. She melted into his arms a fluttering excitement rising in her stomach.

"I've wanted to do that for a long time," whispered Michael.

Carrie was stunned. She touched her mouth reflectively where his lips had burnt into hers so fiercely. Before she could help herself she reached up and brushed his lips with her fingertips. For once she was stumped for words and what to do. From nowhere, Ernie's words came flooding back to her and echoed in her mind 'for happiness you need look no further than your back yard.'

"May I write?"

Carrie nodded, not trusting herself to speak.

"You'll reply?"

She nodded again and this time found the energy to move, "Yes. Goodbye, Mr. Lawrence."

"Michael!"

"Michael." She turned at the door to look at him once more. "Come back. Come back safely." She disappeared into the hallway of the Nurses' Home.

Michael remained there staring at the door until the driver tooted on the car horn. He took a deep breath and returned to the car a huge smile spreading across his face and he began to chuckle. He was soon laughing in delight as the car drove away.

Carrie scrambled up the stairs to her old room and peered out of the window. She watched the car drive away. Pemb pushed open the door, "So that's Mr. Michael Lawrence... say no more, my lips are sealed."

"He kissed me," said Carrie incredulously. "He kissed me. The bloody nerve of the man," and she started to giggle.

Elizabeth Revill

BIRMINGHAM

CHAPTER FOURTEEN

Birmingham

Carrie was still chuckling when she joined her friends for the goodbye gathering in the communal sitting area known as the Arthur Halstead Room, named after a doctor who had pioneered new birthing methods at the Maternity Home.

Kirb was saying a few words to the assembled nurses and doctors. She paused as Carrie entered, "About time. We thought you were going to disappear without a word."

"No chance of that."

"You're cutting it fine, Lew. We were just saying how we were going to miss you," added a nurse from her corridor in the Nurses' Home.

"No chance of that," interjected Pemb, "We'll keep in touch and hopefully see some of you next year."

"As long as you don't pull rank on us," grinned another. "You'll be senior to us then."

"Where's Hawtry?" questioned Carrie.

"She left yesterday. Said nothing to no one. You're welcome to her. Bronglais will be a happier place without her," muttered another.

"She's not that bad," defended Carrie. "We'll cope."

The farewell meeting dissolved into hugs and goodbyes and promises to write, which settled into silence as Sister Toomer walked in, "Ah! I'm glad I caught you. I just wanted to wish you both well. Birmingham is lucky to have you and if you don't like it I'm sure there'll always be a place for you here."

"Yes, Sister. Thank you, Sister," they choroused.

Just then a runner burst into the room. "Lew, Pemb, taxi's here."

Carrie took a last look around the room at the faces she thought she might never see again, grabbed Pemb's hand and blurted, "Bye," as she dashed from the room. The horde of nurses followed to the steps of Bronglais and giggling like schoolgirls waved goodbye to the taxi until it disappeared from view.

Pemb fell back in her seat as the cab rounded the corner and the Nurses' Home was no longer in view. "It's a brand new start. I wonder what Birmingham's like. I've never been to a big city before."

"Well," said Carrie philosophically, "We'll soon find out."

The journey passed uneventfully apart from one, last moment of panic that maybe they had forgotten something when Pemb exclaimed, "Oh, I almost forgot. This came for you," she reached into her pocket and pulled out a letter. Carrie looked at it eagerly. It was from John. "It's from my brother. Forgive me a moment while I read it."

"Go ahead. I may just take a nap. I'm exhausted already." Pemb leaned back in her seat and closed her eyes peacefully while Carrie read the news from home. The epistle, it was much more than John's usual note, brought her up to date with everything she had already heard from Michael Lawrence. When she reached the end of the letter she squealed aloud rousing her friend from her slumbers.

"What? Whatever's the matter?" queried Pemb.

"It's my brother. He's getting married. In two weeks. He wants to know if we can make it to the wedding."

"That's quick. So much for you and your intended matchmaking. I thought you'd ear marked him for me." Pemb laughed, "It's just as well. I don't think I could face the early mornings. Nursing's bad enough, as a farmer's wife I'd be expected to cook as well and I'm not too good at that either!"

"Get on with you! But you're right it is a bit soon."

"A shotgun marriage, maybe."

"Maybe. Do you think we can get time off?"

"I don't know. We can but try."

"Seems a bit cheeky to ask for time off as soon as we get there."

"It is a special case though. We can ask. They can only say 'no'. Will your Mr. Lawrence be there? You've not said a word about your get together."

"No, he won't be there," Carrie said wistfully and proceeded to tell Pemb all about the meeting including the stolen kiss.

An hour later the train puffed into Snow Hill Station, Birmingham sending clouds of glorious smelling white steam billowing up into the sky. The pistons and engine grinded to a halt with a whistle and a hiss. Carrie stuck her head out of the window and looked down the platform. Porters were ready with trolleys and opening the doors. "I'm glad our trunks went on ahead. It'll be bad enough battling with the two cases I've got."

"Two? I've got three. Don't ask me how. I had to borrow one from Kirb," exclaimed Pemb.

"We'd better get to the baggage wagon quickly or there'll be no porters left." Carrie struggled with the door and jumped down onto the platform. She signalled to a porter who progressed to the guard's van where the bags were stored.

"Okay, Ducks," grinned the man as he struggled with their baggage, "Where to?" He had a flat nasal twang and his voice seemed to rise at the end of his sentences. Carrie had never heard an accent like it and had to stop herself from laughing.

"Taxi rank, please."

The man expertly manoeuvred the loaded cart towards the station exit and almost collided with a thin-faced nurse in a blue cape hurrying onto the platform.

"Sorry, Ducks. Didn't see you there," apologised the porter.

"Hawtry!" blurted Pemb in surprise.

"Sorry, I'm late. I meant to get here to meet you but got delayed. Welcome to Brum as the locals say."

"Thanks," said Carrie not knowing what to say next. They followed the porter to the black cab rank where there was a small queue.

"What's the hospital like?" asked Pemb, eventually breaking the silence.

"Busy and bustling like the city, not that I've had a chance to explore yet. Thought I may wait until you had some free time before I do that."

Pemb just managed to put a smile on her face, "Fine. Sounds good." It came out more sincerely than she could have imagined.

Hawtry extended her hand, "I know we've had our moments but I'm hoping we can start with a clean sheet. Deal?"

"Deal," responded Pemb and the two shook hands.

The next cab arrived and their suitcases were loaded. Carrie fished in her purse for some change but the porter refused the tip, "I'll not take from nurses, salt of the earth you are and twice as good. Keep your money. You'll need it here on your wages. Good luck." He gave them a wink and wheeled the trolley back into the station to look for more well heeled customers.

"Dudley Road Hospital please," Hawtry ordered the cabbie.

The taxi pulled out into Colmore Row and Carrie marvelled at the size of the buildings and the impressive limestone Cathedral, which faced them. The streets seemed to be filled with people rushing around. It was obvious that life moved at a faster pace here than at home or indeed in Aberystwyth. As they travelled Hawtry briefed them on what they could expect. Their week would be a mixture of working the wards and lectures. They were entitled to one day off a week and one weekend a month, which from the sound of it, would be devoted to studies and homework.

"My brother's getting married in two weeks and we've been invited to the wedding. Do you think we'll be able to go?"

"It's possible. Let's see what we can fix up for you once you're settled in."

Pemb glanced across at Carrie, her eyebrows raised. It seemed that Hawtry had undergone a change for the better. Cynically, Pemb wondered how long it would last.

CHAPTER FIFTEEN

Winds of Change

The cab drew up outside the Nurses' Home attached to Dudley Road Hospital. It didn't have the leafy splendour of Bronglais or the beauty of village life in Wales with its rugged mountains and lush green fields but it had a certain dusty charm.

Carrie gazed about her at the huge billboard hoardings on the opposite side of the road advertising Woodbine cigarettes, and Ovalteen. A stark contrast, she thought, knowing that cigarettes hadn't helped the plight of her friend, Gilly.

Hawtry barked an order to follow her and the two probationers dragged their cases onto the pavement.

"Can't we get any help with these?" asked Pemb, struggling with her oversized bags.

Hawtry stopped and nodded, "Hang on there. I'll see what I can do."

Carrie paid the cab driver and sat on her case.

"Haven't you done enough sitting?" mused Pemb. "I can't wait to stretch my legs and get walking, blow the cobwebs away."

"My mother always said, never stand when you can sit and never sit when you can lie," replied Carrie, "Makes perfect sense to me."

"Sounds like the recipe for a heart attack to me," rejoined Pemb. "What do you think of the place?"

"Don't know till we get inside. Looks a pretty impressive building though. Do you think they'll run out of hot water in the mornings?"

"I wouldn't put it to the test. Just as well to be cautious."

The dusty pavements began to look drab in the fading afternoon light. However, Carrie was surprised that there were so many trees lining the unkempt streets, which thought needed a good sweep. She'd noticed they'd passed a park on route and determined to walk there at the first opportunity she got.

"I'm surprised there's so many birds here," observed Pemb. "Sparrows, starlings, pigeons..."

"Looks like we'll have a dawn chorus to rival any at home." agreed Carrie. "Did you notice the park?"

"I did. Looked like a place of sanity amongst the city

madness. But did you see the shops?" replied Pemb her eyes gleaming. "Lots of clothes and shoe shops and that was just one street. Imagine what else we'll find when we go to explore."

The conversation paused as the door opened and five young nurses in caps and capes came laughing into the street. One of them smiled brightly at the two waifs on the roadside. "You waiting for help?"

Carrie nodded.

"It won't be long. We just passed Walter with his trolley bulldozing down the corridor. Good luck!" She smiled and ran after her friends who turned up the road to the hospital gates.

"Who's Walter, I wonder?" murmured Pemb.

"I expect he's the equivalent of Cyril," suggested Carrie. "What do you bet he's old and crotchety with a fat belly and bald head?"

"Just how I like them!" grinned Pemb.

There was no more opportunity for chat as Hawtry came out followed by a tall, friendly faced man with a shock of black hair.

"Got that wrong then," teased Pemb.

"Right, let's get this lot inside and help you feel at home," winked Walter. "I understand you're on the third floor."

"That's right," said Hawtry. "Room 45. Two doors down from me. I've got your roster here and it looks like you're in luck. You did say your brother's wedding was in two weeks?"

"Yes," Carrie replied hopefully as she followed the precariously loaded trolley swaying into the foyer.

"They've given you both that weekend off. If you ask I'm sure you can swap duties with someone to give you the Friday, too. Would that help?"

"Certainly would. Thanks Hawtry."

Hawtry managed a smile and Pemb thought uncharitably, again, 'This'll never last!'

Village life in Crynant was changing. Many of the young men had joined the armed forces in hopeful innocence yearning for excitement and adventure. Women who had always tended their houses and looked after their families were labouring on farms. Several younger unmarried women had gone to work in the ammunitions factory in Cardiff. Gradually jobs, which had been dominated by men were taken up by women; ship building in Cardiff docks, the iron and steel foundries in Merthyr Tydfil, mechanical work and building sites, even coal mines were now a female domain.

Women from all over the country joined the ATS. Land Girls arrived to take up posts on farms depleted by workers who had joined the war effort. The first contingent of bewildered evacuees arrived from the cities. The children were taken away to village halls where they awaited selection by families who had volunteered rooms vacated by the men in their homes. Some would be lucky in their placements; others would not fare so well.

Confusion like a propagating mushroom shook out its spores at Gelli Galed. Ernie felt as if he was caught in a quick step whilst doing a waltz. Thomas was sorting out his affairs and packing his case in preparation for leaving for Plymouth where he had chosen to serve in the Navy. John was finalising the last minute arrangements for his wedding to Jenny.

"You can't go till Sunday," he told Thomas. "After all, you are to be my best man. I'll have no other."

"Cwat lawr, John. You're fussing worse than mam-gu. I'll be here for your wedding."

"Is our room ready for us?" John quizzed Ernie.

"Aye, the bed's made up and aired. Space is made in the wardrobe and chest of drawers. It's a real bridal suite."

"What about Carrie? Who's picking her and Pemb up from the station?"

"I'll be there," continued Ernie.

Trix looked up from the rag mat and watched each person in turn as they spoke. She wasn't used to such a commotion. At the mention of Carrie's name she stood up and wagged her tail.

"Her train arrives at three fifteen, but you'll have to meet the Land Girls in the village hall. They're expected at four. Michael Lawrence has offered them Old Tom's cottage on the proviso we get it up and together. It was the last thing he said before he left."

"What? But the place hasn't been cleaned."

"Yes, it has," said Ernie wearily.

"But how did you manage with your hand?"

"And where have you been since last week? It's all mended and healed. I'll be back milking cows before you can thread a needle."

"The way I thread needles we could be waiting a long time, then. And what about your suit? Have you got anything to wear? Don't forget to shave."

"Will you stop fussing? I've got your Da's blue chapel suit that Carrie fixed for me and if that won't do I can always join up again."

"Join up?" exclaimed John in horror.

"There, there, joking I was. Did your sense of humour drain out with the bath water?"

"Sorry, Ernie. I just want everything to be right."

"It will be. Now, who's going to groom Trix?"

"Trix?"

"Duw, Duw you're worse than a parrot. Are you always to be repeating what I say?" John opened his mouth to reply but Ernie cut him off, "Never mind, I'll do it. She needs to look smart for Carrie and the wedding. I've got a lovely pink ribbon somewhere." And he wandered out before John could worry him with any more of his nervous fears.

Trix trotted out after Ernie. She was more than curious at all the fuss. In the yard she allowed herself a vigorous brushing until her coat gleamed. She even permitted a pink satin bow to be tied to her collar and followed Ernie to the barn where Senator was brought out to be harnessed to the cart. Thinking that there was no more excitement to be had she began to slink off to the track. Ernie whistled shrilly, "Oh no you don't. I'm not having you going off and rolling in fox dung or anything else. Come here."

Trix padded back agreeably and was startled to be lifted into the back of the cart when she was used to running alongside.

"I think Carrie will be pleased to see you at the station too," Ernie said to her. "Just sit tight while I get my jacket."

Trix cocked her ears at the sound of Carrie's name and sat to attention, waiting patiently for Ernie's return.

He bumbled out, calling to John, "And don't forget to fill the kettle. They'll be ready for a fresh brew after their journey. Do you want anything from town?"

John's reply was garbled. Ernie just shrugged his shoulders and climbed in the cart. He clicked his tongue and they rolled out of the yard and onto the mountain track.

"Where's Ernie?" asked Thomas as he came in the kitchen.

"Gone to fetch Carrie and her friend. It will take him over an hour to get there."

"Damn! I wanted to go with him," grumbled Thomas.

"He's only just left. If you run you'll catch them up," said John.

"I don't need any second bidding," laughed Thomas as he grabbed his cap and ran out to the yard.

John looked at his reflection in the mirror. "Changes are coming thick and fast. I just hope I'm up to it." As he spoke he smoothed back his hair. The stud holding shirt and collar together pinged with the effort and they separated like feuding brothers. John laughed, "A fine groom you'll make if you can't even look tidy," and he got down on his hands and knees to hunt for the wayward stud.

Trix was excited. Senator and the cart were secured. Thomas bought two platform tickets and Ernie led Trixie into the station. She'd never smelled such enticing scents before. But she somehow knew her best behaviour was expected and so, resisting the urge to explore the unfamiliar territory with her nose, she sat at Ernie's feet to wait for the train. Thomas chattered animatedly. He hadn't seen his cousin since he'd left for Australia and he was more than a little curious about her friend Pemb whom he'd heard so much about.

The guard came out with his flag and whistle as the train chuffed into the station. Carrie was hanging out of the window. She began waving frantically as soon as she caught sight of Ernie and Thomas. Trix sprang to her feet, her tail wagging fit to bust and she barked happily. The train hardly had time to stop before Carrie'd opened the door and was jumping out. She gave an unladylike whoop of glee and with her hair flying out from under her hat, threw herself into Ernie's arms and gave him a huge kiss. "Ernie! I've missed you!"

"Ieuchy dewriath," he blushed all of a fluster as she turned to Thomas.

"Thomas, you're looking grand," and she hugged him hard before turning her attention to Trixie who was now nearly demented with pleasure at seeing Carrie. Carrie knelt down and allowed her face to be covered with sloppy wet licks. She giggled in delight as she ruffled the dog's fur and patted her, "Okay, Trix. I've not forgotten you. I've missed you too."

"I thought you were bringing a friend," asked Ernie.

"Goodness, I nearly forgot." Carrie turned as her friend Pemb struggled out from the train clutching both their bags and coats. "This is Pemb. Pemb meet the unique and lovable Ernie, and my cousin Thomas."

Pemb dropped the bags on the platform and once she'd

extricated her hand from the sleeve of Carrie's coat, which had somehow got entwined with hers she put out her hand.

"Glad to meet you both. I've heard a lot about you."

Ernie flushed in pleasure, "I can see why they call you snowball," he added.

"So can I," said Thomas admiringly. "Here let me take that." He picked up her case and steered her to the exit.

Carrie looked bemused, "And what about mine?"

Ernie laughed, "I'll take that, you'll have enough trouble walking to the cart, the way Trixie's dancing around you."

Carrie picked her way out of the station dodging Trixie's little jumps of affection and pleading eyes. "We'll go for a lovely walk when I get back, Trix, I promise. And I'll make a proper fuss of you."

The proper fuss, however, would not wait until they reached Gelli Galed. As soon as they were in the cart Trix was up and in Carrie's lap.

"You better give in gracefully and let her lick you dry. There'll be no peace on the ride home, else," chortled Ernie who rejoiced in seeing Carrie again. He dabbed at his eye and seeing Thomas's questioning gaze explained, "Smuts in my eye, from the train."

Thomas nodded knowingly and the wagon set off, a bubble of happy chatter rolling along the street to the village of Crynant, the mountain track and Gelli Galed.

John was waiting on the verandah. As soon as he caught sight of the cart he dashed indoors to place the partially boiled kettle on the range before racing back out and into the yard to meet them.

John helped Carrie down. Brother and sister scrutinised each other with quiet reserve. "You've blossomed, cariad. Grown into a beautiful young woman. Duw, I've missed you."

Carrie opened her arms and hugged her brother, "I've missed you too." She let him go and his hair fell into his eyes. She pushed it back gently; "I've got a cure for that. A little bit of Vaseline will soon have that quiff trained." She tucked her arm in his and the two walked back to the verandah happily at ease with one another. Ernie smiled as he watched them. There was something different about the two of them, different and healthy. They had moved on. He helped Pemb down and apologised, "You'll meet John properly inside. They've not seen each other in a while. Always been close."

"That's all right. They must have heaps to catch up on. I know what it's like when I get back with my family and I'm one of seven!"

Gelli Galed rang with joy and laughter that night and the lights burned long. Even the house seemed to welcome Carrie home.

Pemb squashed in with Carrie amidst giggles and complaints. "We better go top to tail," advised Pemb wisely. "That way we'll have more room. That is, of course, if we ever get to sleep."

"If you're prepared to have my foot in your mouth. Don't say I didn't warn you. I have a reputation for kicking like a mule."

"Kick me and I'll kick you back," joked Pemb. "Now, shut up and go to sleep," she said snuggling down.

There was a light tap on the door.

"Yes?" answered Carrie.

John's voice asked, "Can I have a quick word, fy merch 'i, before you go fast asleep? I know what you're like. One whiff of the country air and you'll be comatose."

"Excuse me, Pemb," said Carrie trying not to step on her friend, "I won't be long." She grabbed a wrap and opened the latch on her door. "What is it?"

"I just need to set things straight, that's all," said John awkwardly.

"Why? What's happened?"

He stood there a while hardly daring himself to speak. "I'm embarrassed and ashamed but you have to know the truth. Everyone else will in time."

"Whatever are you talking about?"

"I'm getting married tomorrow..."

"Yes, to Jenny Davies," finished Carrie.

"It's all a bit quick and sudden..."

"I don't see a problem, if you're in love and..."

"No," he cut her off, "That's just it. Jenny and me well... she's having my baby."

"I see..."

"It shouldn't have happened but it did. Jawch, she was my..." he coughed in embarrassment. "She's a good girl Carrie. I was her first... and she mine," he added sheepishly, "She loves me and I care for her."

"Do you love her?"

"It will come, I'm sure. We have friendship and I'll do right by her. I just wanted you to know that's all. I didn't like to say in front of your friend. I don't want you thinking any the less of me."

Carrie put her arms around him and soothed, "That would never happen. As long as you're happy then I am too."

John nodded, "I am. She'll make a good wife and mother."

"And will you make a good husband and father?"

"I'll do my best."

"Then, that's all right then. Congratulations! Now, get to bed or we'll all be fit for nothing in the morning." She gave him a kiss and tiptoed back in her room.

Pemb was breathing deeply in the first phase of sleep. 'Didn't take her long,' thought Carrie as she managed to squeeze herself back into the bed. She allowed herself an impish smile, 'I'm going to be an aunty,' she thought with pleasure. 'Imagine that?' And with difficulty, she engineered herself into a half comfortable position and drifted away on a pillow of dreams.

CHAPTER SIXTEEN

Realisation

"Ernie! Where's the boot polish?" shouted Tom.

"John's got it," came the curt reply. "Duw, Duw someone's hammering at the door. Can you answer it Tom? I'm not dressed."

"Neither am I. I don't want to crease my trousers more than necessary."

"I'll get it," called Carrie as she wrapped her robe around her.

Gelli Galed was a volcano of confusion and excitement. Members and honorary members of the Llewellyn clan were running backwards and forwards like a colony of insects in a disturbed ants' nest. Thomas was practicing his speech in between checking that the rings were safely in his pocket.

"Jawch, man, that's the seventeenth time in a minute. Now leave it be or you *will* lose them," remonstrated Ernie.

To say John was nervous was an understatement. His breathing was so heavy he'd popped his collar stud four times and had now lost it... again! Pemb watched the antics in wide-eyed amusement. Her keen eyes saw where the elusive stud had hidden to avoid capture and plucked it out from under the rocking chair.

"Here," she said amiably, "Let me fix it." She helped John's collar unite once more with his shirt and raided the pigskin stud box on the table. "I'll keep one in my purse as a back up," she promised wisely. "Now, finish dressing and I'll do your hair. What time is it?"

"Not time enough," chortled Ernie. "It's an hour we've got before church."

"It'll take us half an hour to get there. We'll never be ready," wailed John.

"Yes, you will. Now, take a deep breath and calm down. Anyone would think you're about to be executed the way you're carrying on," laughed Pemb.

"He is," called Thomas. "It's last day of freedom."

Trixie, unable to settle in the mayhem took the opportunity to retreat to the comparative quiet of the yard. She nosed open the door as Carrie entered followed by two young women. Thomas shouted in embarrassment and ran out clutching his trousers. John looked sheepish as Pemb was attacking his famously unruly hair with a dab of Vaseline. The new arrivals laughed at the chaotic scene in front of them.

"Sorry, I didn't know what to tell them so I asked them in," apologised Carrie.

John recognised the two Land Girls who had arrived the day before and were being housed in the farm worker's cottage at Hendre.

"Looks like we've caught you at a bad time," giggled a golden haired girl in dungarees and Wellingtons who went by the name of Daisy.

"Didn't Sam Jeffery organise your chores today?" queried John.

"We haven't seen him. He was up early had to go to Neath for something. Apparently, he's going to a wedding this morning," said the other one called Laura.

"In that case," said Carrie, "I suggest you forget your chores for today and get yourselves changed and join us for the wedding. You'll have no sense out of my brother for now."

"Yes, yes," agreed John. "We'll pick you up at Hendre on the way down."

"That's one way to get to know the locals. We'll be there. I'm Daisy, by the way," said the golden haired girl, "And this is Laura."

The glossy haired brunette smiled in acknowledgement, "That's me."

"I'm Carrie, my friend Pemb, Ernie and the lad who left holding his pants is my cousin Thomas. I believe you already know John."

"We met yesterday, at Hendre with the farm manager. We'd better get a move on if we're to get ready on time. See you."

The girls left and Carrie noticed the time, "Eek! I'll never be ready. Pemb you have to sort my hair! By the way, what is your name? I can't introduce you as Pemb all the time."

"Carol, my twin and I were born on Boxing Day so we were christened Christine and Carol... for Christmas carol. Now go and get dressed unless you're intending to wear that."

Carrie took the hint and dashed out of the kitchen to the stairs nearly knocking Thomas over as he returned, fully clothed and looking quite handsome. "I'll go and harness Senator."

"No, you won't," argued Ernie. "I'll do that. We don't want you smelling of horses and hay. Besides I need a bit of peace. A few more minutes here and I'll be ready for the asylum."

Before anyone could object he was gone.

The wagon progressed down the track with all occupants in their formal Sunday best. Even Senator had been groomed until his coat gleamed and he had his mane plaited.

The cart pulled up at Hendre where the two Land Girls were waiting in their finery. Thomas jumped down to help them up. Then, the dray continued on its way to the chapel. John pulled at his collar nervously and swallowed hard as they approached the hallowed building.

Several villagers, friends and family were already waiting. "No going back now," whispered Thomas as he secured Senator to a post.

"Thanks for nothing," retorted John. "Have you got the rings?"

"Aye, I have. Now, look smart and let's get inside."

Carrie jumped down and was immediately surrounded by aunties and her grandmother who all wanted to hear her news. Pemb stood back and smiled. It was heartening to see so much love. It made her think of her own home and that made her feel a little sad. But, she had no time to dwell on that as Carrie pulled her forward to introduce her to everyone.

"Dera, cariad. It's in we must be getting or there'll be no seats left," urged Ernie. Carrie extricated herself from her grandmother's hug and followed Ernie into the church. It had been decorated very simply with autumn garlands and miniature sheaves of wheat, very fitting for a farmer.

The organist played a medley of old hymns before the signal was given and he launched into the familiar notes of the Bridal March. John looked back and caught his sister's eye. Carrie winked encouragingly at him and he smiled. His smile grew broader as Jenny processed down the aisle on the arm of her father. His heart began to thunder in his chest. She looked beautiful; serene and glowing with an inner light, a purity, which made him gasp in appreciation.

Megan, the only bridesmaid, followed behind in an apricot silk dress. Thomas studied her admiringly but his gaze drifted back to Pemb standing with Carrie in the third row. Megan saw his eyes shift and tried to see whom it was that had taken his attention from her. When she saw the curvaceous snowball blonde next to Carrie, her smile set in a fine line and unexpectedly, Megan felt pangs of jealousy churn inside.

John faced Jenny in front of the altar and as he gazed at her gentle face and sweet smiling lips he realised that he had turned a corner. This was right. It felt right and he knew it *was* right. His heart stopped racing and a feeling of peaceful serenity washed over him. So much so he almost didn't hear the Reverend Richard's next words.

"Where are the rings?"

Jenny turned to look at Tom who was staring at them both with an idiotic smile on his face. John hissed, "Thomas, the rings."

Shaken from his reverie Thomas started guiltily and searched in his pockets for the wedding bands. Amused glances passed between members of the congregation as Tom pulled out his handkerchief and the two rings went spinning in the air. He caught one but the other jumped from his grasp and rolled towards the front pews. Thomas like some demented cartoon character cried out, "Got it!" and slid along the cardinal-red waxed tiles after the elusive ring, which came to a halt at Pemb's feet. She bent down to recover it at the same time Thomas stretched out his hand. For a moment their fingers touched and Pemb firmly picked up the wayward gold band and offered it to Thomas. Stuttering his thanks Thomas retrieved the wilful piece of jewellery and gave it to the Reverend who placed them on his open Bible.

Thomas turned back and mouthed, 'Thank you' and blushed redder than a ripe tomato. Pemb smiled back shyly. The interchange didn't go unnoticed by Carrie or anyone else. And Megan felt again, in the pit of her stomach, that spiralling knot of anxiety that comes with both fear and envy.

The Star and Garter was alive with well-wishers and family members who were all enjoying the buffet lunch in the Lounge bar. Someone had brought in a record player and its tinny music acted as a backdrop to the chinking glasses, gossip and laughter.

Thomas raised his glass to Pemb at the bar and smiled as she returned the gesture. Fired with courage from the beer he had consumed he began to make his way towards her when Megan stepped between him and his destination.

"Aren't you going to ask me to dance? It's usual for the bridesmaid and best man to have at least one dance together."

"Aye, if that's what's expected," he replied. "I'm not one to go against tradition."

Megan stepped up to him and took his hands. She pushed

her body close and gazed into his eyes. She was irritated to see that Thomas kept looking back at Carrie's friend and was not paying her the attention she had been used to and that she had taken for granted.

Thomas, ever the gentleman, did what he felt was his duty and as soon as the music was over he extricated himself from Megan's arms and excused himself. Megan scowled as she watched him join Carrie, Pemb and the Land Girls. Pretending not to care she joined Jenny's family and exchanged pleasantries but all the while her eyes followed Thomas. Megan felt her eyes well up and scurried out to the ladies toilets to recover her composure. She was not going to give anyone the pleasure of seeing her upset. In truth she couldn't work out why she was suddenly feeling like this.

Carrie went across to her new sister-in-law and gave her a hug.

"We're family now, Jenny fach. I wish you and John everything you wish yourselves."

Jenny flushed with pleasure. "It's all happened so quickly. I never imagined that someone like John would look at me."

"Go on with you. He needed taking out of himself and you were just the person to do it. I have to be thanking you here or I think he would be condemned to a life of farming and bachelorhood. We need another woman in the family."

They continued to chat like old friends. Carrie had that way with her that made anyone feel welcome and she could talk to any person regardless of status and make him or her feel important. As they chatted, Thomas took Pemb by the arm and excused himself from the Land Girls, Daisy and Laura.

He took her out into the back courtyard. "Sorry to take you away from the party but I wanted a quiet word."

"Go ahead. I don't really know anyone anyway."

"I don't know what Carrie's told you about me..."

"You've no worries there - it's all good stuff. I feel as if I know both you and John quite well. Oh, and of course Ernie."

"She may not have said, but I'm leaving Gelli Galed tomorrow."

"Oh?"

"I'm joining up. Most of the young men in the village have already gone. I thought I would do the same. See what else life has to offer and maybe get a little more respect around here."

"I don't understand..."

104

"I just wanted to ask..."

"Go on."

"If you're willing I'd like to write to you. I know we hardly know each other but I feel there's a connection between us and I would like to keep in touch."

Pemb beamed, "I'd like that, Thomas. I'd like that very much," and she took his hand. They looked searchingly into each other's eyes and for one moment seemed lost in time.

Megan returned to the bar and looked around but could not see Thomas anywhere. She had resolved to tell him how she felt before he went away and to apologise for playing games with his feelings for too long. But he wasn't there. A quick check around the room revealed that Carrie's friend was also missing. Her stomach began to churn and whirl inside her as if her very energy was spinning the wrong way. She had to find him. She went to the front door of the Public House but he wasn't there. The street was practically deserted except for an old taxicab heading down the street.

Megan pushed her way back in and moved towards the courtyard. She opened the door and saw Thomas and Pemb with their heads close together in the midst of a kiss. She turned swiftly and retreated back to the bar. Tears began to stream down her face. Carrie noticed and came to her friend's side.

"What is it? What's the matter?" Carrie took Megan back to the Ladies room and faced her friend. "Megan, what is it?"

"Oh, Carrie; I've been so stupid and selfish and now it's too late."

"What are you talking about?"

"You know I've always had a thing for John and when he started seeing Jenny I went out with Thomas, only as a friend, just to try and make John notice me. Make him jealous. But it didn't work."

"Yes, I know. I told you what I thought about that. Thomas deserves better than that. He was totally besotted with you."

"Not anymore. And now it's too late. I've pushed him away. He's off to Cardiff tomorrow."

"Why? What's happened?"

"I saw him, with your friend. In the courtyard kissing."

"Pemb?"

"Is that her name? Their heads were so close you wouldn't have got a fag paper between them."

"No... I can't believe..."

"It's true. I'd just made up my mind to tell him how I felt

and that I've behaved badly. I don't know what happened I suddenly realised how lovely he is and that if I didn't say anything he'd go off and never know. I've been an idiot."

Carrie took her sobbing friend in her arms and hugged her. She didn't know what to say. It's true she hadn't approved of Megan's tactics but if Pemb had really caught Tom's eye then no one would be more pleased than Carrie.

"Here dry your eyes. Come on." She handed Megan the hanky she had stuffed up her sleeve. "You'll have to tell him. He needs to know. I don't want him leading my friend on."

"He's not like that. He's straightforward and honest. I'm the one who's been playing games. I really think I've missed my chance."

"Get yourself tidied up. I'll go and speak to Pemb. You talk to Thomas and then you'll know."

Carrie returned to the party and saw Thomas and Pemb entering from the courtyard, arm in arm. They did look very comfortable with each other. Carrie scooted up. "Pemb, a word. Sorry, Tom I'll get her back to you soon. I promise." She steered her friend back out to the courtyard as Megan returned.

"What's all this about?" queried Pemb.

"Just a sisterly word, that's all. Are you and Thomas...?" She trailed off as she saw Pemb blush.

"He's asked if he can write to me. Carrie, he's so lovely. You really didn't do him justice when you spoke of him. ... Why?"

"Nothing. You know me. Nosey to the end. I had an inkling that there was some sort of chemistry between you."

"Was it that obvious?"

Carrie nodded, "That obvious."

"Oh dear. Can we get back now?"

"After we've smartened ourselves up a bit. Your lipstick's smudged," she added pointedly.

Megan went to Tom as soon as she saw Carrie and Pemb retreat to the Ladies. "Tom. Can I speak to you?"

"Of course, Megan fach. What is it?"

"I owe you an apology. I've behaved badly to you and although I thought I didn't want a relationship I've changed my mind. I'd love to be your girl. If you'll have me."

Thomas was stuck for words. " ... Megan love... Why didn't you say so before? I always had my eye on you but you were so taken with John I never thought you'd look at me like that and I didn't want to be second best."

"You're not second best. You're *the* best. I've been stupid and I've just realised that it's you I want."

"I'm sorry, Megan. I carried a torch for you for so long. A week ago I would have been ecstatic to hear you say this. I wouldn't be joining up that's for sure."

"You don't have to go. Stay here. We can start again. Give me another chance. Please."

"I can't. I've just asked Pemb if I can write to her when I'm away. She was only too pleased to say, yes."

"Write to me too. Please. I'll make you change your mind. You'll see."

Thomas hesitated as he gazed into Megan's haunted eyes. He had wanted her for so long and now... Now, he was confused. "You can write. But, I'm not promising anything."

Megan smiled, "It's just to have the chance. Just the chance."

Tom turned his head and saw Carrie and Pemb return to the bar. "Excuse me now. We'll talk again." And he went to join his cousin and her friend.

Megan bit her lip. She felt so utterly foolish. But she determined she wouldn't give him up without a fight. Satisfied that she'd made a decision she tossed her head and rejoined the party.

The Landlord of the Star and Garter hammered the counter and Thomas stepped forward to speak.

"I'm not going to make any more speeches but I'm sure before we wind things up that all of us here want to wish John and Jenny the very best in their married life together. I'd like to ask you to raise your glasses in a toast. To John and Jenny."

The assembled company chorused, "To John and Jenny," and swallowed down a mouthful of whatever they were drinking. Suddenly the outside door opened and a tall woman entered carrying a baby. The room fell silent as all eyes turned towards her.

"I wouldn't have missed this for the world," she said. "It's not every day my young nephew gets married." She proudly walked to John and Jenny. "I'm here to offer my congratulations." She shook Jenny's hand who looked enquiringly at John.

"Jenny. This here's my Aunty Netta."

CHAPTER SEVENTEEN

Netta

The wedding party stopped abruptly. Time seemed to stand still and everything moved in slow motion until small pockets of people sought the corners of the room and relinquished their silence in a fevered burst of excited whispering.

Mam-gu almost swooned and Gwenny caught her mother's hand and approached the proud stiff bearing of iron backed Netta. Carrie gasped and almost dropped her drink. Her free hand grasped Pemb so tightly that her nails left red imprints on Pemb's palm.

Pemb looked around totally bewildered, unable to work out what was happening or who the woman clutching a nine-month-old baby could be. Thomas was quick to take Pemb away. They moved outside the pub so that he could explain the extreme reaction Netta had provoked from everyone.

Carrie was among the first to regain her composure. She tilted her head, like her mother, and walked to Netta her hand extended in friendship. There was a flicker of understanding in Netta's eyes and she gratefully returned Carrie's steadfast gaze.

"So this is your..." there was a barely imperceptible pause, "and Jacky's baby?"

"Aye. It is. He's a fine strong fellow with lungs to match when he wants them."

"What have you called him?" Carrie asked reluctantly, almost afraid of what the response would be.

"Jake."

"Not Jacky?"

"No," Netta's reply was measured. "I thought about it but believed one Jacky was enough so I picked a name that was close but not too close."

Carrie looked into the face of the gurgling infant. He was a handsome child with Jacky's dark colouring and unmistakable eyes. Carrie shuddered as her mind filled with images from the past. Regaining her equanimity she questioned Netta, "Are you staying?"

"I don't know. I may look tough on the outside but whether I can brazen out the stares of villagers and their undoubted gossip I've yet to see. I thought perhaps I'd stay a week, see Mam and Gwenny, perhaps get to know my new niece-in-law. Would it bother you if I did?"

"Do as you wish. I shan't be here."

"Oh?"

"Nothing mysterious. The family will tell you. I'm away tomorrow. Only came back for the wedding."

Netta nodded. She didn't probe further. Aunt and niece eyed each other before politely shaking hands. Carrie turned to look for her friend and Netta took Jake across to meet his grandmother and Aunt Gwenny.

The guests had recovered sufficiently for the party to progress but Carrie still felt uncomfortable. Her face was flushed and she needed air. She couldn't see Pemb anywhere and so moved to the courtyard and found a bench to sit on whilst she recovered her equilibrium. It was here Ernie found her.

"That was a tough encounter for you, cariad. You did right."

"You know me too well, Ernie." She hesitated, "Was it right?"

"The child can't be blamed for the father's deeds but..."

"But...?"

"But... I'm saying nothing. It's good that you're away tomorrow."

"Ernie! You can't stop there. You know something, I know you do."

"Let's say, no one knows for sure. It's just a feeling."

"Feelings you've been right with before," Carrie retorted.

"Let's wait and see. I could be wrong."

"Perhaps. But I'd trust your instincts over and above anything and anyone."

Ernie paused. He studied Carrie's earnest expression and relented. He was about to impart his feelings and the premonition he'd experienced but was thwarted by the arrival of Pemb and Thomas.

"There you are!" exclaimed Pemb. "Thomas has just told me the story."

"And one not to be repeated anywhere," admonished Carrie curtly.

"No, of course not. I only wanted to say how I sympathised and understood. If ever you need to talk..." The sentence remained unfinished as Carrie rose and attempted to tidy her unruly hair, which had been constrained for far too long and was rebelling against her hat.

"I won't. But thanks for the offer. Come on, Ernie you owe me a dance." She tugged at his hand until he followed her back into the pub.

"It's two left feet I've got, Carrie. Never been one for dancing; except a jig when I hit my head or burnt myself."

"Then it's time you learned," and she pulled him away from the courtyard and back inside to the party.

"So, what was it you were about to tell me?" questioned Carrie.

"Maybe, I should leave well alone," muttered Ernie as he struggled to remember, which foot went where. Carrie scrunched her face up as he trod on her toe for the second time. "I told you I'm not a dancer. Esgyrn Davydd! You'll have no toes left. They'll be blackberry juice by the time I've pulverised them into the floor. My feet are good for walking and treading grapes and no more."

"Oh, Ernie," smiled Carrie and then winced once more as his boot collided with her shin. "You're right. This was a bad idea. If I'm to be able to do my duty when I get back we'd best sit this dance out."

"Sorry, cariad. I did warn you."

It was past midnight when the Star and Garter closed its doors and the merry revellers celebrating John and Jenny's wedding rolled home like scattered skittles.

Senator's load was heavy as he plodded up the mountainside. The lamps on the side of the cart swung in the velvet black of night and the stars twinkled brightly promising a bright future for the young couple and all stargazers.

Thomas and Pemb secretly touched fingers that unable to resist stretched into a full firm grasp. Pemb placed her snowball curls and head onto Tom's shoulder. Carrie peeped out of the corner of her eye approvingly. John and Jenny were quiet but cuddled together and Carrie felt that at last John would forget his unhealthy possessiveness toward her.

The Land Girls, Daisy and Laura, sang quietly in harmony "Somewhere over the rainbow" and the rest of the passengers hummed along until the cart reached Hendre and they jumped down.

"Good luck, you two," shouted Laura.

"Yes, if you can survive the first year you'll be fine," added Daisy.

The girls ran up the track leading to Old Tom's cottage and Ernie urged Senator forward. The cart was strangely quiet. All that could be heard were the rumbling of the wheels on the rutted track and the clip clop of Senator's hooves. Ernie attempted to fill the void with some less than tuneful whistling and was immediately shouted down.

"Cwat Lawr, wuss. It's enough to make the bones of the dead rattle in their graves," laughed Thomas.

Ernie grinned lopsidedly and fell silent. It felt good and it felt right but he still had his concerns.

CHAPTER EIGHTEEN

Resolutions, Goodbyes and Prophesies

Carrie patted Senator on the nose and nuzzled him as she alighted from the cart before making a fuss of Trix who was jumping around her in a frenzy.

Thomas helped Pemb down and the two decided to take a moonlight stroll a little way up the track. John and Jenny held hands in a contented silence and walked toward the verandah.

"Night all," called John as he and Jenny went indoors.

"Goodnight and thanks for everything," added Jenny before disappearing through the door.

Ernie unhitched the cart and began to lead Senator to the barn.

"Not so fast," chided Carrie. "There are things you have to tell me..." She left the rest of the sentence unsaid.

"Jawch! A man cannot escape your prying mind and tongue," joked Ernie.

"You started it," laughed Carrie, "Said there were 'things'..."

"Many a time my mouth has run ahead of my brain and tripped me up," agreed Ernie, "This is one of them." He stopped and studied Carrie quizzically. "I can see I'll have no rest tonight until you are satisfied. Come to the barn and we'll talk there. Loose talk can raise wild imaginings and I don't want anything misconstrued by the others." With that Ernie led Senator off to his stable to bed him down for the night. Carrie ran after him grabbing at her hat, which wanted to divorce her head. Trixie dutifully trotted after the pair; her curiosity aroused. She was determined not to lose sight of her beloved Carrie and to spend as much time with her as possible.

Thomas and Pemb had settled on a rock on the mountainside. They were gazing at the lovers' ceiling in the lustrous night sky.

"I had a feeling that Megan... is it Megan? I've met so many people today..."

"What about her?" asked Thomas.

"I just got the impression that maybe I was treading on her toes. That you and she, well - you were promised or something."

"We went out but Megan only ever had eyes for John. She only stepped out with me to try and catch John's eye but it didn't work. After John and Jenny got engaged. She ditched me like a sack of teddies."

"I'm sorry."

"No need to be. I was hankering after someone who didn't want me and meeting you... well, it's as if I've known you years. I suppose that sounds silly?"

"No. I warmed to you as soon - as soon as I laid eyes on you."

"Then it was meant to be and I was right to say what I did."

"What's that?"

"Megan, after seeing you and me getting on so well. She said she'd made a mistake and wanted to get back together. I told her, no."

"Thomas, are you sure? I'm no man stealer and I don't want to upset anyone."

"Pemb, at this moment it feels right, is right and hopefully we will see each other again, God willing."

"I almost forgot; you leave tomorrow, too, don't you?"

"Cardiff. I'm joining the Navy."

They sat together in silence. There was no need for words. The moon's silver beams lit the ground and gilded their upturned faces full of shining hope.

Carrie sat on a bale of straw as she listened to Ernie. "What a terrible dream."

"Unravelling the meaning was hardest."

"Why do I get the feeling that there's more?"

"I know you Carrie, heart as big as a bucket. Be careful, don't take on more than you can handle and your aunt..."

"Which one? Netta?"

"Aye, the one with the ramrod back and baby."

"What about her?"

"Not now, but I've a feeling she'll bide her time before striking like a viper. Don't trust all she says. She has grand designs and if she doesn't follow through the child will."

Carrie shivered. She didn't know what Ernie meant but she trusted his words and promised herself she would be careful.

"What about John and Jenny? Will they fare well?"

"John and Jenny will do well but…"

"But?"

"Enough has been said and I've said too much. Just remember that if you go to London, and I suspect you will, be nice to a man called George."

"Why?"

"He could save your life.

Jenny lay snuggled up on John's shoulder in their marital bed. It felt strange away from her home and beginning a new life, strange but exciting too.

John lay at her side, his eyes open and lost in his thoughts. Jenny whispered, "John?"

"Yes?"

"Are you happy?"

"Happiness will come in barrelfuls, of that I'm sure. I always said love would come and when I saw you today in the church I almost choked with pride. Yes, fy merch 'i, I am happy."

Jenny smiled, and a small tear escaped her eye. She took John's hand and placed it on her flat belly. "We must talk to him or her and let it know we care."

John patted her tummy before turning to face her. He drew her up in his arms and kissed her tenderly, her heart soared. This kiss was one of true love.

The next morning was one of chaos and manic joy and laughter. Senator was taken from his comfy barn and instead of being allowed into the field was once more harnessed to the cart. Carrie's and Pemb's bags were loaded first, followed by Thomas' haversack and battered leather case.

Trixie barked demanding a place on the cart with the travellers. Ernie succumbed, "It's no peace we'll be having unless we allow her up," he admonished.

Thomas laughed and picked up the collie depositing her in the back with the luggage. Thomas turned to his cousin, John and clasped him in a warm embrace. "I suppose this is it, wuss. Look after the farm and your Jenny. I don't know when I shall be back but keep a place for me."

"There'll always be a place for you here. You know that. If you change your mind you can return and have your old room back. And that's a promise."

Not trusting himself to speak, Thomas hugged his cousin. He leant forward and brushed his lips against Jenny's cheek before clearing his throat. "Don't be standing any nonsense from him Jenny, fach. Start as you mean to go on."

Jenny smiled shyly and nodded before turning to Carrie and Pemb. "Lovely to see you again and to meet you, Pemb. You are welcome any time."

"Thank you. I hope to be back. Good luck in your married life," rejoined Pemb before clambering into the cart alongside Thomas.

Ernie climbed up into the driving seat and looked down at Carrie facing her brother and Jenny. "You'd better shape it. The train won't wait and you've a long journey ahead of you. Have you got the sandwiches I packed?"

"Yes, Ernie. In the carpet bag."

Ernie turned stiffly but could see brother and sister out of the corner of his eye. Knowing it was their turn to say goodbye he wondered what would be revealed to him.

Carrie put her arms out to John and they embraced. John's eyes misted up, "Jawch, it was good to see you, gal and your friend."

Carrie nodded and clasped her brother tightly saying nothing. She turned to Jenny and whispered in her ear, "I shall be thinking of you and praying for you and the baby."

Jenny had a sharp intake of breath and glanced at John who nodded, "I didn't know that you knew…"

"The glow is unmistakeable," murmured Carrie, "Don't worry. No one else knows."

The two women hugged and for a moment their unruly curls mingled as one as the sun caught the burnished tresses in a fiery glow.

Jenny turned back to John who placed his arm protectively around her shoulder. "Safe journey to you all. Let's trust that when we meet again things will be as good as they are now." As Jenny uttered those words a cloud edged over the face of the sun. Ernie clicked an instruction to Senator and the cart began to rattle its way down the track whilst all the occupants waved madly until John and Jenny were just specks in the distance.

On the way down the track they passed Laura and Daisy who waved their goodbyes and the cart trundled on into the village of Crynant and onto Neath railway station.

Ernie placed Carrie's bags on the rack and took her by her shoulders, "Now, I know you. Don't go doing anything foolish now will you?"

"Like what?"

"Going to nurse on the front lines or something as stupid."

"All I'll say is I won't promise anything then, I can't be held to account."

"Duw, you're a stubborn little tyke."

"Now, where have I heard that before?"

"Look after yourself, cariad, because none of us can." Ernie's eyes misted over and he gave Carrie a warm hug.

"Go on with you. You'll have me in tears if you keep on," muttered Carrie as she stepped into the train.

Trixie gave a sharp yelp and Carrie stepped back down onto the platform, "Whatever am I thinking? Not saying goodbye to my most important friend and companion." She knelt down and made a final fuss of the collie who instead of her laughing smile, looked subdued and forlorn. "I'll be home again at Christmas, Trix. Just you see. You need to take care of John and Jenny now, and our Ernie."

Trixie put her head on one side in that engaging way that all collies have, gave a little bark of acceptance and wagged her tail.

"Understands every word you say, cariad. So Christmas it is. Go on, get on board before I make a clown of myself."

Carrie re-entered the train and took her seat. She glanced down the platform and saw Megan flying toward them.

But, oblivious, Thomas and Pemb were saying their own goodbyes. He crushed Pemb to him and drank in the fragrant perfume of her hair. Megan stopped and with tears coursing down her cheeks left as quickly as she had come.

"I'll write and tell you, which regiment and where to contact me."

Pemb nodded, "Just promise me you'll be careful, very, very careful."

Thomas forced a smile, "Now, get on the train before I drag you away with me!"

The guard came out and waved his flag blowing his shrill whistle and the train chuffed out of the station with Pemb hanging out of the window until Thomas could no longer be seen.

She flopped down, "Carrie, you totally undersold Thomas. He is..." she sighed, "Very special."

CHAPTER NINETEEN

Schemes and Dreams

Netta preened in front of the mirror in her old bedroom. She turned her head to admire her profile. She had worn well, of that she was sure. It was in the genes. She glanced at her make shift crib, a drawer in her dressing table and fixed her eyes on the bright eyed baby.

"Well, little Jake. I made a mistake in trying to rid myself of you. You are mine. Mine and Jacky's and in time you will have your legacy." And with that she began to fiercely brush her hair.

"Netta!" her mother's voice assailed her from the bottom of the stairs, "We need to talk."

Netta threw down her hairbrush and gathered the baby up in her arms. He began to wail.

"Leave Jake, it won't hurt for you to let him cry."

But, Netta was already unfastening her bodice to feed her son. She called back, "I'll be down once I've settled him."

Netta grabbed a pillow from the bed and sat in a low chair, the pillow on her lap, and began to feed her infant. He sucked greedily and Netta was drawn to his eyes; eyes that seemed knowing. She spoke softly and soothingly to her young son, "Duw, you are so like your father. Been in the world before, you have. Like your daddy would say, 'we must tread careful now, if we are to get what we want.' And get what we want, we will." With that she began to croon a Welsh lullaby. Her little one closed his eyes, and when he was resting peacefully and sucking no more, she laid him back in the drawer, tidied her dress and went down the stairs to hear what her mother had to say.

Thomas stepped out of the recruiting office into bright sunshine. He patted his pocket with his enlistment papers and whistled as he walked to the wharf to survey the many ships similar to the one on which, he had agreed to sign up for a tour of duty. He stood on the docks and gazed at the many vessels moored there. A young sailor, in full kit, jostled his arm as he lay down his naval bag. He smiled at Tom, "Thinking of joining up?"

Thomas nodded, "Got my enlistment papers here."

"We need good men. Don't leave it too long."

"How long have you been serving?"

"Just completed my training. Tough it was too. I'm off on tender to join the HMS Royal Oak in Scapa Flow."

"Where's that?"

"The Orkney Isles. What about you?"

"I've come from a farm. Want to see a bit of the world and serve my country."

"You'll do that all right. What's your itinerary?"

"Fill these in first. Come back and get my passport checked and then, if I'm accepted..."

"You will be... They need every man they can get."

"Then, Boot Camp."

"I expect you'll have accelerated training like me. Hope you don't get sea sick?"

"Nah. I've sailed to Australia and back. I've got sea legs."

"Then that's a bonus. Good luck."

"You too. What's your name?"

"Matthew, Matthew Crane."

"Tom, Thomas Davies."

The two shook hands before Matthew picked up his bag and headed for the gangplank of a small naval service boat. Thomas watched young Matthew board the vessel, who turned back to wave at Tom. Tom raised his hand in a salute as he studied Matthew's fresh young face full of hope.

"Now, Tom. Time to make a move and let the family know what's happening," and he headed for the Telegraph Office.

Ernie was clattering about in the scullery when Jenny walked in, "Oh Ernie, there's no need for you to do so much now. I can do the cooking and housework chores."

"Thank you, Jenny, but I like to feel useful. And besides, you will need all your time for the little one that's coming."

Jenny looked shocked, "You mean John has told you?"

"No, but you have that look. It's unmistakeable. Honeymoon baby it is, isn't it?" And he gave her a broad wink.

Jenny flushed with embarrassment and smiled shyly, "Then, Ernie, until I'm blown up like a balloon we'll share the duties. What do you want me to do?"

"I'll wash this lot and you can dry and find their homes. It'll do you good to find out what goes where. John likes a tidy house. Then you can feed the chickens while I see to the stock."

"And, then?"

"That'll be enough for now. I'm sure you'll find other things to do."

"That I will and at ten o'clock I'll do the fry up."

"Agreed," smiled Ernie. "Let's get cracking then."

Nervous, quiet little Jenny began to feel more at home and started to see her role as mistress of Gelli Galed. She burst into song. Ernie stopped to listen in admiration. She had the sweetest voice hitting the notes pure and true.

"Why we have ourselves a pretty songbird. You'll rival the song thrush and blackbird with tunes like that. No need of the wireless when we can listen to you."

Ernie attempted to join in, less melodically, but pulled up short as his voice cracked on a high note. "Esgyrn Davidd, I'd better give up on breakfast warbling or I'll be shot for a crow." He cleared his throat; "I'll leave the singing to you, tempted as I am..."

"Tempted as you are to what?" questioned John as he strolled in stretching.

"Sing," responded Ernie.

"Jawch no! His vocal chords are as rusty as a bent nail. He sounds like he's grinding iron with his teeth. Can't stand the cacophony, especially in the morning," mused John.

"Ah! But Jenny on the other hand has the voice of an angel."

"Has she? I've never heard her sing," muttered John.

"Go on. Sing a line, let your husband hear what he's been missing."

"Yes, go on," encouraged John.

Hesitant at first but gathering courage once the first lines were out, Jenny sang at the top of her voice and from her heart. John listened in admiration and amazement, "You have a beautiful voice," he said in wonder, "A voice that deserves to be heard. Why didn't you say?"

"You never asked and besides it's never really come up. Before we... we got married, I was going to go to music college."

"Oh Jenny, how selfish... I never asked you if you had any plans or ambitions..."

"And I never said. Things change," she said philosophically, "My life is here now, with you and the baby. My ambitions have changed. I want us to be happy. All of us," she added eyeing Ernie.

"But is there anything you want?"

"No, except..."

"What? Tell me?"

"I'd love to have my piano at the farm."

"And have it you will. We'll see to it, won't we, Ernie?" And with that he crossed to Jenny and hugged her tightly.

Ernie smiled; this was good. This was very good, indeed.

Carrie and Pemb attended their first of many seminars in the hospital's primary lecture theatre. The course they were following was intensive, covering anatomy, physiology, hygiene, as well as bacterial infections, respiratory illnesses, and infectious and other communicable diseases. They compared their timetables and notes. Four days were to be spent in the working environment and two in lectures.

"I've got Wednesday off," smiled Pemb, "How about you?"

"Monday," frowned Carrie. She pursed her lips, "I wonder if there's any way we can work it to get the same day?"

"Speak to Hawtry. She may be able to help."

"What do you need?" asked Hawtry overhearing them as she passed the lecture theatre.

Pemb stepped forward, "We'd like to get our days off to coincide. Can we do that?"

Hawtry studied the two timetables. "Maybe, but you'll need to change your ward duty rotas. What you have are the same groups of lectures but you also work the same ward, hence different days off. If you want the same days off you'll have to get someone to switch wards with one of you."

"Oh, thanks, Hawtry. At least we know what we have to do," replied Carrie.

"That's going to be difficult. We both like the Gynae ward," muttered Pemb.

"Yes, but I want eventually to specialise in Chest and would prefer to move there or Men's Surgical."

"I thought you were keen on Gynae?"

"Yes, well I am finding it interesting but don't want to get stuck with women's bits and pieces."

"I know we saw enough of that at the Mat Unit!"

"Let's check the main board."

The two friends headed for the Admin Block to see what could be changed.

Megan sat in the parlour at Gelli Galed. She was puffed out after the climb from Hendre where she had left one of her mother's Arab horses. The track was too steep and full of loose stones and she didn't want to risk the horse taking a tumble.

"Tea, I need tea. For pity's sake give me tea," she languished.

Jenny laughed as she stirred the pot, "Just a minute more and it'll be ready. Do you want a drink of water?"

"No thanks, I'm heaving my heart out as it is. Only tea will cure the stitch I've got in my side."

"Oh, Megan, you are funny. You should have been on the stage," laughed Jenny.

"Funny you should say that. I've been thinking, what with Gwynfor gone off to war along with most of the young men in the village, maybe I might try my hand at entertaining. Mam always said I was a drama queen. Talking of drama, and young men... have you heard from Thomas?" The question was almost casual but it was the real reason why she had climbed the mountain to the farm.

"Why yes," replied Jenny in all innocence. We had a telegramme from him. He's been accepted into the Navy and is doing an intensive training course. He sails from Cardiff a week Friday. I think he's on HMS The Prince of Wales."

"Oh? Do you know the time?"

"Um... Let me think. I thought it said two o'clock, to give time for those on leave to make it back to their berths. I can check if you like?"

"No, I won't put you to any bother..."

"No bother."

Jenny went into the kitchen and retrieved the telegramme from behind the Ormalu clock. She announced as she returned, "Yes, as I said, two in the afternoon." She passed the missive to Megan who read it avidly.

"Thanks."

"What are you going to do?"

"I'm not sure yet." But Megan knew exactly what she was going to do.

CHAPTER TWENTY

Admissions and Admonishments

Carrie started her shift on Men's Surgical delighted to have been able to swap with another nurse suggested by Hawtry. She found the attitude of many of the men a refreshing change from some of the women in Gynae who did nothing but complain.

As she stepped out to do the routine round of blood pressure tests a young Scot, Hamish MacDonald, teased her novice status. "Blimey, better watch out. This one looks like she'll pump up more than your arm."

Other male patients chortled and joined in the fun."Nurse. I need a blanket bath, nurse," called Teddy Smith, "Something's been leaking in the bed"

"I've got my op on Friday, can I book you to give me a shave?" winked another.

"Sorry, it's my day off. I'm not too good with a cutthroat razor. If I do it you may be left less of a man," she joked.

If Carrie was at all fazed by the innuendo, she didn't blink. She continued professionally, joining in their banter and laughing with them. She was so nimble and quick on her feet that pretty soon, when anyone saw her scurry around the ward, the beds would erupt in a verse of, "Run rabbit, run rabbit, run, run, run." It seemed to become her theme tune.

Carrie sat in the Nurses' Station rubbing her feet that throbbed as hard as a big bass drum. Hawtry popped her head in through the door.

"Major emergency. You're needed on the ward now."

There was a clatter and crash as a trolley was rushed into a side room and a shout for nurses to attend echoed around the ward.

Teddy Smith and Hamish MacDonald propped themselves up in bed to watch the frenzied activity in the isolation room.

Carrie hastily thrust on her shoes and dashed to the room ignoring the chorus of voices in the ward.

What she saw when she entered was to live with her forever. A young man about John's age was bleeding profusely from a severed arm. His right leg was horribly mangled, as was one side of his face. The shock of seeing him pulled her up short reminding her of her own father and his Janus face as he had called it. However, she quickly recovered her composure and clinically professional once more listened to the doctor's instructions, which were instantly obeyed.

"Nurse Llewellyn, we need three pints of 'O' negative, now. Put another four in reserve"

"Yes, Doctor Challacombe."

"Staff Nurse Hawtry, take this sample to the Path Lab for matching."

"At once, Doctor."

Both nurses hurried away. The man was making a hideous moaning sound that made the other nurse in attendance, Nurse Clarke, almost faint. She stood immobile, frozen, and unable to tear her eyes away from the grotesque sight in front of her.

The doctor barked again, "Morphine, 15 milligrams. You'll need to set up an IV line." Nurse Clarke remained rooted to the spot. "Nurse Clarke!"

The nurse was transfixed her mouth opened in a 'oh' of horror. Dr. Challacombe crossed to her and slapped her hard across the face bringing her to her senses. He repeated his instruction and Nurse Clarke sped off to get the required dosage.

Dr. Challacombe turned to his junior aid, Don Goodwin, "What in God's name happened?"

"An ambulance was called to Snow Hill Station, Sir. He threw himself off the platform onto the track. A train was approaching..." he trailed off; the evidence of that act lay before them.

Morphine was administered and Carrie soon returned with the blood, which was drip-fed intravenously into the patient's veins. She asked quietly, "What's his name?"

"His ID says, Stephen Crighton," replied the aid.

The doctors attended to the young man's wounds attempting to staunch the flow of blood. His arm was cauterised, bandaged and wrapped. His leg was splinted and cast. Carrie took the young man's hand and spoke soothingly to him over his grunting moans, "Come now, Stephen, gently does it. Let me clean your face."

Flooded with compassion she tried to clean the grit and dirt from the injured side of his face and all the while she soothed with tender words of concern.

Dr. Challacombe looked at Carrie in admiration. He turned to his aid, Don Goodwin, "It takes a real nurse to do that. Real talent. We may treat the damage but she will heal his soul." Carrie was oblivious to the compliment focusing on the dying patient's needs.

"Do you think he'll survive?" questioned Don.

Dr. Challacombe shook his head, "He's lost too much blood. Even if we can replace it, the shock to his body is so severe. I don't expect him to last the night."

"And yet you have treated him as if he'll live..."

"And so we should, Don. We have sworn to save lives and even if the prospect is a tough one we must rise to the challenge and try."

As he said that the young man was struck with an extreme attack of rigour. He shook from head to toe as Hawtry reappeared. She sent Nurse Clarke for more blankets and a bottle and Carrie continued to minister comforting words of encouragement. Suddenly, in a final spasm the young man opened his good eye and fixed on Carrie, he struggled to speak as blood frothed from his mouth.

"Shush now, don't talk. You'll need all your strength, Stephen," murmured Carrie.

Stephen convulsed, his back almost flexing into two and he uttered his last words, "Thank you." He shuddered and died.

Dr. Challacombe closed the one good eye and Hawtry pulled the sheet up over the young man's head. Carrie swallowed hard.

"Nurse Llewellyn."

Carrie looked up at the doctor.

"A word of advice. You have a natural talent but try not to get too emotionally involved." Dr. Challacombe paused, "Even so ... good job, Nurse. Good job."

Thomas stood on the dockside shuffling his feet. His new boots would take some getting used to. He looked handsome in his naval uniform. His newly made friend, Evan, was smoking a last cigarette before they were due to board HMS Prince of Wales and begin a tour of duty.

A shout went up from the end of the pier, "Tom! Thomas!" called the female voice. Tom looked around and squinted his eyes in the morning sun and stared in amazement as the golden rays hit the burnished conker tresses of Megan. She was waving like mad at him. Thomas tentatively raised an arm in surprise.

"Who's the girl?" asked Evan. "I thought there was no one special..."

"There isn't, well... um..."

Megan darted down the steps and ran along the wharf, her hair streaming behind her. She stopped in front of Tom and sought to catch her breath.

"Thank goodness I'm not too late."

"I don't understand," murmured Thomas. All the while Evan looked on quizzically.

"I didn't traipse all the way to Cardiff on a whim. I've something to say and say it I will," she puffed.

"Say on, gal, say on," cheered Evan.

"I made a terrible mistake...."

"And I said...." interrupted Thomas.

"Ssh! Let me finish. I made a terrible mistake. I thought I knew what I wanted, I didn't. What I was dealing with was a bruised ego. I didn't realise what I had until it was too late. Thomas, you are the only man in the world for me and I didn't want you going off to war without knowing that. Or knowing this."

Megan tossed down her bag and pressed her body up against Tom's. She wrapped her arms around his neck shook her incredible tresses and kissed him deeply and passionately on the lips. So fierce was the kiss that Tom's knees began to buckle. He didn't resist and found himself responding with an equal amount of fire.

Megan slipped her arms back to her side, "I treated you horribly and miserably and I promise I will never ever do so again as long as you will give me another chance. There, I've said it. No shame Mam would say, but I don't care."

There was a blast from the ship's hooter and sailors that had been standing on the dock with family and friends said their last goodbyes and began to move toward the gangplank.

"Oh, Megan, I told you..."

"I know, Pemb. But you've only known her five minutes and with me, well, we already have a lifetime of memories. I don't want any promises. Just a chance to keep in touch and remind you of how things could be... Nothing more." Megan stared hopefully into Tom's eyes. He was now very confused but before he could say anymore there was another sharp blast on the ship's horn.

Tom's eyes flicked toward the ship and back at Megan. Before he could say anymore Megan stood on tiptoe and kissed him again, this time tenderly and with love. Thomas didn't fight it.

Finally, he knelt down and retrieved Megan's purse, "All right, Megan fach, write to me and we'll see what happens but I am making no promises, no offence."

"None taken. I just want that chance."

Tom nodded and picked up his bag. He and Evan made their way to the gangway. As he stepped on the boardwalk he looked back and saw Megan's face her eyes shining with tears and her lustrous hair glinting in the sun. He raised his arm and waved before disappearing into the bowels of the boat.

Megan, bit her lip to prevent the tears from falling. She waited until the boardwalk was raised inside and the ropes cast off. Only when the military vessel had begun chugging out of the harbour toward open water did she think about moving. And when she set off there was more of a spring in her step, a lightness that comes from hope.

Evan waylaid Thomas as he boarded, "So, who was that very tasty morsel? If you're not interested then please, do me a favour and introduce me next time she surprises you."

Thomas laughed, "I'd have given anything to have her act like that with me a few weeks ago but she spurned me, was more interested in my cousin, then when he wed another and I met someone else, it seems she changed her mind."

"She is beautiful."

"And so is Carol."

"Carol?"

"Nurse Carol Pembridge, and she is one of twins."

"I like the sound of that more and more," grinned Evan. "You must be quite a dark horse..." The rest of the sentence was left unsaid as the Tannoy announced that Muster would be in fifteen minutes. They just had time to find their births and get ready for the drill.

Netta sat stiffly around the table with Gwenny and her mother. They were deep in discussion. "At least think about it," argued Gwenny. "It makes sense. You have little Jake. You can look after Mam too."

"I have an opinion and a voice Gwenny," remonstrated her mother. "Netta, will you at least think about it. Scandal is soon forgot especially when more comes along to take its place. You won't have to work. You can spend the time with your baby and me. I have enough to look after us all."

Netta's eyes glinted greedily but she still said nothing.

"It's been over two years. My Archie and the girls need me. I can't keep to-ing and fro-ing forever."

Netta sniffed imperiously. Things were working out exactly as she wanted but she knew she mustn't give in too soon.

"You've been here over a month now, have the villagers shunned you?" Gwenny queried.

"No, but..."

"But what?"

"They whisper and point."

"That will stop. Just give them time."

"And what happens if Mam becomes ill. Where will I live? The house will have to be sold and divided between us all."

"That's hardly a problem. I'll put a clause in the will that as long as you are living here the house cannot be sold. It will be your home until you leave this mortal life."

"Hmm." Netta paused, "Let me think on it. I'll let you have my decision tomorrow. I don't think any of you appreciate what I will be giving up."

Gwenny sighed and rose from the table, "Tomorrow then. I hope it'll be the right answer for I'll have no husband left if life continues as it is."

Jake began to wail from upstairs and Netta stood up to attend to the child, she added, before leaving, "I think we may be able to work something out. Until tomorrow."

CHAPTER TWENTY-ONE

Nightmares and truths

Jenny lay in the dark tucked into John's embrace. His deep rhythmic breathing assured her that he was asleep. She ran a hand over her firm belly, barely beginning to pop. She found it hard to believe that she was going to be a mother. Her home in the village seemed a million miles away. She still couldn't understand why John had picked her. He could have had the pick of the village girls and the newly arrived Land Girls. But, question it she wouldn't and she drifted off into a dream filled sleep.

Jenny was dressed in a gossamer silk dress, which floated as she walked through a meadow of buttercups and ox-eye daisies. She carried a small bundle and sat on a tussock of grass as the tiny baby began to cry. Nursing the child to her she was surprised to hear an unfamiliar drone in the sky. An aeroplane passed overhead. It dropped buckets of blood across the field and the buttercups became scarlet poppies. Her baby stopped crying.

John ran through the meadow toward her and snatched the little one. He began to cry, tugging at his hair in abject sorrow and tossed the infant back at her, which was dead. Turning abruptly, he shouted at her, "We will never speak of this again and you are no longer my wife."

Jenny awoke with a start. A slick sheen of sweat covered her and tears were fresh on her cheeks.

John stirred beside her, murmuring sleepily, "What's wrong?"

Jenny bit her lip, "I had a terrible dream that our baby died," she struggled to suppress the fresh tears conspiring to spill down her cheeks.

"That's nonsense. It's not going to happen."

"And you said our marriage was over."

"Now, you're being silly. It's just a dream. A stupid bad dream," and he began to kiss away the tears that were now running freely. The kisses became more passionate and they locked together, urgently in a fierce embrace. United in love, John whispered tenderly, "It will never happen Jenny. I love you."

Jenny clung tightly to John, a joyousness rising in her that love had indeed come to their union as he had predicted.

New tears of happiness bubbled up as they drifted back to sleep in a warm, contented slumber.

Gwynfor's regiment was undergoing intensive training. He was learning to assemble, load and fire his rifle in record time. It was a far cry from Bronallt in Wales where the biggest things he'd handled were a hoe and pitchfork.

The drill sergeant patrolled behind the raw recruits bellowing out orders. Gwynfor or Jumbo, as he was known to his friends, was sweating profusely. He paused to wipe off a bead of sweat that promised to trickle into his eye.

"Slacking soldier?" roared the drill sergeant, Louis Mackay.

"No, Sir," came the prompt response.

"Good, because just one second distraction can mean the difference between life and death. Do you want to die? Do you understand?"

"No, Sir. Yes, Sir," affirmed Gwynfor.

"Right. And again," ordered Mackay.

The soldiers as one lowered their weapons, dismantled them, reassembled them, loaded and fired at the distant target.

Later after training, Gwynfor sat with the rest of his squad polishing his boots until they shone like polished glass.

"Hey Jumbo," called Samuel Griffiths, "Don't mess up again. We did thirty minutes more because of your nonsense."

"Sorry," murmured a contrite Gwynfor.

"Leave him alone, Sam. We've all been there," said Leigh Taylor.

"Yeah? I just want to make sure it won't happen again. With anyone," Sam threatened.

Leigh rose and sat next to Gwynfor, "I should give up now," he said referring to the boots. "Unless of course you're intending to look up some female's skirt."

"What?" asked a shocked Gwynfor.

"Ah, it's nothing. Just a bit of fun. The more those babies shine and you stand in the right place with a female you'll see right up their legs." Leigh gave a low wolf whistle, "Know what I mean?"

Gwynfor blushed profusely, "I wasn't... I mean I didn't..."

"Didn't know? Well you do now. Fag?" Leigh offered him his pack of Players.

"Na, I don't smoke," replied Gwynfor.

"Give it a few weeks and you will. Great for relaxing especially after a training session like that. Go on," and he thrust the pack at Gwynfor who slowly removed one. He tapped it on his tin of polish as he had seen other soldiers do and tentatively put the end in his mouth. Leigh struck a match and Gwynfor puffed and blew the smoke out in a puff.

"Blimey, you were telling the truth. You ain't never smoked before have you? Not even behind the bike sheds," Leigh teased.

"How can you tell?" asked Gwynfor.

"A smoker, a real smoker does it like this, see," and he demonstrated taking a huge mouthful of smoke and sucking it down into his lungs before letting it stream through his nostrils like the vapour from one's breath on a cold winter day.

Gwynfor attempted to copy Leigh and took a drag of the cigarette and swallowed, drawing the smoke deep into his lungs and immediately coughed like a donkey, braying so hard he was unable to catch his breath. His face turned crimson with the effort. He managed to choke and spluttered out, "Them things will bloody kill you."

Leigh laughed, "You've got to work at it, you'll do better next time. Persevere it'll do you good."

"Can't see it does me any good to heave my guts up," rasped Gwynfor.

"They help, honest, doctors recommend them. If they were bad for us, would they be on sale?"

Gwynfor couldn't answer that and in his memory there was a faint stirring as Ernie's words came back to him. "Don't go taking up smoking..." But he buried Ernie's wise words and took another puff of the cigarette. He felt it added maturity and glamour to him, like one of the actors in a film or on one of the many billboards advertising various cigarette brands, and he made up his mind to persevere with the habit. He was convinced it would add to his allure.

In Birmingham, Carrie and Pemb had the weekend off. They decided to use it well with a shopping trip into the town, followed by a trip to the cinema and a meal out. The day began leisurely enough as they searched for something suitable to wear. They were both heartily fed up with their uniforms and while Pemb organised some breakfast, Carrie went downstairs to the pigeonholes and collected their post.

Excited at seeing so many letters for each of them she grabbed them and ran back up the stairs hardly pausing for breath.

Carrie darted down the corridor and slid along the polished floor skidding to a stop outside the kitchen, "Pemb!" She shrieked, you've got a letter from home and I'm sure this one is Thomas' writing. The other is addressed to the two of us. I bet it's from Kirb."

"Yes, and what's the fistful in your other mitt?" smiled Pemb snatching the proffered envelopes.

Carrie scanned the writing, "I think this one is Jumbo."

"Jumbo?"

"Gwynfor. And this one looks like home. I think it's Ernie's hand. And this..." she paused.

"Don't tell me, Michael?"

"I think so."

"And the other?"

"Maybe Lloyd. I'm not sure."

"What's the postmark?"

"It says Aberwrystwyth".

"There you are then. Must be him. Here eat up while it's still hot." Pemb passed Carrie a bacon and egg sandwich. "Get that down you. It wouldn't surprise me if things got scarce in the war. You know food and such. I bet you'll miss the farm then."

"I miss it now," says Carrie with her mouth full.

"What? You'd want to go back?"

"Not at the moment. I love what I'm doing. But some day...." she smiled wistfully.

"You've got butter dribbling down your chin," Pemb giggled.

Carrie wiped it off, "I'd better get the grease off these paws before I start opening letters."

Carrie finished her sandwich with relish and then wiped her chin again before washing her hands. She raised an eyebrow and put Michael Lawrence's letter to the back of the pile.

"Saving the best till last?" winked Pemb.

"Something like that," admitted Carrie.

Carrie pored over Ernie's letter. He wrote as he spoke, like her Aunty Annie, in pictures. She giggled at his descriptions of Trixie and Bandit. The two critters seemed quite enamoured with each other. It was a very odd friendship. It appeared that Jenny's pregnancy was progressing well and villagers accepted that it was a 'Honeymoon baby'.

Ernie worried that John could have swinging moods and one minute he would be love and light and the next scowling like a thundercloud on all around him. That was when Jenny would suffer, not physically but emotionally as his demeanour affected them all. Carrie didn't like the sound of that but imagined it was something to do with his new responsibilities of being a husband and prospective father.

Ernie, however, spoke more clearly. Carrie bit her lip, she hoped Ernie's assessments were unfounded as he finished the letter with, "I worry Carrie. Worry about the prospective child. Lately, John is like two people in a single body. One is kind, loving and thoughtful, the other a great brutish bear who has been caught with his paw in the honey pot. He lashes out at anyone. Even Bandit and Trix have caught the tail end of his boot. Then he's remorseful, I wonder at the real reason for his buried anger. It's more than overwork and I worry." He closed the letter wishing her well. Carrie frowned, what to goodness was wrong with John? Was he drinking? Like their father? She decided to write back later on and include a letter for John. As to what she'd say she didn't know but just prayed the words would come right.

News from Aberwrystwyth was encouraging. Lloyd had kept her up to date with events at Mary's Teashop and news of the Maternity Unit, Bronglais. She was surprised to see that Lloyd had been turned down for the air force because of his disability. Carrie was stunned, a disability? What disability? She had never noticed anything different about the handsome Geography student. She learned that he had contracted polio as a child and one leg was affected. This was barely noticeable unless you looked for it as he wore special boots to make his legs the same length. Carrie had to admit that in all honesty she had never noticed. But what he said next really surprised her. It seemed that he had done well in his finals gaining a first class honours degree in Geography and Geology and was to transfer to Birmingham University to complete his Masters in Education and Welsh and hopefully take a teaching post.

There was a strange flutter of excitement in her tummy. Was this nervous apprehension or trepidation? Did she want him in Birmingham and what would he expect of their relationship?

Gwynfor's letter was next. He had completed an accelerated course of training and was being shipped out to France. He was not allowed to say too much in the letter, some words had already been blacked out and censored but they were on their way to an area that was surrounded by neutral Belgium and the neutral Netherlands. As Gwynfor continued describing his newfound friends a strange uneasiness settled in her heart. Carrie had a prickle of discomfort working it's way into her mind. The more she thought about it, the more she worried and for some reason Ernie popped into her mind. Was this some sort of premonition? Carrie knew that this letter would need answering immediately otherwise she didn't believe Gwynfor would ever get to read it.

"Shame on you Caroline Llewellyn!" she said aloud.

Pemb looked up from her missive with a dreamy smile on her face; obviously her letter from Thomas was a good one.

"Something wrong?" Pemb questioned.

"No, I'm not sure."

"Well, either there is or there isn't."

"Maybe nothing, just an odd feeling. You read on I'll tell you later."

Finally, Carrie opened the last letter. Her hands trembled as she shook out the fine paper and her eyes feasted on the beautiful copperplate handwriting of Michael Lawrence.

"Dear Sweet Carrie,

I hold your last letter in my pocket close to my heart. I have read it so many times that I know all the words inside out. My only concern is that it may disintegrate with the constant reading. I beg you to send me another before this one dissolves in my hands."

Carrie afforded herself a smile and a warm flush of pleasure tingled through her body.

"I am proud to be serving in our Air-force and have pleasure in telling you that I am a Wing Commander with my own squadron of Hawker Hurricanes. Training has been tough and I know that we will soon see action on a much grander scale."

He talked some more of his comrades and without giving away any sensitive information. He continued to praise her and encourage her in her chosen career before ending, "I long for the day when I can return to the beautiful Dulais Valley and yearn for our next meeting. I hold your face in my mind every night before I sleep and I am frightened in case I forget the curve of your chin, the contours of your lovely countenance and that fantastic wild, untameable hair. I hope most sincerely that our friendship will grow strong and that in deed you may be mistress of Hendre as you always dreamed and that if you are I will not be far away. Until the next time with love and respect, Michael."

One little 'x' lay under his signature. There was a P.S. 'By the way the 'x' is no accident'.

Carrie laughed aloud and devoured his words a second time before replacing the letter in the envelope and putting it in her bag. She too, was to read it again many times until she could recite it like a top class actor.

There was a hush between the two as they made their way to the bus stop to travel into the centre of town. Pemb and Carrie were lost in their thoughts until Pemb announced, "Come on, Lew. We are supposed to be having fun not attending a wake. I'll tell you my news if you'll tell me yours."

Pemb recounted her news from Thomas, "He tells me he's seen Megan and is a little confused but still wants to write to me. He knows I don't want to come between him and anyone else. I think he just needs to sort himself out, but it's a lovely letter." She went on and gave Carrie her news from her family and sisters from home. By the time they alighted they were in a partying frame of mind and completed their shopping with giggles and good humour before queuing up outside the cinema in Birmingham New Street. They were pleased that the blackout on cinema entertainment had been lifted. They both needed a suitable distraction from work and this new and ever threatening war.

Netta had come to an agreement. She smiled in satisfaction things were working out well for her. She would remain with her mother to care for her and Gwenny could spend much needed time with her own family. Little Jake had an inbuilt baby sitter, which allowed Netta some freedom. She decided to set up a business from home. She had plenty of training in Millinery and felt sure she could accomplish a small business in the locality. People would come initially from curiosity but by then would appreciate her talent. And although her mother didn't know it her mother would be funding it.

"I don't see why you need to work," complained Mam-gu.

"Think of it," urged Netta. "Me a milliner and you were a lady tailoress, you can help me, and learn alongside me. It'll be fun."

"And where's the money to come from? You need materials for a start and how will you get people to order?"

"Firstly, we'll make some sample hats. I'll advertise locally in Segadelli's and in Neath. You can keep an eye on Jake when I do that."

"And the money?"

"You did say that you had enough for us to live on without me working, well we can manage for now and then, when my business is up and running I'll pay you back and more. What do you think?"

"So, I am footing the bill?"

"Don't put it like that, Mam. Think of it as an investment. You won't regret it."

Netta's mother sniffed uncertain of what to do but Netta was persuasive and enthusiastic, "Trust me, Mam, it will be fun. It will give you a focus and I'm convinced we can do well."

"And when is this to start?"

"Now, today. I'll get the bus to Neath and visit the drapers and market. If you give me your passbook I'll get the money we need. I'll just need a signature from you of authorisation."

Netta smiled as her mother dutifully took her passbook and handed it to Netta, who handed her mother paper and pen. "Mustn't forget the letter that I have the right to draw money for you."

Her mother scrawled the authorisation and Netta tucked the book and note into her bag. "I've expressed some milk into a bottle. It's in the larder and I have prepared some oatmeal for Jake when he wakes. He should sleep for a while. With a bit of luck he won't even know I've gone."

Netta donned her hat and coat and iron backed strode out of the house to wait for the Neath bus. A thin smile played around the corner of her mouth. Things were progressing just as she had planned. Jacky would be proud of her.

Hawtry was to give a piano recital in the Nurses' Home at Dudley Road with invited guests. Nurses and doctors had gathered alike and were sitting waiting expectantly. Carrie and Pemb had front row seats.

Hawtry stood outside with Griff from the pharmacy. They were deep in conversation. Griff passed her a small bottle of white liquid. "Go careful with that. Not too much just the stated dose. I can't keep doing this for you. It could cause you some terrible problems."

"I know. But I'm late again and the stomach cramps I get are unbearable. I just need a little something to nudge my period along. You do understand don't you? Plus, how can I give a recital if I am ill? This will get things moving."

Griff looked concerned. "You need to get yourself checked over by a doctor if this keeps happening."

"I will, I promise. Thanks Griff."

Griff shrugged his shoulders and made his way back along the corridor toward the building's exit. Hawtry ran along to the ground floor kitchen. She made up a dose of the supplied ergot and swallowed it down. She looked at the label Griff had put on the bottle and muttered, "Just to be sure," and made up another dose and drank that down too.

She smoothed down her uniform and made her way back to the common room and piano. Hawtry entered the room and there was a ripple of applause as she sat at the Grand piano, flexed her fingers and did a quick ripple of the keys up and down.

Carrie whispered to Pemb, "This should be good. I hear she's a really accomplished pianist."

"So, I've heard. She kept that hidden at Bronglais. In fact she's not half bad here, as a person, either."

Carrie smiled. It was good that Pemb was giving Hawtry another chance.

Hawtry nimbly ran her fingers across the ebony and ivory keys as the dramatic opening of Rachmaninoff's piano concerto number two burst forth and melodically filled the room.

Hawtry didn't need sheet music and she swayed with emotion, closing her eyes as she played. Her body was at one with the piano expressing both her dramatic interpretation of the music and showing her complete involvement with the piece.

The more than appreciative audience were enraptured with the private concert and Hawtry played the notes with a passion as if her life depended on it.

Carrie studied Hawtry's face and was convinced that the nurse was wincing in pain as if suffering some inner anguish. Her eyes drifted to the pedals that Hawtry pumped for the necessary nuances in the concerto. She took a sharp intake of breath as she saw a rivulet of blood trickling down Hawtry's leg.

Carrie nudged Pemb who was immersed in the music and came to sharply, "What?" she whispered.

Carrie indicated with her eyes and by inclining her head to the floor underneath the piano. The rivulet had become a river and was pooling beneath Hawtry's feet. Yet still she played seemingly oblivious to the tide of red staining the floor and polluting the front of her skirt. Her normally pinched face became tighter and paler until her skin seemed almost translucent. Her playing became more frenetic and built to a climatic end. The audience applauded madly in appreciation but Hawtry remained seated unable to move.

People began to whisper. Carrie leapt up to shield Hawtry from questions and Pemb began to usher the audience away.

"That's all for now. Please leave quietly as Nurse Hawtry isn't feeling too well." Most left quickly, but some noticed the congealing puddle of blood and began to mutter quietly as they left the common room.

Hawtry slumped forward onto the piano causing a ripple of curious murmurs. One of the doctors, Dr. Harvey came to Carrie's aid.

"Okay. There's nothing to see. Let's give the woman some privacy and space".

Carrie acknowledged the doctor gratefully before whispering to Hawtry, "Is this what I think?"

Hawtry nodded.

"Can you stand?"

Hawtry shook her head.

"Pemb, can you get a wheelchair, quickly?"

Pemb pushed the last of the audience out and closed the door firmly, "Where will I get one?"

Doctor Harvey was busy checking Hawtry's pulse and temperature, "In reception, downstairs. Hurry."

Pemb needed no second bidding and scurried away.

Hawtry collapsed forward onto the piano keys, which plink plonked, and she began to weep. "I've been so stupid".

"Ssh, save your strength," advised Carrie.

"Do you know what she's done?" probed Doctor Harvey.

Carrie nodded, "Hawtry is it all right if…."

Hawtry acquiesced, "You'd better tell him."

CHAPTER TWENTY-TWO

Courage and trouble

Netta busied herself in Neath, calling first at the solicitors Phillips, Pugsley and Pugh, that both Jacky and Michael Lawrence had dealt with but each lawyer was vastly different in his dealings. Phillips could be moulded and bribed if the price was right. Pugsley was straight and honest in his conduct and obviously had no idea about his corrupt partner. It was Phillips she had come to see. She sat in the spacious reception area studying the elegant but tired wallpaper design before moving her eyes across to a set of three paintings. She was particularly drawn to one of a collection of giggling women in a meadow all wearing hats. Netta took a pencil from her bag and jotted down a few notes and simple sketches in her notebook. She was engaged in this when the door to the office that graced the front of the building opened and Mr. Phillips bade farewell to an imposing female client.

"Thank you, Mrs. Griffiths. I shall see that your wishes are carried out."

The woman nodded stiffly before exiting the building. The receptionist glanced across at Netta and seeing Mr. Phillips acknowledge the waiting client with an incline of his head, announced, "Mr. Phillips will see you now."

Netta secreted her notebook in her bag and followed Mr. Phillips into his office.

Leonard Pugsley emerged from his room and saw Netta disappearing inside and closing the door. He scratched his head and wondered why the woman was there but quickly forgot as his next client was ushered in.

In the next office Phillips pulled out a chair and bade Netta to sit, "Well, well. I wasn't expecting to hear from you again."

"I'm sure you weren't. Wouldn't that make life easier for you?"

"Not at all, not at all." He gestured her to sit, "What is it I can be doing for you?"

"A little clarity, Mr. Phillips. A little clarity."

"Yes?"

"Hendre."

"What of it?"

"Is any of it or part of it still Jacky's?"

"I thought you understood that a bill of sale had been produced for Hendre making the property that of Mr. Michael Lawrence."

"Yes, yes. I know that. But what of the children's claim?"

"It is coming before the courts shortly, proving that the sale was made in an illicit and therefore illegal manner. I do believe the parties concerned have resolved the issue between them and things are proceeding satisfactorily to that end."

"But what if there was a witness?"

"A witness?" Mr. Phillip's eyes gleamed greedily.

"Yes. If someone witnessed the deal struck by Bryn and Jacky and declared it was seemingly legitimate and that Bryn was made well aware of the consequences."

"I'm not sure. As far as the law is concerned it would still be null and void."

Netta smiled tightly and continued, "And also that the witness could state that the sale to Michael Lawrence was absolutely legal allowing no recourse by the Llewellyn family. Then that sale would employ a second bite of the cherry as you lawyers would put it."

Mr. Phillips licked his already moist lips, "Go on."

"I'm sure you remember Mr. Phillips, the codicil put on the agreement, which maintains that if Jacky Ebron were to have an heir that half the payment again would be liable on the agreement. That money would come to my son, Jake. It won't hurt the Llewellyns only Mr. Lawrence."

Mr. Phillips hesitated, "I'm not sure..."

"Come, come Mr. Phillips, you do remember don't you?" Netta removed a crisp five-pound note from her purse and placed it on the desk in front of her. "Surely, you remember?"

Mr. Phillips smiled, "I seem to recall something but it's a little hazy." He slid his hand across to the note and Netta immediately covered it with her own-gloved hand.

"Tut, tut, Mr. Phillips. Do you remember the agreement or not? If you do, then I believe I will have an outstanding payment to make to you." Netta removed her hand.

Phillips pocketed the money and acquiesced, "Yes, of course. How could I be so forgetful?"

"We will talk on this further. Shall we say, Tuesday next at three?"

Phillips stood and bowed, "Of course, dear lady."

"Then we have a deal?"

"I will only be following through on the Bill of Sale's small print." Phillips winked at her. They understood each other. They shook hands and Netta left his offices proudly and optimistically. She had a newfound arrogance in her step.

Netta set off down the High Street until she reached the Co-operative building society. Clutching her mother's passbook and letter of authorisation. She entered. Fifteen minutes later she emerged, patting her bag containing one hundred pounds in fresh notes. It had been easier than she thought and now she was a permanent signatory on her mother's account.

It was perfect. Her visit was completed with a visit to the market and draper's stall and the high-class tailors and milliners in Castle Street. Soon, Netta would have almost everything for her needs. Her lips couldn't help but smile. Her plan was coming together. She felt guided, guided by Jacky's spirit and to that end it justified all her actions and future schemes. Jacky, she knew would live on in her and Jake.

Jenny opened the window wide before changing the sheets on the bed. A puzzled frown crept onto her face as she noticed some blood spots on her side of the bed. Dismissing it as some too vigorous lovemaking from the previous night she gathered the sheets up and began to spread the freshly starched cotton ones over the feather mattress.

Jenny leaned out of the window and gazed down the mountainside to the valley below. She could see the Land Girls working in the fields below at Hendre and took a gulp of the revitalising fresh air.

She scanned the horizon for John and could just distinguish him in discussion with Ernie in the lower meadow at Gelli Galed. Her smile grew and her heart felt full, overflowing and plumped to bursting point with the abundance of love. She took another breath but was attacked by a sharp stitch like pain in her side.

"Duw, I mustn't overdo it," Jenny murmured to herself. The pain passed and she continued changing the bed albeit more slowly and less vigorously than she had begun the chore.

Gwynfor was stuck in the barracks in France. Sergeant Major Hawkins was briefing them. "It is imperative that we do not wage war as was done in 1914. It is intended to be quick and fast."

"And not as costly," whispered Leigh.

"Something to say, soldier?" snarled Hawkins.

"No, Sir."

"Good because if you know our brief perhaps you'd care to come up front and tell the squad."

"No, Sir. Sorry, Sir," Leigh responded.

"The new strategy is focused on Naval blockade and army encirclement. We will work with the French. Germany's economy is weak. We have been assigned to holding defensive positions and together with a naval blockade we will avoid a blitzkrieg and loss of life and win this battle by attrition."

Gwynfor rolled his eyes.

"Something wrong, soldier?"

"Sorry, Sir, I don't know what attrition means," apologised Gwynfor.

"Tell him, soldier." Hawkins pointed at Samuel Griffiths.

"Wearing down of enemy troops in order to destroy, Sir" Griffiths barked back.

"Correct. A war we will win. Our hopes for quick success are with you, the largest of our British Expeditionary Force. You will march to the defensive lines of the canals in Belgium forming lines with the Belgian army. The key word is defend."

The briefing continued with a final pep talk to the young rookies by which time Sergeant Major Hawkins had stoked the fire in their bellies and excited their patriotism. Gwynfor was going to see action, the first of the war. He did not know that the Germans would be drawing them into a trap to be sprung in the Ardennes.

Gwynfor leaned back in his bunk. His kitbag was packed and waiting. He just had time for a smoke before they would be called to rally.

Jenny lay quietly on the bed. John was snuggled in close to her. He placed a protective arm across her growing tummy. The baby kicked. Jenny's eyes opened wide with pleasure,

"John feel. The baby. The baby kicked."

John opened his eyes and beamed in pleasure, placing his hand where Jenny led. He felt a movement and the wonder of the new life filled him with awe and admiration.

"Jenny, fach," his eyes filled with tears, "That's ours. Our little one. We are so blessed." He kissed his wife's cheek and kept his hand on her stomach. The action prompted him to say more. "Jenny... I don't know what to say. I know I have not been myself lately. These moods are not like me. They remind me of dad, but I don't drink..."

As ever Jenny soothed and placated him, "You have so much to do and organise. It's not surprising you can be an old curmudgeon at times."

"It's no excuse. I shouldn't shout at you for flaws within me. I do love you, Jenny."

They embraced and held each other close.

"Maybe, you should get yourself checked out. See Dr. Rees. Maybe he can give you something to help you relax. It's not good when you are up half the night and then work all day. No wonder you are exhausted."

"Just what are you suggesting?" bristled John, his temper rising.

"Nothing," faltered Jenny. "I just meant that you are so tired at times that it can make you a bit..."

"Short tempered. I know," said John relenting. "I'm sorry, cariad, I nearly went off again. Perhaps you are right. Perhaps, I do need something. I'll see how I feel in the morning." John sighed and protectively cuddled Jenny. Her eyes remained open. Jenny knew there was something wrong. She turned to John and fondly caressed his face and hair.

"Something's worrying you." It was more a statement of fact than an accusation.

Jenny's fingers gently palpated John's scalp, when he suddenly jumped and pulled away. Jenny looked puzzled, but John relaxed and allowed her to continue probing and examining his head.

"John? You have a lump here. Did you know?"

"Probably nothing. I'm not one for making a fuss. Probably banged my head on the barn door or something."

"Ah." But Jenny wasn't satisfied. Her face looked worried in the light of the moon that cast its odd shadows on the old bedstead.

The next morning breakfast was a quiet affair. Ernie studied the young couple as Jenny served eggs, bacon and hot toast. Her eyes looked sore from lack of sleep. John yawned. His eyes were heavy. Neither looked rested.

"You feeling all right, wuss?" probed Ernie gently.

Jenny stopped as she bent over with a mug of tea for John. She gave a sudden gasp. The hot tea spilled over her hand as the mug tumbled from her grasp.

John scraped his chair back quickly to avoid the steaming liquid, "Jenny?" The love and concern in his voice was apparent for all to hear.

She doubled over clutching her side before crumpling to the floor. Strong arms lifted her up and carried her into the parlour. Ernie followed quickly and frowned when he saw the blood running down her leg.

"Get her lying down, quickly. We need to prop her feet up. And get the doctor. Now."

John fled from the parlour and Ernie tried to make Jenny comfortable. He held her hand and spoke gently.

"Now, don't be giving us all a scare, young lady. What have you been doing? Too much I'll be bound."

"Nothing I shouldn't," whispered Jenny her face drained of colour and her eyes brimming with tears. "Please Ernie, can you get my mam?"

"I'll try and catch John."

Ernie raced from the room. Trixie's eyes followed curiously and she rose from the rag mat and padded out after Ernie.

John was leading Senator into the yard.

"John, can you fetch Jenny's mother?" Ernie called.

John nodded and mounted the stalwart horse and set off down the track.

Trixie looked wistfully after John and then trotted back into the kitchen. Hearing soft whimpering coming from the parlour Trix nosed her way in through the door to Jenny's side and licked her hand.

"Now, what are you doing in here?" scolded Ernie.

"Leave her," murmured Jenny. "It's a comfort having her near."

Trix rested her chin on the side of the couch and fixed her soft brown eyes on Jenny. Ernie sighed and dragged a chair alongside her.

"Jenny, fach, why didn't you say?"

"Say what?"

"That you've been having pains. You have, haven't you?"

"I thought it was all part of pregnancy."

"Not yet, not now. It's all too soon."

"Ernie, if anything happens..."

"Nothing's going to happen, to you," reassured Ernie.

Gwynfor sat entrenched in a hide with his friends. They chatted amicably whilst keeping a watchful eye on the land ahead. Any movement or advance by enemy soldiers and they would spot it first.

"So. Have you got anyone special waiting for you at home?" quizzed Leigh Taylor with a wink at the others.

"Nah! I'd like there to be but she's not for me. She doesn't want to be courted. And you?"

"I've got a girl. But I don't know if she'll wait."

"Depends how long this damn war lasts," rejoined Samuel Griffiths.

"They said it would be over by Christmas," offered Leigh.

"Can you see that happening?" asked Gwynfor.

"We can hope," affirmed Matt.

"Yeah. Don't want to be stuck here for months on end," replied Leigh. "Do you think we'll see any real action?"

"Who's to know? If Sergeant Hawkins has his way we'll be in, out and onto another posting," muttered Gwynfor.

"I'd rather see some fighting. That's what we've trained for. Something to tell our families and kids," complained Sam.

"What's that?" whispered Leigh as he spotted some movement through the hide and across the defending line.

"What?" hissed Samuel, suddenly alert.

"Thought I saw something," replied Leigh.

"What sort of thing?" asked Gwynfor.

"Don't know. Probably nothing."

The young soldiers scanned the land ahead for any further action. They saw nothing and continued to chat but in a more heightened state of alert at least for the time being.

Across the empty space between their line of defence and the canals, a German platoon settled, watched and waited.

Landser Kurt Schultz watched the intervening space between his platoon and the British troops with a spyglass and reported to his corporal, Geifrieter Heinrich Baeker. "Ich sehe Bewegung". He called as he saw a flurry of activity.

"Lassen Sie mich wissen, wenn Sie keine Waffen zu sehen.' The corporal demanded to be told if his Private saw any weapons.

"Herr."

"Wenn Sie das tun, zu schieBen, um zu toten."

The young German soldier looked at his Commanding Officer who gave a cursory nod emphasizing his order. Kurt Schultz paused momentarily before affirming the command. Kurt Schultz had not fired a bullet in this war let alone killed someone.

Across the space Gwynfor and his comrades continued to chat and Gwynfor was receiving his fair share of teasing.

"Go on," laughed Leigh, "A big bloke like you and you've never done it?"

"Well," hesitated Gwynfor, "Not really."

"What do mean, not really? Either you have or you haven't?" joked Sam.

Gwynfor decided to be honest, "I came close, once, round the back of the café in the village but we got caught," he admitted red-faced.

"I don't think you're alone there. I suspect there's more than a few virgins in this squad," exclaimed Leigh, "Fag?"

"Don't mind if I do," accepted Sam.

"Got one for me?" asked Gwynfor, "I'm all out."

"Aye, as long as you've got a light," returned Leigh. "My matches are soggy. Left them out last night on my mess tin."

The three rookie soldiers leaned back with the cigarettes stuck in their mouths as Gwynfor fumbled for his book of matches. He retrieved the battered book from the bottom of his pocket and ripped one from the pack and struck it on the emery surface. It ignited quickly exploding like a beacon and Leigh bowed his head to light his cigarette.

Across the expanse the light shone like a flare and Kurt Schultz spotted the light in the distance. He lifted his rifle.

Gwynfor passed the burning match across to Samuel who inhaled deeply drawing on his newly lit cigarette as if his life depended on it.

Kurt Schultz took aim, watching the flickering light.

Gwynfor brought the match to his own cigarette hanging from his lips and began to puff on it.

Kurt Schultz fired.

Gwynfor dropped like a stone as the German bullet hit him right between the eyes. His friends looked on in horror and threw their own cigarettes onto the dirt floor and ground them out.

"Help, we need some help here," shouted Sam who had dropped to Gwynfor's side and was cradling his head.

"It's too late," whispered Leigh, placing his fingers on Gwynfor's eyelids, closing them and shutting out the glazed expression of shocked surprise.

Kurt Schulz put down his rifle quickly. His heart was

yammering like a coyote baying at the moon. He wiped his hand across his sweat-laden brow, shuddered and was promptly sick where he stood. Killing another human being didn't sit well with him, at all. The repercussions on his psyche would continue until the winter of his life.

CHAPTER TWENTY-THREE

Making waves

It was a sombre day. Grey stretched interminably across the sky. No one could see where the clouds ended and the sky began. Everything was solemn and dreary as if the heavens knew something the rest of the world didn't. The damp air threatened rain.

A military vehicle travelled up the track to Bronallt. The wheels spat out lumps of gravel as they slid to a halt. A soldier in full uniform left the vehicle and walked slowly toward the farm's front door.

He knocked officially, and as the door was answered removed his beret. He apologetically delivered a telegramme and exchanged a few words with Mrs. Thomas. The colour washed away from her face as she took receipt of the letter. A wail began to escape from her that turned into keening sob. Megan flew to the door and supported her mother, now on the brink of collapse.

The subdued soldier replaced his beret and marched back to his vehicle. Megan watched the vehicle leave before helping her mother indoors and closing the front door against the wild winds.

Megan struggled up the track from Hendre. The wind was blowing ferociously streaming her lustrous locks into a mutinous tangle.

Tears had frozen on her cheeks. She tightly clutched something in her hand, which the wind was trying to prize from her chilled grip. She pulled her coat tightly around her to keep closed every chink where the gusts could travel.

She tried to prevent her tresses being tangled in the roaring wind and Megan hurried her steps. She stopped in the yard when she saw Senator and the cart. There was no sign of Ernie, John or anyone else.

Trixie appeared from the porch and gave Megan a warm welcome, "What's the matter old girl?"

Trix looked consolingly at Megan and made a funny little noise in the back of her throat, as if to say, "Something wrong here."

Trix padded back to the porch and mounted the old wooden steps. The gentle collie looked back at Megan and urged her to follow. She gave a small bark.

Megan rushed up the steps and pounded on the door, which was opened by Ernie, who admitted her.

The cosy parlour was busy and had been made into a makeshift sickroom. Mrs. Davies was at her daughter's bedside. Ernie stoked up the log fire in the grate. Dr. Rees was checking Jenny's pulse and heart. John stood aside his eyes filled with tears. Jenny looked at her new husband her expression one of concern and love. She pushed herself up.

"Lie still, Jenny fach. Don't waste any energy," soothed Mrs. Davies. "You will need all your strength."

John stepped forward his eyes wet with tears, "Please Dr. Rees, save Jenny and our baby, please."

Dr. Rees stood up to his full height and peered over his glasses, "I'm doing all I can, John. Get some water onto boil. Ernie, prepare something nourishing for her to eat."

"I'm not hungry," insisted Jenny.

"It's what you need, or will do," remonstrated Dr. Rees, "And Megan you can go and help," he said ordering Megan out with the others.

Mrs. Davies, if you can leave your daughter a moment. Mrs. Davies looked anxiously at Jenny.

"It's okay, Mam, doctor knows best."

Mrs. Davies patted her daughter's hand. I'll be in the kitchen. If you need me, call."

Dr. Rees sat on the makeshift bed and smoothed down her face and hair. Jenny grimaced again as another wave of cramps washed over her.

"Now, Jenny, you need to listen carefully. What I am going to say may seem strange but I am going to ask you to have a few drinks."

"What of?"

"Alcohol."

"But doctor, I don't drink, have never drunk." Jenny was shocked.

"If you do I can arrest the labour. Your muscles should stop contracting. Alcohol will relax those muscle cramps. If the baby is born, it is unlikely to live. We don't have the capabilities to keep it alive. If we can get a few drinks inside you, your muscles will relax and may offset labour and you might, just might save the child."

Jenny nodded her eyes bright with tears.

"Whatever it takes, doctor."

"And another thing. You mustn't allow yourself to get upset over anything that could raise your heart rate and pump adrenalin through you as that too could trigger an early labour."

Jenny bit her lip anxiously, as Dr. Rees called for Ernie who appeared instantly.

"Is there any liquor in the house?" queried Dr. Rees.

A puzzled Ernie is about to speak when the doctor urged. "No questions. What's available?"

"Um, I've got some brandy and there's a couple of bottles of whiskey."

"That'll do. Bring them and ginger pop or anything to sweeten it up."

Ernie nodded and was back in an instant with the bottles.

"And a glass please, Ernie." Ernie disappeared again.

Jenny turned her huge eyes on Dr. Rees, "Doctor, I'm worried about John."

Dr. Rees turned his questioning gaze back on Jenny.

"What is it, Jenny fach?"

Jenny spoke hesitantly, "He's got a lump on his head," she indicated with her fingers to her own head.

"And?"

"And I think it has something to do with his changing moods. Sometimes he finds it hard to control his temper." There. It was out. Jenny attempted a smile.

"Now, don't you worry. I shall be lecturing the rest of them out there in a moment."

Ernie knocked politely and the doctor opened the door. Ernie set out a couple of glasses. Ernie hesitated.

"It's all right Ernie. I'll explain in a moment. Gather everyone in the kitchen." Ernie nodded.

Dr. Rees poured a triple shot of brandy into the tumbler and filled it to the top with ginger pop.

"Here, drink this."

"Will it hurt my baby?"

"It may save your baby's life."

Jenny took a sip of the strong liquid and screwed up her face. The doctor laughed.

"Oh, Jenny fach, there's funny you look. Keep drinking. I want it all gone. And then I'll give you some more." He chuckled as he left the parlour to meet the others.

Dr. Rees entered the kitchen and noticed the melancholy mood. His eyes searched John's who stepped forward anxiously.

"We've just had some shocking news." John handed the military telegramme to Dr. Rees who read the stark announcement.

"My God, what a tragedy. Such a young man." He looked across at Megan whose shoulders were trembling uncontrollably. "Now, don't tell Jenny. Nothing must upset her. She is to have complete bed rest."

"But..." started John.

"Nothing must upset her, John. Nothing. It's vital at this stage. You asked me to save your wife and child. I hope to do that," Dr. Rees continued to explain what he was doing to Jenny when her beautiful voice flooded through the wall.

Jenny sang her heart out, "Calon lan ynllawn daioni. Tecach yw na'r lili dlos, Does ond calon lan all ganu, Canu'r dydd a channu'r nos." Megan who had never heard Jenny's sweet voice looked on amazed. And Ernie puffed up his chest in pride.

The group returned to the parlour. Jenny had nearly finished her drink. He face was flushed and she welcomed them all in. Jenny looked at them all happily and requested, "Come on! Join in!"

Mrs. Davies began to sing shakily and one by one they all joined in on another chorus of the famous hymn, except for Ernie. Trixie nosed her way through the door and wagged her tail at everyone followed by Bandit.

The doctor prepared another concoction for Jenny and gave it to her. Jenny giggled and took a swig. Ernie gulped a deep breath and tried to join in the final verse and chorus. His voice grated like a corroded geyser. Trixie turned tail and fled followed by Bandit flapping her wings.

The melancholy dissolved, everyone sang and laughed together.

Jenny flopped back on her pillow still clutching her drink, which Dr. Rees firmly removed. "There, there that's enough now, Jenny fach. We don't want you to be sick."

Jenny allowed the glass to be removed and Dr. Rees checked her over. He smiled as he removed his stethoscope from her chest.

"Good," he murmured quietly, "The labour has stopped."

"Have I done well?" Jenny asked plaintively.

"Exceedingly well," affirmed Dr. Rees. "Now, you rest and sleep if you can." They all trooped out of the parlour.

"Ernie, can you take Megan and Mrs. Davies back into the village?"

"Aye, aye. What about you?"

"I'll be along in five minutes. I just want a word with John."

Ernie nodded deferentially and left followed by Megan. Mrs. Davies shifted uncomfortably in her seat and looked anxiously at the doctor.

"You can visit when ever you want. Can't she, John?"

"Of course," John nodded.

"Good, now if you could leave us please," instructed Dr. Rees. Mrs. Davies rose reluctantly and went out into the yard.

"Now, John I have to impress on you, Jenny is in a fragile condition. We have managed to stop the labour. I wouldn't normally advise alcohol to a pregnant woman. But, in this instance it has worked. However, she mustn't do anything. Nothing at all. It's bed rest with her feet up. And," he laid the weight of importance to his final words. "She must not be upset in any way, shape or form. You have a bad day. Keep it to yourself. As far as Jenny is concerned, everything is sunshine and flowers. Do that and you may save both your wife and baby."

John acknowledged sheepishly, "Dr. Rees..."

"I haven't quite finished. I want a quick look at you, now."

"Me?"

The doctor strode across to John and began what seemed to be a cursory examination of his heart, pulse and chest. Then Dr. Rees began to palpate John's scalp. He soon found the lump.

"Hmm, When did this come up?"

"The lump?"

"Yes."

"About a month ago."

"John, come to my surgery tomorrow. We need to investigate this further."

"But..."

"No buts, this could be serious. Jenny needs you. You have to do this for her."

John reluctantly acquiesced.

"Right. Now, we're done. See you tomorrow at nine."

Dr. Rees stooped under the low kitchen archway and left for the yard.

It was another busy week on the wards and Carrie was relishing the change from Gynae to Men's Surgical. She was blissfully unaware of all that was transpiring at home in Crynant. She found the male patients uplifting. It seemed nothing could dampen their spirits. Her long-term patient, Hamish MacDonald, who always started the ward off singing, "Run Rabbit Run", was a fireman with a broken pelvis and leg, who was likely to be there for another two months. Carrie had dubbed him, 'The Cheeky Chappie', so she was surprised when she arrived on the ward to discover his bed was empty.

She asked the Ward Sister, Brenda Friend, where he had gone. Sister Friend replied in the abrupt manner she employed with Juniors.

"Mr. Macdonald has some kind of encroaching respiratory illness and has been put into isolation until we can ascertain what's wrong. It also means, Nurse Llewellyn, that you are the last member of the team who will have to undergo some tests and have an X-ray. You're expected in clinic at six."

Believing the conversation over, Sister Friend began to turn away but Carrie couldn't help herself and blurted out.

"Oh. I was hoping to visit Hawtry."

Sister Friend turned and scrutinised the young woman in front of her and relented a fraction. "If you're lucky you may be able to grab some time today. Meanwhile, the patients need to be prepared for the doctor's rounds."

"If I work through lunch, is it possible for me to leave an hour early?"

"Don't push your luck, Nurse Llewellyn. I will check the duty roster and we will speak later. In the meantime attend to your duties."

The conversation was over and Carrie busied herself, checking patients' stats and ensuring their charts were correctly filled in.

She was anxious to see Hawtry, as well as drop in on Hamish. So she was delighted when Sister Friend called Carrie to the Nurses' Station

"Yes, Sister?" smiled Carrie eagerly.

"You're in luck, I have an extra nurse coming on duty at three. If you want to work your lunch, and I don't recommend it, I can let you go at four. Be sure to be on time tomorrow."

"Yes, Sister. Thank you, Sister." Inwardly Carrie could hardly contain her joy and began to hurry away.

"Don't run!" thundered Sister Friend and gave a little grunt of satisfaction as she saw Carrie's skipping step dwindle to a brisk walk.

At four o'clock, Carrie scurried off duty and went to visit Hawtry who was in a private room off Women's Gynae. Carrie tiptoed in.

Hawtry was propped up on a pile of pillows, with a drip in her arm. Her face was pale and her eyes fluttered open as she felt the presence of another in her room.

Hawtry smiled at Carrie, "Thank you for coming. You didn't have to."

"I know. I wanted to. So, what's been happening?"

"Not a lot," came Hawtry's thin reply. "It's hardly the most exciting place to be. The cabaret for the day is the morning round."

"What's happening to you? What did you do? Why?" questioned Carrie.

"Which question do you want me to answer first?" mused Hawtry.

"Sorry, just curious, I am."

"Well, you'll know soon enough, anyhow and it's best you hear the truth from me rather that some exaggerated version of it."

Carrie sat quietly, and Hawtry continued. "I am scheduled for surgery, tomorrow."

"Oh?"

"They wanted to see if everything settled down. It didn't, so I am to have a hysterectomy."

"Oh, Hawtry, I'm sorry."

"Don't be. It's my own fault. I'm sad that I'll never have kids. But there, it's no good complaining about the inevitable; a bit like trying to sing a song when you don't know all the words. You bluff your way through," sighed Hawtry.

"I am sorry, really," insisted Carrie.

"I believe you. One thing you've always been is honest."

"So, what happened?"

"It's not something I'm proud of or even wanted to do but..."

"I won't judge you. I've had enough of that sort of treatment in my own lifetime," reassured Carrie.

Hawtry took a deep breath to steady her nerves. It was clear that she had great difficulty in talking about it. "My mother," her tone was even but there was an undercurrent of emotion waiting to bubble out, "She... er... she has a huge problem. My father, um, he left home because of it and gave no financial support to her at all and my brother doesn't want to know," Hawtry paused.

Carrie urged, "Go on... I lost my mother when I was just a little girl and my father died in tragic circumstances when I was fourteen."

Hawtry blinked, and struggled to continue, "Mum often used to have strange swinging moods. We just thought she was quirky, hormones and stuff. Or put it down to her fondness for the odd drink. It was okay when I was at home. I could keep an eye on her but she had actually developed epilepsy. Dad couldn't cope and he walked out. My bother felt stifled and followed. That left mum and me." Hawtry sighed. "I was due to get married and my fiancé, he... he was happy for mother to live near us. I would give up nursing as was expected and required. He'd ensure everything would be fine." Hawtry stopped and her voice began to break. "Then he came down with that damned disease... It's so hard to watch someone you love die."

"I know."

"That's why I made it my specialism, to do my bit and try and make a difference so no other would have to suffer as I had. It was fine when I could study near home, but of course it couldn't last."

A nurse interrupted them to check Hawtry, who went quiet and flinched as her IV line was changed. A notice was placed above her head, which read: NIL BY MOUTH after 12:00. The nurse exited and Hawtry turned to Carrie, "Turning into a bit of a confessional," she quipped.

"You don't have to tell me if you don't want to."

"No. No, it's all right. I need to tell someone and I believe you are the best."

"So, my mother wasn't ill enough to go to hospital. I didn't want to institutionalise her, and had no close family. There was nothing for it I had to pay for care. She couldn't work. No one would give her a job. She used to take in little bits of washing and ironing, anything she could, but I was the main provider and my salary was completely insufficient, as you can imagine. So..."

Carrie took Hawtry's hand and squeezed it gently. This movement precipitated a flood of emotion in Hawtry.

"God forgive me. I would sell my favours. Not regularly and I wasn't cheap. I... I hated myself at first. Scrubbed myself raw after the first time just couldn't seem to get clean."

Carrie nodded sympathetically. She knew exactly what Hawtry meant.

"The frightening thing is, it gets easier to say 'yes' and do it again. As soon as there was a danger of discovery I'd move in an attempt to protect my reputation."

"What about the ergot?"

"That was stupid. Didn't happen often. I had some gentleman friends who refused to wear any kind of protection. It was then I'd get caught and then I'd resort to clinical means to help me. I did it once too often. The last one being the worst."

"What are you going to do?"

"The game is up, now. After surgery and recovery I shall go home."

"But you can't spend the rest of your life in a care situation you have too much to give. Your knowledge is immense and you are a damned good nurse. I know, I've seen you in action."

"Thank you. I don't know what else to do."

"Hawtry, you're not thinking," Carrie sensibly pointed out. "You don't need to prostitute yourself anymore. You have other talents at your disposal."

"What?" Hawtry was puzzled and her interest aroused.

"You are an amazing pianist. You don't just *play* the music; you *are* the music. You feel the notes in such a way that it touches our souls."

"But, how can that help me?"

"What's to stop you giving private tuition? Many parents would love their children to learn under someone as talented as you."

"Oh, I don't know."

"At least think about it. What qualifications do you have?"

"Um, the usual grades from when I was studying."

"Then, I'm sure it wouldn't take much more to do a teaching diploma. Come on, at least think about it. It could buy your freedom."

"Do you know? I may just do that. Thanks, Lew."

Carrie beamed, she really felt as if she might have made a difference.

"I'll be off then, promised myself I'd pop in and see one of our patients who's gone down with some respiratory illness. Then I've got an X-ray at clinic since I have been in contact with him."

"I'm surprised they let you work without checking you out first."

"I don't think it's serious, just a formality. Anyway, you keep thinking about what I said and I'll be across after your surgery to see how you are."

"Thanks, Lew," smiled Hawtry and lay back on her pillows and closed her eyes.

Carrie almost skipped out of Hawtry's room until she saw the eagle eyes of Sister Friend settle on her and so proceeded calmly out of the ward and onto Chest.

The click clack of her metal heels echoed efficiently on the wooden parquet flooring. Carrie clicked to a halt at the edge of the ward as she watched the emergency team scurry into a side room. Curiously she stepped into the ward. She was horrified to see one of the doctors pumping away on Hamish's chest. She bit her lip and tried to find someone to speak to, but everyone seemed to be in the fireman's room. Carrie tiptoed away subdued and thoughtful.

She made her way down to the basement and the X-ray department and approached the clinic desk where a friendly face greeted her. "Yes, Nurse?" enquired the receptionist.

"Llewellyn. I'm here about the X-ray and test."

"Ah yes, you're early. Not to worry we have a gap and can see you now if that's okay?"

"Fine," murmured Carrie.

"Take a seat. Someone will be with you shortly."

Carrie sat on one of the hard upright chairs laid around the area. She didn't have long to wait and went in for an X-ray and follow up blood test.

She came out muttering to herself, "I don't have any blasted TB I'm supposed to be immune."

Carrie returned to the Respiratory Disease Ward and went to look for Hamish. His bed was empty.

"Excuse me," Carrie stopped one of the Junior Nurses on the ward, "Can you tell me what's happened to Hamish MacDonald?"

The junior shook her head sadly, "He passed away about thirty minutes ago. I'm sorry. Was he a friend?"

"Do they know what caused it?"

"Something called Emphysema. At least it wasn't TB or we'd all be in isolation."

Carrie turned away sadly, feeling more than dispirited she made her way to the Nurses' Home.

Carrie trundled up to her room and threw herself on her bed and sobbed. She cried like she had for that pig all those years ago when it was slaughtered to feed the harvesters. She remembered its screams of terror and how she had tried to drown out the sound with her singing. She was overwhelmed with a feeling that she was to see more death than she had bargained for and remembered the words of advice received, from Dr. Challacombe, "You have a natural talent but try not to get too emotionally involved."

"How am I supposed to do that?" questioned Carrie. "I care, I can't stop caring." It was to this scene that Pemb arrived who took Carrie into her welcoming arms and let her weep.

CHAPTER TWENTY-FOUR

Life goes on

Carrie recovered from the shock of Hamish's death and was relieved to discover that she had no serious respiratory infections. It was as she had been told. She had inherited an immunity from her grandmother, which boded well for future studies in Chest Medicine.

Hawtry was gaining strength daily, although it had been touch and go at one point during the operation. Life seemed to be progressing normally.

Carrie hurried down to the lobby to pick up her and Pemb's post. She had three notes, one had been delivered by hand and she recognised the handwriting on all three.

Carrie bounced upstairs where she shoved Pemb's pile of five letters at her. Pemb handed her a mug of tea and they both sat on their beds to read their mail.

Every now and then, Pemb would whoop or giggle, while Carrie remained serious faced. She was studying a letter from Megan and her face was crumpled in sadness.

"So, Carrie fach, I only wish you were here. My grandmother on Mam's side continues to have failing health and you know how much I have always thought of her. And obviously, Mam and Dad are not dealing well with the news of Gwynfor's death. We are waiting for his body to be returned and then he'll have a burial with full military honours. Do you know I can't remember the last thing I said to him? I hope it was pleasant and not me being my usual teasing self. Isn't that terrible? How can I not remember my last conversation? I know I wished him well and told him to come home safe but what else? Oh, Carrie, I am sorry to burden you with this. My heart is heavier than a milkmaid's load. You must know what that's like; you have your own family problems what with Jenny almost losing the baby. Carrie, she was as pale as pale, with as much energy as a dishrag. John was being strong but we could all see how worried he was. Anyway, I'm sure you know all this so I'll ramble on no more. Write when you can, Carrie. I look forward to your letters. I am also thinking of joining ENSA. It's a recently formed service. The Entertainment National Service Association. I want to do something. I'm not going to waste my life in the mountains of Wales. I've always been good at singing and dancing, had a flair for acting. Give me your blessing Carrie and write soon."

Carrie scrunched up the letter in shock. Gwynfor dead! How terrible. But she was pleased that at least they had a pleasant final meeting and that she had agreed to let him write to her. And Jenny. Why hadn't John said anything?

Pemb looked up from her letter, "Everything okay? Carrie?"

Carrie's eyes filled with tears that threatened to burst forth, "Jenny nearly lost the baby and Gwynfor's dead," she blurted out.

"What? Carrie tell me."

Carrie passed her Megan's letter to read for herself. She tore at the next one, but couldn't relax and enjoy its contents. She shoved it back into its envelope and put it aside for later when she knew she'd be calmer. She opened the third missive and recognised Lloyd's neat small hand. She quickly studied the envelope again, no stamp. Lloyd must be in Birmingham.

At Gelli Galed John was preparing to visit Dr. Rees again in his surgery, anxious not to worry Jenny he said he was getting some supplies and Ernie would be on hand to look after her.

Laura and Daisy, the Land Girls were already busy in the fields preparing for a late harvest. Grain needed threshing and grass demanded cutting to make hay for the animals in the approaching winter and he needed to be there, too, to help and oversee the work.

"I'll be back as quick as I can, Ernie," called John as he started off in the cart.

"You do what needs to be done. Don't worry; I'll look after Jenny. Get yourself fixed. Better to have a spinning top that's kept humming rather than one that rolls on its side."

"Ernie you have the strangest expressions, where you get them from I don't know," laughed John. The cart trundled off down the hill.

Within thirty minutes, John had reached Crynant. He stopped in the crescent outside Dr. Rees' house and secured Senator. He marched up the drive and knocked on the door. The diminutive Mrs. Millicent Rees answered the door and ushered John into the surgery waiting room where he took a seat.

He picked up a copy of National Geographic and began to thumb through it. Time passed quickly and John was called in to Dr. Rees' surgery.

"Ah, John," announced the doctor peering over his half spectacles. "You've not eaten?"

"No, doctor, nothing since last night. And I don't mind saying, I'm ravenous."

"Well, if we can get this done, you can get yourself off to Segadelli's and have a fry up. That should soon set you up. Come and lie on the couch and turn over."

John did as he was asked.

"I just want to double check," said Dr. Rees, as he gently palpated the lump. "Good. It doesn't seem to be fixed. It's moveable. That's a good sign. Sorry I couldn't deal with it properly yesterday but I hadn't got the right anaesthetic, you understand."

John grunted and clenched his fists so that his knuckles went bone white.

"I'm going to try an aspiration, now this shouldn't hurt."

Dr. Rees inserted a needle into the lump and drew some fluid from it. There was some clear liquid, which then turned cloudy and bloody. "Hmm." Dr. Rees stopped and scratched his head, "What do you want me to do?"

"Get rid of it Doc, if you can."

"I'll have to shave your hair around the site. It won't look pretty."

"That's the least of my problems. Do you think this is what's been causing my unreasonable bouts of temper?"

"Could be. Have you had any headaches, vomiting?"

"I often start the day with a thumping head but that improves as the day goes on. And I have felt nauseous sometimes and when I've been sick my head feels better."

"Right. I'm just going to clip the hair around this to prepare the site. Okay?"

"Just do it."

The doctor deftly removed the hair and pasted the lump with iodine. "Now, I am going to inject you and you may feel a sharp prick then it will soon numb."

Dr. Rees injected John's skull around the lump, with anaesthetic. John winced and grabbed hold of the sides of the examination table. "In a moment I will make an incision and see what I can. If I don't like what I see I may need you back to do this under full anaesthetic."

"Just do your best, Doc," urged John.

The good doctor made an incision into the lump with a scalpel and pulled back the skin. He studied the small growth above the limbic cortex and using a pair of forceps manoeuvred the globule of fatty tissue out from the gap. There was a spray of blood. Dr. Rees dropped the offending tissue into a kidney dish and cleaned the area thoroughly before suturing the wound and covering it with a dressing.

"Okay, now. You, I'm afraid must stay here a while and recover..."

"But..."

"No buts. Do as you're told, let me help you out. I will clean up and Millicent will make you some tea. Sit and rest."

Dr. Rees helped a groggy John to his feet and gently led him to the waiting room. He returned to the surgery and scrubbed his hands and arms once more. He picked up the kidney dish with the globule of tissue and surrounding bloody connective strands. He sliced a thin piece from the lump and placed it on a slide and did the same with some of the connective and surrounding tissue. Dr. Rees straightened up and exited his room and went out and sat with John.

"We were lucky, John that the lump was accessible. That is a very good sign. I have taken some slides of the tissue and will examine them under the microscope and see if I can learn anymore. The position of the lump was exerting pressure on the Limbic cortex, hence the headaches and mood swings. I can't be a hundred percent but I feel this is a benign growth. I don't expect you to need any more surgery. You will just need to return to have the stitches removed. Give it ten days, but I will check you again in three days to ensure you are healing. When the anaesthetic wears off you'll have a thumping head and it will be sore for a few days, too."

"So, it's good news then, doctor?"

"Let's hope I got it all or it could grow again."

"Oh, don't say that!"

"Let's look on the bright side."

"Aye, worry about it when it happens that's what Aunty Annie'd say!"

"Annie is a wise woman. Okay, if you go into the kitchen Millicent will make you that much needed cup of tea and may even give you something to eat."

"Thanks Dr. Rees. Don't think I could face the stares in Segadelli's."

Dr. Rees nodded and turned to his next patient, a miner with a hacking cough. "Well, Gareth come through."

Netta had set up a workshop in her mother's parlour and she was fashioning a variety of millinery. There was no doubt that Netta was talented. Her hat designs were chic and had great flair. There were many different patterns and she used her accessories wisely. Her mother, too, was learning how to mould and steam the bases into shape to give Netta the frameworks to build on.

"Mam, I am going into Neath and will visit some of the milliners there and department stores that have a hat section. I may be able to sell some and get some advance orders."

"That would be good," sniffed Mam-gu. "It would be right to receive some recompense for all this hard work."

"Then will it be all right for you to look after Jake when I go? It'll make my life much easier."

"Aye, I'll nurse him in the shawl. Make sure you leave some milk for him."

"Of course. I'll feed him before I go and I have already expressed some in readiness it will keep cool in the larder. Mind you feed him at the right temperature."

"And who are you telling about babies. Remember, I've had four!" admonished Mam-gu.

"I know, I know!" exclaimed an irritated Netta.

"Hmm! Just making a point."

Mam-gu continued fashioning and steaming the base she was working on. She studied her daughter. She was under no illusions about Netta and felt that she wasn't to be completely trusted.

Netta began to select some of her most captivating designs and placed them in hatboxes. She groomed and preened, "I have to look smart or they won't take me seriously. I should also wear one of my own creations." Netta picked a cheeky cloche design with a flower and partial veil. She nodded approval. "That'll do nicely. Right, now for young master Jake." Netta began to unbutton her bodice. The movement was well timed as little Jake began to wail upstairs.

Megan was on her way to London. She had a strange flutter of excitement rippling through her stomach. She enjoyed watching the scenery go by. She passed dusty smoky stacks and back yards that faced the railway lines interspersed with green fields and countryside. To look outside it didn't appear that there was a war on. Everything looked seemingly normal; whatever normal meant thought Megan.

Megan pulled out her letter from ENSA inviting her to an audition at The Garrick Theatre in London. She then dived in her bag and took out her audition speeches and ran through them one more time. She knew the passages inside out. The required Shakespeare piece as Ophelia from Hamlet, a piece from The Women's Town a 1902 comedy that her grandmother recommended she do, a poem by Edward Lear, The Jumblies, and she had the music for a song, written in 1926, My Sweetheart's the Man in the Moon.

The journey was long and arduous but Megan didn't mind. She had plenty to occupy her on the journey. She'd written to her grandmother who had encouraged her to pursue her dreams and now, she was penning a letter to Thomas and hoped that he would reply in kind.

Eventually the train rumbled into Paddington Station. Megan gazed about her in wonder. The station was bigger that any she had visited at home and with so many platforms. She wondered how she could find her way to the venue and if she dared afford a taxi. Taking courage in both hands she ventured to the taxi rank and joined the queue.

Fortunately, she did not have to wait long. The chirpy cabbie asked, "Where to love?"

"Garrick Theatre, please." Megan sat back to enjoy the ride.

The cockney cabbie was chatty and Megan began to feel less nervous. She marvelled at the sights and sounds, the amazing shops and the abundance of people. She never knew there could be so many in one place.

The cabbie soon announced, "Here we are love, the Garrick Theatre." Megan took the money from her purse and paid the cabbie, generously telling him to keep the change. The cabbie gave her a salute in thanks and whizzed back off into the London Streets.

Megan gazed up at the imposing building with its arched foyer entrance and pillars and balustrade above. Outside was a large Plane tree and Megan was surprised to see so much greenery in a big city. She ran inside the building, "Excuse me. I'm Megan," she took a deep breath, "Langtree. I'm here to audition for Mr. Basil Dean and ENSA."

The Box Office Lady checked her list, "Megan Langtree you say?"

Megan nodded; she hoped her newly chosen name would bring her luck. It certainly made her sound less commonplace and she knew that a lot of stars changed their names to something more memorable. Megan Langtree sounded better than Megan Thomas.

"Ah yes, I see. Please go round to the Stage Door and see the doorman. He will show you to the Green Room. Wait there until you're called."

Megan deftly left the foyer, her heart thumping, and made her way to the Stage Door. She tentatively knocked and pushed it open.

"Megan Langtree?"

Megan nodded; half wishing she had given her real name.

The stage doorkeeper stepped out from his position, "Box Office rang. Follow me." The old boy led the way to the Green Room and ushered her in. There were a number of hopefuls sitting there who looked up expectantly as she entered.

"Kettle in the corner, make yourself a drink and wait till your name's called."

Megan sat and surveyed the room and the other occupants. There was a tall willowy blonde who looked bored and was playing with her nails, a plump girl with a mop of dark curly hair, and a good looking young man who smiled engagingly at Megan who beamed back.

"Here for the auditions?" the young man asked.

Megan nodded and the other girls looked up curiously.

"Would you like a cup of tea?"

"No thanks. I don't think it would help me sing; clog up my vocals, although I wouldn't mind a glass of water."

The young man jumped up and got Megan a glass of water. "Grainger, Grainger Mason."

"Megan Langtree", responded Megan. She suspected that the young man had also given himself a more theatrical name.

A voice came over the Tannoy and everyone jumped, "Pamela Belkin to the stage please." The willowy blonde rose clutching her sheet music and left the Green Room.

Strains from a tinny piano filtered through into the Green Room and the blonde's strident voice rang out. The inmates of the Green Room couldn't hear clearly but were aware of mumblings coming from the stage and a pause. The Tannoy rang out again, "Polly Purvis to the stage please".

Megan whispered, "Good luck."

"Thanks," answered Polly and left Grainger and Megan together.

"So, auditioning?"

"Yes," answered Megan shyly. "It's my first time."

"You'll be fine. What are you doing?"

Megan told him and he nodded approvingly. "They say they're planning more productions after Christmas in all sorts of places. Their first concert in September was a great success."

"That was in Surrey wasn't it?"

"Yes, apparently it went really well and the pay is good. They have plans for reviews and concerts all over the world. We may be in with a chance."

"Let's hope."

The Tannoy crackled out, "Grainger Mason to the stage, please."

Grainger rose, "Wish me luck... say do you fancy a cuppa afterwards?" Megan nodded amiably. "Great, I'll meet you back in here," he said.

Grainger rose and left. Megan was alone but not for long as another three hopefuls took seats in the Green Room. She was now beginning to feel nervous. A churning sensation akin to fear was rumbling in her gut. Soon her name was called, "Megan Langtree to the stage please."

Megan stepped out and followed the waiting Stage Manager to the wings. The lights blazed on the performance area shrouding the audience in darkness. Megan stepped out.

A disembodied voice called out. "Give your music to the pianist please."

Megan tilted her head and walked across to the piano, she told herself, 'Come on Megan, you can do this.' She handed the pianist her sheet music. The introduction rang out and Megan launched into her version of the song. Her voice was sweet and strong.

She was stopped on the second chorus, "Good, good. What pieces do you have for us?"

"Ophelia from Hamlet, one from Women's Town and The Jumblies by Edward Lear."

"We'll have the Shakespeare first," came the anonymous voice.

Megan threw herself into the role of Ophelia and got through to the end. Her confidence growing she breezed through her comedy piece and finished with the Jumblies.

"Miss Langtree, do you dance?"

"Yes."

"What levels?"

"I can do basic ballet and tap, elementary jazz."

"So you can hold a step?"

"Yes."

"Can you come back at four? We would like you to work with our choreographer. But you need to go to our headquarters at Drury Lane. There's a proper dance studio there. You won't be alone. We need to see how you move."

"Yes. Thank you."

"Don't thank me yet. See you at four. Call June Priest to the stage please.

Megan left the stage in a daze, she was thrilled to be recalled and allowed herself to get a little excited. Maybe this was it. This was her chance. Megan returned to the

Green Room and smiled at Grainger who rose and joined her.

"How did it go?" he asked.

"Okay, I have to go to Drury Lane at four."

"Me, too."

"That's great!"

"Let's see if we can find a Lyons Corner House, my treat, to celebrate."

They left the theatre and made their way to the Strand after enquiring of a passer-by where the nearest teashop was situated.

The bell jangled as they entered and Megan admired the Art-Deco style. Waitresses in black uniforms with starched white aprons waited on tables and Grainger bagged a table and seat near the window.

"So, Megan Langtree tell me about yourself."

"Not a lot to tell really. I doubt I'd be here if it wasn't for my grandmother. She helped me choose my pieces. I'm hoping that I have good news for her and it will buck her up. She's getting on in years and is none too well." Megan continued chatting about her home and upbringing and confessed Langtree was not her real name.

"Still, it sounds good. My name isn't Grainger either, it's Arthur and I've always hated it. Grainger is my mother's maiden name seemed like a good idea to use it."

Megan learnt he was from a family of eight and they were all boys. Three were still at home in Surrey and his four older brothers had joined the armed forces. Megan told him about her brother, Gwynfor. The time passed pleasantly enough and the two made their way back to the Drury Lane Theatre for their recall audition.

There were ten women and five men waiting anxiously. Some wore professional dancewear. Megan frowned, she had brought her dancing shoes but otherwise she had on her ordinary clothes.

The female choreographer quickly assembled the eager talent to the dance studio. "I will show you some simple moves and I want you to repeat them one at a time across the floor. Then you will learn a short tap routine and perform it. Finally, music will play and you will each improvise to it and try and form a collective piece. I am not looking for stars but those who can work well as a team."

Megan took off her shoes and put on her ballet flats for the demonstration of the sequence of moves, which she felt she accomplished well. She changed into her tap shoes and performed the simple routine with ease. Lastly, she took off her shoes to dance barefoot and began to feel the music being played, which was Morning from Peer Gynt. Megan was reminded of a cat waking and stretching and improvised freely with the piece and was amazed to find the other dancers picked up on her idea and gradually the body of dancers almost seemed to move as one.

The chorographer clapped her hands and selected eight, four young women and four young men. She dismissed and thanked the rest and told them to try again at the next rounds. Both Megan and Grainger were selected. Grainger winked at her. Things were looking good.

Carrie and Pemb had managed the same day off duty. Christmas was approaching and they were both looking forward to a few days home at holiday time. They decided to do some gift shopping in the town and had agreed to meet Lloyd in the Kardomah in New Street.

The two friends, arm in arm, marched around the compact town centre. They alighted from the bus in Colmore Row, walked through the Churchyard of the Cathedral and cut through to Corporation Street and Lewis's big Department Store.

"Your money's burning a hole in my pocket," exclaimed Pemb. "Have you seen the clothes?"

"I can see," murmured Carrie, "But that's not what we're here for."

"I know, I know. I've got all the family to buy for."

"And I need help to pick something for John, Jenny and Ernie and of course the new baby."

"No one else?"

"Who else is there likely to be?"

"Mmm, maybe Thomas or..." Pemb teased, "Michael."

"Yes, maybe I should get something for Thomas."

"And what about Michael?"

"He's away. He would never get it."

"He may surprise you. He seems like that sort of man. 'Tidy', as my mother would say," laughed Pemb.

"We'll see," said Carrie primly. "Let's look for Jenny first."

"That should be easy. Whatever suits you should suit her, you are the same colouring."

"Hmm!" Carrie dragged Pemb toward a display of scarves and hunted through them.

"Look at this one!" pointed Pemb. "Emerald green, excellent with your hair. Try it and see."

Carrie lifted up the sparkling silk scarf and tried it against her hair. It was perfect. They both nodded and Carrie made her first purchase of the day. She had it gift wrapped and disappeared to the Gents' Section to hunt through the rails. She didn't see Pemb sneak back and select another green scarf, which she had wrapped for Carrie.

Two hours later loaded with shopping they entered the Kardomah and found a table. Their feet were burning with all the walking. The waitress approached and took their order for two coffees and pastries. They were just tucking into their Belgian Buns when the coffee shop bell jangled and the familiar figure of Lloyd entered. He spotted the two nurses and waved before crossing to join them.

"It's my lucky day, two beautiful women to keep me company and no competition. Who is going to tell me about this city and what has been happening to you both?"

The friends fell deep into conversation and were soon laughing together. "So, I'm not the only one coming to Birmingham, Peter and Joshua start at the university after Christmas."

"And what about James?" asked Pemb.

"Ah, they always like the tall dark ones," mused Lloyd.

"Not necessarily," flirted Pemb.

"No? James has gone on to Oxford. What about you? Are you able to get home at all? For Christmas?"

Carrie noticed that Lloyd seemed equally at ease with Pemb as he did with her and was hoping that might ease the situation as she decided she had to tell him that they could be nothing more than friends. She watched as Lloyd told a joke and Pemb clapped her hands delightedly. There was definitely a spark between them, one that wasn't present, she didn't think, between Lloyd and herself. He was fun and nice enough but she finally admitted he just wasn't Michael. She also remembered their original meeting when he had tried to get into the bumper car with Pemb and then came back for her when his friend James beat him to it. The friends agreed to visit the cinema together to see, 'The Lion has Wings', starring Merle Oberon and Ralph Richardson, on the nurses next night off. Carrie made up her mind there and then that she wouldn't be going.

On the bus on the way home, Carrie broached the subject of Lloyd. "What do you think of Lloyd, Pemb?"

"He's lovely, why?"

"Better than James?"

"James was just a bit of fun, a friend, nothing serious. Why?"

"No reason."

"Lew, I know you, what are you thinking?"

"I'm thinking I don't want to lead him up the garden path. We can be friends but nothing more."

"He'll be mortified."

"I don't think so."

"Well, I think so. Look how he's always written to you."

"I still think I was only second best."

"What? Then who was first?"

"You!"

"Rubbish, why do you say that?"

"You like him don't you?"

"Yes, but..."

"No buts. Picture night. I want you to go alone. Then you'll find out. I'll send him a note explaining."

"Are you matchmaking?"

"Sort of."

"What about Thomas?"

"What about him? You're not promised to him. He's away at sea. Anything could happen. I can't believe I'm saying this but, Lloyd is here and now. You're far better suited to him than me."

Pemb was quiet for a moment and then nodded. "Holding a candle for Michael?" guessed Pemb.

Carrie smiled, "If I get involved with someone else it will only complicate matters. You'll be doing me a favour."

"All right, but only if you're sure. And I am worried about Thomas. As for Lloyd, I don't want to be second best."

"I don't think for a minute that that's the case."

The rest of the journey continued quietly. Pemb was subdued and Carrie was lost in her own thoughts writing the letter to Lloyd in her head.

Megan was entrenched in rehearsals and loving every minute of it. Grainger was in the same company and they had developed a revue type show with sketches, songs and dances. Megan studied the list of proposed venues for the concert, she noticed that one was to be held at Scapa Flow in Scotland and pressed the Stage Manager on it, "Are we scheduled to do that one?" she asked pointing at the list.

The Stage Manager studied his list. Yes, two nights in Scotland, one in Plymouth and another two in Surrey. Then I believe you may be going further afield.

Megan was ecstatic and resolved to write to Thomas to make sure he'd be there in the audience.

"Good news?" asked Grainger.

"Yes, we're going to Scapa Flow and that's where my... a dear friend is stationed."

"Oh?" said Grainger, trying not to show any sparks of envy. "Best get in touch, let him know we're coming."

"I intend to," smiled Megan, shaking her conker tresses. "I will write him a very long letter," she purred. She didn't see Grainger's frown.

Carrie, too, was writing a letter to Lloyd. She believed she had written the truth and gave Lloyd and Pemb her blessing. She hoped that she had read the situation correctly and signed her name with a flourish, sealed the envelope and placed it on her desk, ready to send, when she got an opportunity.

She was looking forward to going home for Christmas. Jenny would be five months pregnant and it would be lovely to see everyone, especially Ernie, and of course, John whom she believed was now truly over his obsession with her. She studied her pile of parcels in the corner of the room and checked that she had something for everyone. She knew she needed to write Christmas cards but somehow couldn't get around to it, it was a chore she hated but she knew if she didn't do them, then no one in the family would receive Christmas wishes from the Llewellyns. John would never remember.

Pemb entered their room and flopped down. She tossed a letter at Carrie and an open one addressed to both of them. "It's from Kirb, she's moving to London. Going to the London Chest Hospital. That's where you want to go eventually, isn't it?"

"It's what I'd like to do. But, we've still got masses to learn here."

"Still it gives us something to aim for."

"I didn't know that you were interested in respiratory illnesses? Oh, I know you said after Gilly, but I thought that was just a reaction at the time."

"I'm interested in everything. All I know is I don't want to be a midwife; women's bits and pieces and screaming their heads off. No, not for me."

Carrie laughed, and proceeded to read Kirb's newsy letter.

Netta walked down Castle Street to the solicitors and entered the offices of Phillips, Pugsley and Pugh. She waited in reception until she was called.

Mr. Phillips fawned over her as she entered, "Why, Miss Llewellyn, please take a seat."

Netta sniffed disdainfully and sat opposite the portly solicitor at his desk.

"I came to see how you are progressing with the case."

"Yes, well, it's not as easy as you would think. It seems Mr. Lawrence and the Llewellyns have got things sewn up pretty tight. Because the original sale of Hendre, by Jacky, was deemed illegal by the court; there is not a lot I can do."

"What about the first payment received by Jacky. Has anyone managed to trace it yet?"

Mr. Phillips shook his head. "At the moment it has not been found and when it is, it will be returned to Mr. Lawrence and the property will revert to the Llewellyns. I'm sorry not to have better news."

"But there must be something we can do. What about my idea of the small print in the sales contract? A second bite of the cherry?"

Mr. Phillips shook his head, "I'm sorry, but unless something else comes to light..." he didn't complete his sentence.

Netta pursed her lips grimly, "There's more than one way of skinning a cat. If so, I will find it."

Netta rose and stiffly left the office. As she closed the door the solicitor breathed a heavy sigh of relief.

Netta proceeded down the High Street and into the Co-operative building society. She took out her mother's passbook and helped herself to some more of Mam-gu's cash, the last had gone on materials and setting up her company. This payment was for her nest egg.

Showing not a prickling of conscience she then strode off down to the department stores and milliners that had taken some of her creations and collected payment for goods sold and took another handful of orders, which she promised to deliver the following week.

Finally, her last stop off was the Police Station. She sucked in a deep breath and entered the old stone building. PC Rees was at the desk.

"Ah. Constable Rees. I'm hoping you may be able to help me."

"If I can, Miss Llewellyn," promised the constable.

"Jacky Ebron."

"Ah," sighed the policeman.

"I know the money on his person was returned to my nephew and niece, and quite rightly too. I wondered what had happened to the rest of my fiancé's possessions. He had a back pack and a bedroll."

"Yes, I remember. I'm not sure. It may still be in the evidence locker."

"Could you check for me, please? As I was affianced to him I would like to collect the rest of his possessions, he had a watch too, I believe."

Constable Rees left Netta at the desk and disappeared inside the offices. He returned a few minutes later with a box. "This is all I can find. This and his bedroll."

"I'll take both."

Rees passed Netta the box and returned for the bedroll. He took out the Property Book and indicated where Netta should sign to say she had received the items.

Netta forced her rattrap mouth into the pretence of a smile and signed. She left smartly, carrying Jacky's property. She was going to enjoy sifting through it.

Picture night was soon upon them. Carrie had posted her letter to Lloyd and she felt easier in her mind. He was a lovely young man and she hoped that she had indeed read 'the signs' correctly.

"How do I look?" asked Pemb and she gave a twirl.

"Lovely," gushed Carrie. "Now, you go ahead and have a wonderful night."

"I'm still not sure about this. And I do still like Thomas. It's all a little confusing."

"Maybe tonight will make it clearer."

"What if it doesn't?"

"You won't know unless you go and try," said Carrie philosophically.

"And what are you going to do?"

"Have a long hot bath and relax with a magazine and I have letters to write."

"To Michael?"

"Maybe."

"Will he be home for Christmas?"

"I doubt it. His last letter was heavily censored, a lot of it was blacked out, but I believe he's doing a lot of reconnaissance missions in preparation for a new campaign."

"Let's hope he stays in the air." Pemb pinned on her hat, "Right, I'm away. See you later."

Carrie settled down for her evening in and donned her nightwear for comfort. She went to run her bath and as she luxuriated in the hot steamy water she found herself drifting off into a world of daydreams and fell asleep.

Time passed and Carrie's body dropped lower and lower into the bath. Her head began to sink under the water. There was a hammering on the door and Hawtry's thin voice penetrated through the door. "Lew? Are you okay in there?"

Carrie took a mouthful of water as she was roused from her slumber and coughed violently. The water was now only tepid and she began to shiver, she managed to call out, "Yes, thanks. Getting out now."

"If you fancy a nightcap, tap on my door," called Hawtry.

"Will do." Carrie was visibly shaken. If it hadn't been for Hawtry knocking on the door, Carrie felt she would have slipped right under the water and drowned. It was a shocking thought and spurred her to get out of the tub and dry herself off. She was feeling faint and wobbly; maybe she was coming down with something?

Carrie deftly wrapped her mane of tangled curls into a towel and emptied the bath. She opened the window to clear the condensation from the room, vowing she would never let that happen again.

Ten minutes later she was hugging a mug of hot chocolate and chatting with Hawtry. She didn't mention that she could possibly owe her life to her.

"I'm on the move again, Lew," explained Hawtry.

"I thought you liked it here."

"I do, but it holds too many bad memories now."

"Where are you going?"

"I've taken notice of what you've said, I'm leaving for the London Chest Hospital, where I can use my skills to full advantage and," she added carefully, "I will set up some private piano tuition and advertise when I get there, give lessons when I have time off."

"Good for you. That's great news. You'll see Kirb there. She's a staff nurse now and that's where she's gone."

"She'll be none too pleased to see me, then. There was no love lost between us."

"That was then, you've changed Hawtry. We can all see that. Gilly saw it and Pemb too, now."

"Well, maybe. I'll just tread carefully to begin with."

"Pemb and I have already told her that you're a different person. She'll give you another chance. When do you go?"

"Christmas. I'm popping home to see mother for a few days and start on the wards Boxing Day. Not much time for goodbyes or anything. I want you to know, Lew, that if it hadn't been for you," and the thin faced nurse's eyes welled up with tears.

"Listen, it's nothing and anyway we may see each other again."

"Oh?"

"It's my ambition to go to The London Chest Hospital I want to study respiratory diseases like you and make a difference, if this lousy war will let me."

Hawtry rose and crossed to Carrie and hugged her hard, "Thank you."

"Go on with you," mumbled Carrie, surprisingly touched. "I'd better scoot. I need to get settled before Pemb comes back and turns our room upside down."

Carrie smiled and drained the last of her drink.

"I'll see to that," said Hawtry obligingly. Carrie smiled. Hawtry certainly had changed.

Carrie bid her goodnight. She stepped out and entered her own room and flopped on the bed to wait for Pemb. She didn't have long to wait. Pemb whirled in breathlessly excited and beamed at Carrie.

"I take it the evening was a success," mused Carrie.

"The film was okay, a lot of propaganda if you ask me."

"I don't mean the film," prodded Carrie.

Pemb blushed, "Well, yes. Lloyd was a perfect gentleman. He had taken your letter to heart and yes, he thinks a lot of you but acknowledged that there was a spark between us. He also understood about having a man in the forces..."

"And?"

"And, I'm seeing him on my next night off, but we both insist, next time we go to the pictures, you must come too."

Carrie hugged her friend. She was delighted for her."

"You'll have to write to Thomas."

"I will. Thanks, Lew."

"Don't thank me, just do the right thing and be happy." Carrie didn't tell her about her near accident in the bath. As nothing had happened, it was no use worrying anyone.

CHAPTER TWENTY-FIVE

Scapa Flow and Old Friends

The young sailors gathered in anticipation of the entertainment concert organised by ENSA that was taking place that evening. There was a bubble of excitement in the audience and backstage. It was Megan and Grainger's first concert.

Thomas sat with his friend Leigh in the middle of the pack. The music struck up with the recent hit, 'Jeepers Creepers.' The ensemble of performers danced onto the stage and sang out the song. This segued into a comedy sketch and left Megan alone on stage. She launched into, 'My heart belongs to Daddy'.

Thomas craned his neck, he recognised the burnished conker tresses and couldn't quite believe what he was seeing. Evan nudged him, "Say, she looks remarkably similar to that girl who visited you in Cardiff. Do you think it is?"

"I'm not sure," Thomas replied, "But it does look like her. What is she doing here?"

"Well, if it is, you ought to make yourself known to her, don't you think?"

"Maybe," agreed Thomas and watched the action more avidly.

Megan attracted admiring glances and wolf whistles, which she acknowledged with a little curtsey.

The show continued and the final number rang out, which culminated in a mass of appreciative applause. The cast took their curtain call and bowed delightedly as the audience shouted for, "More".

As the sailors burst into lively chatter, Megan stepped out from behind the curtain and took the microphone. She spoke evenly and the audience became hushed once more.

"I'd just like to say to each and every one of you that we are so proud of the work you are doing and I have a special message for Able Seaman Thomas Williams."

Evan gave Tom a dig in the ribs, "That's you, boyo!"

Thomas sat up, fully alert.

"If you've a mind I'd love to speak to you before we leave."

There were loud catcalls and whoops from the sailors. Those that recognised Tom made suggestive gestures to him and shouted the odd derogatory remark. Evan pushed him up. "Go on, wuss; you'll regret it if you don't."

Thomas stood up and pulled off his hat and tentatively pushed his way through the seated sailors and others in the audience and walked slowly down the aisle toward the stage. One by one the assembled service men fell quiet and all eyes were on Tom as he processed towards the pretty entertainer on the stage.

The silence was so deafening that the squeak of a mouse would have sounded as thunderous as a lion's roar. After what seemed like an eternity Thomas reached the stage. He had forgotten everyone watching him and this encounter. His eyes were fixed on Megan. He stopped and looked up. Megan's face radiated with love and she jumped right off the stage and into his arms. The audience went absolutely crazy. There was cheering and clapping and some threw their hats in the air.

Megan kissed him passionately and the men went wilder, whistling and stamping their feet.

She stood on tiptoe and whispered in his ear, "Does this mean, I'm your girl?"

Tom swung her around, "Oh yes, yes, yes!" They fell into a rapturous embrace drawing even more applause from the crowd.

The two suddenly became aware of their now very public display and shyly stopped their performance and ran off to the side of the stage giggling delightedly.

The men in the audience began to disband, Megan did not notice Grainger's black scowl as he saw the two of them kiss.

Megan tucked her arm in Tom's and led him away to find a little privacy and they sat together quietly as people drifted away from the area.

"Did you get my letter? Saying I was coming?"

"No. It hasn't arrived yet but post is slow getting here, it's even more out in the sticks than Crynant."

Megan was almost afraid to ask, "What about Pemb?"

Thomas sighed, "She's written regularly but her last letter told me that she was walking out with a university student, Lloyd something or other."

Megan's eyes brightened, "Do you mind?"

"Funnily enough, no. She's a lovely girl and I knew her for such a short time. I think it was all a reaction against you and events at the time."

Megan lowered her eyes, "We all did a lot of stupid things, no one more so than me. Will you forgive me? I have so much making up to do."

"Megan, fach. You were the light of my life."

"Am I now?"

"Oh, yes," sighed Tom and crushed her to him.

"Then it's all been worth it. I am never going to let you go."

They embraced once more and the ship's horn sounded.

"I have to get back. When will I see you again?"

"We have another Scottish date tomorrow before heading for Plymouth. You can write to me care of ENSA. Here."

Megan took out a scribbled address from her pocket and passed it to Tom. "Do you have any time off due?"

"Nothing yet. We're working through Christmas. If this war is over by the end of the year then who knows, I may get back to Gelli Galed."

The ship's horn blasted again and Thomas stood and kissed Megan once more. His heart was on fire. He walked backwards letting his eyes linger on her until he could see her no more and was engulfed by the body of men returning to ship. He didn't even mind the teasing, jeering comments that flew past his head. Nothing could break his spirit or destroy his feelings. At this moment he felt invincible.

Netta had just finished feeding Jake. He fixed his dark eyes on his mother's face and then his eyelids closed and Netta placed him tenderly into the drawer, where he slept.

She laid out the box and bedroll on the bed and her mother's passbook and emptied her purse. She counted out the money she had collected and selected a large white five-pound note and put it to one side. Then she placed the rest of the money in a small cash box alongside her mother's passbook and locked the tin, hiding it away amongst her underwear, taking care not to disturb Jake.

She eyed the box for some moments before opening the cardboard container. She emptied the contents on the bed, there was a gold watch, which she recognised as Bryn's; a small magnifying glass in a velvet pouch, a notebook and pencil, a box of matches, an old fashioned black leather purse and a tobacco tin, a ball of string, a penknife, a bill folder and clip, and a piece of wood for whittling.

Netta grabbed the watch. This could be useful. She wouldn't dream of passing it back to the Llewellyn brats. No, she could pawn this and make some cash.

She tossed the string to one side. The penknife she would keep for Jake. Netta opened the purse and emptied it. There were a few coppers, sixpence, a silver three-penny bit, two crowns and four gold sovereigns. Netta eyed them greedily.

They would come in useful. She retrieved her cash box and placed the loose cash inside, along with the black leather gent's purse. She picked up the bill folder and clip; it was empty, except for a piece of paper. Scrawled in Jacky's hand it read: The Metropolitan Equitable.

Netta's eyes gleamed. Was this a clue?

She opened the matchbox. It contained only matches, some spent. Netta tossed it aside. She picked up the tobacco tin and opened it. It contained some cigarette papers and loose tobacco. Netta frowned; she didn't remember Jacky ever smoking. She turned over the cigarette papers and pulled one out that was protruding, there was more writing, HPBS and ARBS.

Netta turned to the notebook. There were several entries and notes all in numbers. Netta determinedly set her lips in a hard line. Was this the secret as to where the money from the first payment for Hendre had gone? What other secrets did these notes contain?

She unrolled the bedroll, which revealed some items of clothing and a small tin. Netta opened the tin. It contained some photographs, which she studied curiously, two keys, a gold wedding band, papers and a letter. She took out the missive, read it and gasped with shock. She couldn't believe what she was reading.

Carrie was looking forward to a short break at home. She had been given four days off but had to work Christmas Eve, Christmas Day and Boxing Day. That didn't matter at least she'd get home and she knew Ernie would make sure she had a proper Christmas there, albeit late, and immediately penned a letter home telling them when she would be arriving.

Pemb had been luckier and had managed to get her days off through the Christmas period, it seemed that Lloyd had invited her home to meet his family and she was both excited and nervous about it.

Carrie was always told that Christmas time on the wards of a major hospital was wonderful and very different from the Christmas at the Mat. Unit in Aber. The nurses would travel around the hospital carrying lanterns and wear full uniform including their capes and sing carols. One of the doctors would dress as Santa. She was quite looking forward to it.

Christmas Eve arrived and the Nurses' Home was a flurry of activity with nurses leaving for their holiday break. Staffing was slashed to a minimum and Pemb had already left with Lloyd. Carrie sighed. She had an hour before she was due to go on duty. She studied the carol sheet in front of her with all her old favourites and hummed happily. She glanced out of the window and saw the first woolly snowflakes begin to drift from the sky. It was certainly cold enough for snow and the sky had that unmistakeable pink hue. A white Christmas would be perfect as long as the snow didn't settle and cause travel chaos for when she wanted to journey home. She made a quick plea to the heavens above and changed into her crisp, clean uniform.

Carrie arrived on duty and was redirected by the Ward Sister to the lobby. Gathered there were about twenty nurses. She was given a lamp containing a flickering candle. Dr. Challacombe was dressed as Santa and carried a large sack, which he later placed on a small trolley decorated like a Christmas Sleigh. The group of nurses began their rounds in the children's ward.

It was magical. The children who were well enough sat cross-legged in the play and education room and the nurses assembled and sang the carol, "Away in a Manger." Everyone joined in and the little patients' upturned faces glowed with a happy expectancy that added that special sparkle to Christmas. Dr. Challacombe ho, ho, hoed and gave out gifts to the ready and waiting outstretched hands. From there they moved into the ward, where the children were too ill to leave their beds and the nurses sang some more.

Carrie was particularly taken with a small blonde girl of about five years of age who it seems was suffering from leukaemia. The little girl beamed in delight at all the nurses and whispered her thanks to Santa many times, so much so that Carrie was quite moved with compassion that filled her with emotion.

The nurses processed through the wards and the hospital before disbanding and returning to duty. Carrie felt quite elated after this and nothing could dampen her spirits, not even the fact that one old boy, Archie Campbell, on Men's Surgical had just suffered a massive coronary and died.

Sister Friend instructed Carrie to lay the body out and the vessel that had housed the spirit of Archie Campbell was wheeled into a side room and Carrie prepared the body for the morgue and family viewing.

Carrie picked up the bar of green Palmolive soap and resolved that this was a brand she would never buy for herself. It always seemed to be the favoured brand in hospitals and used for just this purpose. She washed him with care, combed and tidied his hair, and shaved him cleanly. Carrie then attempted to close his mouth, which gaped open showing his toothless gums. Realising she needed his dentures she returned to his bay on the ward and picked up a box containing teeth.

Carrie struggled and wrestled with the set of dentures finally managing to force them into Archie's mouth. 'No wonder he never wore them' she mused. They must have been very uncomfortable. Archie lay there, mouth still agape displaying a ridiculous grinning smile.

"He'll have to do," she muttered and wheeled the gurney out from the prep room and into the lift to take the body to the morgue.

When she returned to the ward, she was assailed by a wail from old Billy Goodwin who was in the next bed to Archie, "Nurse, where's me teeth? They were in a box. I can't find them to eat me supper."

Carrie stopped in horror and responded, "Just being cleaned, Billy. I'll get them for you."

Carrie, struggling not to giggle raced back out of the ward, into the lift and down to the mortuary where she recovered Archie's body and had an extraordinary fight to remove the dentures from his mouth. She finally wrested them from Archie's grinning jaws and dashed to the sluice where she scrubbed and disinfected the choppers before rinsing them carefully.

Smiling, she returned the teeth to their rightful owner and smiled sweetly, "There you are Billy."

"Aw, thanks, Nurse," muttered the grateful chap as he took the offered dentures and easily popped them into his own mouth.

'If only you knew where they'd been,' thought Carrie. But Billy was none the wiser and what he didn't know wouldn't hurt him. Still, it was something to tell the family at home. She was sure the story would amuse them.

Christmas day was busy and the wards were short staffed, so nurses did double shifts to help things run smoothly but it left them inordinately tired although the time went very quickly.

The twenty-eighth of December arrived and Carrie overslept. She was glad she had already packed her bag to go home and rushed to get ready. She gathered her parcels together and struggled down the stairs to call a cab. If she relied on the bus she knew she might miss her train. As she waited, Dr. Challacombe passed her in the lobby.

"Off home, Nurse? Do you need a lift?"

"Thanks, but I have ordered a taxi."

"Get Walter to cancel it. I'm off to Snow Hill Station. You're welcome to ride with me."

Carrie hesitated and glanced at her watch. She was cutting things fine. She smiled brightly, "Thank you. It's much appreciated."

"I'll take these," said the doctor and Carrie tapped on the window at reception.

"Walter, can you cancel my taxi? Dr. Challacombe is giving me a lift."

Walter nodded and said, "Watch yourself with that one. He has an eye for a pretty nurse."

Carrie responded, "I think I'll manage."

She stepped outside. Snow was falling thickly again, carpeting the frozen ground. It looked as though it would settle and she hoped it wouldn't delay her journey.

Dr. Challacombe was placing her things in the boot of his green Sunbeam Talbot Ten motorcar. "Okay, door's open. Hop in."

Carrie opened the passenger door and slipped inside. The vehicle was quite luxurious and not like any car she had travelled in before. She sank comfortably in the leather seat. The doctor set the wipers going to brush away the snow curtain manifesting on the windscreen.

The journey passed quickly, and Dr. Challacombe came round and opened her door, "There you go. I'll just get your things, Nurse Llewellyn."

Carrie stepped out and acknowledged the doctor. "Thank you so much. I may have missed my train but for you."

"You're welcome. Maybe, you can thank me when you get back."

"Sorry?"

"A drink out or dinner together maybe?"

"Oh well... er I don't know."

"No need to make your mind up now. Just think about it. See you when you get back."

Carrie blushed, it seemed Walter was right and she wasn't quite sure how to handle it. She nodded and promised, "I'll think about it."

Dr. Challacombe, smiled, "That's all I ask. Now, which platform do you need? I'll help you with those."

Despite Carrie's protestations, Dr. Challacombe lifted her bag and accompanied her to the platform. "There we are. Have a good trip."

"Yes, doctor. Thank you, doctor."

"Oh tosh! We're not in hospital now, call me, Andrew."

"Thank you, doctor... Andrew."

The doctor gave a mock bow and saluted Carrie before leaving her on the platform. He whistled brightly as he walked. It was 'Run, rabbit run.' Carrie couldn't help but smile.

Gelli Galed was delighted to welcome Carrie home and just as Carrie had predicted Ernie had prepared a second Christmas meal just for her. A decorated tree stood in the parlour surrounded by gifts and even the bricks and mortar of the house seemed to extend a yuletide welcome to her. John's old room had been turned into a nursery and Jenny had shown she wasn't only talented in music but was creative with a paintbrush. She had enjoyed painting the baby's room colourfully with murals depicting fairy tales and nursery rhymes.

Jenny's pregnancy was now showing and she was taking things steadily. John appeared happy and both Carrie and Ernie prayed that things would continue in this way. Life was joyous.

The family gathered in the parlour to open their gifts. There were oohs and ahs of delight. Jenny loved her emerald scarf. Ernie was delighted with his new cap, and John more than satisfied with the new watch that Carrie had bought. "To make up for losing Dad's," she said.

John had been whittling wood and made a number of delightful wooden toys, a rattle and mobile to hang over the crib of little wooden butterflies. He'd also fashioned in wood for Carrie a beautiful model of a collie dog. Carrie was thrilled with it, and hugged it to her. Trix looked up at her adoringly with her soft brown eyes and whined gently in her throat. Carrie cuddled the dog so Trixie was allowed to stay in with the family and she stuck closely to Carrie's side. Her eyes watched Carrie's every move. If Carrie rose from her seat, Trix stood up. If she left the room Trix followed. It was clear the old dog was not going to let her out of her sight.

John went to put the kettle on the range and peered out of the window. It was almost dark, yet only three-thirty in the afternoon. He put on his coat, scarf and hat and trudged out of the front door to retrieve the post. An icy blast of air hit him in the face. It wasn't snowing but the sky looked ominous threatening arctic conditions. The flock of sheep were safe in an outbuilding as were the small herd of cows and handful of pigs. The livestock were secure and well fed. The chickens had taken themselves off to roost in the hen house and John shut the little gate keeping them in and then progressed down the yard and part of the track to where the family's post box was situated. He opened it up and retrieved a handful of mail. It was too cold to go through it there and with his breath steaming in the frigid air, like a snorting bull in a Matador's arena, he marched back to the house that was now blessed and filled with gaiety and laughter.

The family were in full flow playing The Minister's Cat and clapping together. John removed his outdoor clothes and plodded in to join them clutching the mail. There were a few late Christmas cards and some bills, a letter from Thomas and a brown official looking envelope bearing the MOD's motif. John turned it over curiously. It was addressed to him. He opened it.

"The minister's cat is a magnificent cat."

"The minister's cat is a naughty cat."

"The minister's cat is an opulent cat."

"The minister's cat is a powerful cat."

"Noooo."

The game stopped and all eyes turned to an ashen faced John.

"What's the matter, John?" queried Ernie.

"I've been called up. I have to report in three weeks for my medical."

The effervescent atmosphere withered away like a leaf dying on a tree. No one knew what to say.

That evening they sat around the kitchen table. The fire blazed on the range and the discussion was gloomy, of war and the farm.

"I'm surprised," murmured Ernie. "Thought you'd be exempt."

"I possibly would have been if I didn't have you and Sam Jefferies at Hendre. And don't forget we have the Land Girls so we are more than well catered for. It was to be expected. I just didn't think it would be so soon."

"I'll manage the stock and look after Jenny. You have no worries there."

Jenny smiled, "I'll be all right. Mam will visit and Ernie's better at looking out for me than I am myself. But I will miss you, John."

"And I you," said John fiercely and he squeezed and kissed her hand. "You will have to take care of both of you. I wanted to be here for the birth, looks like that is denied me now."

"We'll write regularly. Rest assured," comforted Ernie.

Carrie had said nothing. With Gwynfor gone and Thomas and Michael in the forces she wasn't sure what to do or say.

"Well, cariad, you've said very little. What are you thinking?" pressed John.

"I'm... I'm astonished it's happened. I thought you'd be safe here and to say I'm not worried would be a lie. But you have to do your duty as do we all. I will pray for you and only ask you to keep in touch."

"I'm not as good as you with a pen and paper, but I promise I'll try. And now, no more. Let's enjoy the rest of your visit. I think I'm hungry. How about some turkey sandwiches or some of that soup you've made Ernie?"

Ernie duly rose from the table and heated up the succulent stew and began buttering the bread.

Jenny looked up anxiously at Carrie, "He'll be all right, won't he?"

"He'll be fine. You just need to make sure that you are okay too. Rest assured, any time I have off, I'll try and visit. You can trust in that."

Jenny smiled feebly. It was clear she was bereft at the thought of John leaving, but they were soon to have other things on their mind.

Trixie lifted her head off the multi-coloured rag mat in front of the range and whined softly.

"What is it old girl?" asked Carrie and bent down to ruffle the collie's fur. Trix licked her hand and settled her head on her paws and closed her eyes. "You can sleep with me tonight, Trix like you used to. I don't see much of you; may as well make the most of it while I'm here."

"You spoil her, cariad. She'll be expecting the same favours from the rest of us if you do that," complained Ernie.

"Go on with you. She'll keep me warm. It's freezing tonight. By the way, where's Bandit?"

"I don't know. She's usually in by now warming her wings and cwtched up with Trix by the fire," exclaimed Ernie. "I'll go see."

"And I think I'll turn in for the night. I'm as tired as a mother hen with a brood of chicks. I'll see you all tomorrow." John bade them good night. He went up the stairs closely followed by Jenny, which left Carrie and Trixie at the table. It wasn't long before Ernie returned cradling the little duck.

"Little wretch was by the water barrel, almost frozen solid. We need to get some warmth into her and I'll get her a tot of brandy." He handed the duck to Carrie who cuddled it to her.

"You're a bit big to go down my front now, Bandit. Let's see what we can do."

Carrie picked up an old jersey of John's hanging by the range and made a sort of nest out of it as Trix looked on curiously. Carrie grabbed a cardboard box that had held a present and popped paper inside topped with the sweater and rested the duck on the top. Bandit gave a croaky quack and shook her feathers. "Come on, don't give up the ghost now. You're made of stronger stuff than that, my Bandit," Carrie admonished.

She placed the box at the side of the range as Ernie returned with some brandy and a dropper. "Leave her on the rug in front of the fire – just in case she flies out onto the hot coals. After all, we don't want roast duck, do we?"

Carrie removed the box and set it as Ernie asked and he administered a couple of drops of brandy to the cold bird. Bandit shook her head and blinked her eyes at the warming liquid.

"She'll be all right now. Just needs to rest up and get warm," advised Ernie. "Now, cariad are you off to bed now? Or are you going to tell me all that's been happening to you?"

Carrie smiled and proceeded to tell Ernie all her news and about life on the wards in Birmingham.

The lights burned late at Gelli Galed and it was past one o' clock before Carrie mounted the stairs to bed followed by her beloved Trix who jumped on the foot of her bed and curled up at Carrie's feet.

At round four a.m. Carrie was roused from her slumber by a twitching and shivering dog. Trix made funny little mewling noises in her throat and her eyes rolled in her head. Carrie was instantly alert and smoothed down her old friend. "What is it Trix, what's the matter?"

Trixie turned her loving eyes on Carrie and gently licked her hand. She gave a little shudder and a sigh escaped her.

"Trix!" called Carrie, "Trixie?" But there was no response. Carrie hugged the old dog to her as the tears coursed down her cheeks, "No, no, no. Don't die, please. Trixie, no." But she knew it was no good. Carrie wept as she never had before and cradled her faithful Trix whose head lolled to one side.

Carrie rose from her bed and wrapped the loyal family dog in an old dressing gown and tiptoed down the stairs with her. She sat stubbornly staring into the dying embers of the fire, still holding tightly to her beloved friend. Gelli Galed would never be the same for her again.

This was how Ernie found her when he returned at six to make the tea and begin preparing breakfast. "Oh, cariad, you must let her go."

Carrie shook her head, her rebellious curls flying.

"She was your friend, and lived for you. Be thankful she had a good life. She'll always be around you, with you and when your time comes you will meet her again."

"Oh, Ernie, why? Why now? Why did she go now? Everything's changed."

"I believe she was waiting for you to come home. She wanted to spend her last moments with you and she did. Come; give her to me. Wrap up warm and we'll bury her by the water butt in the barn. She loved to sleep there in the sun. It was her place."

Carrie relinquished her hold on the old dog and Ernie took the body of the trustworthy collie out to the barn. As he left there was a flurry of wings and Bandit quacked. Carrie smiled, "At least, you've survived, but you've lost your best friend. We all have."

The smell of frying bacon filled the kitchen but Carrie had little appetite and when John emerged rubbing his eyes he wondered at Carrie's dark eyes and sad expression.

"What is it, cariad? What's wrong?" asked John his face full of concern.

"Trix is gone," she said sadly.

"Where? What's happened?"

The account of the events of the night tumbled from her mouth and John gently hugged his sister. "I'm so sorry," he sighed, "I know what she meant to you, more than any of the rest of us. We'll have to get another."

"You can never replace Trix," said Carrie quietly.

"No. Not replace her. But the farm needs another dog, another collie. One we can train up like Trix. It won't be Trix but in time you may come to love it like you did Trixie."

Carrie continued to stare ahead and the tears continued to stream down her cheeks.

They had a simple ceremony in the yard and Ernie made a cross, fashioned out of iron. He etched in the metal, 'Trixie beloved of us all.' They said a prayer and with heads bowed spent a moment remembering the magic of the captivating collie, her gentle nature, her comforting presence and how she had come to the rescue on more than one occasion. Carrie touched the cross fondly and left a kiss on it and they all trooped back into the house. John put the kettle on almost tripping over Bandit who was flapping around on the floor and Ernie disappeared out of the door.

The mood was solemn. People spoke only when necessary and nothing seemed to be able to lift the spirits in the house. Even Jenny was upset at the loss. She had found Trixie loving and kind and would also miss her dreadfully.

Carrie vanished up the stairs to pack her bag, as she was due to return to Birmingham later the next day. John put the soup on to warm up and smiled weakly at Jenny, "It'll be all right my love. You'll see."

Carrie was soon back down the stairs, she looked fresher and had dabbed some powder on her face to mask her red eyes. The door blustered open and Ernie entered clutching a tiny little scrap of a thing. "Here we are. I knew that one of Trixie's offspring had, had pups at Hendre and Sam Jefferies had two of the litter left." He passed the fluffy bundle to Carrie and the little collie puppy set to licking Carrie's face and in spite of herself she had to smile.

"Best think of a name for her. Something to suit; I'll have her trained up the next time you see her. What's it to be?"

Carrie looked at the gentle freckled face of the little black and white pup and made an announcement, "Let's call her Bonnie. She's pretty and her name is a sign of hope in this mad world."

"Bonnie? Bonnie," considered Ernie. "It suits her. Bonnie it is."

At that point Bonnie took the opportunity to urinate on Carrie's lap and it sent everyone into gales of laughter.

"Best get her house trained. How old is she?" asked Carrie.

"Eight weeks, just old enough to leave her mam." Ernie looked at Carrie and chortled, "You better go and get changed."

Carrie passed the puppy to Ernie and dashed back upstairs to change her damp skirt.

CHAPTER TWENTY-SIX

Goodbyes and Promises

The next day Gelli Galed was busier than an ant's nest. Carrie was frantically trying to find her rail ticket, which she seemed to have misplaced.

"If you're anything like mam – it will have fallen to the bottom of your bag," pronounced John wisely.

Carrie picked up plump little Bonnie and gazed into her face. "You haven't eaten it, have you? Trix was a terror when she was young. Always chewing things to pieces and always *my* things if I remember rightly." The pup responded by giving Carrie a thorough wash all over her face. "I wonder if you'll remember me when I come home next?" she mused.

Carrie passed the squirming, fluffy bundle to Jenny who cuddled her in delight, "She'll remember you. I'll show her your photo every day!"

Carrie laughed, "And you dear, Jenny; you take care of yourself and whoever's in there!" She patted Jenny's tummy, "I'll expect a full report on you, John and all Ernie's activities as well as little Bonnie."

"I'll write, I promise."

"Now, I must find my ticket or I'll be going nowhere. When is your piano arriving?"

"Mam has got some movers to bring it here the end of next week."

"Keep playing; it may rub off on the little one and then you could still realise your dream of music, take exams and teach locally. That would give you an interest."

"Aye, in between changing nappies and feeding a baby!" laughed Jenny.

"Haven't you got to see Mam-gu?"

"I promised I'd call before I went for the train. Is Netta still there?"

"I believe so. Got her own millinery business now."

"Really? Hmm." Carrie did not relish meeting Netta again but knew it was something she had to get over.

Carrie tipped out her bag on the table and foraged through all the items.

"Duw, Duw, what a concoction of stuff," protested Ernie. "What do you need all that for?"

"Just things that might be useful."

"A thermometer, hair pins, some old toffees and a minto..."

"You can have those - if they're not gone off. Ah!" Carrie pounced on her ticket that was stuck to one of the oozing sweets.

"Now, put it where you won't lose it," advised Ernie.

"It's going in my purse," affirmed Carrie. "Come on, Ernie; shape it. And brush your hair, you look like you slept all night on a straw bale," grinned Carrie as she shovelled everything back into her bag.

"Well, I did," laughed Ernie, "Best bed ever."

"Best bed for the mice and rats too. Are you sure there's none nesting in there with you?"

"Go on with you. Is that case ready?"

"Yes, just got to say my goodbyes."

Carrie turned to Jenny and gave her a hug and fondled Bonnie's head. She called for John who ambled into the kitchen yawning. "You're another one who looks as if he's quarrelled with a comb!" exclaimed Carrie.

Brother and sister eyed each other, lovingly and hugged. "Take care of Jenny now and be careful when you join up," whispered Carrie

"I will, I'm hoping I still may get an exemption, when I go for interview. The farm is too much for Ernie to manage alone."

"Well, let me know what happens."

They hugged again and Ernie took Carrie's case out to the cart. The snow that had settled was too little to cause a problem, just a few icy patches that needed watching. John and Jenny put on their coats to wave goodbye and Bonnie sniffed and ran around the yard sending the chickens into a clucking frenzy.

Carrie climbed into the cart, wiped a stray tear from her eye and forced a smile. "I love you all. Let's hope when next we meet, this lousy war will be over!"

Ernie climbed up and clicked Senator into action. The cart began to trundle down the track to Crynant.

They were soon in the village and outside Mam-Gu's house.

"I'll wait by here. Say your goodbyes and we'll get off to the station. Don't want to miss your train."

"Don't fuss, Ernie. Worse than a washer woman, you are," admonished Carrie.

"No, just careful and sensible."

"Hm, as careful and sensible as walking blindfold through a field of cow pats."

"What's that supposed to mean?"

"I don't know. It's one of your sayings. You work it out. I won't be long."

Carrie stepped down from the cart and walked up the path to Mam-gu's house and knocked on the door. Her grandmother answered and fell to hugging her and gushing with questions and loving comments before welcoming her in and closing the door.

"Well, well. Let's take a good look at you. Quite blossomed you have, a proper little lady."

"I don't know about that," blushed Carrie.

There was a creak in the hallway and the forbidding, austere frame of Netta filled the doorway to the kitchen.

"Why Carrie, what a surprise," her aunt attempted a smile, which looked more like the grinning maw of a shark about to attack its prey.

"Aunty Netta," replied Carrie curtly. "I won't keep you. I just popped in on my way to the station, to say hello."

"Nonsense, you must have a cup of tea and a Welsh cake. Netta, put the kettle on the range," ordered Mam-gu.

Netta attempted to hide the scowl that was ready to break out and bit back the acid retort craving to burst from her lips.

"So, nursing full time then, are you?" questioned Netta.

"Yes, in Birmingham. It's an amazing city. I'm learning all the time. Can't get enough."

"Good for you. I'm glad you've found your niche."

More pleasantries passed between them and the subtle undertone of hostility was not apparently obvious but when little Jake began to wail, Netta thankfully took leave of her niece and left her mother and Carrie together.

Carrie pointed at the hat bases littering the table and her grandmother explained about Netta's millinery business.

"So, Netta is staying then?"

"It looks like it. She has me involved in the business and I'm almost in hock for the materials, but I have to say, I think it is working well for her. Everyone deserves a second chance, don't you think?"

Carrie smiled and shook her spangled curls. "Yes, indeed. Well, Mam-gu look after yourself and I'll see you next time I'm home. Say hello to Aunty Gwenny for me."

"That I will."

Grandmother and granddaughter hugged and Carrie left and climbed back into the waiting cart.

"Well?" questioned Ernie, "What did you learn?"

"Netta's staying. She's started her own millinery business."

"Hmm, I wouldn't trust her no more than I would to trudge across a field gone wild and not see a nettle."

"What are you thinking?"

"She's up to something. I'm sure."

"Well, I'm trusting you to see that no harm comes to us or our farms and land. You'll keep me informed?"

"Aye. I will."

Ernie clicked to Senator and the old horse clip clopped off toward the station.

The sky turned that rosy colour, which threatened more snow giving credence to the old saying that if snow stays on the ground it's waiting for more. Ernie and Carrie's breath streamed like smoke in the cold frosty air. Senator's breathing made him appear like an angry warrior horse as warm vapour steamed from his nostrils like a marauding stallion.

"Looks like you're getting back just in time. It's been threatening more snow for some time and we've escaped lightly. I reckon with the remnants of the last snowfall lurking in the hedgerows that it'll be more than a dusting tonight. We could have a couple of feet."

"Well, as long as I get back safe. I don't care."

"You will. You have a bright future ahead of you. There, it's said and you take note. All the best laid plans can fall to disarray."

"Whatever do you mean, Ernie?"

"Nothing to worry about. A star student nurse you'll be. I promise you that. And happiness will envelop you. Just worry about the snake in the grass and don't let it strike."

"You talk in riddles sometimes, Ernie Trubshawe. I can't fathom you out."

"Nor will you have to. Justice will prevail. I'll say no more. When the saddle's on the horse, all will be revealed."

And try as Carrie might she could prise no more information from her trusted friend. They soon reached the station and the cold icy blasts of wind that ferreted its way through their clothes meant little time was wasted on the platform.

Ernie's face glowed red and his nose was almost ready to sprout a dewdrop had Carrie not passed him her handkerchief. She hugged Ernie before boarding the train. Little was said. The love in the embrace spoke louder than any words. Carrie settled herself in the carriage and blew a kiss to Ernie and the guard waved his flag, the whistle shrilled out and the train chugged out of the station.

Back at Gelli Galed John was preparing to go to Cardiff

to meet the Enrolment Officers. He was nervous and hoped to be able to persuade them that he needed to be at the farm. There was too much at stake. He didn't want to leave Jenny. And he worried about leaving Ernie even with the capable Land Girls who were doing a grand job at Hendre. It was Ernie that offered him a possible solution.

"I've been thinking John. The farm needs you."

"I know that. But what am I to do?"

"I believe if you visit Dr. Rees and get him to swear a statement in your favour."

"I don't understand?"

"Jawch! You've had surgery. They may not accept you if they believe the problem could recur. That, together with running two farms. It's worth a try. The fact you still bare the scars should help."

John accepted the lifeline he'd been offered and fingered his bald patch where the hair was just sprouting again and smiled. Ernie could be right. He resolved to visit the doctor that afternoon.

"Of course, John bach. It would be wrong to leave Jenny and the farm. You are needed at home and the surgery to remove the growth should be enough to exempt you, especially as there is a chance it could come back, although we both hope that won't be the case," said Dr. Rees.

"I don't want folks thinking I'm shirking my duty."

"No one will be any the wiser. Besides, if all else fails you could always claim to be a conscientious objector."

"I don't think so. I'll go with your letter."

"And I'll write it now."

Dr. Rees picked up pen and paper and drafted a letter detailing John's surgery and prognosis. He sealed the envelope and shook John's hand.

"Let me know what happens."

"I will." John bade the good doctor goodbye and returned to Gelli Galed. He patted his pocket, housing the missive, almost as a form of good luck. He would be leaving for his enrolment meeting the following day.

Netta clambered aboard the bus that would take her to the North of the country, to Anglesey. Jake was wrapped up tightly and clasped around her body in a shawl. She carried a small overnight bag with various papers taken from Jacky's belongings. She hoped the trip would be fruitful and clear up the mystery of Jacky's missing money. Her mother believed she was on an errand of mercy visiting a sick friend. Netta didn't want anyone to know the reasons or truth behind her journey.

The bus pulled out of the coach station and began its winding journey to North Wales. Netta was unable to resist looking at the photographs that Jacky had kept, showing him sitting with a young attractive woman standing at his side holding a small baby. She studied the birth certificate in her possession in the name of John Maitland. Could this be Jacky's real name? No wonder no family had come forward at the news of his death. Who would equate Jacky Ebron with John Maitland? In some way, she hoped she was wrong but, then she also knew it may be the key to further rewards, especially if the building societies checked out and there were accounts in his or John Maitland's name. But she needed to prove her rights to ownership. Jake might possibly be key to that and there maybe some more work for Mr. Phillips.

It was a bleak day in Anglesey. No one could see where the sky ended and the clouds began. Everything was washed in grey. It was beginning to get dark and Netta needed to find somewhere to stay. Somewhere that would take her and little Jake. She stepped off the bus and waited to retrieve her bag as it began to drizzle with rain. Anglesey seemed to reflect her mood and the hopelessness she felt. Netta knew she'd have to snap out of this depression if she was to achieve her aims. She picked up her bag and walked toward the taxi rank studying the miserable buildings in the oppressive gloom and shivered in the fading light.

Netta took a cab to a small guesthouse, Windy Ridge, close to the town but on the road that led toward the wild and rugged cliffside. Mrs. James, the landlady was more than happy to take Netta and the baby, especially as Netta was sporting a wedding ring. She even offered to baby-sit if Netta needed to attend to business. Netta smiled graciously and accepted. She needed time alone tomorrow and Mrs. James would help her perfectly. Netta began to spin her web of deceit and beguiled Mrs. James with her own brand of flattery. "It is so kind of you. Being widowed so young and with a small infant I sometimes am in despair."

Mrs. James had a catch in her voice that made her sound as if she needed to clear her throat and she was more than sympathetic to Netta, "I quite understand." She clicked her tongue disapprovingly, "People can be cruel. I should know. I lost my Hywell two years ago and since then those who were my women friends have avoided me believing I would try to steal their husbands. I'm no scarlet woman, but insecurities in these hard times can make folk do strange things. Anything I can do to help. I will."

"Why, thank you. My husband, Penry, died in a mining accident when I was pregnant with little Jake. It was a shock to us all and I nearly lost the baby because of it. He had an estranged brother from Anglesey. I was hoping to make his acquaintance as well as sorting out some of his financial affairs that he left behind."

"Let me see, I can't promise, but I know a few people in the town, what was his brother's name?"

"Maitland, John Maitland."

"Never? If it's the same John Maitland you'll not be in luck."

Netta pretended to look disappointed, "And to think I've come all this way..."

"Never knew John had a brother. He left to look for work, was prepared to walk onto London if need be. You should speak with his wife, Sarah. Left her alone he did. He sent money home regularly for her and young Owen. Then the money stopped and no one knew why."

"Does she live close to here?"

"Why, yes. That's how I know her. At Pleasant View, she is, in Chapel Road. It's just around the corner. Is there anything else you need to know?"

"Thank you. You've been very helpful, if I think of anything..."

"Don't be afraid to ask. Now, what are you doing for supper tonight?"

CHAPTER TWENTY-SEVEN

Learning curves

Dudley Road Hospital was busier than ever when Carrie returned to duty. Pemb and Carrie had barely any time to catch up on their news. Illness had struck many of the hospital staff and nurses were hard pressed, many working far longer hours than they should.

Exams were also looming and the time sped away from them.

Carrie was rushing down the corridor past the operating theatre. A dreadful smell pervaded the air and Dr. Challacombe peered out through the door and spotted Carrie. "Nurse, over here."

"I'm late for duty."

"This won't take a minute. Please."

Carrie briskly walked across, "What is it?"

"Close your eyes and hold out your hands."

"No. Why?"

"Just do it."

Reluctantly, Carrie tentatively held out her hands with her eyes closed. She felt something warm and slippery being placed on her palms.

"Right, now open your eyes."

Carrie did so and saw that the doctor had placed a freshly removed lung into her cupped grasp.

"You want to specialise in Chest. Tell me, where is the growth?"

Carrie peered at the unhealthy organ in her hand. "You've got to be joking. It's pitted with calcification and tumours."

"Let that be a lesson to you. This is the lung of a smoker."

"And that's the terrible smell?"

"It is. You shouldn't smoke."

"I don't," Carrie protested.

"Then don't start." Dr. Challacombe removed the lung from Carrie's grasp and disappeared back into the operating theatre.

Carrie dived into the nearest toilet and scrubbed her hands to rid herself of the feel of the lung and the blood that covered her palms. Seeing that diseased respiratory organ was enough to put anyone off smoking for life. She shuddered, then noticed the time and raced off for Men's Surgical.

Netta had left young Jake with Mrs. James and she walked down the street to Chapel Road. She found the neat terraced house called 'Pleasant View'. She noticed the polished brass letterbox and scrubbed front door step and taking a deep breath forced herself to smile as she knocked on the door with its brass lion head door knocker.

Netta was rewarded with the sound of energetic footsteps approaching. The door opened. A comely young woman, many years younger than Netta opened the door. She was slim and attractive with dark curling hair. "Yes?"

"Sorry to disturb you. Are you Mrs. Maitland? Mrs. John Maitland?"

A catch entered her voice and she said almost too eagerly, "Yes, have you news of him?"

"Not exactly. I think he may have duped us both. May I come in?"

Sarah's face became ghostlike and haunted. She bit her lip and Netta entered. As she walked into the cosy house she took in the neat furnishings and clean décor.

Sarah showed Netta into the parlour and invited her to sit, "You have news of Jacky?"

"You called him Jacky too?"

"Why yes, he always preferred it to John. What is this all about?"

"It's difficult. I don't really know where to begin," murmured Netta. "I need to know were you legally married?"

Sarah flushed, "We lived together as man and wife. Everyone thought we were married and we were going to go out of town and get wed once he found solid work. He always wore a wedding ring."

Netta pulled the ring from her pocket, "This one?"

"Yes, how did you come by this?"

"I'll explain that later. You must have been very young... did you have a child?"

Sarah's eyes welled up, "I was only sixteen when I met him. I was living in Cwm then. Jacky was working in Betwys. When I became pregnant, my parents wanted nothing to do with me and we came here to Anglesey. To start afresh he said and have no questions asked. Why? Who are you?"

"I'm Jacky's wife."

Sarah looked stunned and her face crumpled into tears.

Netta moved across to the weeping woman and took her in her arms and held her until her sobs subsided.

"I'm afraid he wasn't honest with you or me. Did you say you had a child?"

Sarah nodded, "A boy, we called him Anthony."

"Where is he now?"

Sarah began crying again, "He contracted Meningitis a year after Jacky left. We lost him."

Netta's eyes gleamed with pleasure at the news. "How terrible. How have you managed?"

"To begin with, he sent money home regularly with a short note. I've kept them all and then suddenly they just stopped. I didn't know what to think. I suppose stupidly, I hoped he'd come back."

"Sounds like Jacky. He came to work for my brother and we married. I have a son, Jake. I left him at my lodgings as the information regarding you has only just come to light. I found these in his drawer." Netta took out the photo and birth certificate. Sarah took them and studied them.

"We had the photo taken just before he left. I can't believe he'd do this to me. Where is he now?"

"Gone. I don't know where. I thought maybe he had returned to you. But that was wrong. He's probably wooing some other poor woman and fooling her as he did us. Have you not thought of going home? You have no child now. You are single. I'm sure your parents would be pleased to see you."

Sarah was puzzled by the change of tack. "I don't understand..."

"The thing is, Sarah, may I call you Sarah?" Sarah acquiesced with a nod, "The thing is, he swindled my brother's family out of a large sum of money and things are difficult at home and with an extra mouth to feed..."

Sarah hung her head. "I know Jacky wasn't always honest in his dealings with folk. That's why he went looking for work out of the area. Yes, he's sent me money but not any huge amount. Sorry."

"No, no. It was just a faint hope."

"He did tell me he'd money put by but I don't know where."

"Not to worry. I'm sorry to have brought you such bad news."

"It's all right. I haven't seen him in such a long time. I even thought he could have joined up."

Netta cleared her throat, "This house, is it...?"

"Rented."

"Ah."

"Do you know, maybe you're right. Maybe, it is time to go home, put things in order. If they don't want me I can always come back."

"I think that's wise and I'm sure your family will welcome you. Also, when trying to find you I didn't want your name besmirched and told my landlady that I was married to Jacky's estranged brother. No one will know what has transpired between us."

Sarah half smiled her gratitude, "Thank you. Do you want some tea or anything?"

"No, no. I'll be getting back. I suggest you start packing. Get yourself home to Cwm."

Sarah nodded quietly. She rose from her seat. Netta stood up and walked back along the passage to the front door trying desperately to stop the smile spreading across her face.

Although the day was bleak to Netta it seemed as if the sun had broken through the clouds and was shining its golden light on her.

Netta stepped out revitalised.

Sarah bid her goodbye and closed the door disappearing inside full of despair. But, she also had a lifeline and she marched upstairs determinedly and took down a case from off the top of the wardrobe. Perhaps, it *was* time to go home.

Netta briskly walked into the town. She opened the notebook written in Jacky's hand, with references to places and numbers. There was a building society agent in the town. For the solicitor Elwin Jones, she would have to travel to Bangor. She couldn't believe her luck that the Police had never opened the bedroll to find these items or if they did they did not realise the significance of them. She glanced at her watch. She had an hour left before retrieving little Jake and moving on. She would put it to good use.

John stood before the enrolment board. The panel of four passed the forms and Dr. Rees' letter around. Eventually, the Chief Enrolment Officer, Captain Reginald Dykes looked up. He addressed his board, "We are in agreement Gentlemen?" The panel assented and Captain Dykes addressed John, "In view of the letter from your G.P. and," he indicated John's head, "the very obvious surgery and its implications; also, the needs of your farm, the panel has agreed that you will not be suitable to enlist although, because of your willingness to fight for your country," he paused and John's heart began to pound, "We reserve the right to contact you again should we need good men and true. That's if this wretched war drags on. But for now Mr. Llewellyn you are free to go."

John turned smartly on his heel, military style, and walked out. His heart was thumping in excitement. He could hardly wait to return home and tell Jenny.

New Year had come and gone. Carrie couldn't believe how quickly the days turned into weeks and weeks became months. She would have plenty of anecdotes to regale the family with as well as her nursing friends in the hospital. Only the other week she had been on night duty, doing her rounds; it was eerie on the ward, deathly quiet. The hospital was short staffed and she was alone. She had swapped duty with Pemb who wanted to see Lloyd and so Carrie had taken over Pemb's night shift on Women's Surgical.

A strange unearthly cry came from one of the beds. Carrie froze. She picked up her torch and began to pace around the ward shining her torch discretely on the occupant of each bed. All seemed to be sleeping soundly. Carrie tiptoed quietly to the last bed and another strangely frightening groan was heard. Carrie shone the light onto the bed but there was no one there. She directed the beam to the side of the bed next to the locker and tried to stifle the scream that readily rose to her lips. The female patient had slipped out of the bed onto the floor and looked utterly grotesque, her mouth was agape revealing toothless gums and her head was as bald as a baby's bottom. The woman's wig had flopped onto her chest like some attacking giant rodent ready to gnaw at her breast. Carrie hesitated momentarily before she hastened to the woman's aid and hauled her up, and back into her bed. Carrie was silently cursing, thinking that Pemb could have warned her that this patient had no hair. The sight of that ethereal, pale face had shocked her as much as if she had seen a ghost. Later, however, she laughed about it but at the time she was very scared.

Pemb and Lloyd's relationship was progressing well. It seems Lloyd's mother had given the stamp of approval to Pemb and the couple spent every spare moment together but they always included Carrie in whatever they did. That is, if she wanted to accompany them, which for obvious reasons she didn't. But, sometimes, when she felt it was right she would join them. In fact, when they were short of cash they all would get onboard a number eleven outer circle bus and ride around the whole circuit to where they had alighted.

They would take some pop and fruit and sit upstairs on the back seat. The bus conductors never seemed to mind, as long as they took their orange peel and apple cores home. They could stay warm and enjoy the city lights as they travelled around. They were doing just that, when Pemb started to reminisce about events at Christmas. Pemb began giggling.

"What's so funny?" queried Carrie.

"I was just thinking. Lloyd, remember the car?" This comment set Lloyd grinning. "Tell Carrie, you tell it better than me."

"I don't know about that," replied Lloyd.

"Well, one of you tell me, please," admonished Carrie.

Pemb and Lloyd burst into giggles. Carrie joined in even though she didn't know what they were laughing about. It was a while before Lloyd could speak without spluttering into giggles again. "Pemb and me, we don't have much money, as you know. We have to make our own fun. Like now, riding round on the bus. We can manage the pictures sometimes and that's a luxury. Well, we were out walking in the village and it was bitterly cold. Pemb's little nose was red, just like Rudolph."

"Get on," laughed Pemb.

"Well, we passed a big house, a real fancy one and it had a garage, with a big car and the door was open. We didn't see the harm so we snuck inside the garage. We didn't risk getting in the car."

"Good job too," interjected Pemb.

"Who's telling this story?" reminded Lloyd good-naturedly.

"Sorry, go on."

"We got out of the icy wind in the garage but had nowhere to sit so we sat on the running board on the passenger side. Just enough room for our two bots."

"Yes?" encouraged Carrie.

"Well, there we were all cuddled up when someone comes into the garage from the house. We froze and kept as quiet as a whisper when to our horror, whoever it was got into the car and started it up. We didn't dare move. Then, the car reversed out of the garage and down the drive with us still sitting there feet up in the air as if we were on a swing."

"Then, what happened?"

"We had to jump off so as not to be seen, and both landed in the slush on our bottoms. That'll teach us!"

"Ruined my coat!"

"You and your coats," chuckled Lloyd.

"I've spoiled two – the other time was when we went into

a shed on an allotment and sat on some sacks. You were covered in cement dust and me in fertiliser. We looked like a pair of tramps."

They laughed again just as the bus conductor called out, "Terminus."

It was time to get off the bus and walk back to the Nurses' Home. The three friends tucked their arms in each other's with Lloyd in the middle and marched on.

Carrie mused happily to herself that she had been right about them both and was delighted to see her friends so happy together. She prayed in her heart that she, too would be as lucky, but there was an anxious churning in her stomach that made her feel ill with trepidation that something bad was going to happen. She remonstrated with herself, 'Duw, girl. You're getting like Ernie." But try as she might she couldn't shake off the feeling of malaise stirring inside her.

Elizabeth Revill

CHAPTER TWENTY-EIGHT

New life

At Hendre, John was pacing the kitchen in a frenzy. "Jawch man if there were carpet in this kitchen it would all be worn through by now," advised Ernie. "There's nothing you can do. Sit down, have a cup of tea and wait. Pacing's going to make little difference to Jenny now. Dr. Rees is with her and the midwife."

John tried to settle in the chair as Ernie suggested but two seconds later he was up and pacing again.

"You are making me giddy to look at you. If you can't sit still go outside and do something useful to take your mind off it."

A pitiful wail escaped from upstairs. Ernie looked at John's face full of concern. "Go on, off with you. I'll call you if something happens."

John looked anxiously at Ernie, "The last time this happened it was my Mam and she died," murmured John blinking back the tears.

"Well, this isn't your Mam and nothing is going to happen to Jenny or the baby. You'd better start thinking of names, and if you want something to do, go and fetch Jenny's Mam from the village."

Another terrible scream ripped out. John went to the door. "I'll be outside. Call me."

John fled from the house followed by Bonnie who was looking sturdier and growing quickly. She scampered along beside him jumping up every few steps wanting to be petted and fussed.

Dr. Rees stood in attendance sympathetically. Jenny groaned as the pains of Hell were upon her. The midwife, Bethan Owen, called "Doctor, the baby's head. It's crowning."

"I'll take it from here. Another push, Jenny."

"I can't, I'm tired, please," she groaned as another contraction hit.

"Push, Jenny. Push! One last push and the worst is over. The shoulders will be through. Come on!" encouraged Bethan.

Jenny grunted and then with a final squeal the baby slipped out slippery and wet.

Its lusty cry reverberated around the bedroom and Jenny burst into tears.

201

"It's a girl, a beautiful little girl. Jenny you have a daughter," beamed Dr. Rees.

"John. I want John," murmured Jenny.

"I'll call him," offered Bethan.

Dr. Rees cleaned the baby and wrapped her up, before giving her to Jenny.

"Thank you, and Bethan thank you for all your kindness."

Bethan flushed with pleasure. She opened the pine door and called down the stairs, "It's all over, Jenny's asking for her husband."

"Jawch!" exclaimed Ernie poking his head up the stairwell. "I'll get him."

Ernie ran out into the yard, skidding and sliding on the puddles in the yard, "John! John, it's here!"

John turned from playing with Bonnie. His face creased into a huge grin.

"Hurry up! Jenny's asking for you."

John hurried across the yard. Bonnie thinking it was a new game scampered beside him almost tripping him up.

"What? What is it?" called John.

"Why, it's a baby, a little baby."

"You can be so twp at times Ernie. What sex?"

"Oh, I don't know."

John flew past Ernie who had stopped stock still, before gathering his wits and chasing after John. One of his waistcoat buttons burst off like a tiddly-wink and spun in the air before landing in a muddy puddle. "Aw, Duw," he muttered as he bent to retrieve it.

John scurried indoors and sprinted up the twisting stairs. He pushed open the pine door and pulled off his flat cap and stared in dumb amazement.

Jenny lay propped up on pillows holding a tiny baby at her breast with a shock of gold red hair. Bethan was sponging down Jenny's forehead as Dr. Rees washed his hands. He turned and smiled at John. "You have a healthy daughter, seven pounds two ounces. What are you going to call her?"

Jenny looked at the midwife and smiled, "Bethan. We're going to call her Bethan."

John's face creased in a smile and he dashed to his wife's side and took her hand and kissed it. "Thank you, my lovely. Oh thank you." John laughed and glanced across at Dr. Rees, "I worried... I thought, you know, I worried..."

"I know," returned Dr. Rees. "You thought of your mother."

John nodded.

"Oh, John," whispered Jenny. "I'm fine. The baby's fine. Bethan's fine. But you..."

"I'm fine too, Jenny, now!"

John knelt at her side, and as his father had sworn some years before, John's words echoed those of Bryn. "By all that's Holy. You and Bethan are the most important to me now. You and the farm." And his eyes filled with tears of love and emotion. "Wait till we tell Carrie."

"Aunty Carrie," prompted Jenny.

There was a knock at the door and Ernie popped his head round, "Is it all right if I come in?"

Ernie was welcomed in and his cherubic face glowed in delight. "It's a healthy baby you've had and the seal on a loving marriage."

"That's one Hell of a prediction, Ernie," smiled John.

"Not from Hell though, I hope. More heaven based," chortled Ernie.

There was a huge kerfuffle and squawking outside. Ernie peered out into the yard to see Bonnie investigating the chickens and being chased by an irate cockerel who pecked at her.

Ernie scooted to the door, "It's off I'll go to rescue her or we'll be having a blind sheep dog." He bolted out of the door leaving the others laughing after him.

Bethan put on her coat, "I'll be round again tomorrow. You need to rest now."

"I'll second that," affirmed Dr. Rees. "She needs a nice cup of tea, plenty of fluids and rest. And I'll be back tomorrow afternoon."

Carrie was anxious to visit home and meet Jenny and John's new arrival; the baby girl they had decided to call, Bethan. It was right that John had been given a reprieve from his call up. John had huge responsibilities organising work at both Hendre and Gelli Galed. Ernie attended to the stock, and John together with Sam Jefferies organised the Land Girls' work force. Jenny's time would now be taken with the baby. Carrie couldn't wait to see her new niece.

The war had not had a huge effect on life in Britain but all that was to change with a concerted bombing programme or Blitzkrieg by the Germans on major cities, including Coventry, Plymouth, Birmingham and more alarmingly, London. Ernie's prophetic words were to come ringing home.

CHAPTER TWENTY-NINE

Home visit

Carrie was excited about returning home. She and Pemb had managed to get four days off. Pemb was visiting her extensive family and taking Lloyd to meet her parents. Carrie was hoping to become acquainted with her baby niece and catch up on all the village news.

She scrutinised the letter in front of her and read it again as the train chugged on, puffing through dusty towns and lush green countryside. Megan was on leave for a week and she hoped that Carrie would find time to meet up. Megan's outpouring radiated love for Thomas. Carrie hoped that this relationship would last and that Tom's heart would not be broken.

Carrie stuffed the letter back into her bag and took out another letter written in the masculine but elegant handwriting of Michael Lawrence. Many words had been blacked out in the interests of National Security but Carrie understood that Michael had led a number of missions; all successful, and more dangerous assignments were approaching. It was apparent to Carrie that Michael was in the front line of duty and she feared for his safety.

The train pulled into Abergavenny, where people milled on platforms changing trains. Carrie was amongst them. She boarded her connection to Neath and settled in a vacant carriage that wasn't empty for long.

Two able seamen smiled at her as they entered the compartment followed by a handsome man in a beige trench coat and brown fedora trilby hat. He tipped his hat to her. She acknowledged him with a smile.

The young sailors laughed and joked and took out a pack of cards and invited the other occupants to join them in a game. Carrie politely refused, "Thank you, no. I only know Top of the Bus and Snap, and I'm sure that wouldn't engage your interest." The sailors laughed.

The other gentleman commented, "Top of the bus? I believe that's what we call, Ride the bus."

"I wouldn't know," smiled Carrie.

"I've only heard it called that by a friend of mine, one whom I'm off to visit actually." His tone was cultured and he seemed personable and friendly but Carrie had a prickling of misgiving about the good-looking stranger.

"And where are you headed?" he asked casually.

"Neath," Carrie answered honestly.

"What a coincidence," he beamed, "So am I. We are to be travelling companions. Grainger Mason at your service." He extended his hand, which Carrie reluctantly grasped, "Sorry, I didn't catch your name..."

"That's because I didn't give it," Carrie promptly responded.

Grainger sat back in his seat at this rebuff. Carrie felt guilty at appearing rude and so continued, "Caroline Llewellyn."

Grainger considered for a moment before adding, "No, it can't be. Surely not? You aren't known as Carrie are you?"

Carrie stiffened at the familiarity.

"Only, if so, I have heard so much about you."

"And how pray would that have happened?"

"We have a mutual friend, Megan. Megan Langtree."

"I know no one of that name."

"No, of course. You would know her better as Megan Thomas."

To say Carrie was stunned was an understatement. Now, she would be forced to make small talk with this man until they reached Neath.

Grainger appeared to be open and friendly but there was something about him that reminded her of Jacky. Maybe it was the dazzling smile like a film star or the dark eyes that glittered astutely as if appraising her. If this was the case, then she was being unfairly prejudiced against the man. Carrie tried to swallow her fluttering of anxiety and managed a smile, "Megan was my best friend at school."

"Yes, I know. I have heard about your escapades in the meadow and the hay barn and the famous story of Bull Rock. Why, I feel I know you." He then, added, "Extremely well."

Carrie gave an involuntary shiver. The gushing flattery was so reminiscent of Jacky that she had to struggle to keep her face impassive. Never-the-less Carrie managed to remain polite and the time did pass. She responded as she felt she needed to, but without being effusive. If Grainger noticed a hint of reticence in Carrie's manner he didn't show it.

The young sailors continued to joke and lark around and Carrie had begun to wish that she had accepted the invitation to play cards. She was also beginning to wonder about the relationship between Megan and Grainger and how Thomas fitted into the picture.

"Megan, she's just wonderful isn't she?" asked Grainger.

"We've always got on," answered Carrie in a measured tone, "How is it that you know each other?"

Carrie was treated to an oration about ENSA and their shows. Carrie then realised that Megan had mentioned him but only as a friend. The way Grainger was speaking, it was apparent he wanted something more.

Carrie made a mental note to advise her friend of this in the kindest possible way. Megan needed to be alerted. Carrie was afraid to call it an obsession but that's how it was appearing to her.

The train steamed into Neath and Carrie allowed Grainger to retrieve her bag. They left the sailors still laughing in the carriage and exited to the platform, where Ernie awaited who welcomed her with a huge hug.

"Is there anywhere I can get a taxi?" Grainger asked politely.

"There's a rank just outside the station." Carrie hesitated, "We are going on to Crynant and could give you a ride to the village but I am not sure how you will fare in getting to Bronallt from there."

Ernie studied the young man curiously but said nothing. Grainger nodded, "Not to worry. I'll grab a cab. I may see you again then, at some point."

"You may." Carrie courteously shook hands and Ernie watched.

Grainger picked up his case and with his Trench coat flapping headed for the main doors.

Ernie lifted Carrie's bag and began to walk slowly toward the station café.

"What are you doing? Why aren't we going?"

"We will. I just want to be sure that young man is on his way."

"Why?"

"You have no need to ask, because you felt it too."

Carrie pursed her lips and frowned. It was one thing wondering about the man. It was another having her intuition confirmed.

Ernie scrabbled about in his pocket for some change when he ordered two cups of tea at the café.

"Here, let me get those," insisted Carrie. "I'm better off than you and you can tell me what you sensed about Grainger Mason."

"That his name? Bit grand isn't it?"

"He's an actor."

"Oh yes?" Ernie raised an eyebrow, "And if he's good at it he's doubly dangerous."

"Why do you say that?"

"He'll be able to act his way out of any situation."

"Hmm! And conmen are good actors."

"Exactly. Although, I don't think he intends conning anyone. Deception is more his line."

"Isn't that the same thing?"

"No. I don't think money is at the root of it. You warn Megan. She needs to be wary of him."

Carrie fell silent as she digested this prediction. She changed the subject, "And what of John, Jenny and the baby?"

"I wondered when you'd ask. Let's say, we all have choices. We are masters of our own destiny and once this union was blighted by dark happenings but now it is blessed, as you will no doubt be relieved to hear. They are doing well and looking forward to your visit."

"Well, they won't have long to wait. Ernie, can we go now? I can't wait to see them and little Bonnie."

"Ha! Not so little now. Proper replica of Trix she is. Same gentle temper and quick to learn. You'll see. You'll love her!" Ernie rose from his seat and lifted Carrie's bag. "Come on, now. We should be safe."

They left the station café and walked to the exit. Ernie put his fingers to his lips. Grainger Mason was just getting into a cab.

They paused and watched the cab pull away. Ernie frowned, "That man fills me with an odd feeling. I wonder... Is Megan actually expecting him?"

Carrie walked to the waiting cart deep in thought. Ernie, too, was quiet as the cart rattled along the roads to the village until they began the ascent up the mountain track. Then Ernie broke out into a cheerful whistling.

Carrie turned to him, "I'd forgotten that."

"What?" He stopped whistling.

"You never could hold a tune whether singing, humming or whistling. Duw! It's good to be home."

Carrie's arrival was greeted with great interest by Bonnie. She was now longer limbed and her muzzle more shaped. She had the same freckles on her nose as Trixie. Her coat was longer still retaining some of her baby fluff. She jumped up and gave her the traditional dog welcome of licking her all over her face.

"Not on the lips! Not on the lips," squealed Carrie twisting her mouth to one side to avoid Bonnie's soft, pink tongue. "You're as bad as Trix! She was forever washing my face as if I needed it."

"Liked your soap she did, Trix. Always smelled of honey," smiled Ernie. "Go on with you," laughed Ernie as Carrie squealed again, "You're enjoying it really."

"Enough," giggled Carrie. "Now, I'll have to wash before I meet my new niece."

John and Jenny stood on the porch in readiness, waiting to meet Carrie and Jenny was clutching a small bundle swathed inside a shawl like a sling, in true Welsh tradition.

"Carrie, fach. I can't believe it," grinned John. "Duw, you're so grown up now and so much like mam."

"If that's the case, then I'll take that as a compliment."

Brother and sister eyed each other before hugging. Carrie pulled back and beamed at her brother, "Never mind me. Look at you, a father. Who would have thought it?"

Jenny smiled delightedly and embraced Carrie without squashing the baby.

"Oh, do let me see," pleaded Carrie. She gazed upon the tiny little face with rosebud lips and golden red hair. "Bethan, Bethan Llewellyn. It's a good name. She's got your eyes John, and Jenny's lips. She'll be a little beauty, a heartbreaker when she's older."

"I hope not," mused Jenny. "I can't see John welcoming any man into the house. She's the apple of his eye. Do you want to hold her?"

"Isn't that what aunties are for? Of course I do."

And with much billing and cooing, Jenny relinquished her precious bundle to Carrie and they went inside.

Megan was more than surprised when Grainger arrived at Bronallt. Surprised wasn't the word; she was also somewhat annoyed that he had taken the liberty of turning up on her doorstep with his weekend bag.

"Grainger! This is a surprise..." Her tone attempted to mask her irritation but didn't quite succeed.

"I've come at the wrong time," his manner was apologetic. "If you didn't want me to visit you should have said but you did say that if I was ever around this neck of the woods, to drop by."

Megan didn't remember saying any such thing and why Grainger should be in 'this neck of woods' as he put it, she couldn't fathom.

"Who is it?" called Megan's mother, Nancy.

"It's Grainger from my theatre company, Mam."

"Don't keep him on the doorstep. Invite him in, for goodness sake."

Megan stepped aside to admit Grainger who removed his

hat and smiled beguilingly at Megan's mother, "Why your beautiful daughter must take after you. I can see where she gets her good looks from."

Nancy flushed with pleasure, "Come in, come in and sit down. Megan put the kettle on," she ordered.

Grainger sat with his case and surveyed the room with its elegant mahogany furniture and brocade curtains. The room boasted money, of that he knew with Megan's mother breeding racehorses.

"Duw, what are we thinking? Let me take your coat."

Grainger rose and removed his trench coat. He sat once more on the comfortable moquette chair. He sat in there as if it were made for him.

"Where are you staying, Grainger?"

"I don't know, I haven't thought. Maybe the pub in the village, The Star and Garter, is it?"

"No need to do that. We've plenty of room here. With Gwynfor gone..." There was a slight catch in her voice as she said his name. "You can have Gwynfor's room."

"If you're sure?" It was not asked as a question but as a statement of fact, an acceptance.

"Of course. Can't have Megan's friend staying in the village. What will people think of our hospitality?"

Grainger smiled. He determined to win over Megan's mother. He knew this would help in winning Megan too. There was just the hiccup of Thomas and he was sure he could deal with that as well. In fact, he had already begun...

Megan forced a smile as she entered the room carrying a tea tray. "Grainger, I hope you don't mind but I promised I'd be visiting friends today to see their new baby..."

"That's all right. I can always come with you."

"I'm sure Jenny and John won't mind," interrupted Megan's mother.

"Oh, I don't want to intrude," added Grainger.

"Well, I am also visiting my dearest friend and we will be gossiping like old washer women."

"That must be Carrie Llewellyn, we travelled on the train together," smiled Grainger.

"There you are, he knows Carrie so it won't be a problem," continued Megan's mother.

Megan was uncomfortable and didn't know what to say. She certainly didn't want him present when she saw Carrie.

Grainger noticed her thoughtful expression, "Don't worry about me, Megan. I know what it's like when friends get together. I'll settle in and get to know your mother a little better. Next time, you visit her I'll tag along. After all you didn't expect me."

Megan's relief was obvious. She practically gushed, "That's great. Yes, next time, come with me next time. Carrie and I have so much to talk about and you'll be so bored."

Nancy looked at her daughter but didn't pass judgement but she could tell that something was amiss. "Well, Grainger let me take you to your room and you can tell me all about your shows and future bookings. This way." She rose and beckoned Grainger to follow her.

Megan stopped her mother, "Mam, I'll be going now. I'll see you all later."

"Don't be late. Remember, we have a guest."

Grainger looked back at Megan and winked cheekily before following Megan's mother out of the door and up the stairs.

Megan grabbed the opportunity before anyone had a chance to change their minds and fled from the house. She saddled Cobalt and kicked her heels and galloped off toward Hendre and Gelli Galed.

"Megan!" exclaimed Carrie and hugged her friend, as she greeted her on the porch. Carrie peered over Megan's shoulder, "Are you on your own?"

"Yes, why?"

"Thought you may have had Grainger in tow."

"That man! He turned up on my doorstep and Mam has invited him to stay. Not what I wanted."

"I thought you'd asked him."

"No, he just arrived out of the blue. It's hard to be rude to him. I have to work with him; we're in the same touring company."

"Then if I were you I'd speak to the powers that be and try and change," interrupted Ernie who had walked up and heard the exchange.

"Why Ernie? What do you know?" questioned Megan suspiciously.

"Nothing. Nothing at all. It's just a feeling and a feeling Carrie shares."

"Is that right?" asked Megan as she pulled away from her friend's embrace.

"It's not for me to say," Carrie replied.

"We've been friends long enough. Say whatever you want."

"Well, he seems personable enough," began Carrie.

"That's what I thought too, when I first met him... but?" Megan pressed Carrie.

"I don't know. Perhaps I'm being uncharitable but there were things about him. Reminded me of Jacky. I feel the young man is not what he appears to be."

"And I'll go further than that," added Ernie, "I wouldn't trust him. There's deception and illusion all around him. He's someone of whom you need to be wary. And more worryingly, he's very taken with you."

"And don't I know it? I've been evading his arms since we started touring. There's no man for me except Thomas. Grainger knows that and yet he still continues to push it."

"Hmm, careful he doesn't put between you."

"Tell me Ernie, what do you know?"

"Just be careful, Megan fach. Carrie's right. The man is not all he seems."

Megan shivered, "Never mind all that. Come Carrie, I want to hear all your news, and of course, to see Jenny and John's new baby. I hear they've called her Bethan?" Megan tucked her arm in her friends and the two went inside the house, followed by Ernie.

Jenny was sitting nursing little Bethan. Her face was flushed but there was a serenity about her that made Carrie's heart burst with pride.

"We have a visitor. Megan's come to see Bethan."

Jenny smiled and offered, "Would you like to hold her Megan."

"No, not me, I'd be afraid of dropping her on her head. I'll just look and enjoy her, thank you. Anyway, she's sleeping fast. Don't want to wake her."

"She won't break. Babies are tougher than you think."

"If I have any they'd better be born with a miner's helmet on. I'm such a clot when it comes to things like this."

"Go on with you." Jenny rose and disentangled herself from her shawl and passed the sleeping baby to Megan.

Megan's face filled with delight and she began making soothing noises to Bethan, who opened her eyes at the movement. She soon closed them again and Megan beamed in pleasure. "She's so adorable. You're a lucky woman, Jenny."

"You'll be a mother yourself one day," continued Jenny.

"Me? I've not got a maternal bone in my body," rejoined Megan.

"You'll be surprised, when it's your own it's so very different," laughed Jenny.

"I'm sure Thomas will think differently," added Carrie.

"Thomas! I've a bone to pick with him, next time I see him," remonstrated Megan. "Do you know, he used to write every week, I haven't heard from him in over a month. It's not like him. I mean; I know he's on active duty but he's always found time to write."

"How do you know he hasn't?" queried Ernie.

"Because I haven't received any letters."

"That doesn't mean he didn't write them," said Ernie pointedly. "Be careful of your facts before you judge him."

"What are you implying, Ernie?" asked Megan quizzically. "Just what are you suggesting?"

"I'm just saying if you want the relationship to continue – keep writing to him and post the letters yourself."

"That's the problem. I don't always know where he is. He moves around a lot."

"Never mind. Your letters *will* reach him eventually and be sure to tell him you haven't received his."

Megan turned to Carrie, "Is he always as annoying as this?"

"This is quite mild for him. He's the master when it comes to riddles," laughed Carrie.

At that moment Bethan decided to exercise her lungs. Her little face crumpled up, turned red and her rosebud mouth opened into a huge 'O'. The squeal was enough to set Jenny's milk running and she quickly retrieved her squalling baby and disappeared up the stairs unbuttoning her blouse as she went.

John laughed, "Do you know, I never thought I'd say it but when I see Jenny and our baby feeding, I love it. I just absolutely love it. It makes me fill with... I don't know, what's the word?"

"Love," everyone chorused.

"Yes, love." John smiled, "now if you'll excuse me. I must get out. I have some sheep ready to lamb and don't want any mistakes there. You know, I swear the first thing on a lamb's mind when it's born, is to die. I have to force it to the teat and it struggles and stretches its feet, pushing away, as if it's the last thing it wants to do."

"Ah, but once attached it's beautiful to see," added Ernie. "I'll leave you girls to chat. I dare say you've a Pandora's box of gossip to share."

"Without the ill effects I hope, Ernie," grinned Carrie.

"Jawch! You know what I mean," chortled Ernie as he waved his hand and pulled his beret down on his head and left.

"And I must be off too. I'll take Bonnie with me and see

you both later. Megan. Carrie." John touched his forelock politely and followed Ernie out from the kitchen.

Carrie pulled her friend Megan to a seat and sat with her at the table.

"Come, tell me all your news and about Thomas."

"Well, things seemed to be going well."

"And? Come on don't clam up now," urged Carrie.

"After we, well... sorted things out. I heard from him regularly and I wrote to him telling him every venue we played just in case he could be there. Although, I know that's unlikely. But the letters just stopped. I don't know what's happened or even if he's okay." Megan's eyes suddenly filled up, "Oh, Carrie, what if he's dead?"

"No, no. He's not dead. We would have heard. It's something else..."

"What? What could it be?"

Carrie spoke really slowly and chose her words carefully, "How do you receive your mail?"

"The Stage Manager collects it from the Post Office. We have a special P.O. Box number."

"Does he deliver the letters?"

"He used to."

"What happens now?"

Megan looks nonplussed, "Usually Grainger collects it and passes it out."

"Hm."

"What are you getting at?"

"Next time, I suggest you go with him. Or offer to take your turn."

"You don't think...?"

"I don't know. But I don't believe Mr. Grainger Mason is all he seems and he does have a thing for you."

"You think he's fielding my letters from Tom?"

Carrie remained silent.

"You do!"

There was a pause and Megan quietly fumed her anger building, "Wait till I see him. He just turns up at the farm and..."

"Don't say anything."

"What? Why?"

"Don't give him any warning. If I were you I would carry on as if nothing had happened. Next time mail arrives suggest going with him. If he makes excuses why you shouldn't. Give in, but follow him discretely... Then when you turn up if he has nothing to hide, no harm has been done." Carrie shrugs, "Doesn't that make sense?"

Megan nodded thoughtfully, "You know I will do that and maybe more..."

"What are you suggesting?"

"I think I am going to apply to transfer to another ENSA company. Get away from him completely. He really is starting to worry me."

"That may not be a bad idea, but keep it quiet. I don't think it would help if he found out."

Megan shook her burnished, conker coloured tresses assertively, "That man, you know I agree with you, something isn't right. But, that's enough about Mr. Grainger Mason. What about you? Tell me what has been happening to you."

Carrie chuckled and began to recount anecdotes and events from her time spent at the Maternity Unit and the Birmingham hospital. They were soon giggling uncontrollably like a sack full of sisters on their way to a school dance. Megan took a deep breath and tried to bring some calm to the conversation.

"So, Pemb has your student friend, Lloyd, in tow. Does she make a habit of that?"

"No. It wasn't like that. It was my idea. I pushed them together."

"Why?" quizzed Megan. "There's something you're not telling me," she accused.

Carrie hesitated, "I'm not sure if I should say this..."

"Go on," urged Megan, "You can't stop now."

Carrie rolled her eyes heavenward; Megan was always very good at winkling out information and Carrie decided she'd have no peace until she told her friend about her friendship with Michael Lawrence. But it came with a warning, "Don't you dare say anything to anyone. It's just friends, we are. I don't know if anything will come of it."

"Come on, Carrie, after all that's happened you need to be straight with the man."

"He knows. I think."

"Don't let him slip away. You must let him know how you feel. Don't make the same mistake I did."

"I won't. I haven't heard from him in a while. I hope he is all right," and a worried frown impressed itself on Carrie's sweet face. "I just have this awful feeling, a sinking in the pit of my stomach."

Elizabeth Revill

CHAPTER THIRTY

Thunder in the Skies

Michael Lawrence strode out onto the runway and glanced up at the bruised sky, threatening more unsettled weather. The clouds rolled and churned. A rumble of thunder was heard in the distance.

A young aircraftman came running out, "Wing Commander Lawrence! Sir!"

Michael looked up enquiringly. The young recruit puffed up, "A letter, Sir. Postmarked Birmingham."

"Thank you, Parfit." Michael took the envelope and studied the handwriting. He smiled as he recognised Carrie's flowing round hand and placed it in his inside pocket, which he patted with pleasure. He would read it later.

Michael walked back toward the main building on the runway and made his way inside. He ran up the steps and into the briefing room where six young airmen waited for their orders.

They jumped to attention and saluted as Michael entered.

"At ease, gentlemen."

The men visibly relaxed but remained alert. Michael's face remained gravely serious.

"We've had some major successes but mustn't become complacent. This mission is the toughest yet." He glanced at his watch, "We have been assigned to destroy German ground troops and protect Luxembourg where columns of Germans are on the offensive. They are gaining ground in France, Belgium, Poland, and Holland. Their sustained attack must be stopped. They are out to conquer Europe. We must not let that happen. We, together, with Bomber Command are sending thirty-two planes to stop them where they stand."

Michael stepped up to a blackboard and grabbed a piece of chalk quickly drawing a flight plan and detailing their formation for the tactical manoeuvre to arrest this two pronged attack by the Third Reich.

"What time, Sir?" asked a fresh faced airman known as Dobby.

"Eleven hundred hours. That gives you two hours to prepare and get any messages home that you need to."

"Will you be there, Sir?" questioned another, called Burton.

215

"Aren't I always? When you fly, I fly. Dismissed."

The airmen left in a flurry of excitement and Michael sat behind the desk to take a moment to read Carrie's letter and attempt a reply. He would summon one of his men to take it to the mail before they left. He knew the letter would be censored and struggled to write something that made sense and would be considered safe. He also knew, as he did each time before a mission that he might not come back.

Netta now back in Neath sat opposite Mr. Phillips and passed him Jacky's birth certificate and other papers. "So you see, as I explained, Jacky deposited and sent the first payment from Michael Lawrence into a Building Society in Bangor. I need to prove my entitlement to this, especially as Jake is Jacky's son. Can you help? You will be well paid."

"Have you registered the child? And listed Jacky as the father?"

"Yes, but there lies the problem. His real name was Maitland. Is there anything you can do?"

"Hmm... Leave it with me and I'll get back to you."

"The Llewellyns won't be able to claim it will they?"

"Do they know about it?"

"No, of course not."

"Then, we may be able to do something. I have an idea."

"But..."

"Miss Llewellyn, let me see what I can achieve. You will be hearing from me." Mr. Phillips rose and extended his hand, which Netta took as she stood up and faced him.

She gave him a warning, "Remember, the knowledge I have of the deals that you made with Jacky could be very damaging if they came to light."

"I am sure we understand each other and that will not be necessary. Good day, Miss Llewellyn."

Netta managed a smile with pursed lips and stiff backed, glided out from the office.

Mr. Phillips sat down. Netta Llewellyn was a difficult woman to shake off but this new evidence could well prove useful and profitable. He walked to his shelf of files and removed one titled, Jacky Ebron. With a stroke of his pen he added a hyphen and the name Maitland and began to study the folder contents.

Michael flew in formation with four other planes at twenty thousand feet. Five thousand feet above them eight spitfires grouped in pairs covered the twenty-four Hurricanes as they crossed the English Channel on route to Luxembourg.

A British Warship had been spotted that was under attack from the Luftwaffe and Michael gave the order to defend the battleship whose aircraft guns were valiantly firing at the enemy aeroplanes. He issued the order to engage before they could proceed onto their mission.

The Germans surprised by the appearance of fighter-bombers manoeuvred from their position of attack, peeled off one by one and engaged with the Hurricanes. The unscheduled air battle was to prove both successful and costly. The six German aircraft were out numbered but hungry for blood. All too soon, Parfit's Hurricane was damaged; holes in the fuselage, a broken wing and one engine on fire it dived into a droning spiral and crashed into the sea. Parfit managed to eject but Michael was sad to see the young airman fired on and slump in his parachute. There was no doubt about it; the young man was dead.

Michael had no time to ponder on this as a Messerschmitt homed in on him and started firing. Michael dodged and turned, dived and soared in a ballet of aerobatics trying to shake off his attacker.

Two wing men came to his aid but not before a bullet found its mark and fractured his fuel tank. Fortunately, it didn't ignite, but fuel began to drip.

The Messerschmitt warplanes finding themselves outnumbered abandoned their attack on the warship and tried to defend their territory. They managed to take out one more Hurricane, which exploded in a fireball. Burning fragments plummeted to the ocean below. The German fighters soared up and away, disengaging from battle and retreating to the safety of their homeland.

Michael alerted his fighter squadron. His orders were that they were to continue with the initial mission so they proceeded along to the coast of France and headed for Luxembourg. It was all too clear from the air that the German army was in a comfortable position to strike and take the country.

Armoured tanks raised their guns to blast the British airmen from the skies. The bombers peeled off to attack the ground forces and began to bombard the lines of marching troops.

Michael's Hurricane began to lose power. He looked in alarm at his fuel gauge, which was spinning wildly as more petrol streamed from his tank. He was losing power and losing height. He struggled valiantly to pull his plane out of a nose dive. The sound of the engine changed dramatically as it plummeted toward the ground. It whined in complaint as it tried to fly. Michael knew he had to eject or die in his plane. He managed to get a message out before being blasted out from his cockpit. The parachute engaged and Michael drifted down into enemy occupied territory.

Things were manic at Hendre. Little Bethan was screaming her head off, her tiny face screwed up tight and redder than a robin's breast. Jenny was trying to soothe her little one and becoming more and more frazzled as the baby refused to be calmed. Carrie was running late and hurriedly gathering her things together. Bonnie was barking, Bandit was quacking and Ernie was scratching his head in disbelief at the mayhem in the house. John was in deep discussion with Sam Jeffries, Manager at Hendre and the Land Girls were waiting to receive their instructions for the day.

It was to this hullabaloo that Megan arrived with Grainger in tow. Ernie opened the door to admit the couple. Laura, one of the Land Girls turned to see the new arrivals and gasped in astonishment, "Arthur, Arthur Mason. Whatever are you doing here?" and she didn't look pleased to see him.

Grainger started guiltily and flushed with colour, "Laura!" he exclaimed. Suddenly, everything went quiet, even the baby stopped crying and everyone looked curiously at Laura and Grainger. Bonnie eyed Grainger and growled softly in her throat.

John glanced at Laura and back at Grainger, "You two know each other?"

Megan studied Grainger's face curiously, "Do you?"

"I'm sorry," interjected Laura. "Are you two together?" She was addressing Megan.

"No! We just work together."

A flash of annoyance rose on Grainger's face and then was gone.

"In that case," continued Laura, "Are you here to see me?" she questioned.

"No, no. I'm just visiting a friend. I had no idea you were here," he responded.

"May I suggest we take this outside? May we?" Laura asked John.

John nodded and Daisy added, "Go on, Laura. I'll get our duty roster. Go ahead."

Grainger and Laura went out of the kitchen to the yard leaving many puzzled looks behind them. Ernie nudged

Megan, "Get to the truth of that," and he jerked his head in the direction of the couple, "And it may help you."

Megan nodded and crossed to her friend, Carrie. "I'm so glad I haven't missed you. I was terrified you'd have left."

Carrie grinned, "No, you made it in time and more interestingly, as Ernie said, it looks like there *is* a story to tell there." She indicated the two in the yard who now appeared to be arguing. "Ernie's taking me to the station. Do you want to come for the ride?"

"Not with him trailing after me," Megan grumbled.

"We may be able to fix that," said Ernie.

Jenny interrupted, "Sorry, everyone but now that Bethan has calmed down I am going to try and get her to sleep."

"Of course," agreed Carrie.

John crossed and gave his little baby daughter a kiss on the top of her head and tenderly touched Jenny's cheek, "Now, don't you go tiring yourself out. Why don't you take the opportunity to put your feet up and have a sleep, with Bethan?"

"Thank you, I will," murmured Jenny, "But I must say goodbye to Carrie first." Jenny gently embraced Carrie but when little Bethan's face puckered up. Jenny beat a hasty retreat up the stairs. "Sorry," she called out after her.

Carrie laughed, "Now, where was I? Oh yes, my bag's in the hallway." Bonnie sat at Carrie's feet and looked soulfully at her. "Duw, you are so like Trix." Bonnie cocked her head on one side and listened. Carrie knelt down and embraced the dog that responded by licking her face. "I shall miss you. Don't forget me," she ordered.

"John, do you need Bonnie?"

"No, why?"

"I thought she might like to come with us in the cart to the station," said Ernie.

"Fine. But, don't you go without letting me hug my favourite sister."

"Why? How many have you got?" giggled Carrie.

John wrapped his arms around his sister, "Try not to leave it so long, cariad. You're an aunty now and little ones soon grow up."

A scream interrupted the goodbyes. Sam Jeffries strode out to the yard followed by Daisy. Ernie stopped the rest from following. "Just wait a moment. Leave them to it, a second. Carrie, make sure you've got all your things."

"I have."

"Then, you both wait a minute. I'll take these to the cart and see if young Mr. Mason can make his own way back…"

"But, Ernie…" protested Megan, looking worried.

"Let me deal with it. It will be fine," asserted Ernie as he picked up Carrie's luggage and went out to the waiting cart. He kept his eyes lowered to the ground and his ears open as he loaded the two bags.

Grainger was desperately trying to placate Laura. "I promise you, I did not know you were here. I am merely visiting a friend."

Sam Jeffries tried to intervene, "I don't know what's going on here and," he raised his hand silencing them, "I don't want to know. Daisy, Laura, you both have work to do. Deal with this in your own time."

Laura was now almost crimson with anger, "I need to get my lunch box." And she stormed back inside leaving the assembled company embarrassed and uncomfortable.

Ernie spoke quickly as he saw Grainger attempting to follow her. "I don't think that's wise. Give her a moment. In fact, I will be taking Carrie to the station in a minute or two and I know Megan wants to see her friend off…"

"Then, I'll come with you," suggested Grainger.

"No. They want to talk. You know what young women are like. They want to share their secrets. We'll have no sense from them, sillier than boots on a dog. Let them have their time. Why don't you walk down with Sam and meet Megan in the village? It seems more sensible. It will give the other lass time to calm down."

Grainger was about to complain but thought better of it and nodded agreement.

"I'm walking down now. Ready?" asked Sam Jefferies.

Reluctantly, Grainger began to move toward the gate and the track. Daisy, called out, to Ernie, "Tell Laura I'll see her back at Hendre at two."

John emerged from the house and ran to catch up with Sam and Daisy. He waved at Ernie as he passed.

Ernie made his way back to the house to find Laura sobbing in Carrie's arms, "Jawch! There's more than a tale to tell but tell it you should, if not for yourself but for this young woman here," he indicated Megan, who was standing silently and looking shocked, before he continued, "Not to worry, Carrie. Megan will come with us in the cart to the station, and so will Bonnie. She didn't like the look of young Grainger Mason either."

"I'm sorry," blurted Laura, "This is hard for me but Arthur…" she began sobbing again.

"It's all right. Don't talk if you don't want to," soothed Carrie.

"No, it's fine, really. I can't make a scene like that and not explain," said Laura as she tried to control her sobs.

"Take a deep breath," ordered Ernie, "That's it, and another. It should make you feel calmer."

Laura shook her golden hair and gratefully received an offered handkerchief from Megan. She dabbed at her eyes and blew her nose loudly. "I'm sorry, it was just such so unexpected seeing him here."

"Go on," encouraged Ernie.

"Arthur is from my town, the same area. We went to the same school. He was quite popular, always in the school plays. We became reasonably friendly," Laura paused and struggled to keep her voice even, "Unfortunately, he became very possessive, abnormally so. I wasn't walking out with him, courting or anything but he constantly pressured me to spend time with him." She hiccupped another sob, "He was obsessive and attempted to put between all my friends and me." Laura sighed again, struggling to contain her emotion; "He was very clever about it, making me look paranoid. His obsession was frightening. I joined the Land Girls to escape him. His friendship was stifling."

Ernie commented, "That's not friendship."

"No, at times it was scary and I often felt threatened by him. Once I thought... I thought..." Laura started to cry again.

"You thought he was going to rape you," finished Ernie.

"Yes. How did you know?" said Laura with astonishment.

"Ernie knows a lot of things," added Carrie.

"But, what do I do? Now he knows I'm here..."

"I think you'll be safe for a while. He has his sights set on someone else, now. Megan, are you listening?"

"What do I do? He's staying at my house."

"Firstly, don't reveal what you know and try not to change your attitude to him or it will raise suspicions and he'll wonder what's under the bed sheets. No, lull him into a false sense of security. If he believes you know nothing. It will be better for you and Laura." Ernie pulled off his beret and scratched his head, "I'm thinking we need to make a plan. Come on, girls. Get yourselves to the cart and take Bonnie. I want a word with Laura."

Carrie and Megan went outside to the cart. Ernie looked at Laura gravely, "Did you ever tell the police about this harassment?"

Laura shook her head, "No. I wanted to but what could they do?"

"Probably, not a lot. But you need to get it documented. I don't think he'll bother you again, yet, now he has his sights set on young Megan."

"She needs to be careful, very careful," warned Laura.

"Wait here until I get back. I'll give your apologies to Sam and Daisy. And I'll come with you to the police just to get the incident recorded. It's then we must see if we can get you another placement just as a precaution, you understand?"

Laura nodded, tearfully, "Yes, Ernie. Thank you."

"Now sit by here and make yourself a cup of tea. I'll let Jenny know that you're down stairs and she will pop down when she has Bethan settled."

Ernie with his staccato walk stuttered along the passage and up the stairs. He tapped lightly on Jenny's door.

"Yes," Jenny answered softly.

Ernie entered and explained everything to her and she promised to check on Laura once Bethan had finished feeding.

Ernie returned, "Now, don't worry. We will see you are kept safe. I believe the man returns tomorrow. Don't have anymore to do with him."

"I can't run forever, Ernie. This is so unfair. I'm happy here. I don't want to leave."

"I know, and there may be a way around this. Now, drink your tea before you start hiccupping again or you'll slop it all over your dungarees," with that Ernie left Laura and hurried to the cart outside.

The cart progressed slowly down the track, everyone was silent including Bonnie who sensed the seriousness of the situation and thrust her chin on Carrie's knee. In the distance Ernie could see, Sam, Grainger, John and Daisy heading for Hendre. "Now then girls, I want lots of laughter and chatter. You're an actress, Megan. Come on, you can do it. Act like you know nothing about Laura's misfortune. It will be better for you if Grainger thinks you know nothing. Sing or chatter as loud as possible," and with that Ernie launched into a droning rendition of Sospan Fach.

Carrie and Megan, shaken from their subdued state suddenly squealed with laughter and proceeded to drown Ernie's less than tuneful singing with their complaints. Ernie smiled. This would work, he thought to himself. Megan herself began to sing and Carrie clapped her hands as if being entertained. As the cart rattled past the quartet, Megan waved gaily at Grainger, "See you in Segadelli's!"

Grainger smiled back, a look of relief replacing the

haunted look he had on his face. He raised his hand in acknowledgement. The others called out their goodbyes and good wishes to the girls. The cart continued past and went on down the track with Megan valiantly recounting an event from a past production that had caused her much mirth and merriment. Ernie whispered back, "Now then, Megan don't overdo it." Then, he chortled loudly as if something very funny had been said and the wagon continued on its way.

"Okay, ladies. Well done. Our Mr. Mason will feel safe from discovery now."

"But, what do we do?" questioned Megan fearfully.

"Firstly, we get Carrie to the station."

"And then?" asked Megan anxiously.

"When are you going back?" Ernie requested.

"I have another two days of leave left."

"And, I have a plan." Ernie unwrapped a Nuttall's minto and popped it into his mouth. He sucked contentedly leaving the young women looking curiously at each other.

"We'll have no sense from him now, till he's finished that sweet. It's as if the world stops. Nothing comes between Ernie and his mintoes," laughed Carrie.

"Now, that's not fair," spluttered Ernie in between each chew. "These are Nuttall mintoes made with delicious treacle, sugar and butter. They're for savouring."

"They ought to put you on their tin!" laughed Carrie. "It's all right. We'll let you munch in peace."

Ernie's jaw yawningly struggled to get through his sweet and before he was allowed to unwrap another, Megan pleaded, "Come on, Ernie. What's your idea?"

Ernie smiled inscrutably and tapped the side of his nose. "Patience, ladies. I'll soon tell all."

CHAPTER THIRTY-ONE

Impasse

Carrie hugged Ernie one last time before bending down and ruffling Bonnie's head. The young collie bitch gazed soulfully at Carrie. Embedded in the dog's eyes was the same deep emotion and understanding that Trixie had possessed.

"You have a winner here," murmured Carrie.

"Aye. That we do, Carrie fach. That we do. Now, onboard the train or it will be steaming off without you."

Carrie turned to her friend and opened her arms, "And you be careful. Take Ernie's advice. Remember what we talked of; don't let Grainger fetch your mail anymore. I'm sure he's the reason you haven't heard from Thomas. In the meantime, I will write to Thomas and explain. Maybe he hasn't been receiving *your* letters either. I expect Grainger offered to put them in the post for you?"

Megan frowned, "Yes, you're right." She bit her lip nervously, "I am in a mess aren't I?"

"But not for much longer," Ernie wisely offered.

The stout guard came striding out onto the platform and raised his flag and whistle. Carrie stepped aboard and closed the door. She peered out at her friends, "And don't go leaving Gelli Galed before I come home again," she warned Ernie.

"Jawch! I'll have to go sometime, cariad, but for now I'm content."

"Thank God for that," said Carrie relieved.

The portly guard raised his flag and blew on his whistle and the train began to chuff its way out of the station. Carrie waved for as long as she could, before flopping down onto the seat. She had the carriage to herself and she pulled out some writing paper and a pen from her hand baggage and gazed thoughtfully out of the window. She would pass the time by writing a few letters; the first one would be to Thomas.

The Neath offices of Phillips, Pugsley and Pugh were drenched in sunlight. The professional rooms of the main players in the partnership had opened their windows to let in some fresh air. Mr. Pugsley however, was engaged in trying desperately to encourage a wayward wasp out of his room and was surprised to see the stiff backed figure of Netta

Llewellyn approaching and entering their building. He succeeded in helping the stinging insect on its way and was about to close his window when he heard the organised clip of Netta's boot heels on the wood floor outside his office door as she passed and knocked on his partner's door. Mr. Pugsley didn't know why but having seen Netta visit his partner on a number of occasions he felt the need to remain at the open window and listen.

He heard greetings and pleasantries exchanged and was about to close his window when he heard a rustling of paper. And Mr. Phillips' voice saying, "Take a look."

Netta's eyes glinted with feral delight and she pursed her lips in a smirk as Mr. Phillips handed her a document. Netta opened it and gasped, it was a copy of Jacky's last will and testament.

"It had completely slipped my mind that I had drafted a will for Jacky before his last visit. It was very remiss of me." Mr. Phillips winked at her, "It states quite clearly that his name is Maitland but that for his own purposes he is also known as Jacky Ebron."

"Does this mean we can access the money in Bangor?"

"Of course. As you can see it states that you are his beneficiary and after you, any child you may have from your union."

"What about the Llewellyns?"

"What about them?"

"Will they hear anything of this?"

"Come, come Miss Llewellyn," and he clicked his tongue, "How are they to know anything about this?"

Netta acknowledged Mr. Phillips with a pleased nod.

"Naturally, there will be a fee for doing this…"

"I shall see that you are well paid. What now?"

"I will approach the Building Society, on your behalf, with copies of all documents including Jacky's real birth certificate. I believe you will be more than content with the almost guaranteed outcome."

"Almost?" questioned Netta tartly, her nettle sharp mouth showing dismay.

"Don't worry, all will be well."

Netta nodded again, looking more gratified, "Then, I will await the outcome. You will send your bill?"

"Once the money is received. There will of course be two separate accounts to settle, one for the firm and…"

"…And one for you," finished Netta.

By this time Mr. Pugsley's eyes were almost popping. He could hardly believe what he was hearing.

Netta by comparison was almost shuddering with delight. She appeared taller and more imposing, now she was obviously well satisfied with the result. "Then, I believe our business is concluded, for the moment," she said grandly.

"I will be in touch," responded Mr. Phillips drawing the meeting to its conclusion. He opened his door with a flourish and Netta departed with precision.

Mr. Pugsley, in the next office, hurriedly stepped down from off the chair in the window and drew his seat back to his desk. He sat down looking thoughtful. He would have to work out very carefully as to how he would use this knowledge. This sort of corruption and blatant disregard for the law did not sit well with him. He was a moral man. Now, what *could* he do? He knew the money in question should rightfully be returned to his client, Michael Lawrence.

Michael Lawrence's bumpy landing had not gone unnoticed by German ground troops. Already an armoured car and two patrol jeeps were speeding their way along the country roads to intercept the baled pilot.

Michael drew in the silk from his parachute and studied his surroundings. He hunted for somewhere to hide the huge swatch of material. In the distance he could hear the approach of military vehicles and knew instinctively that they were searching for him. He hurriedly bundled up the parachute. The wind wasn't helping, making it difficult for Michael to get it into some sort of smaller package. He scoured the field in which he'd landed and headed for the hedgerow. At least he could try and conceal it there. There was nowhere else. Michael made a break across the meadow and stuffed the silk canopy and harness in the middle of the hawthorn bushes and tried as best he could to disguise its presence. Once done, he raced to the gate, leapt over it and made a dash for a small piece of woodland where he hoped to find sanctuary.

Breathing heavily, Michael struggled through the brambles and searched around him for a place to hide. Ahead of him he could see what appeared to be a large oak tree. He sprinted for it dodging the overhanging branches of other specimens. He looked up at the leafy canopy and paused. Could he clamber up and secrete himself amongst the branches? Had he left a trail through the woods that could be followed? What would he be able to see from the top and could he remain still and not be seen? He glanced behind him. Then shook his head vigorously. Something had happened to his ears when he ejected from his plane and the subsequent explosion. He listened, but could hear nothing. He hoped this deafness was only temporary. Taking a chance, he retraced his steps and covered the ground where his tracks were visible on wet ground. He churned it around and strew detritus over the muddy patch and then carefully picked his way back.

Michael assessed the tree. He hadn't climbed one since he was about fourteen. He grabbed hold of a lower branch and swung like an acrobat onto the sturdy limb and then began to clamber up the trunk and through the branches. He shook his head again and clamped his nostrils shut and blew hard in an attempt to unblock his ears. He was rewarded with a soft popping noise inside his head but still could not discern much sound. It was as if everything was in a fog. This was worrying. He needed to hear and with this level of loss he could be put in grave danger.

Michael finally reached the top of the tree and had a great vantage point of his surroundings. In the distance he could see the patrol vehicles and armoured car heading in his direction. He scanned the area and spotted a barn the other side of the woodland adjacent to a farmhouse cottage. He decided to sit tight, hope he wasn't detected and then under cover of darkness make his way to the buildings he could see.

Michael's heart was thumping loudly enough that he felt it could be heard outside his body. He settled himself as comfortably as possible and waited.

Carrie gazed out of the window as the train rumbled though the countryside, the repetitive clickerty-clack of the wheels on the rails and the swaying motion of the carriage had a soothing effect that soon had her eyes closing and Carrie gently floated away on a cloud of visions and dreams.

She dreamed she was in the bell tower of a church overlooking a few houses at the edge of a wood. She heard the sound of marching feet approaching. An engine rumbled in the distance. Carrie leaned out to see a contingent of German soldiers and two armoured trucks drawing closer to the church. Amongst the troops was a British airman being forcibly pushed along.

Carrie leaned out through the opening in the turret and scrutinised the line of men. There was something familiar about the airman. A sudden gust of wind blew and before Carrie could stop it her nurse's cap flew from her head and fluttered down into the courtyard below. The hat landed at the feet of a German officer who looked up and saw Carrie's blaze of fiery curls. He shouted out and other infantrymen raised their eyes, as did the British airman.

Carrie gasped and cried out, "Noooo! Michael!" She was instantly awake. Fortunately, she was alone in the carriage. Her heart was beating wildly and a thin speckling of sweat adorned her forehead. She tried to quell the coiling serpent of unease rising to her mouth, and was filled with churning fear. Somehow, she knew that her dream was significant and she was convinced that Michael was behind enemy lines and a prisoner of war. Carrie prayed that she was wrong.

The train rattled on through country stations. Carrie was no longer lulled comfortably into slumber. She picked up the letters she had penned and lingered on the one she had written to Michael. She opened it up and wrote a few more lines in a P.S. and before she had time to change her mind she replaced it in the envelope and sealed it, just as the train chuffed into Snow Hill Station.

Carrie gathered her things together and left the steaming iron monster. She hurriedly forced her obstinate curls under her hat and struggled across the platform to the street exit. Her ticket was clipped and she arrived on the pavement in Colmore Row when to her horror an air raid siren began it's mournful wail cutting through the traffic noise. People scuttled frenziedly toward the station and temporary air raid shelters situated close by.

Carrie looked wildly around her. She seemed to be carried along with a throng of people surging forward to find safety. The siren continued its wailing drone. Cars and buses pulled over and people alighted and hurried toward what they perceived to be a secure and safe area.

A large man in a trilby hat jostled against her, "Careful, bab. You need to get to the shelter, and quickly. Follow me."

"Surely, it's just a drill or something?"

"Not this time. They test the siren out at one o'clock each day." He glanced at his watch, "It's twenty past five. This is not a sound test."

Carrie stopped to listen and heard the whine and whir of plane engines. She hurried after the portly chap, clasping her bag tightly. There was a loud explosion somewhere behind her. She jumped in fright and moved all the faster. A little girl was sitting on the pavement clutching a teddy and crying. Carrie stopped and paused by the small tot. Carrie searched around her with her eyes and saw a distraught mother scouring the road and screaming in anguish.

"Hilary!"

Carrie took the tiny child's hand and cajoled, "Come on,

Hilary. Mummy is looking for you." Hilary stopped snivelling and looked trustingly at Carrie. She stood up and Carrie struggled through the crowd to the frantic mother and reunited them. The mother burst into tears and thanked Carrie profusely. There was another explosion and the three raced on amidst the hustling crowd to where they hoped they would find sanctuary.

The air raid shelter was gloomy and filled with families, children and business people all crowded together. A porter from the station took a harmonica from his pocket and began to play a mournful melody. A rough voice shouted out, "Let's have something a bit more cheerful, mate." The tune changed from a sad song to a chirpy upbeat version of 'Jeepers Creepers' and one by one people began joining in and singing together as bombs showered down outside.

The shelter shook and people flinched but bravely sang on. The barrage of blasts subsided and everyone fell silent and waited. The siren went again sounding the all clear and people gathered their belongings together and cautiously started back up the steps and back outside into the streets.

Carrie bade farewell to the little girl and her mother and carried her bag back to Colmore Row to find the taxi rank. She wanted to get back to the Nurses' Home quickly and didn't want to have to wait for a bus.

Plumes of smoke drifted up from in the direction of Aston, and Erdington, which was close to the city centre and on chatting with the cabbie it appeared the area of Nechells had also been hit. The taxi driver was seething with anger, "Damn Germans, do you know what they've done?" Carrie remained silent and listened. "I think they were targeting Fort Dunlop, you know, the rubber factory. What a stink that would have made. Casualties would have been enormous. But, they got it wrong. Bastards."

Carrie looked confused, "Why? What happened?"

"Our fire fighters. Brave men came to put out the blaze and I'm damned, if they didn't start bombing and firing on them. What sort of humanity is that? No conscience. It's against the rules."

Carrie thought that there were no rules in war but agreed that it was a despicable act as the black cab pulled into Dudley Road and drew up outside the hospital. Carrie paid the driver and hurried into the Nurses' Home. She felt she had time to unpack and have a bath before duty shifts changed and everyone would be chasing the hot water. She ran into the vestibule and popped her letters in the post tray and checked her own pigeonhole for mail before going to her room. There was nothing. She sighed, wistfully and dashed up the stairs. She ran into Pemb, who was preparing to go on duty.

"Did you hear the air raid warning?"

"Heard it? I was in it."

"No?"

"Yes, it was frightening and I was told that the Germans were attacking the firemen who were trying to douse the fires."

"Bastards! Sorry, there's no other word to describe them. I've got to run. Speak to you later," and the blonde snowball hastened down the stairs and out to the hospital.

Carrie unlocked her room and dropped her bag on the bed. Her thoughts turned to Michael and her expression became anxious. She just had a gut feeling that something was wrong.

Chapter Thirty-two

Enemies

Michael was still sitting up the tree. The woods were now swarming with soldiers. Twice one had stopped at the base of the trunk and twice he had escaped detection. He wondered how long his luck would last and his hearing was still impaired. He realized how dangerous that could be for him.

One foot soldier gave a shout as the silk of Michael's parachute was discovered and the platoon knew then they were in the right area and began to do a more concentrated search on the ground. They raked through the leaf litter trying to find evidence of tracks before moving off toward the farm building in the distance. Michael watched and waited.

He saw the troop roust the occupants, two men, three women and two children, from the farm, out of the house, and line them up outside the barn whilst they systematically searched the house and outlying buildings and barns. The older farmer protested and he was bludgeoned to the ground. A female relative ran to his aid and she too was struck, down. Michael clenched his fists at the wanton brutality. There was nothing he could do. He was helpless. He wondered how long it would be before they moved on or worse returned to search the area again.

Michael stretched uncomfortably trying to make his movements as small as possible. He didn't want to alert anyone to his presence by the shaking of the tree. A black crow alighted on a branch and eyed him curiously. Michael tried to shoo it away and the raucous bird flew up its harsh, grating cry reverberating around the woodland. Michael thought it an unfortunate omen. Crows were harbingers of death and Michael had a strange foreboding that he was going to experience death close at hand. He hoped it wasn't his. The bird flew off to part of the thicket that housed a rookery and the devilish birds perched silently as if in judgement. The phrase, a murder of crows sprang to his mind and he prayed this premonition wasn't a prediction of his future.

The afternoon sunlight was turning to dusk and Michael watched as the troop of soldiers left the farm and retraced their steps through the wood and back toward their camp.

Momentarily he heaved a sigh of relief. He had avoided capture but for how long? He knew he had to move and get shelter. He wondered if the farm was the safest place to head for?

The group assembled outside the farmhouse had retreated indoors. The older gentleman had to be carried and supported inside. Michael hoped that this might make the family more sympathetic to him if he was discovered.

Slowly, he picked his way down through the branches and shinned down the stout trunk. He jumped down lightly to the ground and stopped. Anxiously, his eyes searched the woodland around him. He tentatively broke cover and zigzagged through the trees toward the lonely farmhouse.

Neath solicitor, Leonard Pugsley was working late. He waited until he heard the next office door click shut and waited. He heard the familiar clip of Mr. Emlyn Phillips' heels click down the corridor. Mr. Pugsley rose and observed from the window and watched as Mr. Phillips with his silver topped cane walked away from the building and down the street. He knew that now was his chance to find out what his partner had been up to regarding Netta Llewellyn and false wills.

Mr. Pugsley stealthily crept from his office and opened the door to his partner's rooms. He hunted through the box files on the shelf until he found what he was looking for. He noted the addition of the hyphen from Ebron to Maitland. He returned to his office and sat at his desk and opened it, becoming engrossed in its contents. His eyes almost popped as he devoured every note, every letter, every document and was stunned by what he learned. There was enough evidence in the file to effect legal proceedings against Phillips but how could he do that without it affecting his practice? But, then if *he* were the one to expose Phillips, surely it would reflect well on him? The senior partner of Phillips, Pugsley and Pugh sat back in the chair, and thought for a while as the arguments raged inside his head.

Mr. Pugsley removed some documents and made notes on items he had found. He also took out a copy of the very telling Last Will and Testament of Jacky Maitland a.k.a. Ebron. These he put into his active file and locked this in his desk drawer.

He returned to the neighbouring office and was about to replace the box file on the shelf when he froze as he heard footsteps and the tap, tap of a cane on the polished floor echoing in the corridor. Leonard Pugsley knew that the younger partner, Mr. William Pugh had left much earlier and he had watched Netta Llewellyn's lawyer, Emlyn Phillips leave. Cleaners were not due in until much later. So who was it? To his horror the footsteps stopped outside the door. The handle began to turn. Mr. Pugsley hurriedly pushed the closed file on the shelf. The door opened.

"Leonard?" queried Emlyn Phillips in a quietly cold voice. "What are you doing in my office?"

Leonard Pugsley flushed with colour and was completely lost for words. Emlyn Phillips slowly walked toward him.

Mr. Pugsley blustered his apologies, "Sorry, Emlyn I'm working on the Michael Lawrence and Llewellyn case..."

"Yes?"

"I was just about to check in Jacky Ebron's old file to see if there was anything I had missed."

Emlyn Phillips picked the box file from its place, "I don't think so. Anything, you need to know you can ask me."

Leonard Pugsley mustered up enough courage to speak, "I don't think you've been conducting business professionally or honestly."

Emlyn Phillips' eyes narrowed, "Just what do you mean by that? What are you accusing me of?" He lifted his silver topped cane and tapped it lightly into his hand and a menacing note crept into his icy tones.

"Jacky Ebron..." he didn't finish his sentence but raised his arm to fend off the first blow. This was swiftly followed by a second and Mr. Pugsley crumpled to the floor. Blood oozed from his temple.

Phillips was not thinking straight. The surprise of the accusation had brought an immediate response and he had struck out without thinking. Now he knew, he had to cover up this crime and quickly. There was no time to waste. He rifled through his drawers and found a box of matches.

Moments later the office was ablaze.

Ernie sat in the village police station with Laura. The whole sorry story of Arthur Mason's pestering obsession was documented. Pritchard the police was sympathetic. "I've never heard anything like it before."

"What can you do?" asked Ernie.

"Well, it's all on record. If this Arthur or Grainger Mason as he calls himself bothers this young lady again. She can report it and with what we have on file we can give him a formal caution."

Ernie nodded, "That'll do for now. Laura, you get yourself back to Hendre and I'll make it clear that you are being relocated. That should ensure your safety. He won't come looking for you here, then. I'll tell him you are moving on tomorrow. Thanks, Trevor."

Trevor Pritchard nodded and returned to the desk. Ernie and Laura smiled and left the station. "How are you feeling, now lass?"

"Better, thanks"

"You'll be safe, now."

"I hope you're right?" queried Laura.

"I am, I feel you will be safe from his attentions, now."

"What about Megan?"

"Leave Megan to me. We have a plan."

"Where is she now?"

"At home, packing her bag and explaining about young Mr. Mason to her mother, and getting her help in executing the plan."

"Then what?"

"I shall be joining the young man in Segadelli's where he has been waiting," Ernie glanced at his pocket watch, "For two hours now... I'd better rush."

Ernie touched his beret and with his stuttering gait stepped out toward Segadelli's in the centre of Crynant and to Grainger Mason.

Ernie entered the café and glanced about him. Grainger Mason was sitting at a table in the corner. He looked up enquiringly at Ernie, "Where's Megan?"

"Sorry, Grainger. News came that Megan's grandmother is seriously ill with pneumonia. She's not expected to last the week. Megan's gone to see her. She's afraid she won't see her again, else. You understand?"

Grainger paused and forced a smile, "Yes, of course. I know Megan thinks a lot of her. She helped her choose her audition pieces."

"The thing is Megan's mother will be leaving to visit her as well."

Grainger smiled broadly, a smile that didn't quite reach his eyes. It was the eyes that had it, thought Ernie. The eyes revealed the truth or lack of it in the soul. Ernie detected the ice in Grainger's eyes although vocally his tones were warm.

"Then I'd best get across to Bronallt and get out of their hair. They won't want me around when there is a family crisis."

Ernie pretended to agree, "Yes, that's most considerate of you. I expect Megan will need your support when she returns to camp."

Elizabeth Revill

Grainger's expression brightened, "Yes, she will won't she? I'll be there for her."

"I'm sure you will. And now I must take my leave. I have to get Laura to the station."

"Laura? Why?"

"I don't know. She wouldn't explain or talk about it. Except she's arranged to be deployed elsewhere."

"Where?"

"She wouldn't say. Very cagey she was. Said she didn't want anyone to know. I can't think why. Do *you* know?"

"No... No. We had a disagreement, used to know each other years ago. She wanted something more but I was not prepared to be serious..."

Ernie rose and touched his beret, "I see. Well, Grainger. Good luck in your endeavours."

"I expect I'll see you again, I'll be bound to." Grainger drained the drink in front of him.

Ernie nodded and left. The first part of the plan had been executed without hitch. The rest was up to Megan and her family.

235

Chapter Thirty-three

Exams and Investigations

Carrie had closeted herself in her room. Exams were fast approaching. She had to face an oral with the Matron and written papers in anatomy and physiology. She struggled with some of the names; the calf muscle was the gastronemus muscle. Some just didn't seem to make sense, gastronemus sounded as if it was something to do with the stomach. She just hoped she'd remember.

Carrie made herself another hot drink and tried to settle into her studies. She couldn't shake off the uneasy feeling that was twisting and turning in her stomach. Carrie sighed wearily and rubbed her tired eyes that were aching with the strain of revision.

She removed Michael's latest letter and read it again. He told her he had read and devoured her missive and had just got his reply into the post before embarking on a dangerous mission, the details of which were not revealed. She now wished that she had questioned Ernie on his intuitive feelings regarding Michael Lawrence. He could have put her mind at rest, she was sure.

Carrie was finding it difficult to concentrate. Nothing seemed to be going in and sticking. She decided to make up a song on human anatomy to help her remember when there was a terrific hullabaloo outside in the corridor. Angry voices screamed. Carrie got up curiously and started to open her door when someone fell against it and a nurse ended up sprawling at her feet. This was just too much for Carrie in her anxious state.

"Just what the Hell is going on, here? I'm trying to study and I don't need this racket going on outside my door." Carrie helped the fallen nurse to her feet.

"She started it!" screamed the slim brunette who rubbed her bruised legs. The other nurse, Carrie recognised from the wards. She remembered her name was Malone.

"Malone, can't this be settled calmly?"

"Go and take a running jump, Lew. It's nothing to do with you."

"That's what you think," screeched the brunette who Carrie was soon to learn was called Yorkie. "It wouldn't surprise me if he was chasing her, too."

"What?" asked Carrie, now totally confused.

"What are you getting at, Yorkie?"

"Her. This Lew girl. He gave her a lift to the station." She turned to Carrie, "Don't deny it."

Carrie flushed with fury. Her hackles were rising and a temper that had not revealed itself for some time was bubbling to the surface, "Is this infantile display something to do with Dr. Challacombe?"

"See! See! I told you so," shrieked Yorkie.

Malone, "So it's *you*, is it? Andrew has finished our relationship because of *you*."

"Now, hang on a minute," Carrie's voice was threatening to betray her fury. "I am *not* involved with Dr. Challacombe, have no intention of being involved with Dr. Challacombe, and I see no reason why I need to defend myself against you."

More doors on the corridor began to open as nurses came out to listen to the row. Carrie, although no stranger to scenes of her own making, felt embarrassed. "I suggest that instead of acting like two witches, your anger would better be directed at the doctor himself. Talk to Walter," with that Carrie proudly lifted her head and went back into her room. She tried desperately not to slam the door.

She sat at her desk and was visibly shaking. Studies forgotten, there was no way she could focus on her revision of anatomy or anything else. Carrie hurriedly changed into her nightclothes and dressing gown, and grabbed her wash things. Maybe a soothing bath would make her feel better. She hoped the corridor had cleared and listened quietly at the door, waiting for the sounds to subside and the appropriate moment to exit her room.

Tentatively, she opened the door a fraction and peeped out. The majority of nurses had dispersed and returned to their rooms. Of Malone and Yorkie there was no sign. Carrie left her room and headed for the bathrooms.

A shout came from the end of the passage, "Lew!" Carrie turned and saw Pemb returning from her duty. "Knock on my door when you're out, I've got something to tell you."

Carrie nodded and smiled and continued to the bathroom. She didn't trust herself to speak just then. She would tell Pemb all about it later.

Michael was uncomfortable stuck in the hayloft in the barn. He had hidden there under the cover of the darkness. He was feeling hungry and thirsty.

Michael peered out from behind a hay bale and listened. His hearing still wasn't back to normal. He knew he had to be extremely careful. Michael climbed down the ladder into the main body of the barn. He moved carefully to the barn door and was horrified to see it opening. Michael froze, his eyes darting anxiously around. He slipped behind the hencoop and ducked down. Chickens perching on their roost inside the house clucked nervously. The door opened wider and Michael chanced a quick peep at whoever was entering. He was stunned to see a German soldier complete with rifle and bayonet. Michael was stuck. He dared not do anything that might reveal himself. His mind raced, he knew he had to keep very still and he didn't know whether the enemy was alone or not, and Michael had no weapon.

The soldier rested his rifle against the chicken house, disturbing the occupants that complained noisily. The German sat on a straw bale and took a tin from his pocket, opened it and began to roll a cigarette, which he lit with a match from his tin before puffing contentedly.

Another young man entered. He was a member of the family from the house. He remonstrated loudly in French with the soldier for smoking in a barn full of combustible straw and hay. The soldier snorted and ignored the plea to extinguish his roll up.

Michael's French was good but because of his impaired hearing he could only catch odd words.

The Frenchman remonstrated with the German. "Espece d'idiot! You idiot! Mettez cette cigarette. Put that cigarette out. Vous pouvez definir toute la place sur le feu. You could set the whole place on fire."

The response was for the soldier to blow smoke in the man's face after making smoke rings in the air.

"Porquois etes vous ici?" demanded the Frenchman wanting to know why the soldier was there.

The soldier grunted again, and ignored the young man. Michael hardly dared to breathe. Someone only had to walk around the henhouse and then couldn't fail to see Michael crouching down in hiding.

The Frenchman was now completely exasperated with this rude person and he snatched at the cigarette and ground it out with his heel. The German was on his feet and attacked the young man and a scuffle ensued. The German screamed at his adversary, as he floored him and reached for his Astra 600 pistol. Michael sprang out from his hiding place and tackled the German from behind, wrestling him to the ground. The gun went off, twice.

Carrie was luxuriating in the bath and feeling drowsy.

She could hardly keep her eyes open, but she began to feel strange. She was experiencing pins and needles that were the size of ball bearings and suddenly felt nauseous and light headed.

There was bang on the door, "Come on, Lew. I thought you'd be out now," called Pemb.

Carrie shook her head trying to make herself alert, "Won't be long." Carrie pulled herself out of the bath and stumbled for her towel. She needed fresh air and fumbled for the window, which she struggled to open. Her hands seemed clumsy as if they didn't belong to her. Her fingers were feeling like sausages. She finally succeeded in dragging up the sash window and leaned out to gulp fresh air. Carrie immediately began to feel a little better. She wrapped her towel around her. This was the same bathroom that she had the mishap in before.

Carrie opened the bathroom door and stood in the doorway to survey the room. There must be something wrong in here. It was then she noticed the little fan that allowed air from outside to circulate in the room. It was stuffed up with paper to stop it turning. Carrie thought that maybe someone had done that to prevent a draught. Her eyes drifted to the copper geyser that heated the water. Her attention was taken with the pilot light's lazy orange flame. Surely, that flame should be blue? Carrie was concerned.

Another nurse approached the door. Carrie put her arm across the doorway, "If I were you, I would wait for another bathroom. There's something wrong in here. I'm going to call Maintenance. I'll put a note on the door."

The nurse seemed happy to accept this and moved to the bathroom next door. Carrie hurried back to her room and changed into her clothes. She scrawled a note and pinned an 'Out of Order' sign on the suspect bathroom door before tapping on Pemb's door. "Won't be long, get the kettle on."

Carrie ran down the stairs into the vestibule and hammered on the door of the Maintenance office. "Damn!" There was no answer.

She ran to Reception and knocked on the desk. The clerk, Jane Grady, was just putting on her coat. She looked questioningly at Carrie, "Yes?"

Carrie explained as best she could. The receptionist looked sceptical. A note of urgency entered Carrie's voice, "Please, this is no joke. There is something wrong up there. It's not safe."

The woman grudgingly gave way, "I was just going home."

"Please!"

Jane Grady sighed and nodded, "Bill's on duty tonight. He's on a break. I'll get him from the canteen."

"Thanks." Carrie smiled and ran back up the stairs. She briskly made her way to Pemb's room and knocked.

Pemb opened the door, "At last! Come in and sit down. I've made you a hot drink. What's been happening?"

Carrie explained about the suspect bathroom and how ill she had felt.

"That's awful. What do you think it is?"

"I don't know. But, I'm sure we'll know soon enough. Now, what have you got to tell me?"

Pemb put her fingers to her lips and lowered her voice. "Ssh."

Carrie looked conspiratorially around, "What? There's no one here. What is it?"

"You know what they say, "Walls have ears.""

"What?" hissed Carrie impatiently, "Tell me."

"Lloyd."

"What about him?"

"He's asked me to marry him. And I've said, yes."

"Pemb, that's wonderful."

"I know. But you mustn't say. It's a secret."

"You'll have to say sometime."

"Not yet, you know we're not allowed to marry. I need to qualify first and after the war, well, that may be different. I don't want to lose my job."

"Your secret's safe with me."

"Thanks. Tell me, are you ready for the exams?"

"As ready as I'll ever be. And you?"

"You can test me later."

The two friends continued to share their news and sip their drinks. It was going to be a long night.

Michael disentangled himself from the German soldier who fell back on the dirt floor. The Frenchman stood looking dazedly and Michael hobbled up. He'd been shot in the leg. "Je suis desole," he apologised. "Je n'avais pas le choix qu'il allait vous tirez." Michael was trying to impress on the farmer that he had no choice; the German would have shot the young man.

The French farmer looked stunned, "Vous parlez Francais?"

Michael followed what the young man was saying and added, "Oui, mais il y a quelque chose de mal avec mon oreilles. J'espere que c'est temporaire." He tried to explain about his hearing and seemed to get through to the young man.

"I speak English."

"That's a relief my French is …"

"Very good," said the farmer.

"That's debateable. What do we do now?"

"We must attend to your leg and…" he paused, "Get rid of him."

It was Michael's turn to look shocked, "How?"

"Can you walk?"

Michael nodded, he grimaced with the pain and hopped to a straw bale and sat.

The farmer introduced himself, "Henri Pascal." He caught hold of the German soldier's legs and pulled him toward the door, "And you?"

"Michael, Michael Lawrence."

"Well, Michael Lawrence. You must be hungry. And we must be quick. Someone will be back looking for him," he indicated the dead soldier. "We must bury the body and hide his weapons."

"How can I help?"

"You stay here. I'll deal with this and I will send my sister, Adele, to treat your wound and bring you some refreshment. Then we must contact the Resistance to help you return to England." Henri dragged the body out through the barn and outside.

Michael nodded agreement. His leg was bleeding profusely. He was lucky that the bullet hadn't hit an artery. He tugged at his shirttails and tried to rip off a strip of material. It was tougher than he thought. He pulled the cotton fabric up to his mouth and bit into it with his teeth and managed to tear a strip from his shirt. He tied it around his leg as a tourniquet in an attempt to stop the bleeding, biting his lip to stop him crying out with the pain.

The door opened, and a young woman entered carrying a basket containing a dish of olives, an apple, some bread and cheese in a cloth, and a drink of milk, which Michael accepted gratefully. Adele also had a first aid box. She said nothing and looked at his leg.

Adele took a pair of scissors and cut Michael's trousers around the site of the wound and probed it with her finger. Michael let out a cry of agony.

Carrie had fallen asleep over her books. She awoke with a jolt, and shouted, nearly knocking over her table lamp. Pemb was snoozing in the chair. She stirred and stretched, "What is it?"

"We must have fallen asleep. It's almost two o'clock."

"Why did you shout?"

"I heard a cry."

Pemb listened, "I don't hear anything…"

"No, it was Michael. I'm sure of it."

"How do you know?"

"I don't know. Just a feeling. Oh, Pemb, I think he's in trouble."

"It was a bad dream; that's all," soothed Pemb, rising. "We better get to bed and try and sleep. We've got exams in the morning."

"I know. Can't do any more cramming tonight. It just won't stick," rejoined Carrie.

Pemb grabbed her study notes and opened the door. "Sleep well. Don't worry, it was only a dream," and she left.

Carrie removed her robe, switched off the lamp and snuggled into her bed. She lay there quietly her eyes wide open wondering what had just happened. She had a strange nervous sensation fluttering in her stomach and wondered if this was what Ernie felt when had a premonition.

Carrie turned over decisively and closed her eyes. She needed to sleep. She wanted to be fresh for her exam in the morning. But she had this niggling fear twisting and rising inside her. Carrie kept her eyes firmly shut. She prayed hard in her heart for Michael's safety and was rewarded with a flooding calm spreading through her as if she had been kissed by an angel and fell asleep.

Carrie's alarm rang shrilly and she tapped at it with her hand. The bell seemed to sing inside her head and she swiped at it again. It tumbled to the floor still persistently jangling.

"Duw," she grumbled and slipped out from under the covers and grabbed the offending clock and savagely switched it off, "Ding, dong yourself!" she snorted. Carrie picked up her wash things and robe and trundled out into the corridor. There was a queue for the bathrooms. She groaned inwardly. With one bathroom out of commission, the wait time was longer. Carrie went into the toilet block and used their washbasins to freshen up and clean her teeth. She was glad she'd bathed the evening before.

Her hair was being particularly difficult that morning and she couldn't find her Vaseline pot. She knocked on Pemb's door. "Let me have a squidge of your Vaseline, Pemb. I can't find mine and my hair's such a tangle it'll be coming out at the roots when I brush it, else."

Pemb was just putting on her cap. She walked to the

table, opened the drawer and handed Carrie the pot. "I want it back, mind."

"Thanks, I won't be long. Are you going for breakfast?"

"No, I'm too nervous. I'll meet you outside the hall."

"I'll be there in a gnat's wing."

"What?" laughed Pemb.

"One of Ernie's sayings. I won't be long. I'll catch you up."

Carrie flew back into her room and tried to tame her spangled curls. The Vaseline did the trick and Carrie donned her cap, snatched up her pens, pencils and keys. She raced out of her room and scurried after Pemb to the big hall where the exams were to take place.

The huge doors opened to admit the student nurses. Stilling the bubbling nerves that simmered inside her, Carrie tilted her head, wished Pemb luck and walked to her seat. It was crunch time, the first part of the two-year training to lead to her SRN. Carrie was glad they had shortened the course from three years to two. Now, it was up to her.

Michael was re reading Carrie's letter it gave him hope and courage. His hearing was almost back to normal and the German soldier's body had been dealt with and buried. Sadly, the elderly man who had been brutalised by the German patrol had not recovered from his beating and had died. The Pascal family had no love for the Germans and vowed to do what they could to help the British airman now hiding in their cellar.

Adele had managed to remove the bullet that had lodged in Michael's leg. Fortunately, it hadn't hit the bone and just needed time to heal. Painted with Gentian Violet and iodine, bandaged up, it was still incredibly painful but the family had found Michael a stick to help him manoeuvre his way around. It reminded him of the time that Carrie twisted her ankle and he smiled to himself as he remembered her protestations as he lifted her up and carried her back to Hendre.

Just as quickly, a feeling of sadness overtook him; his smile faded as he wondered whether or not he would ever see her again. He decided that if he was fortunate enough to get home that he would pursue her and do whatever he could to win her heart. Michael knew that she was stubborn, strong and wilful so he would have to work at it. But, the reward of having Carrie at his side would be an enduring light in his life.

There was a shout from above. The Germans had arrived.

Chapter Thirty-Three

Further Machinations

Megan had a head start on Grainger. She had visited the Head Office of ENSA and put in a formal request to move theatre companies to back up her letter, which she had handed in to Basil Dean's office.

Megan spoke to the secretary at the main desk who was very sympathetic. She looked through her lists, while Megan waited anxiously.

The secretary, Teresa Sloman, smiled brightly. "You may be in luck. One of our girls due to go to Burma has had to pull out of her tour of duty. She broke her leg and pelvis after falling off the stage."

Megan could hardly believe her luck, "Burma?"

"Yes, is that a problem?"

"No, not at all."

"And I have someone else waiting to be deployed. A Lucinda Elvey who passed her auditions and is waiting for a vacancy. This could be just what you need."

"That's great. When will I know?"

"Now, I'm not promising anything but we will telegraph your company manager. If you are successful."

"Will it be common knowledge at the company?"

"No. I can do it in such a way that you will simply be recalled to Head Office. No one need know why or where you are going and Lucinda Elvey can be rehearsed into your roles, maybe with your help if she arrives before you leave."

"Thank you," Megan was ecstatic.

"As I said, it's not guaranteed but I will do my best."

Megan left the office with a happy step and headed for the station to take the train back to camp. She was feeling more positive, now and much more alive. She just had to play things as if nothing was wrong. She was sure she could pull it off and if she did the first person to hear about it would be Carrie. She would write to her on the train and tell her of the plan.

Carrie and Pemb had returned to their rooms. They had exchanged notes after the exam and both were reasonably confident in how they had performed. They felt they had done the best they could. Carrie took a mouthful of her

Ovalteen when a sudden explosion outside shook the whole room.

The air raid siren sounded out and footsteps were heard running down the corridor. Pemb opened the door and looked out. Off duty nurses were streaming to the stairwell and hastening to the air raid shelter.

One nurse called out, "Get to Camden Street. The Cruikshank Chemical Building. The air raid shelter. Hurry. The sky's red over Brum."

Carrie and Pemb glanced out of the window. The sky was certainly on fire. They left their drinks and joined the fleeing throng. Houses and factories were burning and Carrie thought of the brave firemen who would be valiantly trying to extinguish the flames that were like a beacon to the German bombers. Hamish Macdonald, the fireman who died, inexplicably popped into her head. This image was closely followed by one of Michael Lawrence.

Michael, Lawrence shuffled to the back of the cellar where there was a cupboard with a false back that hid a little hidey-hole, which led into a small tunnel that ran under the house, the yard and surfaced in the middle of a copse where there was a large hollow tree. Michael hoped he wouldn't have to use it. He manoeuvred himself into the space and settled the dummy wall securely into the back of the cupboard, and placed a shielding metal sheet between him and the false panel and waited.

He could hear jack booted men turning over chairs and smashing furniture. A female voice cried out as if struck. He flinched and thought it may be Adele.

It wasn't long before irate German voices filtered down and descended into the underground storage room. Michael remained as quiet and still as possible as soldiers crashed around the cellar overturning packing cases and prising the lids off boxes. The cupboard door was wrenched open and deemed to be empty. Bayonets were thrust into locked trunks and crates. Believing that there was no one down there the footsteps retreated upstairs. Michael could hear the French family complaining about the intrusion and violent ransacking of their property. The marauding army laughed in derision, shouted their orders and satisfied that neither their man nor the British airman was there they left the farm, surmising that their sentry had encountered the enemy and was elsewhere. They would continue to search the surrounding countryside.

Michael waited for what seemed like hours but in fact

was just thirty minutes. The family were being careful. They weren't prepared to risk an unexpected return and had to be sure the enemy was clear of the area.

Henri tapped lightly on the cupboard. "All clear, Michael."

Michael removed the protective metal sheet and false back, and emerged from the gloom squinting in the lamplight brandished by Henri, who spoke with urgency. "We must not delay. When they don't find their man, they will be back. Here." He thrust a bundle of clothes at Michael. "Wear these. We will burn your uniform. Fortunately, your French is good enough for you to get by."

"Where am I going?" groaned Michael as he stretched and rubbed his cramped dead limbs to life.

"Lille. You and Adele will travel together as cousins. I will drive you in the farm truck to the station."

"What about papers?"

"All in hand. The less you know the better. Just in case, vous comprenez, you understand? You will be safer travelling with a woman. They won't suspect that."

Michael inclined his head questioningly, "What happens at Lille?"

"There's a small airfield there. A pilot will be on hand to take you across the channel and to safety."

Michael nodded gratefully, "I was lucky to land here."

"We have no love for the Germans. Even more so, since they murdered my father."

"I understand." Michael approved with a curt jerk of his head, thankful that he had good French, which had been necessary when he worked in Africa.

Carrie was studying intensively for her anatomy exam later that week but desperately needed a break from her revision. She wanted to stretch her legs and get some fresh air so she grabbed her cape and went to collect her mail. She stuffed the letters into her pocket and resolved not to look at them immediately or she knew she would never get outside.

Carrie began to walk around the hospital grounds. She noted nurses on the step of the back entrance smoking. She almost felt inclined to speak to them and warn them of the dangers but knew that her interference would not be taken kindly and would only fall on deaf ears.

Carrie gulped a mouthful of fresh air that was not as fresh as the air from home, around Hendre and in the Welsh valleys. She could taste smoke and not from the nurses' cigarettes, but smoke from bombed buildings that still continued to smoulder from the sudden attack the previous evening. Occasional flakes of ash flew on the wind and crumbled to dust as they collided with windows and walls leaving an unpleasant sooty film on their surfaces. Carrie decided to return indoors, make a hot drink and read her letters. She strolled back towards the Nurses' Home and walked straight into Dr. Challacombe.

"Nurse Llewellyn, I trust you had a good break away."

"Yes, Dr. Challacombe. Thank you."

"Please, off duty I am Andrew."

"Thank you... Andrew."

"And have you thought anymore about my invitation?"

Carrie looked uncomfortable, "Oh, I thought you were just being polite, friendly..."

"So, you thought there was no substance to my request?" Carrie was uncertain how to respond and just looked down, which the doctor took as a sign of shyness. "What should I call you? Nurse Llewellyn is bit formal and quite a mouthful."

Carrie looked him squarely in the eye, "I believe that it's best to keep the friendship on a professional level, doctor."

If Andrew Challacombe was affected by this rebuff he certainly didn't show it. If anything it seemed to make him more determined, "Now, Nurse. I'm sure you don't mean that. Unless of course you really don't like me."

"It's not that..."

"Oh, so you do like me."

"I didn't say that either," returned Carrie.

"Touché," smiled Dr. Challacombe, "What do you say? Will you accompany me one evening to the cinema; that's of course if we still have one standing?" he laughed.

"Dr. Challacombe, much as I appreciate the invitation I do not believe it would be wise of me to accept. I have my study and I have already encountered the wrath of two nurses who objected to my having a lift with you to the station."

Dr. Challacombe attempted to speak and Carrie put up her hand to stop him and much to his amusement she continued, "I do not intend to become embroiled in a war with other nurses for your affections, nor do I want any affections," she hurriedly added. "I do not want any complications in our friendship, working or otherwise and I hope you will respect that." Carrie sighed heavily. There... she'd said it.

"Thank you for making your feelings so plain," mused the doctor, "And I hope you will not be offended if I ask you out again, for ask you out again, I must, as you have now made yourself even more intriguing."

"That is not my intention," insisted Carrie and she turned and fled back to the Nurses' Home to curtail any further discussion.

Dr. Challacombe roared with laughter, her old-fashioned manner and prim attitude both delighted and charmed him. She was easy on the eye, good at her job and her reaction to him quite stirred him up. He wondered, which nurses had fallen foul of her; not that it mattered. He would bide his time and ask her again, when he was ready.

Chuckling to himself he strutted away to the car park, found his car and drove away to his digs.

Carrie hurried up the stairs and back to her room. She flopped forward onto her bed and heaved a sigh. She rolled over and removed the letters from her pocket. There was a letter from Thomas, who was delighted to know the reason why he hadn't heard from Megan. It had explained everything to him. Carrie could hear the relief and excitement in the tone of his letter. His ship was due to dock in Southampton and he had been given a week's leave when he proposed to travel to wherever Megan was based. Carrie smiled, this was good, at least she thought so until she opened Megan's letter.

"Burma!" Carrie exclaimed aloud. She read the paragraph again. It wasn't yet confirmed and Megan might have to rehearse a new member into the company. Carrie prayed that the job change wouldn't happen until Thomas had at last met up again with Megan, again.

Carrie put the letters to one side. She needed a drink. Carrie grabbed her mug and went along the corridor to the communal kitchen, passing the bathrooms on the way. The maintenance man, Bill was just removing the 'Out of Order' sign from the door of the bathroom where Carrie had, had such a frightening experience.

"So, Bill what was the problem in there?"

Bill turned and smiled, "You were lucky young lady, very lucky. Someone had blocked the air vents, the geyser was faulty and spewing out Carbon Monoxide."

Carrie shuddered. The memory of the feelings she'd experienced almost overtook her.

"It's the silent killer," continued Bill. "You can't see anything, or smell anything. It's invisible and deadly. You spotting that lazy orange flame was the giveaway. It's lucky no one died."

"Is it all safe, now?"

"Aye, ducks. It is. I've put a notice inside, *not* to block the air vents. Hopefully, people will listen." Bill picked up his bag of tools and whistled his way off down the corridor.

'Carbon Monoxide,' thought Carrie. She *was* lucky. She would be more mindful in future. She just hoped that her short exposure to the toxic gas wouldn't have any lasting effects or repercussions in the future and she made up her mind to find out more about the subject.

Carrie went on to the kitchen, she groaned inwardly as she recognised, Nurse Malone stirring something on the stove. Tilting her head she steeled herself and breezed into the kitchen as if it were no consequence.

Nurse Malone looked around, "Oh, it's you. The man stealer." She turned her back on Carrie and resumed stirring the soup that was bubbling away.

Carrie bristled at the unjust accusation and couldn't help herself; "Let's get one thing straight, Malone. I am no man stealer and I am not interested in your Doctor Challacombe."

Malone sprang around angrily, the wooden spoon in her hand, splattered drops of tomato soup over Carrie's clothes, "Then why did you accept a lift to the station?"

Carrie looked down at the red splodges on her front and visibly bridled, "I don't have to explain myself to you, but…" and she took a deep breath, "I accepted the lift because I was in danger of missing my train. No other reason."

"But, he's asked you out," she said accusingly.

"Yes, and I have refused. It seems to me that your doctor is at fault here and no one else."

Malone's eyes filled with tears.

"It's better you know now that he is not to be trusted, not an honourable man."

"But, I love him." Malone turned back to the stove her shoulders heaving as she tried to still the sob that threatened to rise.

Carrie, her anger forgotten, put her arm around the distraught nurse, who turned, still with the spoon in her hand, and sobbed in Carrie's arms. Carrie found her cheek daubed with soup where the wooden implement had come to rest against her face. She struggled not to laugh.

Malone pulled away and murmured, "I'm sorry."

"Yes, well… apology accepted. Listen, I'm not one to give advice but I know what's right and I don't think the man is deserving of your love," and she rubbed at her soup stained face.

Malone noticed and gulped, "Oh no. Did I do that?"

"It's nothing that a little soap and water won't cure," smiled Carrie as she placed the kettle on to boil.

Malone dried her eyes, "I know you're right, but it's hard. I thought he would be my ticket out of this place, too bad I fell for him in the process."

"Don't you enjoy it here?"

"It's all right. Not what I expected."

"No?"

"No. But that's me. Do you know I can't stand the sight of blood? What good is a nurse who feels faint at the sight of blood? Even the soup on your face makes me feel queasy. I've been so stupid," and she began to cry again.

Carrie was at a loss at what to do, she didn't know the nurse very well and she found the encounter difficult, "I'm making a pot of tea, do you want a cup?"

Malone shook her head, "No, thank you."

The soup was bubbling and threatened to boil over, "Don't forget the saucepan," prompted Carrie.

Malone took the pan off the heat and with shoulders drooping served it into a bowl. Carrie made her tea and began to leave the kitchen, she felt obliged to say something soothing, "I have to revise but if you ever need to talk…" she left the sentence unfinished and escaped from the kitchen back to her room.

Carrie took a swig of her tea and sat at her desk. She looked at the last unread letter waiting on her bed. She picked it up curiously as she didn't recognise the hand. She opened it. It was from an airman in Michael's Squadron, someone called Burton. Much of the letter had been blacked out. Infuriatingly, the little that was left made little sense.

Carrie dropped the letter, she was very afraid. Something had happened to Michael, she just knew it.

Chapter Thirty-Four

Truth will out

Megan had arrived safely back at camp and was settling in and wondering how she would face Grainger when he returned. She would do as Ernie said and behave exactly as if she had known nothing and would continue with the charade of the story of her sick Grandma that may require her to return home at any time. This would be her official story if she received confirmation of a transfer. The company manager, however, would have to be sworn to secrecy when the time was right. Megan knew she would have to be very careful so as not to arouse Grainger's suspicions.

Megan decided to pen some letters knowing that she was setting a trap she wrote as if she knew nothing about Grainger Mason's activities. This required some creative thinking on her behalf. She wrote to Thomas bewailing the fact that she hadn't heard from him and asking him to get in touch as soon as he could. She said that she knew contact was sometimes difficult and blamed the fact they were both in the services for not receiving any letters. She read it through critically. Yes, it sounded fine. There was nothing to suspect it wasn't a genuine missive.

Back in Wales Grainger had packed his bag and left the Thomas family home muttering his sympathies to Megan's mother and promising he would look after her daughter on their next tour. His thoughts drifted back to Laura. He hadn't expected to see her here. It was quite a shock and he wondered if she would keep her mouth shut. It wouldn't do for her to go spouting off about their relationship. There again, he had been told that she was moving on to another placement and Grainger had no reason to believe otherwise. He suppressed any anxiety he may have felt and continued on his way to the station.

He waited on the platform for his train and the station was buzzing with gossip about the solicitor Leonard Pugsley who had been knocked unconscious in his office, which had then been set on fire. Firemen had tackled the blaze and rescued the solicitor who was now in hospital and suffering from smoke inhalation.

It now seemed that Emlyn Phillips had absconded from his home. The village was full of the scandal especially as

Phillips, a bachelor, was now nowhere to be found. It was rumoured that the police were on their way to visit Netta Llewellyn. Grainger wondered what all the fuss was about in a small mining and farming community such as this.

Grainger's train chuffed into the station billowing out white steam clouds. Grainger smiled. He would make himself indispensable to Megan and in that way make her, his. Grainger boarded the train and found himself a window seat. He popped his bag in the overhead rack and settled down to await the departure. The guard waved his flag and blew his whistle and the train gathered up the steam to chug out of the station. A movement caught his eye and he stared disbelievingly out of the window.

Laura arrived on the platform with Pritchard the Police deep in conversation. Grainger hurriedly turned his face away from the window and slunk down in his seat. He was now a worried man.

Thomas' ship was approaching Southampton. It had sustained some damage in combat and needed an urgent overhaul before setting sail again. Many sailors had been given an unexpected few days leave whilst the repairs took place. Thomas was excited that he had the time off and that he had the list of entertainment venues for Megan. He was all set to travel to see her. He had received Carrie's letter, which explained fully why he hadn't heard from his love and he determined he would give this Grainger fellow a punch on the nose if he caught hold of him. He was delighted to learn that Aldershot was only fifty-one miles from Southampton

Megan had arrived back at camp before Grainger, and had spoken to the company manager, Simon Jackson, who told her that he had received a telegramme from Head Office. It was important for Megan to maintain the story about her grandmother. After her replacement was rehearsed in she was to be allowed compassionate leave and would be deployed back into another company once family issues were settled, at least that was the official version. Lucinda Elvey was due to arrive shortly. They had a show to perform in Aldershot for the Canadian and British troops based there. Megan secretly slipped an old letter from Thomas that she had resealed into the incoming mail tray ready to be sorted and placed in the cast's pigeonholes.

Megan dreaded Grainger's return but knew she could continue the charade for as long as was necessary. To back up her account she would mention her letter to Thomas and see if Grainger offered to post it and collect the mail, then see what happened as Carrie had suggested. She had, had some fun composing this missive. She would, also, be sure to catch him when he collected the post for the company. Time would tell. Megan was convinced that Ernie had been right in his assumption of her fellow actor.

Back in Birmingham the city had been given a short reprieve from the air attacks but all the news on the wireless was of the Blitzkrieg in London. Continued bombing was devastating the city and plans were underway to evacuate all children to the country and areas deemed safe by the government. The war that people had believed would be over in a few months was obviously going to drag on for a lot longer. Carrie was anxiously awaiting her exam results with Pemb, which would then confirm that they could progress to their second year of training and subsequent finals to become State Enrolled Nurses. They were promised results would be with them in a week. This was great news as initially they thought the papers were to be sent away and would take much longer to be marked, but now they were to assessed internally because of wartime difficulties.

News on the wireless was again of the relentless bombing in London. People were using the Underground Stations as air raid shelters and sleeping on mass down there. London was being hardest hit, but bombs were falling on other major cities too, like the ones experienced in Birmingham. The news was of devastating explosions being recorded in Manchester and Plymouth amongst others.

Michael was travelling through the French countryside. Henri was driving and Adele sat alongside. They had been motoring easily along sparsely populated country lanes but were now approaching a small village on route to Lille. Henry groaned. There was a German roadblock up ahead. "Don't speak unless you have to," declared Henri. "I'll deal with this."

The German sentry waved them down.

Henri pulled the truck to a stop and wound down the window, "Quel est le problème?"

The German didn't answer. He walked around the truck scrutinising the passengers carefully. He spat onto the ground and returned to the driver's window. "Papers," he demanded curtly.

Henri fished in his pockets for his documents and handed them across. The soldier examined them slowly and suspiciously and stared at Henri before studying the information and official stamp. He glared at Henri and reluctantly returned his papers, then aggressively slammed his fist into his hand and snapped his fingers at Adele and Michael.

They exchanged a look between them before handing their papers across. The German went through the same routine, taking his time and filling the three with trepidation. He passed back their items and pointed at Michael. "You! Was ist Ihr Unternehmen?" Michael looked confused. He did not speak German. Henri went to reply, but the soldier insisted. "Nein! Er ist zu beanworten." It was clear the officer wanted Michael to speak.

Michael glanced sideways at Henri then spoke, "Pardon, je ne parle pas allemand," affirming that he didn't speak German.

Henri added, "Il veut connaître votre entreprise."

"Ah!" Michael beamed with feigned recognition, so he wanted to know Michael's business. Michael indicated Adele and gushed that she was his fiancée and that they were on their way to catch a train to visit his family. They wanted his mother's blessing to marry. All this was said in perfect French, which Henri translated into German. The soldier snorted and spat again before officiously waving them on. The trio breathed a sigh of relief and continued on their way. "That was lucky," said Michael.

"It was having Adele with us that saved the day," observed Henri. "That and a helping of luck."

"Let's hope that luck holds," added Michael as they sped their way toward the railway station.

Grainger had arrived back at camp and made his presence known to Megan almost immediately. "How are you feeling, Megan? How's your Gran?"

"She's failing, Grainger. I'm hoping to be allowed home soon on compassionate leave. I've asked Head Office and they are agreed. They'll send a replacement to be rehearsed in while I'm away. My only fear is it won't happen in time."

"But..." Grainger spluttered, "You can't go..."

"I'm sorry?" questioned Megan, feigning shock.

"I mean, no one can replace you," he blustered, "We'll miss you."

"It won't be for long. I've just written explaining it all to Thomas so he knows where to send his next letter. Do you know, I still haven't heard from him. I hope he's all right."

Grainger smiled slyly, "I'm sure he is. If not you'd know about it, wouldn't you?"

"No, that information would go to his mother in Australia. Oh, Grainger, why hasn't he written?"

"You know what they say about sailors..."

"Oh, Grainger, that's cruel... I hope you're wrong. Anyway," and Megan kissed the back of her letter, "I'm off to catch the post and see if any mail has arrived for me. Surely, there must be a letter soon?"

Grainger took the letter from her hand.

"Hey, what are you doing?" she queried.

"I've got letters to post, too. I'll take them and collect the mail as well. I usually do, save you a trip."

"That's okay, you've got to unpack. I'll take yours for you," and she smiled sweetly at him.

"That's kind, but I've been cooped up on the train, I could do with stretching my legs. I'll do it. It's no problem."

Megan decided to give in gracefully, "Oh, okay. I wanted to run through my lines before rehearsals tomorrow. See, how I could help the new girl; that's if it ever happens."

Grainger smiled back and touched his hat to her. Megan began to walk slowly away. Grainger shoved the envelope in his pocket and walked away.

Feeling like a character in a play, Megan looked back at Grainger, who feeling her eyes on the back of his head, turned back and waved. Megan smiled brightly and waved back. Grainger continued toward the company office.

Megan waited a little while before discretely following him. She patted another fake letter, in her pocket, which was to be her excuse if Grainger spotted her. She would declare she had forgotten this one and it, too, needed prompt mailing.

Megan watched Grainger surreptitiously. She dodged behind the shrubbery as he paused on the path and looked around. He removed Megan's letter, tore it open and avidly read the contents. Shaking with anger he ripped it to bits and tossed it into a dustbin then, strode out toward the Company Office.

Megan hurried out to retrieve the destroyed communication. She rummaged through the bin and popped the evidence into her handbag.

Grainger had now arrived at the Company Office and gathered up the post from the in tray and skimmed through the mail. Noticing the letter to Megan in Tom's writing he furtively removed it from the pile just as the door opened and Megan breezed in. Megan, what are you doing here?"

"I'd forgotten I had this to post to Carrie," she said waving the envelope.

Grainger tried to secretly push Thomas' letter into his jacket pocket but Megan's eagle eyes saw what he was doing.

"That's for me, I think," she said accusingly holding out her hand.

Grainger was flustered he protested, "I put it in my pocket to bring to you, I said I'd collect the mail."

"Yes, you also said you'd post this for me," and Megan emptied the shredded letter onto the Company Manager's desk. Simon Jackson looked up curiously. The clerk who was busy filing, stopped and watched the proceedings.

"Yes, well I can explain that…"

"Can you? I'm listening."

"I was going to tell you…"

"What? That you'd been fielding my letters and preventing me from receiving them?"

"No!"

Simon Jackson intervened, "Interfering with the mail this way is not only against the law but punishable with heavy penalties. We take a very dim view of it."

Red-faced Grainger spluttered. He couldn't think of anything to say. He mustered a few words, "I was doing it to help you. I didn't want you getting hurt. I know what sailors are."

"I think that's up to me not you," said Megan icily.

Grainger charged back outside calling, "I only did it because I love you."

Simon Jackson looked questioningly at Megan, "What do you want to do?"

"Nothing for the moment. We'll wait and see. Besides I may be leaving before too long."

"And I will send out a company directive that all mail is to be collected from me personally."

"Thanks Simon."

"Are you able to work with him tonight?"

"I'm a professional, aren't I?" said Megan stubbornly and tossed her head, defiantly.

Simon smiled wryly. "I'll be keeping my eye on him from now on."

Adele and Michael were safely on the train. Henri had dropped them and bought the tickets, a single and return to Lille. He had hugged his sister and embraced Michael warmly, "Good luck my friend."

"I can't thank you enough," murmured Michael gratefully.

"Nor I you. You saved my life."

The guard began walking up the platform and slamming the doors. Henri quickly stepped back onto the platform. He touched his cap at the two of them when a shout came from down the platform.

"Halt! Halten Sie den Zug."

Two Gestapo officers walked toward the guard. Words were exchanged and the men boarded the train. Henri stepped back from the train, a worried look on his face. The guard blew the whistle and waved his flag. The train let off a burst of steam and began to chuff out of the station with the two Gestapo on board.

Henri moved down the platform and queried the guard about the men, "La Gestapo, que voulaient-ils?" He wanted to know what they wanted.

The guard shrugged, "Quelque chose au sujet d'un aviateur Britannique. Ils verifient tous les trains et les routes."

At the mention of a British airmen and the fact all roads and trains were being checked filled Henri with fear.

Mr. Pugsley had recovered sufficiently to answer the questions of the police and a warrant was put out for the arrest of Emlyn Phillips. Fortunately, the fire had not engulfed all the files in Phillips' office and Leonard Pugsley's room was untouched. The case notes on John Maitland alias Jacky Ebron were still safely locked in his desk drawer. Rippling with righteous indignation, Mr. Pugsley had sent word to his secretary to attend the hospital bringing with her the relevant documents.

She sat primly at his side taking notes and a letter was composed to the solicitor in Bangor outlining the rightful ownership of John Maitland's deposited money and instructions to forward it to his office. Supporting documents were enclosed as well as a letter from the local constabulary, verifying the claim.

Mr. Pugsley paused before continuing, "Sign on my behalf and now two more letters I will enjoy writing. Duw, Duw there's grand it is that the truth has come out at last. Who would have thought such a tale of deception and barrel of lies would have beset our small town?"

The next letter was to Michael Lawrence informing him that the first payment for Hendre had been discovered, and would shortly be deposited into his bank. Mr. Pugsley advised that when Michael returned to Neath he could call in and the whole bizarre story would be explained to him.

Thirdly, he wrote to the Llewellyns. It gave him great pleasure to tell John Llewellyn that justice was finally being done. That once the money was placed into Michael Lawrence's account then according to the terms of their agreement, John would be at liberty to return to Hendre. His heart was almost bursting with pride at this point. He believed that his actions would redeem his firm in the eyes of the public and the Law Society. He knew that there would be gossip but he also knew that his secretary, whilst not breaching any confidentiality, would support the firm and scotch any misinformation.

His secretary, Glenys Jenkins believing the dictation was over, closed her pad with a flourish and began to rise. "Well, Sir, that has worked out very satisfactorily, if I may say so."

Mr. Pugsley stopped her, "You may, but we are not quite finished, yet. Lastly, Miss Jenkins a final communication to Miss Netta Llewellyn." Mr. Pugsley smiled grimly. Netta was not going to get away with a catalogue of attempted fraud and blackmail. She too would have her comeuppance.

Miss Jenkins sat once more and resumed her shorthand dictation. It seemed that Netta Llewellyn had breached the terms of her probation. Glenys Jenkins was fascinated. How she wished she could tell someone, but she was an honourable woman in a trustworthy position. Her lips were sealed or at least she intended them to be.

Chapter Thirty-Five

Escape

Lucinda Elvey had arrived. She was a fresh-faced young girl with corn blonde hair. She was due to watch the show that night to observe Megan's performance. Rehearsals were set the following day where Lucinda would step into Megan's shoes and Megan would help direct her where appropriate. Lucinda had a bubbly personality and was obviously delighted to be there. She came from Liverpool, but fortunately didn't have an overpowering Scouse accent so audiences would have no difficulty understanding her.

Lucinda found herself sitting amongst a variety of enlisted men who were more than delighted to have a pretty blonde in their midst. She was accomplished enough to enjoy and deal with their attention and not be upset by it.

On stage Megan gave a glittering performance, as did Grainger and the rest of the cast. Backstage things were tense. Megan was trying to ignore Grainger who was constantly studying her, watching her every move. He pleaded with her, "Please, Megan, forgive me. You have to understand that my motives were made entirely through love. You and me, we're perfect together, a fine match. Just give me a chance."

"Look, just get it through your thick skull. I don't want you, will never want you and nothing you do or say will make me want you."

Megan danced back onto the stage followed by Grainger and they enacted a delightful routine where any onlooker would believe they cared deeply for each other. They danced off and the smile left Megan's face.

Grainger persisted, "How can you behave like that with me on stage, if you don't care?"

"It's called acting, Grainger. That's my job," Megan retorted, then bounced back on stage for a solo song.

Thomas had crept into the back of the hall. He took off his hat and watched Megan singing her heart out delivering the song, Stormy Weather. His eyes filled with love and pride. That was *his* girl up there. He resisted the urge to run to the stage and sweep her off it and into his arms. He nudged a soldier sitting next to him and whispered, "That's my girl up there." The soldier smiled and nodded disbelievingly. Thomas didn't care.

The show continued and the audience loved it. When the curtain call came they shouted for more. The cast took another bow before jitterbugging off stage to whoops, whistles and applause.

Backstage Megan sat at her table and mirror and started to take off her costume and make-up. There was a knock at the door and Lucinda popped her head round, "Can I come in?"

Megan nodded, "What did you think?"

"You were great."

"Think you'll be okay?"

"I will *love* it. I can't wait."

"I'm sure you'll be fine."

"I hope so. Are you coming to the Mess?"

"I'll be along as soon as I'm changed."

"I'll let you get on, then." Lucinda left.

Megan fluffed up her hair and slipped back into her uniform. She popped a splash of cologne on and a dab of lipstick, checked her costumes were ready for the next show. She placed her washing outside the dressing room door for collection and switched off the light.

Outside, enlisted men still thronged, chatting and laughing in the aisle. Some drifted away to the Mess and Thomas struggled to get through them to try and reach the backstage area.

Megan stepped out from her makeshift dressing room and started down the steps. The lights went out. "Damn!" she swore softly then two hands grabbed her from behind and she was pushed up against the wall. Grainger pressed against her. She tried to scream but one hand went across her mouth, whilst the other held her fast.

"Shut up, Megan. You know you have feelings for me. You're just in denial. We're meant to be together. You and me. It will be perfect."

Megan's fear suddenly dissolved and she struggled against him and manoeuvred her mouth to bite him hard. She drew blood.

Grainger quickly withdrew his hand. Megan managed to cry out as he hissed at her, "Bitch!"

Thomas had fought his way through the remaining members of the audience and just reached the stage, when he heard Megan cry out. Thomas hurried around the back and saw Grainger forcing Megan to the ground. She was thrashing around and brought her knee up into Grainger's crotch and he yelped out and slapped her hard across her face. Thomas leapt across and dragged Grainger up onto his feet and hit him straight on the jaw knocking him flat. Megan jumped up, crying and threw herself in Thomas' arms.

Grainger stumbled up rubbing his jaw and faced Thomas. He turned to Megan and spat angrily, "This isn't over," then turned and fled from the area.

"Are you all right?" asked Thomas tenderly as he stroked her puffy, bruised cheek.

"I am now," she responded and stood on tiptoe to kiss him. "Come on, let's get to the Junior Ranks' Mess. I need to speak to Lucinda, she's going on for me tomorrow and I'm leaving."

"Can you do that?"

"Simon, he's the Company Manager, he'll understand."

"What about Grainger?"

"I'm reporting him."

Thomas nodded, "I'll come with you."

"Not yet, I want to enjoy the little time we have together. We have so much to catch up on."

Thomas wasn't going to argue with that. He took, with mixed feelings, the news of Megan's transfer to another theatre company that was to be stationed in Burma. He grabbed her hand, "Megan, love, we don't know what's going to happen or what's around the corner. Marry me."

Megan's eyes shone with love and delight, "Oh yes, yes, yes!" she answered and threw her arms around his neck and he hugged her to him.

"Let's do it. Let's do it now."

"We can't. I'm not twenty-one. I need Mam and Dad's permission."

"That doesn't stop us buying a ring."

Filled with happiness and love they held onto each other and the moment.

Michael and Adele sat uncomfortably on the train. They were aware from conversations going on around them that two members of the Gestapo were onboard and trawling through the train checking everyone's identification papers. Michael had escaped the scrutiny of one German soldier. He wondered, would his luck hold?

Adele and Michael exchanged worried looks and whispered together. Adele persuaded Michael to follow her lead. He sat with his arm around her and she laid her head on his shoulder. They looked like a genuine couple and Adele pretended to be asleep.

They didn't have long to wait before their carriage door

opened. The other two occupants of the carriage looked up, anxiously. Adele continued to feign sleep. The Gestapo demanded the passengers' papers. A young Frenchman opposite handed his across whilst a large, older lady rummaged through her voluminous bag to find her I.D.

One of the German duo, a harsh, spectacled man, kicked Michael's cane, which slipped from his grasp and rattled to the floor. Adele opened her eyes. She pretended not to understand what was happening and then made a show of looking fearful. "Qu'est-ce qui se passé? Oh, Mon Dieu. Gestapo." Adele rubbed her eyes and began to search for her papers. A gleam of triumph entered the mealy-mouthed officer's eyes. He snatched at her papers, while Michael searched his pocket before producing his own.

The second German examined Michael's documents and eyed him carefully, "Sprechen Sie Deutsch?"

Michael shook his head, " Non, un très petit peu."

"Anglaise, Englisch?"

Michael again, shook his head in denial. The man returned his papers. He pointed at Michael's leg, "Wie haben Sie schaden Ihrem Bein?"

Michael looked confused, but Adele spoke indicating his injured limb, "Il demande, comment as- tu mal à la jambe?"

"Ah!" Michael nodded in understanding and with apparent relief gushed forth in French.

The officer put up his hand to stop him, "Genug!" Then, he asked Adele what Michael was saying.

Adele explained convincingly that a stout metal nail had pierced his thigh, when he was working on the farm, fitting gateposts, after a horse had kicked the stake he was handling. The men appeared to be satisfied, returned their documents, and moved onto the next compartment.

All in the carriage heaved a sigh of relief. Michael glanced at his watch. It was still some time before they were to reach Lille. He had no idea what to expect there, or if his deception would be uncovered. He'd been lucky four times. How much longer would his luck hold?

John received with delight the news that Michael Lawrence's missing money had been found. He immediately wrote to Carrie telling her that when she next visited she was almost sure it would be at Hendre.

Things appeared to be progressing well at the farm. Official notification had been sent to Michael Lawrence but provision for just such an event had already been made at the solicitors. With Sam Jefferies' help Michael's effects and furniture would be ferried to Gelli Galed and John and Ernie would resume tenure of Hendre. The properties would exchange ownership as planned.

To cover the interest owed on the first payment, Gelli Galed would be occupied rent-free until the end of the war. Michael Lawrence would have the right to purchase should he so wish. No one could imagine the struggle for world peace was to drag on for four years.

More interestingly, Netta and young Jake had vanished and no one knew where they had gone. After receiving Mr. Pugsley's letter and before the Probation Services or Police had a chance to visit, Netta had taken what money she could and left her mother's home in Crynant. Netta had taken advantage of the swift coming and goings of new arrivals to the village. Children from the inner cities desperate for a safe place to live were being lodged in spare rooms. The small hamlet was being swamped with a variety of young outsiders. Much good came from this, as Mam-Gu took in two such children, a brother and sister from Erdington in Birmingham, who told harrowing stories of the bomb blasts in that city. Mam-Gu fretted over Carrie, knowing that she was nursing there in a major hospital. This news didn't escape John, who was filled with grave concern.

John ruffled Bonnie's fur as he collected the mail from the post box at the end of the lane. He was surprised to see a letter addressed to Ernie and hoped it wouldn't be bad news. There was nothing else of interest and John trudged back along the track to Gelli Galed. He sighed wistfully as he reached the house. It was strange, all the longings he had harboured to be back at Hendre were not so important now and John was actually feeling regret at the impending move to Hendre. Gelli Galed, too, had a special place in his heart and held many happy memories.

He mounted the steps to the verandah and was greeted by a grief stricken Jenny. Bonnie sat and looked soulfully at Jenny and whined gently in her throat.

"Whatever's the matter?"

"It's Bethan. She's having difficulty breathing. I don't like the look of her. Her neck is swollen like a bull and she has a fever."

John ran into the house, followed by Jenny and the dog, and up the stairs to the cot in the baby's room. John peered in at his daughter. Her skin had a bluish tinge and she had a watery, bloody discharge coming from her nose.

"Wrap her up, keep her warm and upright and we'll take her to Dr. Rees. We've no time to lose. I'll get the cart."

Jenny hurriedly did as she was advised and nursed her baby close to her. Bonnie yapped uncertainly at all the confusion. "Hush now, Bonnie. Hush. Don't make Bethan cry."

As if immediately understanding, Bonnie became quiet and followed mother and baby down the stairs. John was waiting outside talking to Ernie who peeped at the little one.

"She's got the strangles. Don't let her cough over you. Put a scarf around your mouth to protect you. We'll all need treating too, or else."

Jenny climbed into the cart, "The strangles? What's that?"

"I don't know the proper name, but it's a killer. Hurry. If it's caught in time, all will be well."

John needed no second bidding, he picked up the reins and then remembered Ernie's letter. He removed it quickly from his pocket and passed it to him. "Sorry, Ernie this has come for you."

John crashed out of the yard and down the track to the village.

Ernie looked at the writing on the envelope and recognised the writing as that of his sister. He frowned, why would she be writing to him, now? Ernie knew it would not be good news.

Carrie and Pemb were waiting with other nurses in line to collect their results. The talk was of an important meeting to be held in the Reception room of the Nurses' Home. They just had time to collect their results before attending. There were mixed reactions from the assembled nurses; some were ecstatic with delight, others looked sorrowfully as they knew they would have to repeat the exams. Carrie went striding up to the desk and was given her envelope, but Pemb held back. Carrie looked back at her friend, "Come on, you know you've done all right."

"But what if I haven't?" worried Pemb, "What shall I do?"

"Cross that bridge when we come to it. You'll be fine," Carrie cooed, "Come on."

Pemb approached the table and with a shaking hand received her envelope and the two scooted to the corner of the room to open them.

"Tell you what," said Pemb. "I'll open yours and you open mine."

Carrie hesitated as she had her finger in the envelope flap ready to tear it across. Reluctantly, she passed it across to Pemb, who handed hers to Carrie in return.

"Right, on three. One, two, three!" The two friends ripped open the envelopes and studied the contents.

Carrie screamed, "Oh Pemb, Duw – you've done well. Top of the tree, well almost. Well done!"

Pemb was silent and looked mournful, "Oh, dear," she said slowly.

Carrie's face lost its happy sparkle, "What? What is it?"

Pemb scrunched up her face, "I don't know how to tell you."

"What?" Carrie was really worried now.

Pemb's face changed and she broke into giggles, "You've passed, really well. Look!"

They swapped papers and studied their results and both whooped with joy, dancing around the room in delight.

"Calm down, Nurse Pembridge, Nurse Llewellyn," muttered Staff as she strode past. The two nurses stopped guiltily and then burst into laughter again.

"Are you going to this meeting, Lew?" asked Malone. "If so, you'd better get your skates on. It's due to start soon."

"Thanks, Mal," rejoined Carrie, "Come on, Pemb" Carrie grabbed Pemb's hand and hurried off down the stairs to Reception. They skidded to a halt when they saw Staff turn and glare in their direction. Suitably chastened they walked more sedately down to the meeting.

The hallway was filled with chatter. A shout went up for everyone to be quiet as the hospital Matron arrived to address them. Gradually, the nurses fell into silence and waited expectantly.

Matron looked at the assembled crowd, "I know you are all wondering why you have been called together. And this is a difficult thing for me to ask of anyone, let alone hardworking nurses who already dedicate their lives to helping others." She cleared her throat and continued, "You are all well aware of this insidious war and the toll it is taking on lives. Many of you have spent nights in air raid shelters. Others have diligently done their duty on the wards whilst explosions are happening all over the city. Our capital city has suffered more than most with a continuous blitzkrieg. German bombers are targeting public buildings including hospitals and then striking at the firemen striving to extinguish the flames. A plea has come from the highest order for nurses who are prepared to volunteer to work in London to come forward. This is not an order or instruction from me but if anyone out there is prepared to risk their life by transferring to a London hospital. Please see me as soon as possible and no later than by the end of tomorrow. That's all. Dismissed."

There was a rush of excited chatter as the Matron left. Some nurses drifted away, shaking their heads, others looked concerned whilst some actively and noisily considered the proposal.

Pemb gazed curiously at Carrie. "You're considering it, aren't you?"

Carrie turned to her friend her eyes alight with passion, "You know me too well. To tell the truth..."

"I wouldn't expect anything else, " quipped Pemb with a grin.

Carrie smiled bashfully, "I will go where I'm needed. If I think I can make a difference..." she trailed off.

"There's more to it than that. Come on, Lew, give..."

Carrie studied her friend's face and the fervour vanished from her eyes to be replaced by pain. "It's Michael."

"What? Have you heard from him?"

"I haven't, not for a while..."

"But?"

"I had a letter from someone in his squadron. Most of it was blacked out. Oh, Pemb. I'm sure something has happened to him. I had this dream..." and Carrie began to recount it to her and what she had felt. "And so, if I can help, I will. I am going to volunteer."

"And if you are going, then so am I," affirmed Pemb.

"What about Lloyd?"

"What about him?"

"Won't he worry with you in London? He won't want you to go."

"Lloyd respects me and my wishes. He won't stop me. Of that I'm certain."

"If you're sure?"

"I am. Come on, let's get on Matron's list and then you can show me that letter, we'll see if we can work out what it says."

The two chums scurried away to Matron's quarters.

Michael and Adele were alighting with the other passengers and moving toward the end of the platform. Michael couldn't walk too quickly because of his injury but he also determined to exude a calm demeanour so as not to arouse suspicion.

The two Gestapo officers stood at the gate with the ticket collector who was checking tickets. Every now and again the Germans would demand the travellers' documents and the queue to reach the station's exterior would come to a stumbling halt. The railway man examined Adele's ticket, clipped it and returned it to her. The Gestapo looked curiously at Michael whose ticket was retained by the Railway Official. They watched suspiciously as Michael and Adele quickened their step, as much as they could, in the direction of the town. Michael looked back nervously. The harsh faced German was glaring hard at him. Michael turned back and hobbled on. He took his handkerchief from his pocket to dab at the sweat that was manifesting itself on his face. What he didn't notice was Carrie's letter that came out with his hankie, fluttered out of his pocket and drifted to the floor as his skipping step took him forward. The Gestapo left the station and hurried after them. One man ran to try and catch the envelope that was caught on the breeze as it began to skitter along the road. He stamped on it heavily to prevent its escape, picked it up and studied it. He filled his lungs and shouted, "Halt!"

Adele urged Michael down a side street under an arch and along an alley adjoining a commercial building. They slipped in through a heavy wooden door. Adele bolted it tightly and waited. Footsteps thundered past, stopped and returned. The door was rattled, hard. The men continued to run on down the alley.

Adele turned to Michael, "They know, but how?"

Michael shrugged, "I've no idea," he said breathlessly. "Now what? And what about you? They will be looking for you, too."

"Worry about me later. We have to get you out of here and back to England."

Michael reached for his hankie again and felt in his pocket, "Oh no!"

"What?"

"My letter, Carrie's letter. It must have fallen out of my pocket."

"Carrie?"

"My... my girl at home."

"Oh. Never mind that now. This way."

"Where are we?"

"It's an old carpenters' workshop. Follow me. It leads to the workman's accommodation. He is the one who will get you to the airfield. We must try and change your appearance somehow, or you will have to remain hidden."

"What will you do?"

"I will make contact with the pilot, the less you know the better, in case of capture, you understand?"

Michael nodded, "Take me there."

Adele led the way through the workshop and up a flight of winding stairs. They entered the private quarters of Pierre Leblanc.

Carrie and Pemb stood before the Matron with six other nurses. Matron surveyed the group in front of them. "You are the only ones who have come forward. You are absolutely sure?"

"Yes, Matron," they chorused.

"Very well. I don't know whether to applaud you for your bravery or chide you for your foolishness. But there: you will have the option to continue your studies in London. And if you so wish to return here after the war the transition will be made easily for you."

Carrie stepped lightly from one foot to the other, with nerves, and then tilted her head in the way her mother always did when she was alive and facing some daunting task. Carrie was suddenly filled with an indescribable flooding warmth that made her gasp.

"Is everything all right, Nurse Llewellyn?" asked Matron turning her piercing gaze on Carrie.

"Oh, yes, Matron," replied Carrie boldly. She felt herself flushing with colour that accompanied a spreading calm, until she felt that she glowed with confidence. In that instant she knew she was doing the right thing and that her mother had blessed her for her action. A smile tugged at the corner of her mouth and she found it hard to suppress the mirth that threatened to spill from her lips.

"Any questions?" queried the hawk-eyed Matron. Carrie raised her hand. "Yes, Nurse Llewellyn?"

"When are we to leave and do we have any choice of hospital?"

"Nurses are needed urgently, so you should aim to leave by the end of the week. There are a number of hospitals. The list is here. If you have a preference, please indicate on the sheet, with your signature, and also, sign to say you are doing this of your own volition."

The Matron placed the information on her desk and watched as the nurses crowded around to see. Carrie was more than pleased to see the London Chest Hospital in Bethnal Green was one of them. Carrie didn't hesitate she wrote her name in the box alongside and then signed in the space provided to say she was volunteering without coercion. Pemb did likewise. Of the other nurses, they selected, St. Thomas', Guys, Barts and Mill Hill.

The Matron studied the sheet. "The next thing is to speak

to the Staff or Sister in charge on your ward of duty. Adjustments will need to be made. A number of the London hospitals are being evacuated to the countryside but this is not possible or practical for all. I wish you all well and trust that you will at some point return to us here. Nurses of your calibre will be missed."

This was clearly their signal to go, Pemb spoke, "Yes, Matron. Thank you, Matron." The others offered their thanks and they left together, buzzing with excitement.

As they exited Matron's domain, Dr. Challacombe came striding around the corner, "Well, ladies, what's all the excitement?"

Carrie said nothing, but one of the other volunteers, a bubbly brunette with glasses, spoke up, "We're off to London at the end of the week, to do our bit for the war effort."

Dr. Challacombe raised one eyebrow, "London?"

"Yes," continued the nurse. London nurses have dropped out of the profession in droves, so we've volunteered to help fill the gap."

"You, too, Nurse Llewellyn?" he asked studying her face closely.

"Yes, doctor," she admitted with pride.

"And might I ask which hospital you are going to?"

Carrie hesitated, but Pemb broke in, "We're both hoping to be accepted at the London Chest."

Michael nodded and with a gleam in his eye said before, striding off, "I'll see you there, then."

"What?" Carrie couldn't help her outburst.

Dr. Challacombe stopped and turned, "Chest. It's my speciality. They need doctors too and I have opted for that hospital," he whistled as he walked away and there was a dynamic energy about him as he walked.

The brunette nurse turned to speak to Carrie, "I think he's got his eye on you," and she giggled. Carrie looked none too pleased.

Dr. Rees was visiting Bethan and checking on her progress. Everyone on the farm had been immunised and Bethan was undergoing antibiotic treatment for the highly infectious disease of diphtheria, sometimes called 'The Strangles' by country folk. Dr. Rees listened to Bethan's heart and lungs, "She's a strong baby with plenty of fight. There is no reason why she shouldn't come through this without any damage to her heart. That's one of the biggest fears with this sickness. But we have a mystery on our hands. There have been no cases of diphtheria in this part of Wales for some years. Bethan must have come in contact with someone with the illness and I know of no one likely to have infected her. What is worse, there is a possibility that there is someone carrying the illness without any apparent effects to him or herself."

Jenny frowned, "Bethan hasn't been come into contact with anyone new..."

"Think," urged Dr. Rees, "There must be someone."

"There's a lot of evacuees in the village," offered John, his face white and his arm protectively around Jenny.

"But, we have no evacuees here," added Jenny. "There's only the Land Girls, and we were visited by Carrie."

"Carrie has been inoculated, it won't be her, " continued John.

Dr. Rees agreed, "Is there no one else?"

"No one new... oh wait a minute, Megan was here briefly with a friend from her theatre company, somebody Mason. But he didn't display any signs of a cold or anything."

"A carrier wouldn't show any symptoms but, if he's working in the services, he should have had all his injections as do all military personnel, unless he's somehow slipped through the net. Then, a course of antibiotics would clear the problem."

"Then I don't know," Jenny looked worried.

Dr. Rees stated, "Well, it's someone recent within the last two to five days and we need to discover who it is or we could have an epidemic on our hands. Have I seen everyone from Gelli Galed and Hendre?"

"I believe so," affirmed John.

"Make a check list and run it by me. I'll be out again tomorrow. I hope this is the only case. I've sent a notice around to the midwives so that all young babies can be protected. We must be vigilant. I'll also get in touch with the company Megan and her friend are in, just in case." Dr. Rees looked around the kitchen at the packing cases, "On the move again?"

"Yes, to Hendre. The missing money from Jacky Ebron has been found and we can go home."

Dr. Rees nodded affably, "Well, it's about time. I had heard something to that effect. It's right that the Llewellyns are going home. See you tomorrow."

Dr. Rees left as Ernie came in. He was wearing his travelling clothes and carried a brown paper package under his arm. He stood there stiffly and awkward, then removed his beret.

"What is it Ernie?"

"Duw, this is hard. This has been my home for so long now. Longer than I have ever spent anywhere."

John's face fell, "No, you're not leaving?"

"I've come for my money. I know you've put it by for me all this time. It should be a tidy sum."

"Yes, it is. It's safely in a Building Society and earning you interest, better than stuffing it in a jar or under the mattress."

"I'll need all my money and I will have to say goodbye."

Jenny looked shocked and John sat down, his face crumpled in despair, "No, Ernie. We love you like our own. Why are you leaving? Why now?"

"The letter, the letter you gave me. It was from my sister with a message from my daughter. Jawch, John. I've never seen her. I'd love the chance to get to know her…"

"But why now?"

"My wife, we never divorced. She died two months ago. On her deathbed she relented about having nothing to do with me and gave all the letters I had written through the years to my daughter, Wendy. Wendy, do you know I never even knew her name… Anyway, Wendy has read them and she's sent for me. My sister has written to me enclosing a note from her. It just said, Dad, come home. I have to go John, you understand?"

John slowly nodded and a tear escaped his eye, which he brushed away with annoyance, "Oh Ernie, we'll miss you. We'll miss you so much," and another tear cascaded down his cheek. "Will you be back?"

"I don't know. I'm so much a man of the road. I don't know if I can live and settle in a house now. The barn's the place for me, always has been as well you know."

"When are you going?"

"Now, when I'm ready. I'm not one for goodbyes. I usually just up and go but this family is different and of course there's my money…"

John rose and walked to the sideboard, he opened the cupboard and removed a small metal cashbox. He unlocked it and took out a passbook and a fistful of cash. "I haven't paid this in yet," he said sheepishly.

Ernie accepted it, and stuffed it in his pocket, "One thing I will say, I have been happier here than at any time in my life and although I need to build bridges with my daughter and her family members. I cannot see me being a slippers and pipe man, sitting by the fire, listening to the wireless and doing nothing. I'm hoping to mend what once went wrong, and if I dare say it, I'd like to come back. That's if you'll have me and want me."

John was too filled with emotion to speak and he crossed to his friend, adviser and workmate and clasped him in his arms. Ernie's hands, at first limp, rose up from his sides and he returned the embrace, the paper parcel tumbled to the floor with a clunk.

Ernie broke away, his eyes bright and he flustered, "Duw, Duw, that's enough now of that old nonsense. I'll have to come back to check on Bandit and Bonnie and that beautiful little girl you have. After all, if I'm to be her 'Uncle Ernie' I'll need to visit."

Jenny looked up, tears streaming down her cheeks, "Oh Ernie, You have a place in our heart and a place in our home, whenever you want to return for a visit or to stay, our doors are open to you."

Ernie, not trusting himself to speak, stooped down to retrieve his package, replaced his beret and gave a stiffly, formal little bow. He swallowed hard and left the parlour, walked through the passage and kitchen of Gelli Galed and began making his way through the yard to the mountain track.

Jenny prodded John, "He can't walk all that way. Take the cart and give him a lift. You'll soon catch him up."

John skidded out of the door after Ernie and stopped him, "Ernie! Ride down with me, please."

Ernie glanced back and smiled, he was filled with an overwhelming sense of belonging to the Llewellyn family and more. As he looked at young John, he knew he *would* be back. He also knew that he would be needed here, as more tough times were ahead.

Adele had begun her return journey to the farm; she had borrowed some clothes, wore built up shoes to make her appear taller, padded herself out to look heavier and had cut her hair short, a pair of spectacles completed the transformation and no one gave her a second glance as she boarded the train to go home. For now she was safe. Adele's intention was to go on and become what she hoped was to be an extremely valuable member of the French Resistance. She wouldn't disappoint.

Night had now fallen. Under the covert cover of the starlit skies Michael and Pierre were attempting to reach the small airfield just outside Lille. Arrangements had been made for a small craft to fly in, refuel and wait until midnight. If Michael somehow didn't arrive in time then the aeroplane would leave without him. They were on the clock.

Michael, too, had changed his appearance. He had allowed beard stubble to grow; his normally well-combed hair was in disarray, he had changed his clothes from that of a young gentleman farmer to a labourer. His face was smudged with dirt. He had managed to lose the cane and limped along the lane with Pierre. All the time they moved stealthily, keeping alert and watchful.

"Not too far now, Michael." He stopped and raised his hand. They could hear voices ahead; German voices.

A bored sentry was remonstrating with another soldier. They were on watch and designated to monitor everyone who entered the airfield. Michael and Pierre were in a dilemma. There was only one entrance to the airfield and it was being guarded. There was little hope of entering through a gap in a hedge and crossing the expanse of open ground to the hangars, offices and control tower. Tantalisingly, they could see a small plane standing on the concourse; its engine had just started up.

"Now what?" questioned Michael in a whisper.

"I don't know," Pierre looked worried, "I have a pass that would admit us but will not endure close scrutiny. We must try to think of something. Something to distract their attention and allow us through."

"Like a diversion?"

"Maybe."

"Are you prepared to take a risk?"

"What have you got in mind?"

"We could start a bit of a fracas, pretend to have a brawl."

"Yes?"

"We could be arguing over your treatment of… my sister. You could taunt me with the pass and say you didn't need me. I could grab the pass to go in alone, it would fall on the floor and get dirty and then we could have a tussle and tear the thing in two…"

"That would cover any defects in the look of the thing…"

"We could perhaps be a little tipsy…"

"And then maybe we make up and we're home and dry."

"Do you know, it's so stupid, it might just work?"

"And if it doesn't?"

"Improvise."

Michael and Pierre began to walk toward the entrance. They appeared to be disagreeing over something. They stopped on the road their voices began to rise as they started yelling at each other. Pierre took the pass from his pocket and waved it at Michael, who lunged for it. Pierre roared and shoved Michael in the chest and sent Michael sprawling. The German sentries stopped their own argument and focused on the two men. Michael struggled to his feet and barged Pierre and they scuffled and rolled in the dirt. The pass fell into the mud. Michael snatched at the pass, as did Pierre, and the paper tore into two.

Michael and Pierre stopped and went quiet. Pierre tried to put the pieces together. All arguments seemed to be forgotten and Pierre rose and extended his hand to Michael who took it and stood up. Again, they railed at each other with angry voices over the torn pass. The Germans were watching the proceedings in earnest. They were initially amused by the affray and joked between them their own differences forgotten.

Pierre and Michael appeared to come to some sort of understanding and seeming now, to be more concerned than enraged, calmly neared the gate. Michael tried hard not to limp. The sentries stepped forward and looked the two up and down. Pierre gushed forth in French about their pass being ripped and was very apologetic then, reiterated his comments in German. Michael, too, offered his apologies, which Pierre then translated. The soldiers having seen the fight and the resulting destruction of the pass to the airfield were more inclined to believe the evidence of their eyes rather than being suspicious.

One German demanded to know what the tussle was all about and Pierre launched into an explanation about Michael's sister and Michael's perceived treatment of her by Pierre. The row threatened to break out all over again as Michael accused Pierre of taking advantage of her and being dishonourable in his intentions. The German sentry shouted angrily, "Enough! Genug, Assez!" and fearing another outburst waved them into the airfield. They continued inside onto the concourse still muttering and swearing at each other, whilst inside they were heaving a huge sigh of relief. The two Germans laughed and lit cigarettes, continuing to joke about what had happened.

They moved closer to the small craft and the pilot jumped down to speak to them. This was the correct plane.

However, this action attracted the attention of the guards, who, now, began to stare suspiciously at the interchange between the men. One guard threw down his cigarette and crushed it underfoot and began to move toward the plane. The pilot climbed back in and took the controls. The guard watched as Michael hopped around to get in, his limp very clearly manifesting itself.

"HALT!" The guard's cry rang out. Michael jumped quickly and tried to scramble inside but his leg gave way. The guard raised his rifle. Pierre struggled to help Michael up and the guard fired. Pierre dropped like a stone, a bullet in his shoulder.

"Save yourself," screamed Michael, "Run!"

Pierre hauled himself up and ran. He sprinted across the concourse to the outer boundary and Michael found himself fighting to haul himself aboard. Shooting pains blazed up his leg. The plane began to move down the runway. The guard chased after it. He raised his weapon again. A shot rang out. Michael was hit in the back between the shoulder blades. A surge of adrenalin powered through him and he managed to heave himself inside and crawl to safety. The other guard had now joined the first and they emptied their rifles at the departing craft, which lifted off the ground and soared up into the air.

The pilot called, "You okay?"

Michael groaned, "I'll live." But blood frothed from his mouth, the bullet had lodged in his lung.

LONDON

Chapter Thirty-Six

Home Front and Reconciliations

Carrie looked around her room, now devoid of pictures and personal effects. Her bags were packed and she was waiting for Pemb to return from saying her goodbyes to Lloyd. She had written two letters, one to John and Jenny and one to Michael. She would drop them in the post tray before she left and prayed that her letter to Michael might prompt the MOD or whoever was responsible for conveying official information to let her know what had happened. She preferred to receive a letter from him herself, of course, but she had a need to know. She was even thinking of posing as a relative to discover the truth of the contents of the blacked out letter.

There was a tap on her door. "It's open," called Carrie.

Pemb popped her head around, "It's time. Are you nervous?"

"A little. You?"

"Actually, yes. I've got this awful knotting in my tummy like a rag being wrung out."

"You can always back out."

"No, I want to do it. Like you, I feel it's right. Anyway, Lew, grab your things. The taxi is due in," she glanced at her watch, "Ten minutes."

Carrie picked up her bag and case. She took a last look around her room. "Let's do it." She pulled on her hat.

"Is that all you've got?"

"My case is in Reception and my trunk is being sent on."

"Mine, too." Pemb put her arms around Carrie and hugged her. "A new adventure awaits." She giggled and they left the room chattering excitedly.

Grainger Mason had finally returned to camp. He had been missing for a day and as there was no show for a few days he was dealt with extremely leniently, at Simon, the company manager's misguided discretion. There he received an official warning, which he endeavoured to talk his way through, but to his dismay Megan had already left.

He believed that Megan was home with her grandmother, so he was not too concerned about not seeing her again. He thought she would be back and no one told him otherwise. He threw himself into the rehearsals for a new show and working with Lucinda. However, his mind drifted back to the Land Girl, Laura and he convinced himself that he would be able to discover to where she had moved on, should the need arise. In his twisted mind, he saw nothing wrong with his obsessions. In fact, he enjoyed fantasising, creating various scenarios for himself.

To the rest of the theatre company he appeared very likable and the other members all enjoyed his company, including Lucinda. But Lucinda didn't interest him. Her hair was the wrong colour.

Jenny and John were delighted, it was thanks to Dr. Rees that little Bethan was recovering and doing well. To their relief she was getting stronger every day. They were becoming excited over the prospective move back to Hendre and had already begun packing boxes with their belongings and sorting out which furniture they would take. It would be a straight swap and the Llewellyns were at long last coming home to their beloved Hendre. The only blight on their joy was the loss of their companion, worker and friend, Ernie. John, in particular was finding it very hard. Ernie had been his mentor as far as the farm was concerned and John was the first to admit that Gelli Galed would not have fared half so well without Ernie's guidance.

John needed to let Carrie know, but he was finding it difficult to concentrate. He was beginning to suffer with some blinding headaches. He put it down to pressure and overwork. He knew he needed to get organised and promised himself that if these headaches and dizzy spells continued he would have to see Dr. Rees and John was heartily afraid that the tumour had returned.

Ernie had received an awkward, but warm welcome from his sister, Alice and his daughter, Wendy. He was finding it difficult to settle in Vaynor Penderyn. He missed his life on the farm. He missed John, Jenny and little Bethan, Bandit and Bonnie.

Meeting his grown up daughter was difficult. She had never been allowed to be a part of his life and although he had always made sure to send a letter on important dates to his sister to pass onto her he had never received any reply. He knew now that it was because his wife had held onto them. He was thankful that at least she hadn't destroyed them. It was Alice who always tried to keep him up to date with milestones in Wendy's life.

Wendy was so much like her mother, dark, ebony hair

and eyes to match. She was striking in looks but had inherited Ernie's sense of humour and much more, as Ernie was to learn. She was fascinated to talk to him. Her husband, Oliver had just gone off to war. He had joined the Welsh Guards and had been instrumental in persuading her to get in touch with her father now that her mother had passed. Alice, too, had encouraged her and so Ernie was now back in their lives.

He found it very different trying to sleep in a bed and adjusting to the regime of a well-run Welsh household. This he thought he could cope with, but the constraints on his freedom were more difficult to accept. He missed the appreciation of his knowledge and being needed and valued; he missed the warmth and contact of the Llewellyns and Gelli Galed, even little Bandit and Bonnie. He missed being busy on the farm. They had been more of a family to him than anyone else at any other time in his life. When he thought about them Ernie became full of melancholy.

Breakfast was over and Alice had dropped by on her way to the shops. She lived five minutes away from her niece and was almost as close to Wendy as her own mother. Wendy had given Alice a short shopping list and some cash, so Alice bade farewell and left. Ernie sat silently at the table.

Wendy pulled out a chair next to him. She idly picked at the toast crumbs on the starched white cloth as she struggled for words. "Er... Dad," she still had difficulty in saying it. Ernie looked up and gazed into the mellow, but anxious gaze of his daughter.

"What is it?"

"There's something I need to know and something that I have never been able to talk about, not with Mam or anyone."

Ernie looked interested, "Yes?"

"This is difficult..." Wendy paused and took a deep breath, "I know mam thought you were infected by the devil. But it's clear to me that it's just not true. She used to rant about ungodliness and made me regularly attend Chapel. Not that I minded. I used to enjoy singing in the choir."

"Follow your mother there, then. I have as much tune in me as a grasshopper without legs."

Wendy smiled, "You have a unique way of saying things."

"Aye, I've been told that before." Ernie looked down sadly, thinking of young Carrie stopping her ears in complaint at his singing.

"Are you...?" she stopped again, "Are you fey? Truly fey?"

"Why do you ask?"

"Mam said you had knowledge of the devil that no person should know but..."

"Yes?"

"I need to know because..." and she hesitated again.

"Because, you are like me. You know things, too."

"Yes." The relief was apparent, "There it's out now. I never spoke of it when Mam was alive. I was afraid to, especially after what happened to you. But, surely it doesn't mean I am cursed?"

"Wendy, fach, it's not a curse, although sometimes it may feel like that but in truth it is a gift and I believe it is a gift from God. There's many a person I have been able to help because of it. I just don't broadcast it. Not everyone understands or is charitable about my... intuition."

"I also know that you won't stay." Ernie looked up at his daughter in surprise. "You are not happy here. Oh, you'd enjoy a visit but your heart is somewhere else and I couldn't bind you to us for duty's sake."

"Wendy, you are wise beyond your years. Yes, I have loved meeting you and seeing my sister again. You are my family, but you understand. I don't fit in here. It's funny; all these years I've tramped the roads waiting for the call to come 'home' as I understood it. That's what I lived for. Then I went to Gelli Galed and I was needed like no other place I have been. They have been more than family to me, and yes, I love them all. I am sorry if that sounds harsh."

"No, no. All I ask is you talk to me about your gift, so I understand it better, for I am like you."

"You are, and you need to nurture it and develop it. It can help you in so many ways. Just don't go telling everyone as that brings its own pressures. That's what did for your mam and me."

"I think she knew. She just wouldn't admit it. It was easier not to."

"Aye, that would be just like her."

"Tell me about it, about you and her."

Ernie sighed and filled with love he satisfied his daughter's need to know. When he finished she wrapped her arms around his neck, "Oh, Dada thank you. You have given me more than you know and now you need to return to your other family."

"But..."

"No, it's all right. I feel your heartache. It's the right thing to do. As long as you promise to visit again. Please don't stay away."

Ernie smiled and returned his daughter's embrace, "I won't."

"Go on, get your things."

"You mean my brown paper package."

Wendy laughed, "Yes, your parcel tied up with string."

"What about Alice?"

"Leave Alice to me. She'll understand. Go on, get your bits and bobs," she urged.

Ernie rose and hurried up the stairs a feeling of euphoria flooding through him. He wasn't gone long. He stood before his daughter in his coat and beret with his package under his arm and he handed Wendy an envelope.

"What's this?"

"It's for you. There's a letter of authorisation to access the account. I want you to have it, and the extra money."

"I can't take this."

"Yes, you can. It's your legacy and more use to you now than in twenty years should I live that long." Wendy went to speak, but Ernie brushed away her comments and continued, "It doesn't make up for my absence in your life but it will help make things a bit more comfortable especially with your man at war and baby on the way…"

"How did you know?" Then she smiled, "Of course you know, although I have only guessed at it. I have yet to have it confirmed."

"Confirmed it will be, and you let me know when the baby is born so I can see my grandchild. You promise?"

"I promise, but, Dad about the money…"

"About the money, nothing. It was always for you. Saving I was until the time came. That time is now. It gives me reason to return. I need to earn some more." He pulled his beret down on his head and smiled, "I also know I am needed at Gelli Galed."

"Then you better hurry, before Alice gets back or she'll be about persuading you to stay."

Ernie nodded and clasped his daughter in his arms once more, "I'll be back, cariad. You must believe that."

"I do," and Wendy wiped away an escaping tear, "Goodbye. Now go, before I change my mind and lock you in your room," she mustered.

Ernie gave his strangely stiff formal little bow and exited the house. He breathed in the fresh air, drinking in the atmosphere of the world outside. Today, it was a good day in a beautiful world and he was going home. John needed him.

Michael was rushed to hospital. He had fallen into

unconsciousness and had lost a lot of blood. The bullet had to be removed. He needed a blood transfusion, and quickly. The pilot had landed at a small military airfield, North Weald in Essex. From there, because of his injury, he was driven at pace to The London Chest Hospital in Bethnal Green. They were best equipped to deal with a damaged lung and had the necessary expertise. The military ambulance sped along the country lanes, through Epping Forest, Buckhurst Hill, Woodford, Snaresbrook, Leyton and Hackney, passing bombed buildings and manufacturing areas and factories disguised as something else to fool the German bombers.

Many important industrial sites employed the use of trickery and thus, clouded the interpretation of German aerial reconnaissance images. Germany had been sending spy aircraft over to Britain regularly since 1936 to build a picture of strategic targets should the two countries ever be at war again. However, an illusionist would carefully remove part of the roof of a factory, such as the De Havilland aircraft factory at Hatfield and let off copious smoke canisters. Then, when a German reconnaissance aircraft flew over the industrial complex and took photographs, the resulting images after analysis meant the factory was downgraded from an important economic target to one that had suffered severe bomb damage. At other potential target sites the British had also used canvas tanks, fake aircraft and empty oil barrels to disguise the landscape or to encourage wasted bombing attacks. Airfields were given dummy hedges and ploughed to look like farms and flares and oil drums were lit to mimic bomb damage. Often the image in the photograph lied and distorted the truth, and the judgement was down to the interpreter. It was a vital part of the country's defence.

Michael was raced into the hospital, along the corridors and into the theatre where an emergency surgical team was standing by. His life was ebbing away. It was now up to the surgeons to work their magic and save the young airman's life.

The pilot of the small plane had imparted the necessary information about Michael, gleaned on the journey, to transmit to Head Quarters and he had a name of someone to be notified, Caroline Llewellyn of Gelli Galed, near Crynant, Neath; a nurse who was employed at Dudley Road Teaching Hospital, Birmingham. He had promised Michael he would do this and he was a man of his word. A telegramme was sent both to Carrie in Birmingham and her home in Wales. The pilot had fulfilled his promise.

Michael lay on the operating table, fully sedated. A mask delivering oxygen was over his mouth and nose, and his blood type had been matched. Life saving plasma was being fed into him. It had been delivered by one of the four units that had been set up around London. It was to be an important precursor in the initiation of a National Blood Transfusion Centre. Saline dripped in from another Intra Venous line. The surgeon, Mr. Ingram was scrubbed and ready. The newly arrived Dr. Challacombe was Mr. Ingram's aid and the anaesthetist; Harvey Collier was monitoring Michael carefully. Theatre Nurse Jennings, Staff Nurse Kirby and Sister Peterson were in attendance. Kirby looked at Michael Lawrence's face. There was something familiar about him, something she couldn't quite recall. She shrugged the feeling aside.

Michael's chest had been cleansed. He had been given penicillin. The hospital gown was opened, his chest exposed, and painted with iodine.

The surgeon raised his scalpel and cut.

Carrie and Pemb were getting used to their new surroundings. London seemed exciting. They were looking forward to starting a brand new adventure. It was a place they were eager to explore. They already had their duty roster. For the time being there would be no more lectures. All learning would take place on the wards. Practical experience would be the rule and Carrie couldn't wait to begin.

Pemb was to start on Women's Respiratory while Carrie had been assigned to Men's Surgical. The two friends chatted together, their journey to London had been uneventful and they had been allowed a day to unpack, meet with Matron, take a tour of the hospital and generally look around. Next up was a briefing on safety during air raids when on duty. But first they would finish their tea. They sipped their drinks thoughtfully, totally at ease with each other.

Carrie joked, "One place you don't want to be in an air raid is the Morgue. No one would think of looking for anyone down there."

"So, what do we do? Avoid taking the dead ones down to the basement?"

"Um, I think I'll keep a packet of straws in my apron pocket, with one short one. We can all take a pick. I'll start a trend."

"That'll work."

"Or not," laughed Carrie. "Right, Pemb fach, let's get to it. I don't know how we're going to find our way around here. I'm bound to get lost."

"We can get Kirb to help us."

"Kirb!" shrieked Carrie. I'd almost forgotten. Does she know we're here?"

"Not yet. Let's surprise her."

"Where is she? Do we know her room number or the ward she's on?"

"Where's her last letter? Didn't it say?"

"I'm not sure, probably in my trunk. Can't you remember?"

"We can always check in the office. I seem to think she was in room 49."

"That rings a bell, but we'll double check. Got a defective memory sometimes, head like a colander Aunty Annie would say."

"I know she was full of the fact that she was going to assist in Theatre. Really excited, she was."

"And what about Hawtry? She's here somewhere, too."

"Lew. *We* are here. That's all that matters, we'll find them. Come on, put a spurt on. Let's get to that briefing."

John was pacing the kitchen. His head was pounding. He was feeling nauseous. His vision was blurry and he was worried. He was frightened that the tumour had returned and was not benign. He felt bile rising to his throat, dashed outside, bent over and vomited. He wiped his mouth with the back of his hand. He was shaking as he straightened up. He looked across the yard and shaded his eyes, there was a figure approaching the little gate, a portly little man wearing a beret. He squinted in the morning sun as the figure drew nearer. Were his eyes playing tricks? It couldn't be. The man drew closer. He had a staccato, irregular gait and was holding a brown paper package under his arm. John whispered to himself, "Ernie? It can't be." His mouth dropped open in amazement.

"Duw, Duw. There's a climb. I'd forgotten how tough it was. Been spoilt with taking the cart, I have. Now, now, John. Close that mouth. It makes you look twp."

John hurriedly, closed his lips. But it was soon open again as the questions tumbled out, "But how...? Why...? Ernie, what are you doing here?"

"Oh, well, if I'm not welcome. I'll turn around and go back but I hope you'll offer me a cup of tea first."

"Ernie!" John grabbed his friend, "Ernie!"

"Jawch, wuss. Is there an echo?" Ernie laughed, "I had to come back. I've no money. I need to work and earn some more."

"But, Ernie. Your family, I don't understand…"

"Let's get inside. Put the kettle on the range and I'll tell all." But Ernie had no sooner gone inside when he was set upon by Bonnie, who whimpered and cried in sheer happiness. She was practically quivering with delight. She danced and jumped and wagged her tail in a joyous frenzy.

John scratched his head in confusion and set the kettle on the coals. "Tell me, please. Are you really here or am I dreaming?"

"I'm here, and here to stay if you'll have me?"

"Will I? Oh, Ernie, of course. But what of your own?"

"We've come to an understanding and I will be visiting them, especially with a grandchild on the way, but my heart, my heart and soul is here, with you. And, John you must stop worrying."

"What?"

"The pains in your head. It's not serious. Dr. Rees will tell you. You need to get and see him, soon as possible."

"How do you know? No, don't answer that. Welcome home, Ernie."

Carrie and Pemb screeched with pleasure and jumped around clasping Kirb by the waist. The three friends were ecstatic to be reunited. They all spoke at once and then burst into fits of giggles. "What's been happening? However did you both end up here?" asked Kirb.

"We volunteered, but never mind that. Tell us about London and the hospital."

"Yes, and which ward are you on?"

"Which question do you want me to answer first?" grinned Kirb.

"Sorry, Duw. I'm just so excited to see you," laughed Carrie.

"Me, too," added Pemb.

"I can see I'll have no sense out of any of you for five minutes. All right, you can have your turn next. Oh, Lew, Pemb, I love it here. London is wonderful, even in a blackout. The shops, well, when we have a day off together I'll show you. I have found some fascinating places to visit. The markets, too, there are plenty here in the East End in spite of the war. Chatsworth Road is really alive with over two hundred stalls of bargains."

"Chatsworth Road?" queried Pemb.

"Clapton, Hackney area. It's not far."

"But what about the hospital?" prodded Carrie.

"I was saving the best for last," said Kirb. "It is amazing and there are so many opportunities here. I am doing a stint in the Theatre and I've decided that's what I want to do. I hope to remain as a Theatre Staff Nurse and work my way up to Theatre Sister. You wouldn't believe the intricacies of operations. It is so exciting. We have some incredible surgeons. Only the other day Mr. Ingram removed a bullet from the lung of a young airman. It was touch and go at one point. He had lost so much blood. Poor man, he was recovering from a bullet wound in the leg, too. Got shot down in France, by all account. We get our fair share of injured soldiers here."

Carrie shivered, a strange prickling feeling ran down her neck and spine, "Don't know whether I would cope with that every day. It was bad enough when I saw the injuries of that young man who jumped in front of a train. All that blood. It will live with me forever."

"You get used to it. To me, it is the most fascinating aspect of nursing."

"Mm," enthused Pemb. "I'd love to watch an operation."

"You'll get your chance. There's a gallery where medical staff can observe," continued Kirb, "Now, what about you?"

The three friends exchanged news and chattered animatedly hardly stopping to draw breath. Kirb looked at her watch, "I'd better scoot. Grab myself a bite before reporting for duty. You ought to get down to the refectory and have supper. You don't want all the congealed leavings; they're not very palatable. That's the only thing. The food is okay if you can get to first sitting, later on… well, it's not up to much." Kirb rose from the bench in Reception.

"Wait, what about Hawtry?"

"You'll see her, Lew. She's in charge of Men's Surgical. Knowing her, I expect she asked for you. But, what a difference. Whatever you did to her in Birmingham, she's a changed person."

"She's okay," added Pemb, "Now."

"Oh and we have a new doctor from Dudley Road. He assisted Mr. Ingram the other day. Look I have to dash. I'll see you later." Kirb hurriedly left the foyer.

Pemb and Carrie looked at each other and chorused, "Dr. Challacombe."

"You better watch out," joked Pemb, "He'll be after you."

"Not if I can help it," Carrie said tartly and rose. "I don't know about you but I am going to have a look around, see if I can find my way through this place."

"Aren't you eating?"

"Na, I'm not hungry and Kirb's description doesn't exactly excite my taste buds."

"Hm, I know what you mean. Okay, I'll come with you. Where first?"

"Let's see if we can remember how to get to Men's Surgical and Women's Respiratory first."

They jumped off the bench they were sitting on and briskly walked off. Carrie turned a corner abruptly and almost crashed into a tall Hall Porter wheeling a patient with an IV line toward the lift.

"Oops, sorry."

"That's all right," he stopped, "I've not seen you before, new are you?"

"Just arrived," smiled Pemb.

"Yes, on loan from Birmingham," added Carrie.

"But that's not where you're from. You're a long way from home with those accents."

"Yes, but we are loving it. Very different from the valleys," gushed Pemb.

"We'll be seeing a lot of each other, then. I'm George. George Perkins, Porter. And," he dropped his voice conspiratorially, "If you ever need anything, you know, silk stockings or whatever. I'm your man." He winked at them and trundled away with his load and something flickered in Carrie's memory. Ernie's words came back to her.

"If you go to London, and I suspect you will, be nice to a man called George. He could save your life."

Thirty minutes later, Carrie turned to Pemb, "You've learned the quickest route to Women's Respiratory. Let's see if we can do the same with Men's Surgical. Come on."

They scurried along the corridor and down a flight of stairs and then puzzled about which way to turn. "Um... I think I'm lost," frowned Carrie.

"Are you sure it's on second?" queried Pemb.

"I'm not sure of anything at the moment. Not even my room number."

"Thirty-six. You're in room thirty-six."

"This way," asserted Carrie. "I can feel it, drawing me like a magnet. Follow me."

Pemb sighed and chased after Carrie. They eventually took a sharp turn and found they were heading for the Septic Block. "This isn't right, Lew. Let's go back."

"Ah!" shouted Carrie and indicated a sign. "That way!"

A few minutes later they were rewarded by the sight of Men's Surgical. "Now, do you think you can find it again?"

"I don't know, don't know if I can find the Nurses' Home. I'm so confused."

"It'll come."

"It's all right for you, Women's Respiratory is easy to find."

"It'll be fine. Come on. Let's go back. I'm feeling hungry now. Shall we venture out, see if we can muster up some food, somewhere?"

"There won't be anywhere open now."

"Maybe not, but let's look anyway."

The two friends stepped out into Bonner Road and walked in the direction of Victoria Park. They had not gone too far when the air raid warning siren began to wail.

"Now what?" questioned Pemb.

"Tube station and quickly," advised Carrie.

People streamed toward the underground, they poured from houses. Anxious mothers hurried children not yet evacuated or too young to leave to go ahead of them toward the steps that would lead to safety. Carrie and Pemb were carried along on the swell of the crowd. Although, numerous people were rushing down the steps, no one pushed or shoved. There was an amazing camaraderie amongst the people of the East End who all pulled together in times of crisis.

Safe in the depths of the station, hot and sticky from the excess of body heat, people initially quiet, began talking in hushed tones. One woman in a scarf turban and hair curlers began to sing. One by one others joined in, almost in defiance at the splintering blasts and ear splitting whistles they could hear above ground. The attack was sharp and quick not like some of the prolonged and sustained bombing that sometimes accompanied such a raid.

The woman with the curlers took out a pack of sandwiches and offered one to Carrie and Pemb. "Nurses, ain't yer?" she asked in a cockney twang.

Pemb nodded, "Off duty."

Carrie added, "We were just on our way to find a café."

"Here love, don't be proud, 'ave one," she said, shaking the bag at her. "It ain't nothin' fancy – just a bit of bread and dripping."

Pemb and Carrie looked at each other, and not wishing to appear rude, finally accepted. Carrie took a tentative bite. It tasted surprisingly good.

"Just imagine it's a cracking bit of roast beef. It'll do yer good." She nodded at Pemb, "Go on, love try it."

Pemb, too, took a bite and they both munched contentedly.

"Yer both need a bit of fat on yer." The woman laughed, "We'll be out in a bit. The Gerries are just playing with us. Like to throw us all in a panic and cause chaos. That's what they're about."

The mournful cry of the all clear whined above ground and people gathered themselves together to return to their homes. Some elected to stay put, having brought down bedding to sleep there. Carrie started to realise how smelly the platform could get with its continued use as a dormitory. She was glad to get up the stairs and back outside. It made her feel claustrophobic crammed together with so many others. They bade goodbye to the woman who had shared her food, who shouted, "Nellie. Me name's Nellie an' I 'ope I 'ave no need of your services," she winked.

Carrie and Pemb hastened back to the Nurses' Home. Tomorrow would be a tough day. A new hospital, a new regime and new colleagues to get used to, and as Carrie had said, a new specialised form of nursing. She was hoping to get experience with Tuberculosis patients, commonly called TB.

Hawtry smiled delightedly when she saw Carrie arrive for duty, "I asked for you specially," she told her. "It's very varied here. I think you'll find it really interesting. If you can work your way around the ward, familiarise yourself with the cases, taking temperatures and checking each patient that will be an excellent start. There are eleven on the ward and we have four spare beds. Mr. Wilson is due in surgery at two this afternoon. He must have nothing to eat, but he is allowed a few sips of water. They are performing a pneumonectomy to remove part of the affected lung."

"TB?" questioned Carrie.

Hawtry nodded, "They believe only one lobe is affected and this may be the best approach. They'll know more when they open him up. He's being pumped full of antibiotics. You'll find him in the side room in isolation, or as good as. After recovery he'll be transferred to the Septic Block. Make sure that all necessary precautions are taken before entering and on leaving his room. Doctors' rounds start at ten. The ward needs to be ready. Sister is on her break. She's a bit of a tartar but appreciates good work."

Carrie understood, what was needed and was keen to begin.

"Oh, and watch out for Basil Tennant. He's a bit of a flirt and will embarrass you if he can. He means no harm. Just a bit of a lad. I'll let you make your own judgements on the rest. Oh and bed six will need his dressings changed." Hawtry glanced at her watch, "In about thirty minutes. Gunshot wounds. He's one of our brave boys who has been fighting for our country. Then, there's bed nine, he will need re-dressing, too. We have been trying to prevent gangrene, but between you and me I don't hold out much hope. His leg was badly damaged in a mortar attack and it may have to be amputated."

"How will I know, if there's gangrene?"

"The smell is the first thing, if there's any discharge it will be really foul smelling and, of course, the discolouration of the flesh with the death of the tissue. If it is under the skin sometimes the skin will crackle when touched. Call me immediately if you suspect this and the doctor will schedule emergency surgery."

"Anything else?"

"That's enough for now, use your own common sense and judgement. Get to know the patients. A word of advice, there are a few jokers on the ward, but I am sure you'll manage. And of course Sister Black may want to test you out so be prepared."

Carrie stepped from the Nurses' Station into the ward, which was relatively peaceful. Some patients were dozing, whilst others were reading. Breakfast dishes needed collecting and Carrie decided that would be her first job before she monitored the patients clinically. She fetched the trolley and passed along the row of beds, removing their trays and carefully loaded them. She passed bed six and the occupant turned over from his snooze and opened his eyes. He caught a glimpse of a fiery curl escaping the nurse's cap and propped himself up to watch as she proceeded through the ward. The distinctive tilt of her head and her proud bearing drew a gasp from the patient as he studied the back of her very carefully. Carrie removed the trolley for collection and then returned starting at the end of the ward collecting patient statistics and checking pulses and temperatures.

Michael could hardly believe it. It had looked like Carrie from the back and when he saw her face he knew it *was* Carrie. His heart pounded erratically in his chest. He lay back down, quickly, hiding his face, as if asleep, hardly daring to accept the truth of the situation, desperately wanting to laugh with joy and he waited in anticipation for his turn. His arm dangled down at the side of the bed. Carrie picked it up and felt for his pulse. It was racing.

Concerned Carrie put his hand down carefully and efficiently stepped to the end of the bed and picked up the patient's chart. She studied his stats and then saw the name, involuntarily giving a little cry, "Michael!"

Michael turned over and propped himself up on one arm, "Carrie," he whispered.

Carrie's eyes rested on his face and she gazed at him in delight and disbelief, "I thought you were dead…"

Michael made a pretence of looking at his hands, "No, not yet…"

"No, I mean, I truly hoped you weren't. I'm not dreaming am I? It is you?"

"I'm the one who must be dreaming. The last I heard you were in Birmingham."

"I was." Carrie picked up the thermometer from its cup at the head of the bed. "Look I have to get on, I'll be back to change your dressings. We'll talk more then." Michael tried to say something and Carrie shoved the thermometer between his lips. She looked impishly at him, "I'm in charge here, or rather Sister is!"

Michael mumbled something in response but with the thermometer stuffed in his mouth it was totally incomprehensible. Carrie laughed, as the Ward Sister came past.

"Is everything all right, Nurse Llewellyn?"

"Yes, Sister. Thank you, Sister."

"Have you finished, patient stats?"

"Nearly, Sister," said Carrie removing the thermometer and giving Michael a warning glance as she filled in his chart.

"You have two dressings to change before the rounds."

"Yes, Sister."

"You had better get a move on." Sister Black pursed her lips and moved on down the ward checking Carrie's work. Appearing satisfied, she returned to Carrie. "Bed nine first, Nurse. Then, back to bed six and Mr. Lawrence."

"Yes, Sister." Carrie scurried away and prepared a trolley with kidney dishes, forceps, surgical tape, jug of hot water, basin, cotton wool, iodine and other medical items.

Carrie wheeled the trolley, to bed nine where Sister was talking to the patient, Matthew Elwood. Hawtry was standing at her side. "Right, Nurse Llewellyn you may begin."

Carrie carefully pulled back the blanket covering the cage on the bed protecting Matthew's legs. She gently removed the barrier and studied the bandaged leg in front of her that was obviously swollen. Carrie took a pair of surgical scissors and began to cut away the dressing. The wound was clearly oozing as it was staining the bandage. The smell that emitted from it was putrid.

"Observations, Nurse?" questioned Sister. "It's all right, Mr. Elwood is aware."

"The smell is not a good sign."

Sister nodded, "Continue."

Mr. Elwood winced in pain with a sharp intake of breath. The lint was stuck to the wound and Carrie used the warm water to help ease it off. The skin was a dark green turning black and separating from the discoloured tissue that crackled as she gently touched the wounded area.

Mr. Elwood let out an involuntary cry.

"Sorry," murmured Carrie. Carrie treated the necrosis and cleaned the surrounding tissue with iodine. She prepared a penicillin dressing.

"What are you doing now and why?" queried the Sister.

"The penicillin should help to arrest further festering or spreading of the infection. Once I have cleaned it I am to inform Staff who will contact the Emergency Medical Team to decide if surgery is warranted."

"Very good, Nurse Llewellyn and what do you think they will say?"

"It is not for me to make medical assessments regarding surgery, but my personal view is that it will be necessary."

"Good, good," remarked Sister. "You were right, Staff. I think young Nurse Llewellyn will be an asset to us."

Inwardly, Carrie heaved a sigh of relief. She completed the task in hand, took away the clinical waste to place in the incinerating bin and prepared another trolley to address Michael's injuries.

"How did it go?" asked Michael keeping a wary eye out for the intrepid Sister.

"Okay, I think," whispered Carrie. "What happened to you?"

Michael explained as Carrie tended to him. She listened in fascination to all he had endured as she treated him. She sat on the edge of his bed.

"What will happen now? Will you go back?"

Michael shook his head, "It's unlikely. As soon as I am able I will be returning to Hendre. I don't expect to be in here for much longer."

"You haven't heard, then?"

"Heard what?"

"The missing money. It's been found. You will be returning to Gelli Galed."

It was Michael's turn to be shocked. Carrie imparted all that she knew. Michael sighed, "Then you have your beloved Hendre back, after all."

"Maybe. But, I have grown quite fond of Gelli Galed, too."

"What are you saying?"

"Nothing. Only time will tell, when the cock crows its news."

"Carrie you speak in as many riddles as Ernie."

"Never, no one can cause such confusion or be so wise."

"Yes, he's a complete enigma."

"But a lovely one."

Sister Black's professional stride clicked down the ward, "Nurse Llewellyn, are you finished here?"

Carrie jumped up, "Yes, Sister."

"Good, take Mr. Elwood down to Theatre. Chip, chop!"

Carrie began to move from Michael's bed, but Michael caught her hand. Sister Black frowned at this intimacy.

"You'll be back?" asked Michael.

Carrie nodded and managed a smile. As she moved to Mr. Elwood's bed, Sister Black spoke, "Nurse Llewellyn, a word." Carrie inclined her head. "It is not wise nor prudent to become emotionally involved with a patient, no matter how pleasant they are."

"Yes, Sister."

"Anyone would think you knew the man."

"Forgive me, Sister, but I do."

"Pardon?"

"Sorry, Sister but he is a gentleman farmer from the same village."

"I see," said the fierce Sister, not knowing quite what to say. It was clear she disapproved, her beetling brows furrowed. "Not too well, I hope?" she questioned, "Or you may have to move wards. Now, take Mr. Elwood down."

Carrie scooted across to bed nine and took the brake off from the wheels. She ensured it was safe to move and hurriedly left the ward before she could be questioned further.

Chapter Thirty-Seven

Looking Forward

Carrie gushed enthusiastically with all her information about Michael, Pemb was stunned and she had her own news to tell, Lloyd had taken a first teaching post with a very well recognised Boys Grammar School in Birmingham, it seems he was teaching Physical Education.

"But, I thought he was a geographer!" exclaimed Carrie.

"He is, but he did PE too. On his interview they were expecting a visit from some dignitaries and wanted to put on a display. He got the job and had a day to do it in."

"How on earth did he manage that?"

"Easy, he got the sixth formers to organise it themselves. He didn't know what they could do. And it worked. Apparently, the gymnasts were excellent, real quality. They did well. And he got the kudos."

"Lucky him. So, what's next?"

"He's going to stay at the school and will be taking the whole school in gym and has some lower school geography, but they are all being evacuated from Birmingham to Monmouth."

"Goodness, he does get about."

"Not as much as your Michael."

"He's not my Michael."

"No?"

Carrie hesitated, "No. We have agreed to make peace for the time being and we will just have to see how things work out."

"Carrie Llewellyn, you're a stubborn one. He's the one you gave up Lloyd for, remember?"

"And aren't you glad I did?"

"Don't change the subject, Lew. You're good at that!"

"Talking of changing, I need to do just that. I'm on duty in fifteen minutes."

"And you don't want to be late with Michael on the ward," teased Pemb. "Always on time from now on, eh?"

Carrie batted Pemb, playfully with her hand, "Go on with you." She glanced at her watch, "I really must get a move on. I'll see you at supper."

Carrie arrived on the ward ten minutes early. Sister Black frowned when she asked if she could just speak to Michael for a few minutes. "All right, five minutes," and she stressed the five, "But, note that I don't approve."

Carrie acquiesced, "Yes, Sister."

She hurried to Michael's bed where Hawtry was making him more comfortable with his pillows. She winked at Carrie, "I'll leave you to it. Don't stay too long, you know what Sister is like."

"I know."

Hawtry briskly strode away to attend to another patient. She called back, "You'll need to be saying goodbye soon."

"Goodbye!" exclaimed Carrie, her voice rising.

"They're moving me onto convalesce for a week and then home to Hendre." Michael explained.

"Gelli Galed," corrected Carrie a spark of fire lighting her eyes.

"Or Gelli Galed," agreed Michael, unruffled by her remark.

"Hmm..." Carrie, for once, was stuck for words. "So, what then?"

"They won't let me return to my men. I will be released from duty."

"That's good isn't it?"

"Maybe. It depends what I have to go back to in Wales," he raised an eyebrow questioningly.

"Why, you must work at being a great gentleman farmer, and keep Gelli Galed running successfully."

"And why would I want to do that?" he pressed.

Carrie felt her face flush with colour and she flustered, "Because... Because..." she stuttered.

"Because...?" he asked mischievously.

"Because Gelli Galed needs looking after... it's a good little farm."

Michael let out a yelp of pain and Carrie drew closer to him. "What is it? What's wrong?"

"My leg. Draw the curtains, quickly please."

Carrie did as she was bid and concerned went to the head of the bed. Michael clasped her hand and pulled her close. Carrie gave a sharp intake of breath, the pupils in her eyes dilated and shone. Michael stretched out his other arm and tenderly stroked her cheek. Carrie froze uncertain what to do, but then slowly she began to incline her head toward him. Michael placed his hand behind her head and drew her velvet lips to his. Before Michael could lose himself in the moment Carrie pulled back nervously, she touched her lips that tingled with passion. At that point the curtain was wrenched back.

Sister Black demanded, "What's going on here?"

"Mr. Lawrence complained of a pain in his leg. I drew the curtain for his own privacy."

"And what have you learned, Nurse?" persisted the Sister.

Carrie hesitated, but Michael rescued her, "I didn't feel comfortable with her examining me, because we know each other. I asked her to call another Nurse."

"Which I was just about to do," added Carrie.

Satisfied, Sister Black sent Carrie to attend to another patient and called Nurse Palmer, also on the ward, to examine Michael's leg. Sister Black watched with an eagle eye. "It appears to be healing well. It was probably a muscle spasm. You need to begin exercising the leg, or the muscles will waste. Lean forward," ordered Nurse Palmer.

Michael did as he was told, supported by the nurse and the Sister lifted his pyjama jacket and checked his back. "Hmm." She palpated the skin around the site of the injury. "Does that hurt?"

Michael flinched, "A little."

Sister sucked a breath in through her lips, "I need the doctor to take a look at this. Nurse Palmer make the patient comfortable." The nurse did as she was bid as the Sister pulled the curtains back. Carrie glanced across curiously and Michael shook his head in confusion.

"Nurse Llewellyn, prepare a penicillin G injection."

"Yes, Sister."

Carrie soon returned with a kidney dish containing a syringe and covered with a cloth. She passed it to the Sister. "That will be all, Nurse Llewellyn. Please get ready for the doctors' rounds."

Carrie stepped smartly away. She was now very concerned. Carrie waited anxiously for the doctors to arrive and was surprised to see Dr. Challacombe as part of the team. He winked at her, "Nurse Llewellyn."

"Doctor."

Sister Black looked suspiciously at the interchange and stepped back to allow the medical team to circulate around the ward moving from bed to bed. Dr. Challacombe spoke again, "Nurse Llewellyn, would you like to accompany us? That will be all right, won't it, Sister?"

Sister Black swallowed and forced a brittle smile, "Of course, Doctor Challacombe."

Embarrassed but enthusiastic Carrie joined the group as they progressed around the ward. She listened carefully and answered questions put to her, flushing when she received praise for her observations. They reached Michael's bed.

"Ah, Mr. Lawrence," the doctor picked up his chart. "I

see you are due to be moved to a military convalescent hospital before being allowed home. Then we had better clear up this Staph infection that is attempting to invade your wound. Move forward please. Nurse, help him with his pyjama jacket."

Carrie stared at the bullet wound that showed some small signs of necrosis right at the edge of the site, which had otherwise healed.

"Not too serious, thanks to the intervention of the good Sister. Continue with the G injections every four hours and this will soon be blitzed. Excuse the phrase." Dr. Challacombe gave another of his cheeky winks to Carrie, who looked down self-consciously.

"When can I leave, Doctor?" asked Michael.

"I believe they are scheduling transport either today or tomorrow sometime. It's not yet confirmed. But, you will soon be home."

Michael thanked the doctor and rested back on his pillows as Dr. Challacombe continued his rounds.

Michael tried subtly to attract Carrie's attention, without success. Staff Nurse Hawtry came to his side, "Yes?"

"I need to speak to Carrie," he said pleadingly.

"I see," She pretended to tuck his covers in and make him more comfortable, "After the Doctors' rounds Sister usually takes a break for a cup of tea; sometimes at the Nurses' Station, sometimes in the refectory, I'll see what I can do. Be patient."

The team finished their assessments and began to leave the ward en masse. Dr. Challacombe turned to Sister, you have an excellent nurse here," he indicated Carrie. "Make sure you look after her." Carrie blushed and Sister Black acknowledged with a tight-lipped smile.

The entourage left the ward. Sister Black turned to Hawtry, "I'll take my break, now, Staff. Nurse Llewellyn, bed four needs a blanket bath and Mr. Mortimer must have his dressings changed." The good sister obviously thought that this would keep Carrie busy until her return. "Nurse Palmer, you're wanted in Theatre to bring Mr. Fosse back."

"Yes, Sister," they chorused. Nurse Palmer hurried away immediately.

They watched as Sister Black left the ward. Hawtry stopped Carrie, "I'll do the blanket bath. Michael needs to speak with you, be quick and no one will be any the wiser."

"Thanks, Hawtry."

Carrie scuttled across to Michael's bed, "You wanted to speak to me?"

"Yes, I know you have given me permission to write to you but I want more."

"Pardon?"

"Will you allow me to court you? I want you to be my girl, Carrie Llewellyn. There, I have said it, it's out now." Michael gazed anxiously at Carrie's face looking for some clue of her thoughts or reactions. Carrie had, since she had been nursing, always able to keep her face impassive. She was trained and practiced in the art when faced with horrific injuries or anything else.

Carrie looked down, "Mr. Lawrence, why do you possibly think there could ever be anything between us after our history together?" Her face showed no emotion.

Michael's expression crumpled in dismay and despair, "But I thought. I really thought we had a connection..."

"Did you now? What effrontery!" Carrie lifted her eyes and as she gazed at him she was unable to keep the smile from creeping to her eyes and into her voice. She quickly placed her fingers on his lips to prevent further protests and unable to continue the teasing any longer, she smiled broadly. "Michael Lawrence, you have to get yourself fit and well, I do not want to walk out with someone who is not strong enough to handle farm work."

Confused, Michael searched her face, "What are you saying?"

"I'm ordering you to get better soon and, then I can teach you how to love Gelli Galed and Hendre as I do."

"You mean...?" Michael could hardly keep the joy from his voice, "You will?"

Carrie nodded, "Yes, I'm telling you, yes."

Michael punched the air ecstatically then, winced, "Ow!" followed by an elated, "Yes, she said, yes!" which, he shouted to the entire ward.

Hawtry popped her head around the curtains of bed four and smiled delightedly, she was genuinely pleased for Carrie.

Carrie spoke quickly to Michael, "I really have to get on. We'll talk later."

Carrie briskly stepped, across to Mr. Mortimer and placed screens around the bed before fetching a trolley with the necessary items.

Hawtry caught up with her in the sluice, "Bed bath's done."

"That was quick!"

"I left him to finish off, helps them keep their dignity, although some can be tricky," she smiled, "You know what I mean, like Basil Tennant … Lew, I just heard from the switchboard that they are definitely moving your Mr. Lawrence out later today. Oh, and Sister Black has put you on nights for a week. She's not a bad old stick. Night duty will give you time to write a few letters. These men do sleep sometimes."

Carrie nodded, "Leaving today? That doesn't give me much time."

Hawtry glanced at her watch, "Sister will be back in about five minutes. Give me this. I'll see to Mr. Mortimer, quickly now, go and say your goodbyes."

Carrie briskly hurried to Michael's bed; again she drew the curtains around the bed and placed her finger to her lips for him not to speak. She moved to the head of the bed and gathering her courage she did something she would have deemed impossible a few years ago. She leant across him and kissed him with tenderness and love. Michael eagerly responded and when Carrie finally broke away, her curls were tumbling from her cap. She drew back the curtains with a flourish. Michael was stunned. Then she spoke, "Now, Mr. Lawrence, you have your answer," and not trusting herself to say anymore she turned tail and fled to join Hawtry at Mr. Mortimer's side.

Michael softly touched his lips emblazoned with her kiss and closed his eyes to relive the magical moment once more in his mind. In that instant he truly believed that he had the found the happiness for which he had so yearned. He prayed in his heart that nothing would take that from him.

Carrie's week of nights was upon her and Michael was gone. She enjoyed the solitude and would sit at her desk in between checking her patients mostly soundly asleep and snoring. She padded quietly around the patients' beds every fifteen minutes with her torch, checking them and ensuring the blackout blinds were drawn and that no chinks of light would signal to the Germans that here was a place that needed further scrutiny. All through the night the sound of the air raid sirens would wail their warnings bringing terror to the people of London. Bombs fell regularly over the city and often concentrated on the Isle of Dogs striving to blast the many and varied factories that lay along the water's edge.

On Hitler's instructions they changed from daily raids to nightly ones, targeting industrial areas, cities and civilians. People had been drawn to the relative safety of the underground stations as a place to escape the German bombardment but even that wasn't ideal. Balham tube station in the South West of London had been hit by a 1400 kilo semi armour piercing bomb that penetrated thirty-two feet underground and exploded just above the cross passage between two platforms. Above ground a number 88 double-decker bus travelling in the blackout ploughed into the crater made by the bomb. Water mains, gas pipes and sewage pipes were broken and water flooded down the shafts, swirling through the tunnels further hampering rescue attempts. But the Gerries were unable to break the indomitable spirit of the survivors.

The German fighter planes were particularly active in the East End and Carrie was no stranger to the sounds of ear splitting bomb blasts from enemy aircraft. Thousands were being killed or injured and the surrounding areas were blighted with destruction. Where once stood proud buildings rubble remained. This brought further problems with vermin roaming the streets. They would strive to find shelter alongside the human population.

It was three o'clock in the morning and Carrie paced around the ward before going to the Nurses' Station to make herself a cup of tea. She placed the kettle on the stove to boil and felt something brush against her legs, something furry. At first she wondered if the hospital cat had invaded her ward but when she turned her torch on the intruder to her horror she saw a very large rat scuttling around the kitchen. Stifling a scream she removed the kettle from the heat and turned off the gas. She fled from the small kitchen and shut the door closing off the creature's escape. Carrie loathed rats and could barely control her shaking hands as she rang down to the hospital porter, George. She silently urged him to hurry and answer the call. Eventually, she was rewarded with his voice, "Perkins."

"George?" she could scarcely keep the panic from her voice.

"Yes?"

"Nurse Llewellyn on Men's Surgical. I have a problem. There's a rat on the ward. It's huge."

"Where is it?" he asked, instantly alert his previous sleepiness forgotten.

"I've locked it in the kitchen. What do I do?"

"You've done the right thing. Stay away from there and whatever you do, don't open the door."

"I'm not likely to," responded Carrie, relief flooding through her.

"I'll get my things. I'll be as quick as I can."

Elizabeth Revill

Carrie replaced the telephone and walked back in the ward. She was anxious not to disturb any of her patients, but she couldn't relax. She tried sitting at her desk but her fingers drummed impatiently. She arose and paced the ward again. She was afraid of disturbing the sleeping men and had to contain her nervousness as best she could.

She was soon released from the painful waiting as George arrived. He was clad from head to toe in a thick stiff cream calico suit. He had gloves like gauntlets and was carrying a large stick with a loop, a canvas bag, and headgear that reminded Carrie of that belonging to a beekeeper.

"Show me," he whispered.

Carrie walked him to the kitchen and he peered in through glass window ward side. Carrie shone her torch through the glass and the light caught the creature's eyes shining malevolently as it raised itself up on its hind legs. There was nothing cute or cuddly about this rodent.

"He's a big fellow, isn't he?" George said rhetorically. "Keep the light shining in there. I'm going in."

George placed on his protective headgear and walked to the door, which he opened with care. He shut it swiftly and stared about him. The rat scampered to the corner as George approached it warily. George bore down on the condemned rodent. Finding itself trapped and with a human threateningly bearing down on him looking like something from a Science Fiction novel the rat bared its large, yellowing gnawing teeth and jumped straight for George's throat and face. Carrie struggled to suppress a squeal. The mammal bit into the stiff calico and clung on tightly while George grasped the wriggling creature that ripped at his neck. George deftly twisted the animal's neck and forced its twitching body into the sack bag he had brought with him. He returned to the watching Carrie whose face was creased in revulsion.

"Is it dead?"

"If it isn't, it soon will be," said George.

Carrie shuddered, "How did it get in?"

"It could have come from the sewers or a bombed building and tried to find sanctuary here, probably through an air vent or sewer outfall pipe. Did you see it, fight?"

"It went straight for your throat. If you hadn't got that lot on," she shivered, "I dread to think what would have happened."

"Yes, well, let's hope there's no more."

"Duw, don't say that," exclaimed Carrie horrified.

301

"At least you know what to do now."

"Yes," agreed Carrie, "Call you."

George laughed, "I'll take this monster away and you can have your well earned cuppa."

Carrie had gone off the idea of making tea and instead returned to the ward. She spent the rest of her night duty restlessly and was more than relieved when Hawtry appeared to take over the day shift.

Living in London was proving an adventure to say the least; the violence of the repeated air raid attacks, the acrid smell of burning, the sight of bombed buildings and for the first time since she had left Gelli Galed she truly longed for the tranquil hills of Wales and home.

Ernie looked about him and took a deep breath, inhaling the clean and pure country air. He smiled as he took in the scenery leading from the stony track to the rough road that led to Hendre. Bonnie skipped round his heels, making little rumbling noises in her throat. She jumped up every few moments nudging his hand, begging him to pet her.

"Aw, all right Bonnie, all right." Ernie stooped down and patted the little collie, who was obviously extremely excited to have him back. He straightened up and looked across the lush, green wooded valley and smiled. Ernie felt he had come home. How he would feel living at Hendre, he didn't know? Gelli Galed had become part of him. He had played an integral part in building its success and of that he was extremely proud. Here, there was a detachment from the war. There was safety in the Welsh hills.

He slowly walked back to the cobbled yard where the last cart loaded with packing cases and furniture waited. Senator stood patiently and he whinnied softly. Jenny and little Bethan were already settled in and John was busy unpacking and tidying up the farmhouse. Sam Jefferies was on his way to take his place in Gelli Galed in the house exchange until the time Michael Lawrence returned, which Ernie believed was not too far away. Sam could be heard trundling up the path with his possessions in a small handcart.

Ernie knew that there would be no going back. He would be needed more than ever once John underwent the surgery necessary to relieve the pressure on the optic nerve by the removal of the small, but benign growth that was developing. Ernie took a last look around before lifting Bonnie up to sit alongside of him. He clambered up and flicked the reins instructing Senator to move. The sturdy shire clopped forward as Sam Jefferies arrived in the yard.

He acknowledged Ernie, gasping for breath, "My God; that's a tough climb."

"You'll get used to it," chortled Ernie.

"If I don't have a heart attack first."

Ernie laughed, "See you tomorrow, Sam," and Ernie clicked his tongue and Senator moved off out of the yard, and down the track to Hendre.

Ernie removed his beret and scratched his head, his thoughts were drawn to Carrie and although he wasn't certain, he was convinced that she was now in London and in his heart he prayed for her protection from harm. Ernie felt strongly that big changes were coming; changes that not only involved the return of the Llewellyn's to their family home but changes that would send ripples further afield. The family members and their friends were so intricately involved in each other's lives that the tendrils of the merging relationships were to bring both drama and pain but, he felt assured, great joy, too, would also follow. His thoughts floated off as he allowed himself the luxury of a daydream whilst the faithful horse plodded on down the track. He looked up at the clouds scudding across the sky, chased away by a nimbus mass that was rolling in threatening rain. Ernie mused to himself; the shadows on the moon would soon be eclipsed by rainbows in the clouds and he smiled as he knew Carrie would be coming home, home safely to them all and to her beloved Hendre, once this lousy war was over.

Lightning Source UK Ltd.
Milton Keynes UK
UKOW05f1832290813

216212UK00001B/58/P